The Tower's Shadow

Jericho Series Book 1

James Bonk

Storming Strongholds LLC

To my girls,
AB, BB, and BB.

Books By James Bonk

Jericho Series

1. The Tower's Shadow

2. Book 2 – Coming Soon

3. Book 3 – Coming Soon

Light of the Ark Series

1. Light of the Ark

2. Shadows of the Ark

3. Light of the World

- Isaiah and the Sea of Darkness (standalone prequel)

More Fiction

- Christian's Look Back at Life

Stay up to date on new releases and email exclusive content:

https://hello.jamesbonk.com/signup/

Contents

CHAPTER 1

H e stepped into the office where the two figures that would change his life stood talking. One in the white lab coat of a doctor and the other in a three-piece suit with a chain arching neatly from the left breast pocket. They shook hands and parted ways as he entered. The businessman moved toward the front desk while the doctor stepped back, expectantly waiting for the new patient to check in. The shadows of the hallway shrouded his facial features, but Darren saw a polite smile on the optometrist's face. A flicker of bright eyes through the darkness.

"Mr. McArthur?" a sweet woman said as she stepped out from behind the front desk. She was shorter than Darren, with short graying hair that was curled up neatly. Her red button-up sweater, white blouse, and gold cross necklace gave her a sweet grandmother vibe. She could have passed for Mrs. Claus every Christmas.

"Yes, ma'am." Darren nodded. He looked to her and then back toward the hallway. With his impaired vision, everything seemed a little blurry, but if he focused enough, he could make do. He told himself the unrelenting pain behind his eyelids whenever he closed them for more than a couple of seconds was the reason he stood in the optometrist's office, but really it was his girlfriend's insistence that drove him to get checked out. After a week and a half of bloodshot eyes and horrible sleep, her urging pushed him to make the call.

"Perfect timing, Mr. McArthur. I'm Ms. Barbara. Would you like a cookie?" She extended her hand in greeting. Darren shook it and took the clipboard of new patient forms.

"Cookie?"

"You fill those out and I'll get you one *and* a nice glass of milk to go with it. You prefer skim, whole, vitamin D, or raw?" she asked.

"You serve raw milk?" Darren said, his eyebrows shooting up, and the thought of a cow hidden in a back office or behind the building filled his mind. The pain embedded in his eyes soon stole back his attention.

"Mmhmm," her sweet voice hummed as she swiftly disappeared behind a corner.

"Don't let her fool you. She runs a cookie empire. She makes more addicts out of this office than pharmacies with painkillers," the businessman in the three-piece suit said as he leaned his back on the front desk. He appeared as comfortable as if he were in a recliner on vacation.

"Oh, empire, my foot!" she said from behind the corner. A second later, she came back into view with a tiny plate and coffee cup full of milk. "Now you take your time, young man, but don't you let that warm cookie go cold." The look in her eye reminded Darren of his own late grandmother, who had a way of inserting love even when being stern. Ms. Barbara had the same loving yet commanding way about her.

"Maybe I should have gotten into the cookie game? Medical devices and gene therapy don't hold a candle to the sugar industry," the three-piece suit said with a chuckle.

Before she could respond, the front door swung open and an elderly man entered the room. Large, circular wire-framed glasses that dwarfed the narrow face behind them came into the office with an ear-to-ear smile. His tan, leathery skin showed a lifetime of working in the sun.

"Now, Ms. Barbara, don't you tell me no," he demanded. He mockingly put his hands up, a small white envelope in one hand. "For all you and the doctor have done for me, my wife insisted," he said, handing her the envelope.

"Oh, Almanzo, you're too kind. And how is Laura?" Barbara asked with a matching grin.

"She's just fine ever since the good doctor got her cataracts out. Rode with me for a full eighteen holes this past weekend. And get this, said she never knew how bad my putting was. She said I'm the blind one!" He shook his head but couldn't hide his smile.

Darren found their smiles and friendly banter infectious, but the three-piece suit rolled his eyes as the two leaned in.

"Oh, she didn't," Barbara replied.

"She done did! But aww, raspberries, we both know that woman is right about golf as all else in our lives. You tell that doctor thank you, will ya?"

"Tell him yourself!" Barbara motioned to the hallway.

Almanzo went silent, immediately straightening up as he looked at the doctor. His eyes watered as he stepped forward and hugged the man in the white lab coat.

"Thank you. You've shown me so much," Almanzo said, muffled by the embrace.

He stepped back into the lobby area, keeping his eyes on the doctor as the doctor stayed back. Reluctantly, Almanzo finally turned away from the doctor and walked past the three-piece suit, who mockingly saluted him. Almanzo ignored him as if the sharply dressed businessman wasn't there. Finally, Almanzo flashed a gigantic smile and a wave to Ms. Barbara as he left.

Barbara turned to the doctor in the hallway. They exchanged a glance of satisfaction.

"Well, I'll need another box of tissues if there's any more Hallmark movies," the suit said.

"You hush now, and take a seat next to the nice Mr. McArthur while I get the doctor's signature," Barbara chided as she pulled a thick manila folder from under her desk. She shot an uncertain look at her patiently waiting boss as she motioned to the businessman.

"You sure about this?" she said plainly for the businessman and Darren to overhear. The doctor didn't reply, but turned and walked with her as the two disappeared into the shadows, leaving the suit and Darren in the waiting room.

The man stood as Darren secretly lifted his eyes from the paperwork to look him over. He was tall, at least six-four, with a broad, chiseled jawline. The more Darren observed the man, the more he stared. He was extremely handsome, with short blonde hair perfectly parted and combed to the side, product holding it in place, yet still a natural look. The fitted suit was tight on his upper body. His chest, shoulders, and biceps bulged under the silky smooth fabric.

A moment later, Darren met the man's eyes and quickly looked away. The suit smiled and turned to face him, now shifting his impatience to once again leaning comfortably, as if back on vacation and having all the time in the world.

"Tell me, Mr. McArthur," he said. "What is your enterprise and is it successful?"

"I..." he said, picking his head up. He locked eyes with the man and lost his train of thought. A moment of silence passed as the businessman waited for Darren to continue.

"That good, eh?" He left the desk and put his hands in his pockets, both thumbs sticking out as his fingers comfortably rested inside the tailored material. He walked past Darren to the end of the waiting room and looked out the window.

"How old are you, boy? Twenty-four, twenty-five?" he asked.

"Twenty-five."

"Girlfriend? Married?"

"Girlfriend, but..." Darren stopped himself.

"But... hope for more?" He turned, a smile creeping from one corner of his mouth.

Darren nodded.

"Now, if I may, what would her father say if you asked for her hand? AND, what if he asked you back something like 'what are you all about?' and 'how you doing with that?'"

Darren remained quiet, not admitting that he received glowing approval when he asked for her hand three months ago. None of those questions came up. But finding enough savings to buy a ring was his constant challenge. After paying rent, bills, and a modest date here and there, there wasn't much left.

"Boy, you need to know where you're going if you're ever going to get there," the man said.

"I know where I'm going," Darren replied defensively.

"Great, tell me!" the man jested.

"I'm going to see the doctor so I can get my eyes checked out." Darren let a smile slip out. The man's face dropped, unimpressed with the humor.

"Clever and all-knowing, about right for your age. But I'll tell you what, if you ever figure out your target, you come see me."

"But who..." Darren began as a grin trickled onto the man's face, like he'd been eagerly waiting for Darren to ask.

"I'm easy to find," he said, picking up a magazine from the end table. He spun it through the air like the last playing card from a winning poker hand, dropping it perfectly next to Darren on the waiting room couch.

Looking back at Darren from the cover of *Medical Magazine* was the businessman. Instead of a three-piece suit, he donned a surgical gown as Photoshopped images of DNA double helices surrounded him. His arms crossed and a half smile that oozed confidence. The headline stated "Dr. Thomas Thornhill and his miracle drug."

"Tell her I'll be back later, would ya?" Dr. Thornhill said as he strolled out of the office. Darren nodded, looking back and forth between the man and the magazine.

Barbara came back from up the hall and rustled through supplies at her desk. Darren set the magazine aside and returned to the paperwork, a pain simmering in his eyes as he squinted to focus. But soon, Barbara's smile lit up the room once again and wrapping up the material was easier than before.

"All done?" she said as she extended her hand, and to Darren's surprise, she didn't ask about Dr. Thornhill being gone.

She took the papers back to the front desk.

"He said he'd be back later," Darren said.

"Who? Oh yes, he always seems to come and go, reporting his lab trials or such-and-such," she said as she clicked away at the computer.

Another silence grew in between every click of the keyboard.

"So, how'd you like it?" she said, and Darren looked around, confused at the question. "The cookie?" she clarified.

Darren turned to stone, mortified that Thornhill's conversation distracted him from the wonderful-smelling treat. He took half of it in one bite and his soul felt it was melting faster than the soft chocolate chips. He didn't realize he'd shoved the second half in his mouth when he tried to reply. Only a muffled 'mmmmm' came out.

"Good, eh?"

"Mmmmhmmm." Darren nodded vigorously and then washed it down with the milk, finishing the cup in two gulps.

"Okay. Right this way, Mr. McArthur," she said, popping up from her desk.

"How'd you know my name when I came in earlier?" Darren asked.

"Oh, we see all," she said with a serious tone before a pleasant grin slipped out. She motioned toward the hallway as she continued. "Most of our patients have been here for years. It's easy to spot a newcomer, plus," she dropped her voice to a whisper, "newcomers are the most fun."

"Glad to hear it," Darren said.

Darren turned and began walking into the shadow-filled hallway. Bright white lights and modern furniture gave the waiting area a pearly-white sense of life, more of an art exhibit than an eye doctor's office. However, the hallway leading back to the exam room felt a generation old, giving it the sense of a portal to another world. Old, dark wood panels came up to his waist below dingy beige-colored walls.

"Also, I can see your bloodshot eyes from here. Dear, that has to be painful," she said.

"Yeah, it's not great," Darren said, trying not to rub his eyes now that his mind focused on them.

"But have no fear, for Dr. Abrams is here! I swear it's like he takes you to your healthiest self somewhere in the future and then brings the best back here. A shepherd of true health if you ask me."

"How long have you worked here?" Darren asked.

"Not as long as I've been a patient, but let's not recount ancient history." She winked at him as they entered the exam room.

"Just take a seat?" Darren asked as he studied the room.

"The good doctor will be right in," she said.

He stepped into the office and the same bright 5000k white lights used in the waiting room nearly blinded him after the dimly lit hallway.

"Thank you, Ms. Barbara," he said.

"My pleasure," she said, already a few steps back down the hallway.

He sat in silence, taking in the common office. A small rolling stool rested near a sink and cabinets while a large gray phoropter hung above him from the ceiling, its countless dials ready to test his vision.

Soon, the rhythmic sound of dress shoes striking the hard floor sounded behind him.

"Hello, Mr. McArthur," the doctor said in a low, gentle voice as he entered. "Pardon our dust." He motioned to the dark hallway. "It's actually a lighting trick, so it's easier to upsell patients to the most expensive brands."

Darren's eyes widened in surprise.

"Just kidding. I love those old panels, but alas, they'll be the last to go as we remodel. The front of the office is nice, eh? Another of Ms. Barbara's talents that improves this place," he said as he reached out his hand with a smile.

"It is, and her cookies are wonderful," Darren said, shaking the doctor's hand. The hand was rougher than Darren would have expected, more of a manual labor feel than a doctor.

"Oh my, yes. You know she once had a food company rep in here telling her she could sell a million of those things if she'd license her recipe to them."

"And she wouldn't?" Darren asked.

"Oh, she absolutely sold. She's worth ten times more than anyone else in this town! The funny part is that I can't get her to retire. I think she gets a kick out of serving them to patients. Plus, they're always better when she makes 'em. The packaged kind is good, but you know, kind of eh," he said.

The doctor wasn't as large or handsome as Dr. Thornhill, but he had a calming sense to him, reminding Darren of a younger version of his grandfather. He had passed six months after his grandmother. A powerful yet gentle man that never overwhelmed with size or shouts but always carried a certain confidence. In his grandfather's last few years, his body became a shell of the powerful man Darren remembered from his childhood days, but the times together by the campfire or silently watching the river flow by his back cabin were cemented in Darren's mind. His grandfather had a John Wayne feel to him when he was getting work done around his cabin and the sprawling land that backed up to the river, but when it was time to relax, the bear hugs that held Darren or any of his cousins made them instantly feel protected and safe.

Dr. David Abrams gave off the same feeling of strength and protection, but without the bear hug. He seemed to do it with a single look and a smile. His distinct gray eyes beamed and held Darren's gaze from under the doctor's salt and pepper short hair.

"Good for her," Darren said.

"And for all the patients, but you didn't come to talk about cookies. Tell me what's going on?"

"Glass..." Darren felt the pain flare in his eyes as he thought of it.

The doctor leaned in to listen.

"My girlfriend has been saving glass bottles, old coke bottles, wine bottles, you know. We're cleaning and painting them up. We keep some and give some, but mostly she sells online and at local markets."

"Sounds lovely," the doctor said.

Darren nodded. "Yeah, she's wonderful and has great ideas for how to make something out of nothing. But one bottle, it shattered as I was scrubbing the label off." He held out his hand, showing remnants of a few nasty gashes that were now scabbing over. "But I think some bits got in my eyes. If I blink hard or when I'm trying to sleep, they sting. They just... hurt," he said as he winced.

"Sounds like it. Let's look," Dr. Abrams said as he pulled a small flashlight out of the front pocket of his white lab coat.

Darren tried not to flinch as the bright light moved around his cornea.

"Something is in there. Almost like sand that is scratching at your eyes," the doctor said. He waved Darren to another seat on the side of the room and tapped the device. "Chin here, forehead here."

"Is this the giant poof machine?" Darren asked as he complied with the instructions.

Dr. Abrams quit adjusting knobs. His brilliant gray eyes peered out from behind the equipment, and the smile gave Darren a feeling of ease.

"Sure is. It's best to think happy thoughts so you're not waiting for it to–"

POOF!

A shot of air hit Darren's right eye. Surprisingly, it wasn't too painful given his condition and Dr. Abrams's distracting conversation.

"Okay, next one." The nozzle backed up and then shifted over to his left eye.

"Tell me more about you. Girlfriend? Job?"

"Are you just trying to distract–"

POOF!

The second shot of air struck Darren's eyes.

"Yup," he said. The doctor grinned as he stood up and moved back to the main exam chair. "But I certainly want to learn about those areas and hope they're going well."

"Me too," Darren commented.

The doctor froze and turned toward Darren.

"Tell me more?" he asked.

"Job stuff and future, you know, finances and tying the knot," Darren admitted, then immediately wished he hadn't shared the personal thoughts. "We don't need to talk about these things. I know you're busy."

"I see." He nodded thoughtfully. "Finances can become a blessing or a curse. One of the most hard-hitting questions to answer for yourself is 'Is wealth worth it?'"

Darren nodded, remaining silent as a guilty feeling overtook him. What kind of provider would he be in the future if he couldn't even afford a decent ring?

Dr. Abrams opened a nearby cabinet and shuffled through its contents.

"Ah, here we are. Simple antibiotics, often overused, but in this case, they're exactly what you need. I'll give you the first dose, but you'll need to do these daily. The first few won't be fun. It'll hurt, but the body is amazing. You'll make a full recovery."

"It can't be worse than what it is now," Darren said.

"This will hurt much worse than it does now," the doctor said. "That's usually the case before real healing."

Darren winced, but the calming gray eyes of the doctor gave a sense of solace amid the painful ordeal, like being wrapped in a warm blanket as they traveled through bitter cold.

"If it heals 'em, let's do it." Darren straightened up in the leather chair.

"That's the spirit. You know how antibiotics work, right?" he said, pausing for a moment as he readied the dropper with medicine. "They stop bacteria from multiplying. It breaks down the cells within the bacteria. Once they can't reproduce and the original population dies off, well, it's like a mass extinction event."

"Sounds like a good thing," Darren tried to agree.

"Can be. Bacteria can serve a purpose, but can also be horrible. Reminds us that even horrible things serve a purpose. Okay, lean your head back."

Doctor Abrams held back one of Darren's eyelids and let three precise drops fall.

It felt like fire erupted underneath his eyelids. He shouted and jerked his head, but the doctor quickly put his hand on the younger man's forehead and held him steady. Pain illuminated his eye, burning the socket all around his eye. However, in the heat of the horrid sensation, the gentle, firm hand of the doctor gave him a sense of peace. It calmed him enough to endure the intense feeling until it gradually decreased.

"It stops malicious bacteria, but, unfortunately, kills the good bacteria as well. Such a powerful agent can't tell the difference between good and bad. Both die off."

"There are *good* bacteria in my eyes?" Darren said as he blinked, one eye still searing in pain.

"Lean back. Let's get the other one... *Every* living thing serves its purpose. And unfortunately, when the bad overwhelms or prevents the good from doing its job, well... everything suffers. But thankfully, there is always a remnant of the good left to rebuild. That's a promise."

He let loose another three drops and Darren once again flinched, this time able to hold back a scream. The doctor held his hand on the patient, helping to control and calm him as the pain died down. The second set of drops was just as painful as the first, but the doctor holding him and speaking to him helped.

"Okay, so one set of three drops every day until you use up the bottle. Should be about ten days."

Darren wanted to rub his eyes, but he resisted. Instead, he blinked like crazy as his eyes watered.

"When was your last eye exam?" Dr. Abrams asked.

"Probably high school. I've never needed glasses," Darren said.

"There's a lot more to healthy sight than just glasses, but tell you what, let's start with vision correction and go from there?"

"I'm not sure my insurance covers that, and thank you, but I really should get back to work. My boss is strict on time."

"Free of charge, and you'll need to let those drops settle for a bit until you drive. So before you get another cookie on your way out, what do you say?"

The thought of Ms. Barbara's delicious cookies softened Darren's resolve. He nodded in agreement and the doctor pulled down the large gray phoropter. The silver rings around the little glass holes sparkled against the light as the smooth arm swung down and the doctor positioned it in front of Darren.

"Sure. What can it hurt? But wait, can I even see clearly right now?" He blinked and a tear of excess moisture escaped, rolling down his cheek.

"Sometimes we only see clearly after intense situations." The doctor lined up the large device to Darren's eyes. "Now, lean forward and tell me what you see..."

Darren wiped the tear away and pressed his face against the device. At first, all he saw was black and thought a cover must still be on, but then the doctor's voice seemed to jump down the hallway, like it echoed from a distant cave. White sparkles illuminated the black. Then, the world around him changed.

He was no longer in the black leather exam chair but was looking up at the night sky and desperately trying to catch his breath.

Chapter 2

"They're... coming..." the panting voice of a young girl whispered in his ear as she struggled to catch her breath.

"Who–" he started, but the deafening clang of metal striking an empty dumpster at the end of the alley shot out in the night. It echoed down the alleyway and thundered in his ears.

The voice that left his mouth was odd, not his own but that of a child. Looking down, he saw that his hands were different: younger, smaller, but also rougher, calluses built up as if from years of manual labor, and black edges of dirt and soot outlined his fingernails. Turning, he saw the girl at his side. She couldn't have been more than ten years old.

"They're coming," she urged, pulling his arm. Her frightened look pleaded with him more than words ever could.

He instinctively knew who she was and understood the situation. Like waking up from a deep sleep, his mind sharpened.

"Kira, they're already here," he said.

"Then get rid of it. Maybe they'll go for the food and not us," she said.

He felt his pocket and the crinkle of a plastic wrapper muffled from his dirty pants.

"Mango," he whispered as a memory filled his mind. All of their troubles tonight were because of the synthetic fruit.

"Get rid of it!" she whispered.

"No." His new body and mind took over. "I took it for you. Those monsters can take it from my cold, dead hands."

His hands wrapped to fists as he peered out from behind the foul-smelling dumpster. They were getting closer. A man in a purple robe swung a metal club, striking everything he passed and giving a bell tower-like toll that tracked their fear like a metronome. The booming, hollow echo reverberated against the cracked buildings of the dense city as they searched.

"Kaden, let's go!" she whispered with urgency, shaking his arm.

Kaden.

Hearing his name was like a revelation, a breath of fresh air.

"Kaden!" She pushed him and he finally moved. Holding hands, they darted behind the next corner, moving through shadows and between alleys.

"They hate the sewers. Keep your eyes open," he whispered as they sprinted.

"But we can't," she replied.

"We'll have to," he barked back.

Ahead, he saw a circular cover and picked up the pace. They held hands as they raced, and a glint of hope sparked within him.

But before they reached the manhole, his body stopped running, frozen mid-stride. All the air in his lungs shot out as if only his body stopped and the air carried forward. The intense pain of an invisible, constricting force tightened around his midsection. He struggled against the pain, and soon it released, dropping him to the cold, hard ground. Kira toppled over him and rolled to the alley.

A guttural noise, like a demonic hum rumbling from deep in the earth, sounded from the creature behind them.

"Go," he mouthed to Kira, but she refused to enter the sewer as she looked back at him. They quickly dove into the next alley and behind a dumpster, burrowing into putrid smells and soggy trash piles. Their childhood weaved in and out of the filth in the Outer Ring, learning to keep their clothes in good condition so they'd fit in with the cleaner children of the Inner Ring and its working class.

Now the pair buried their heads into their arms as they tried to stay quiet.

"Rats can run..." a voice rumbled as a man in a purple robe strolled into the alley, as if on a leisurely walk. A dark figure stepped into the alley next to the purple-robed man. Its outline was human-like, but its skin crumpled as it came forward, the sound of rubbing rocks with each subtle movement. The creature paused and smelled the air. Opening its mouth, it seemed to taste the air more than breathe it. Its skin was a cracked charcoal, and the dry, ashy lips curled up, revealing black teeth with a grayish coloring that eerily matched the creature's exterior. The light of a nearby lamp moved across its face as Kaden lifted his head. He saw the gums and tongue, both the same lifeless black as the teeth. The creature's open mouth smiled, sensing food and eager to feed.

"But they can't hide," the purple-robed man hissed.

The charcoal thing waved its hand, and the rubbish-filled dumpster in front of the children flew down the alley. Kira remained in her huddled position, but Kaden picked up his head and stared death in the face. Again, he saw the creature smile in delight as Kaden looked back, a mix of terror and wonder as he looked upon the demon-like stone face above the black robe.

The thing closed its mouth and took a long inhale through its nose. Kaden felt a pull toward the thing, like its breath contained a gravity that pulled him closer.

He forced himself to keep his eyes open, to study the creature of this nightmare. The thing seemed to emanate power, yet its dead, cracked skin took away from its perfect silhouette of muscle. As if a corrupted Michelangelo's David, carved from black marble, a perfect creation, but then dried, burnt, and thrown down a flight of stairs. The charcoal-skin more devoured the light from the nearby street lamps than reflected it. Shadows from deep cracks etched across it like spiderwebs of chipped away stone stole any unique characteristics of the thing's face. A demonic mannequin come to life.

From behind it came another demon, appearing as if a living shadow. It stepped smoothly into the alley, as if gliding on air, and stood behind the first. Kaden stole a look at it and saw the same charcoal skin and washed away features, yet underneath, he could tell there was a difference in the two. Like branches from different trees, they held their own unique colors and curves, but were both thrown in the fire, their flaking burnt shells pulled out.

"Here!" Kaden pulled the package of pale mango slices from his pocket and thrust it forward. He prayed they took the bait as he thought about how fast he and Kira could get to the sewers. But the creature never took its eyes off of Kaden. The second creature now eyed Kira, a wolf eyeing a wounded fawn.

The man in the purple robe stepped next to Kaden, snatching the package from Kaden's hand. A long metal weapon, a club-like mace with a smooth ball on a long rod, hung from his belt. Kaden recognized it, the tool of all Agents, and the source of the deafening hollow sound when they smacked it against the dumpsters.

"Unauthorized rations and out after curfew?" he snapped.

But Kaden ignored the man as the charcoal creature held its gaze. It pulled on the boy with every breath, like waves of gravity rhythmically inching him closer to the thing.

"What's your name, boy?"

He didn't answer.

"You've seen one before?" The man in purple gestured to the metal piece at his side.

Memories from a past he never knew entered his mind. He knew they were not Darren's memories, but those of Kaden, the young boy he inhabited in this dystopian hell. He saw glimpses in his mind's eye, men in various colored robes swinging the piece of metal: a long, thin handle with a solid ball on the end. The heavy object was lethal when swung with force, but the fear that erupted in young Kaden wasn't from the force of the impact, but the crackle that came from the electricity inside. One hit could break bones and paralyze the unlucky soul in its path. And a shot to the head permanently turned the lights out.

Kaden's eyes jumped to the object and then back to the demonic figure, its patience wearing as its lips curled.

"One more time, boy. What's your name?" He removed the mace from its holster and his head tilted up as he looked down at Kaden.

The boy still refused to speak, and the man squeezed the handle of the mace. A bright flicker popped off the smooth metal ball, sending an echoing crackle through the air.

"We're running from our mother!" Kira called out.

He drew back from Kaden and looked toward the girl.

"Oh?" he said unsympathetically.

"There's an Agent that *visits* her. He doesn't like children," Kira said, and painful memories of a backhand striking his face exploded in Kaden's mind.

"*I* don't like children," the man snapped back, and Kaden saw a memory of Kira being shoved to the ground.

"I won't let him!" Kaden jumped up.

The charcoal demon roared a guttural call, and Kaden was pushed by an invisible force back to the cold, stone-covered ground.

"You think you'll find mercy by breaking the curfew laws?" he said with an unsympathetic smirk.

"No, sir," Kira said. "The Agents of Empyrean. Warriors of Order, like you, who seek order and life in Pinnacle's glorious name," she pleaded.

He remained silent as a corner of his mouth curled up, enjoying the praise.

"We seek refuge from those who disobey Pinnacle's grand plan," Kira said.

Kaden sensed the impatience of the two black creatures. The purple-robed man seemed to as well. The smile left his face.

"You caused the chaos that you now seek refuge from." He pointed his mace at Kaden's face. "Your name."

"Darren," he said instinctively.

Kira shot a confused look at him, then quickly tried to hide it. They both remained silent, their mouths tightly shut.

"You seek refuge amid lies." He spun the mace in his hand as he walked in circles. "Now which to let eat, my Spark Club or..." He squeezed the handle and a tiny bolt of lightning popped off the club. The alley lit up, their shadows dancing against the cracked brick walls of the surrounding buildings. The creatures' demonic faces that continued to stare at him and Kira. "Or my Elites... Hmmm," he jested.

The two children moved closer together, Kaden nudging them toward the manhole to make a run for it. Kira squeezed his arm so tight, he felt his wrist tingle.

"I suppose we'll follow procedure," he said as he stepped toward Kaden. However, for the first time, he stepped in between the charcoal demon and Kaden, breaking its gaze with the child. Like a meal pulled from the hungry jaws of a wolf, the creature of black snapped. With one motion, it shoved the man to the side, sending him rolling down the alley, before shooting a claw-like hand at Kaden's throat. It clamped, crushing the muscles in his neck as it picked him off the ground.

The second creature erupted forward as if on cue. Kira ducked behind Kaden, but the human-like thing was too fast. A split-second later, the black stone of a hand held her up by the throat as well. She tried to scream, but the hand closed off her air.

Kaden tried to turn to her, but he was already off the ground. He scratched at the forearm, his fingernails breaking against the ashy black rock. His eyes shot to the side, looking for her, but she was now out of view.

He gulped for air, his lungs burning as his throat screamed in pain. The world started going dark as he felt himself inching closer to the creature. His neck seared in pain, his skin heating as it seemed to meld with the thing's hand.

"You serve me!" the purple-robed shouted.

The black rock of a creature snarled at the man, then it raised its other hand, and amazingly, the man in purple robes flew toward the creature in black. Like a stuffed doll, the creature batted the man's head. Like a bob-blehead doll, it careened off the creature's hand and then bounced off the cobblestone alley. Blood trickled from the man's ears and the black-robed creature slowly turned his head back toward the boy.

Kaden saw the fear in the man's face as he shot off the ground, pulled by the creature. But now, he lay limp on the hard cobblestone ground as his

Spark Club rolled out of his hand and struck the dumpster, a pathetic ping of a noise compared to the once horrifying echo.

Now the creature, fully focused on Kaden again, squeezed tighter and seemed to pull the boy into itself. But a moment later, a cool feeling swept around him.

To him, the feeling was like a gentle breeze passing by. Behind the demon holding him, a blurry figure shot down the alley as if hit by a bus. It flew parallel to the earth and slammed violently into a far wall. From Kaden's fading vision, he saw bits of brick and pieces of the hard, black rock-like flesh thrown into the air.

He heard Kira gasping for air as she held her neck.

She was free.

In a fury, the hand holding Kaden's neck lifted higher and then spiked him to the ground. He saw a brilliant flash of light as his head bounced off a brick. Somewhere within the flash of light, a glimpse of a distant doctor's office revealed itself and then disappeared as fast as it came.

He lifted his head in time to see the creature fly back, striking a solid wall at least ten feet off the ground. The force of the impact left a rough outline of the charcoal demon into the wall. The thing looked to be cracked all the way through, like a broken statue falling from the building, gravity peeling it down. It fell as lifelessly as a rag doll, striking the ground below with an earthshaking thud.

Kaden looked at Kira as she scrambled closer to him. But she wasn't looking at him; her eyes locked on the entrance of the alleyway.

His head screamed in pain and his body felt ten times heavier. A pool of blood formed around him, flowing from a fractured skull and three-inch long gash on the back of his head.

Seeing Kira alive gave him relief at the pain. A moment later, with his last piece of life, he followed her stare to the alleyway.

Something, someone stood there. His vision grew blurry as he tried to make out the backlit silhouette. A thin hooded cape rippled in the soft breeze of the night air.

A flicker of light lit up his vision, and he was back in the doctor's office. His mind reeled. It flashed between the alleyway and the pain on the back of his head, where it had struck the cobblestone ground. Yet another flash, and he recognized the eye doctor's office. Like a strobe light controlling his reality, his mind flashed between the alley and the office as Kaden lost more life every second and he pulled back to Darren.

The silhouette of a man in the alley.

The phoropter in the office.

The two images came into focus, two worlds blending into one.

The last thing Kaden saw before returning to Darren's body were the sparkling gray eyes of the man in the alleyway entrance.

He'd saved their lives.

Those brilliant gray eyes.

With a final jolt, Darren jumped out of the brown leather exam chair, smacking his head on the arm of the phoropter and falling back into the leather chair. Again he stood, shoving the device aside, and behind it were the gray eyes of the doctor.

Dr. Abrams looked back at him as Darren's shoulders rose and fell. His breath settled.

"Tell me, how was your life?" Dr. David Abrams asked him.

Chapter 3

His stomach churned, rejecting the sensation of death and jumping worlds. The doctor swiftly grabbed the wastebasket and slid it under Darren, barely catching the vomit that exploded out.

"It's okay, that happens," Dr. Abrams said.

Darren stood up, his head spinning with confusion. He stepped backward out of the office and into the dark hallway. Dr. Abrams' gentle eyes held his stare and invited him back into the office like a warm blanket on a frigid day, but the disjointed lives of Kaden and Darren jammed his mind, the memories of each life a cacophony screaming in his mind. He wanted to run, to be in his room, to be away from whatever this was that was pulling his brain apart.

Breaking eye contact with the doctor, he turned out of the office. Jogging from the hallway, his eyes locked on the round knob of the exit door, trying to ignore everything else around him and to just leave the place. In his tunnel vision, he caught something. It felt like a brick wall, but as he looked up, he saw the same three-piece tailored suit of Doctor Thornhill. He'd returned, but how long had Darren been gone?

The well-dressed doctor had barely moved, looking down at Darren with a dispassionate blank expression.

Barbara shot up from behind her desk.

"Oh, Mr. McArthur! Are you okay?"

"Fine," he muttered as he scrambled to his feet.

"You look a little off," Thornhill commented, but Darren was already at the door before Barbara could get to him.

He scrambled through the gravel parking lot toward his truck, slamming the door shut behind him. The engine off, he stared at the wheel. His eyes darted back and forth as the memories of his own life meshed with Kaden's life.

"Kira?" he muttered, unsure how he knew her, yet knowing they've been together since Kaden could remember.

His mind was a raging strobe light, catching a flicker of thought and then losing it before another shot into the frame.

The familiar environment of his truck sank into his subconscious. The music playing from the radio and the glowing red numbers on the clock gave his mind a subtle comfort that settled his thoughts and his breathing.

"Agents," he whispered, as if breathing life into a nightmare. The vision of the two charcoal creatures took center stage in his mind. He shuddered and then remembered the way the air felt when the hooded figure effortlessly sent them away. Cool, easy, refreshing.

Looking up from the steering wheel, he turned back to the office. The window blinds were closed. Within the bright light of the exam room, he could see two men.

A moment later, the blinds rotated open, and the gray eyes of Dr. Abrams looked out. Darren froze, wondering if the doctor could see him through the tinted windows of the truck. The doctor seemed to look right at him, holding his view for longer than needed, but then he turned back to the conversation with Dr. Thornhill.

Shadows moved over the parking lot from clouds passing under the sun. Darren continued to look back at the doctor's window.

"What in the world…" he said before putting his truck in gear. The crackle of the gravel drowned out the sound of the radio as he pulled away from the office.

He soon sat at a red light and grabbed his phone. Dialing her number, he waited as it rang, but the generic sound of voicemail came before her.

"The person you are trying to reach is unavailable at this—"

"Come on, Kelly."

The long beep came, and Darren spilled his thoughts as quickly as they came.

"I think I just hallucinated and then had a panic attack of some kind at the eye doctor. It was the weirdest thing. You know those dreams where it feels so real? It was like that, but… but even *more* real. I could smell the stale, warm air of the alley. And my head, I think I cracked my skull there. Well, some monster thing was trying to get us. It strangled us and threw me down, but there was a guy in a hood, like some urban dark superhero. He saved us…"

Darren stopped and finally took a breath.

"Monsters and powers don't make much sense, huh? It felt so real."

He hung up the phone as the truck continued on, the hum of the engine sounding through the cab.

Two miles later, his phone vibrated in the cup holder. He snatched it immediately.

"Kelly, hey–"

"Are you on your way home?" she interrupted.

"Yes… Where are you?"

"Look, Darren, we need to talk," she said.

"You heard my message, right?"

"I did, and… I'm on my way. We need to talk," she said.

"Kelly," he said, but she had hung up. "We need to talk...?" he repeated. "No one says that unless..."

He felt like an idiot leaving a lunatic's message on her voicemail.

The visions of the other life, Kaden's life, echoed like a distant drum in his mind as he finished the drive back to his apartment. He pulled in the parking lot that wrapped around to their doorway. Both of his roommates' cars were there, but there was an empty spot where Kelly always parked. The black asphalt in between two white lines looked hollow in the partly cloudy afternoon sun.

As Darren turned the knob to enter the apartment, he heard his child-hood friends, brothers Chris and Kirk, and their typical banter. Usually, their comical narration of whatever video game was the latest craze, along with various jokes aimed at opponents and each other, made him smile, but now the thought of them being here during a serious discussion with Kelly left a pit in his stomach. A hollow sense that reminded him of Kelly's empty guest parking spot.

"I thought you were eating better?" the older brother Chris said as Darren entered.

"I am," Kirk responded.

"You're having Pop Tarts for lunch."

"Yeah?"

"Bro, those are awful," Chris said.

"Made with twenty-one grams of whole grains. See, it says on the package," Kirk said.

"That's meaningless. What about all the enriched bleached flour and hydrogenated oils?"

The conversation didn't skip a beat as Darren entered. He received a nod from each brother as they continued.

"You're just jelly, a big jar of green jelly."

"I'm not jealous."

"Big jar of green jelly..."

Chris rolled his eyes.

"These things even have protein in 'em," Kirk added.

"They're awful for you, bro. You need to quit all that sugar and junk carbs."

"Oh, and how much sugar is in your morning orange juice?" Kirk fired back.

"That's a fruit. It's good sugar, like honey!"

Kirk waved his hand, dismissing his brother as if his comments were a passing fly. Then he took half of a Pop Tart with one bite.

"And if you're going to eat that junk, why not S'mores?"

"Because strawberry is the best and S'mores taste like plastic," Kirk said.

"Lie. S'mores, best all-time Pop Tart flavor," Chris said, smacking the table.

Kirk pushed back his chair, raising it to two legs. With both hands in the air, he motioned to Darren.

"Come on, D. S'mores or strawberry?"

"Leave me out of this world-changing debate, would ya?" Darren responded.

"No, no, no. You need to back a horse in this race," Chris demanded.

Darren rubbed his eyes. The drops from Dr. Abrams appeared to be working. He didn't feel the violent sting of pain under his eyelids.

"Come on... Give it to him. Strawberry is king," Kirk said, a wide smile on his face.

Darren returned Kirk's eager smile with a sympathetic expression.

Kirk's smile faded.

"No. Don't you dare," Kirk started, shaking his head.

Chris stood up from the round breakfast table like an eager contestant on a game show, ready to see their prize revealed.

"S'mores is the best Pop Tart flavor of all time," Darren said.

Chris dropped to one knee and pumped his fist in celebration.

The forlorn expression on Kirk's face didn't last long. He took another bite. Bits of hardened white frosting with sprinkles and warm red filling fell with crumbs from the pastry exterior. The broad smile returned. Chris stopped celebrating when he noticed Kirk's satisfaction.

"Hey, Kelly might stop by. If she does, you mind going to your own rooms?" Darren interrupted.

"Common area, bro," Kirk mumbled, his mouth still half full.

"I know it's the living room, but come on, help me out here," Darren said.

"Trouble in paradise?" Chris exaggerated, knowing Darren hated that phrase, so he used it every chance he could.

"Something like that," Darren dismissed.

"Oooohhhhh," the brothers said in unison, leaning back in their chairs.

"Yeah, yeah..." Darren said, leaving the common area and closing the door of his room behind him. Pulling out his phone, he put on Beethoven's Fifth to drown out his friend's banter. He cleaned his room, picking up the dirty clothes and organizing his scattered work notes. He was making his bed when he heard Chris call out.

Darren came out of his room and looked through the living room window to the parking lot.

Kelly sat in her car, staring back at them from the guest spot.

"Bro, she okay?" Kirk said, walking beside Darren and peering out.

"She said she *needs to talk*," he said.

The brothers turned to look at each other, then toward Darren.

"This is serious, huh? But you two are legit together," Chris said.

"It's been a really weird morning," Darren said.

With all three men standing in the window looking out at the parking lot, Kelly kept her eyes locked on Darren. She was frozen, both hands still on the steering wheel.

"I'm going for her," he said, turning toward the door, but as soon as he moved, Kelly broke her pause. Slamming the car in reverse, she shot backwards before peeling off in the parking lot.

Darren stopped and felt his heart drop, his chest an empty cavity.

He called her five times that night, but each call went quickly to voicemail. It took over an hour for him to fall asleep. When he finally closed his eyes, he dreamt. The vivid dream put him back in the other world.

In the dream, he was Kaden in the other world again, but now the same as himself in his reality. Booming echoes of an Agent striking the dumpsters sounded all around him.

Kira was near him, also now in her mid-twenties like him. Before he could get a good look at her, she shot off running, leading the way through the alleyways and tight streets in between a mix of patched brickwork and crumbling buildings. He followed, trying to keep up.

She bounced through shadowy pockets in between street lights. Through the shadows, she flashed back and forth from hidden to visible. He ran after her, at first trying to catch her, but soon the echoing boom behind him became so overwhelming that he no longer ran to her but from the deafening noise. Fear pulsed in his veins as his heart raced.

Kira pulled away, but as he tried speeding up, he found his legs slowing. Heat pressed on him from behind and he stole a look back. A wall of fire, like a tidal wave rising from the horizon to overtake the sky, roared toward him. With every deafening boom, the wall pulsed and lunged closer to him.

Faster, faster. The beat picked up and the inferno sped at him. It ripped through buildings, destroying everything in its path as it crept closer to him.

He could feel the heat as he ran, still following Kira's path, but he could never gain on her. She stayed just out of reach. Every time he thought she was close enough to reach out and touch her, she'd turn a corner and Kaden would turn to find her further away.

As she extended the gap between them, the fire behind him grew closer. Inch by inch, he felt the heat on his back intensify. Soon, the back of his neck and legs felt like they might burst open, like his skin was sitting at two hundred and eleven degrees, ready to boil.

Kira accelerated forward and disappeared behind a man at the top of the street. With the moonlight behind him, the man stood with his hooded jacket. The wind whipped at the edges of the jacket. He stood firm and confident, with a sense of relaxation that confused Kaden as he raced to escape the fire.

Kaden sprinted at the man, trying to find Kira's path. The fire licked his feet, but as he approached, the hooded figure held up his hand and stopped Kaden mid-stride. As if frozen in time, one leg outstretched as the other pushed off the ground.

He thought of the fire overtaking him, but there was no fear in the man. The inferno could have been a birthday candle to him. A split-second later, and the hooded-figure was nose-to-nose with Kaden. He came so fast, it was like a blink of light, a blip through space and time.

The overwhelming fear of the fire evaporated as he looked into the man's gray eyes.

Then, the fire caught them. But it didn't burn them. It wrapped around them and Kaden knew it was the man protecting them. A strange power emanated from him, providing a bubble-like shield that held back the flames.

"The fire!" Kaden gasped as he felt the air being pulled out of his lungs by the hungry flames.

The man nodded, as if acknowledging the flames were real and locking eyes with Kaden.

"You're the fire," he said.

Then his gray eyes closed. He leaned his head back, exposing his neck. The flames jumped at him like a hungry wolf on a wounded cub, sinking its teeth into the soft neck tissue. Flames wrapped around his neck and tightened. Soon, the entire wall of fire was on him, his flesh burning, the jacket crumbling away. His skin turned a bright red, like iron in a furnace, then it went black, lifeless. He could have been a charcoal demon.

The man absorbed the entire wall of fire and now stood as lifeless ash. Kaden stood in shock, examining the lifeless statue of charcoal, but as he inched closer, the wind picked up. Flakes of black particles floated away.

As the burnt body left in the wind, the sun rose, bringing light to the night.

Kaden looked up, Kira stood ahead of him, and both turned their gaze to the heavens.

Darren woke from the dream as a voice rang out, "You're the fire." It sounded like a church bell, echoing in his mind even as he sat up panting, sweat covering his face.

Chapter 4

He sat up in bed, letting his breath settle as he felt the damp cold of his sweat on the sheets. It surrounded him like a policeman's chalk outline on his bedding. The light of the sunrise crept into his dark room, and the image of the fire and the man in the hooded cloak faded back.

His vision was blurry and painful as he looked around the room. His mouth was as dry as the Sahara, and the pounding of a headache crept into his mind, an unrelenting bass drum. He opened and closed his dry mouth, wishing he didn't have to leave his room to get water. He felt as though the fire from his dreams had removed all hydration from his creaking joints and sore muscles.

Filling up the largest glass he could find, he sat on the couch and forced all twenty-four ounces down and began to stretch his sore body. The gray eyes from the dream constantly popped into his mind. He dropped into a squatting position as he grabbed his phone, hoping to see Kelly's name, but nothing.

"Good morning, I love you," he texted her. Three bubbles appeared, then quickly disappeared.

"Yooo!" Kirk called out as he came out of his room and went to the refrigerator. His shaggy brown hair was a tangled mess of bed head, matching the scratchiness of his voice. He poured a glass of his brother's OJ and watched Darren stretch.

"Squatty McSquaterson, what you up to?"

"Trying not to feel like garbage. My joints are like drying cement."

"You gettin' sick?" Kirk said, then held up the bottle of OJ, shaking it. "Vitamin C, bro?"

"No thanks," Darren said, glancing at his phone again. No messages.

"Whelp, you probably caught something from that doctor visit. Only sick folks go to the doctor."

"I went to an eye doctor," Darren replied.

"Eh, same thing. Go back to bed. Let it run its course," Kirk said.

"I'm working today," Darren said, shaking his head.

"Oh yeah, the ol' nine-to-five. Well, you enjoy grinding it, and I'm going back to sleep," Kirk said as he downed the glass and then took another swig straight from the large plastic bottle before heading back to his room.

"Caught something..." Darren said as he finished stretching and moved to his bathroom. The cold shower jolted him like a cup of coffee, and slowly, his body began catching up to his mind, feeling more normal. The headache and soreness slowly subsided. Buttoning his shirt, he looked at his phone. Kelly told him they *needed to talk* and then drove away as soon as she saw him move closer to her. Now checking for her response was driving him mad. He resolved to not text or call her again until after work. In between those times, he'd give her space.

Work. He'd been so distracted with the visit to Dr. Abrams and the other world, he hadn't thought about work. If he was ever going to afford the engagement ring, he needed a promotion. The ring and wedding that Kelly deserved was out of his grasp. But now maybe she was out of his. If only student loan payments were as good as a diamond.

He left early for work, hoping to get a few things done before the daily standup meetings began. Early on, he loved hearing about other people's work and being able to update the group, but lately, everyone's thirty-second updates revolved around the same long-term projects. They had built the basis of their analytics platform and now were in the change management phase. Darren's work revolved around studying spreadsheets to measure usage—nothing that his undergraduate medical school-focused degree prepared him for—but he enjoyed the analysis and linking strategy to patient health outcomes, at least when he felt his boss wasn't pestering him about a problem he'd already figured out. In his role, he saw the numbers before anyone, and the latest attempt to gain market share wasn't working. Adoption wasn't happening.

Halfway through the drive, he waited at a red light, and the gray eyes of Dr. Abrams came back to his mind. Traffic was light that morning and he sat at the intersection, his truck the only vehicle in sight. The timer switched the lights and a green left turn arrow gave freedom to the empty lane at his side. He stared at it for what seemed an eternity. The green arrow glowed in the hazy morning, as if inviting him down its path.

Straight ahead was work, an early jump on the day's tasks.

To the left, the glowing green arrow pointed toward the eye doctor's office, and the gray eyes that seared themselves into his mind.

The red lights of the clock next to his truck's radio told him he had time to go by the office.

The green arrow remained.

He thought.

It went yellow and he jammed on the gas pedal, spinning the tires and shooting through the empty intersection. A smoky haze rose from the melted black of his tires pointed toward the eye doctor's office.

"Well, hello, Mr. McArthur!" Ms. Barbara said as Darren entered.

"Hi, any chance the doctor's available?" Darren asked.

"Sure thing. He's wrapping a meeting. Cookie?" she asked as she motioned for him to take a seat.

"No, ma'am," Darren said, sitting on the edge of the plush couch.

As he waited, he heard a muffled conversation bounce down the dark hallway. Dr. Abrams and the other voice went back and forth as if in debate. The voices soon burst out into the hallway.

"Look, all I'm saying is if we go public with your test case, it'll convince everyone, all the investors, PLUS the board," Dr. Thornhill said as he came into the light of the waiting room. He wore another perfectly tailored three-piece suit, this one black with a gray vest and a perfectly folded handkerchief instead of the gold pocket watch chain. The man could have been CEO of the largest bank in the world. He looked so sophisticated, well-off, and refined.

"Thomas, you know my stance," Dr. Abrams replied.

"How about this: talk with Sarah before we do the next bloodwork? You two should consider the impact of your health on the kids."

"I am thinking of my kids, and future generations," Dr. Abrams responded.

"David, your kids will be in middle school soon. I'm betting they know more than you let on. You can't hide endless rounds of chemo, but this, all your vitals are through the roof. You could be the face of a billion-, no, trillion-dollar drug!"

"I have accepted my path, and we're not hiding anything," Dr. Abrams said.

"Oh, cut the crap!" Thomas snapped. "You're one the smartest men I've ever met, but you're the dumbest when it comes to your own well-being. I wouldn't have gotten through medical school if it wasn't for you, but then you hide your life and career as an optometrist? You could bring the secrets of the cosmos to existence within every person's cellular structure, yet you work with spit and mud trying to heal blind eyes!"

"There is nothing more important than helping the world see right," Dr. Abrams said. He was still shrouded in the shadows of the dark hallway, but Darren saw the brilliant gray eyes move from Dr. Thornhill and look straight at him.

"Because once you see, you can't unsee," Dr. Abrams said.

"And you think everyone will just *somehow* see? No offense, David, but if your business came to me for capital backing, I'd say it's about as flimsy as the walls of Jericho," Thornhill said.

Darren leaned in the chair, trying to not be too obvious as he overheard the conversation.

"I don't mind that comparison. An example of what God can do with the faithful," Doctor Abrams said with a smile.

"I'm not joking here, David. I don't understand why you're avoiding the easiest decision of your life. Your story will inspire the world," Thornhill said.

"You're right. However, my decision isn't the easy one; it's the right one. I can see that," Abrams replied.

"David, we're moving forward. You should be the one to tell the world, not because of the money or because you're my friend and mentor, but because I care. Don't let this chance for a better life with Sarah and the kids slip away. Besides," Dr. Thornhill smiled, "enabling unthinkable energy production in the cell was your idea. But if you won't come forward, leading the research, and your example, who knows what the patent board and FDA will think," he said, winking at Dr. Abrams and stepping back. "Your name is on the papers, but it won't be in the media."

"Do your duty," Dr. Abrams said before turning and heading back through the shadows of the hallway toward his office.

Thornhill stood in the waiting area, then turned to Barbara and threw his hands up. "Your boss..."

"He's quite the man, eh?" Barbara replied happily.

"Sure," Thornhill said, moving to the door, but then he noticed Darren. "Oh, back again?" He sat down on the couch next to him.

"Hey, doctor," Darren said.

"Tell me, how's the love life?" Thornhill jested.

"I'm trying to get seen before work," Darren said, trying to change the subject.

"Did you know I own a business consulting firm?"

Darren shook his head.

"I see young men like you all the time. Each one trying to climb the ladder and get the girl."

"Okay," Darren said passively.

"I'm going to stop you there." Thornhill looked down at Darren. "Stand up, kid. That slouch tells me you don't care about yourself."

"Why do I need to–"

"Stand up! And don't let me call you *kid*," Thornhill said in a firm, demanding voice.

Darren complied.

"Look, kid–"

"Don't call me kid," Darren injected.

"Ha! Perfect, you're learning already," Thornhill exclaimed. "You came in here because you have an eye problem, but not seeing the world right is your real problem. Sure, get your eyes checked and deal with my friend's kooky methods," Thornhill said as he watched Darren, who remained silent, a skeptical look across his face. "Life's not that complicated, kid–"

"Don't–" Darren interrupted.

"Now you're catching on. Good!" Dr. Thornhill spoke over him as a smile came out. "I mentor young men just like you, and life's not that complicated. Why should all the best things in life be so difficult to obtain? The secret is, they're not! We imagine it's so hard because we let other priorities get in the way. Take my friend, for example," he said, pointing to the shadowy hallway. "His brilliance? He could be a trillionaire. But he focuses on things that don't give him leverage. If I had his seat, I'd be able to flip this world inside out, but even with what I have now, I've made hundreds of millions through scientific research and entrepreneurship. You know my secret?"

Darren shook his head.

"Mr. McArthur, the doctor is ready for you," Barbara said.

"One sec." Darren held up a finger.

"Control," Dr. Thornhill said, his face going firm with determination as he locked eyes with him.

"Control?" Darren's eyebrows raised.

"Yup, control yourself and you control the world around you. Listen, son, you can drift through this world or you can make what you want. You're trying to get to work early, to grind that extra inch with hopes of recognition, am I right?"

Darren's silence confirmed his answer.

"But listen to your boss next time they speak, I mean really listen to their words. I'm betting they care more about looking good to their superiors than half a crap about *your* career and dreams."

"But I still need–"

"There's more than just promotions, but I'm telling you, take control of your life and those around you will fall into line. Life is about power, young man. It's a have and have-nots world. But the secret is, you *can* go get it!" He patted Darren on the back and left the office.

Barbara shepherded Darren through the hall and toward Dr. Abrams's office. He held his breath as he looked up at the phoropter. Dr. Abrams smiled at Barbara, thanking her, and turned to Darren.

"Rough night, eh?" he said, waving his arm for Darren to enter.

But Darren remained in the doorway. Barbara caught his eye. She smiled pleasantly, then winked at him, holding up a cookie. He let out a breath, relaxing his tense body, and took the cookie. As he thanked her, she left down the dark hall.

"You took the drops this morning?" Dr. Abrams asked.

Darren stood wide-eyed. With all his soreness and the dream of fire, he'd totally forgotten.

The doctor nodded, accepting reality.

"So, one day of instruction falls short? I suppose it's my own fault for not explaining the value of it well enough."

"Could you explain it to me?"

"The drops are quite simple–"

"No. I mean," Darren interrupted and noticed a sparkle in Dr. Abrams's eye, as if a parent anticipating a child's revelation.

"I mean what I saw. That world... I was a totally different person, and your eyes, they were there," Darren said, stumbling to find his words.

The two stared at each other, the doctor's smile now broad as he motioned toward the brown leather chair.

"That's a big question."

"We're not talking about eye health anymore, are we?"

"What makes you say that?" Dr. Abrams sat in the small round swivel chair with four wheels.

"You've done three rounds of chemo and have a wife and kids at home. I overheard Dr. Thornhill, but can't understand why you're still here."

"I've chosen my path. And if it's all the same to you, I like being here. There's value to it, whether patients see it or not." He smiled.

"Was that an eye doctor joke?" Darren said.

"Yes, yes, it was." Dr. Abrams laughed.

"You're here at some hole-in-the-wall office when you're terminally ill, your secretary has a multi-million-dollar cookie empire, and you're making jokes?"

"Once you see, you can't unsee."

"What does that even mean, and another thing, because I can't get around the idea that I was hallucinating. My girlfriend, or maybe ex-girlfriend, won't see me anymore and I'm having dreams of the world in that giant eye device–"

"It's a phoropter," the doctor interjected.

"Whatever it's called, there's a man in my dream whose eyes are sure a lot like yours, and he's telling me I'm responsible for a tidal wave of fire," Darren said.

"Yup." Dr. Abrams clapped his hands. "That's the future."

Darren stared blankly at the doctor.

"What?"

"Your dream was a dream, but Empyrean, that's the future."

"Empira... What?"

"Empyrean. That's the name of the place you went to in the future," the doctor said. His tone was so simple that it confused and infuriated Darren further.

"How f-f-far into the future..." Darren stuttered.

"About four hundred years."

"Yeah... I'm done here," Darren said as he began to stand up.

"You came to correct your vision, and true sight, *your vision*, is about a lot more than eyesight. You're going to help save the world, Darren McArthur, and you're going to do it in the future."

Darren sat in disbelief as Dr. Abrams rolled forward on the stool and then stood up, pulling down the phoropter. As he brought it down, he looked at Darren, and their eyes met. Darren saw the brilliant gray eyes from his dream. The same gray eyes of his hooded savior from the alleyway in the future.

"You're there too. Aren't you?"

"I am."

"I don't understand."

"You look through this and you're there, instantly. Your body is safe here all the while in that chair."

"And you?"

"I'm here *and* there," the doctor said.

"But I'm not me, I'm Kaden?" Darren asked.

Dr. Abrams nodded.

"And you're?"

"Something else," Dr. Abrams replied before switching the topic back to Darren. "You, Darren McArthur, are an ancestor of Kaden McCloud. The same blood. You are Kaden, and Kaden is you."

Darren paused to take it in, then looked back at the doctor. "But who are *you*?" Darren asked.

"Let's get you looking forward," the doctor said as he reset the equipment.

"But this is crazy," Darren said, now away from the chair and stepping backwards toward the office door. "Time travel is... nuts. It's not real."

"Isn't it? There are countless things that are unexplainable by today's science. A flood that covers the Earth, fire from Heaven takes out Sodom and Gomorrah, and the walls of Jericho fall at a shout."

"Those were all destruction of wicked things from a book thousands of years old. You could tell me Hercules jumped over the moon, or some other nonsense. We can't prove or disprove something so ancient."

"Why is the past, or present, so different from the future?" the doctor asked.

"This isn't..." Darren threw up his hands and exhaled. "I'm behind at work, yet I'm debating time travel with an optometrist." He shook his head.

"Your future is waiting for you, Kaden McCloud," the doctor said.

"No," Darren said, stepping back into the doorway. "I've been going along with everything in my life so far, and look where it's led me: seeing a quack doctor talking about the future to heal my scratched eyes? I'm taking control of this situation, and I'm not buying some nutcase time travel."

Dr. Abrams patiently leaned back in his chair and looked at the younger man with sympathy.

"Kaden... Empira-what-cha-ma-call-it. No, just no." He stepped into the dark hallway and left the office without another word.

CHAPTER 5

Darren stared at his monitor, slowly scrolling through the spreadsheet. His finger rose and fell as it clicked the down arrow. It dropped like a hammer with a loud 'click.' His head rested on his other hand, a look of boredom and displeasure, his gift back to the unyielding and endless data before him.

"Hey-o!" A head bobbed above his cubicle wall.

"Hey, Mr. Rondeau," Darren said, snapping out of his daze and sitting up.

"How's it looking?" John said, glancing at the screen.

"Well..." Darren took a deep breath. "If we think sales rise by at least nine percent, we're in good shape."

"Why does it feel like a *but* is coming?" John said.

"*But* I can't find evidence of any similar programs giving a lift near that. And the further I go out, the muddier the data. I can't attribute any sales lifts to comparable programs."

"Segment it down to participating offices?"

"I thought that too, but look." Darren changed windows and showed a line graph with two colored lines that weaved back and forth together. "The blue is in and the orange is out. No difference."

"But that's over a two-year window." John pointed to the date on the x-axis of the graph.

"That's part of the problem. We give this promotion to the sales staff and run quarterly promotions, but it's entirely up to them for when they sell it in. What's worse is we don't have the contract dates; the only lagging indicator is simply the doctor offices start prescribing us more. But we can't use that because then we get into the timing of the office visit versus natural lift from seasonality. It's all convoluted and we change the promotion every quarter."

Darren sat back as John leaned in to examine the graph more.

"Appreciate your work here, really, but we can't go to the core team with a hope and a prayer of nine percent."

"I'm not saying that. I'm saying–"

"You've been at this work for what, six months?" John cut him off.

"Over a year," Darren replied, and he wondered if John sensed how demoralized he was with over twelve months of work and no clear answers.

"You know the work, but you're going to have to dig in further and come up with answers. Bad data is an excuse, not a reason."

"Mr. Rondeau, I'm not saying that." Darren swung back his tone to be more professional. "I'm saying nine percent is the break-even and we have zero evidence that programs have–"

"Have you called anyone in the field? And come on, call me John," he interrupted.

"No, I've been trying to tease this out to give us a source of truth. The data doesn't lie," Darren said.

"But your source of truth is unclear. So, muddy data does lie, eh?" John snickered.

"Yeah, sure. Garbage in, garbage out, but that only backs up my point."

"And for field responses? Those folks are on the ground living this," John said.

"In last quarter's core team meeting, didn't they insist we can't trust field feedback for a data-driven sales lift? You said we have to verify it in the data to not be misled. So I'm–"

"You know we have to balance quantitative and qualitative. It's an art and science," John said then paused. "But in the end, it's all about change management. That's the organizational alignment we need." John looked away from the monitor for the first time, peering over the rows of cubicles. "They're still teaching effective change management in school these days, right?" John asked with a smirk.

"Yes, of course–" Darren desperately wanted to roll his eyes.

"MBAs feel so watered down these days," John said.

Darren slid back in his chair. He had a medical degree and an MBA but now sat as a medical device analyst, eagerly wanting to solve big problems but answering to a boss whose primary goal was to impress his leadership regardless of the methods.

John finally looked away from the sea of cubicles. "You have two years of experience here. It took me twenty to really master this, so you'll have to dig in. You'll see it, and hopefully, it doesn't take eighteen more years, eh, but who knows?" John said, exaggerating a playful smile and slapping Darren on the shoulder.

Darren's face didn't move. He had learned in his two years with the company that John Rondeau loved to cover his stress by acting playful and friendly. But that quickly flipped to passive-aggressive accusations of poor performance when his superiors were in the room. It still bewildered Darren how much time an organization could spend developing work, but one hiccup in the rollout or one unfavorable quote from a high-ranking leader, and a scarlet letter was pinned to the project. He thought he could help the world by influencing the medical field from the inside out, but John's insistence to "massage the data" or "keep digging" was pushing Darren's motivation to the brink.

His boss let down the fake smile and returned to examining the graphs.

"There is a way to segment this data and figure out the sales lift, and I bet it'll be higher than nine percent. We have records of each sales call, plus the contract team has all the records. There's two ideas for ya right there!" John said, looking like his suggestion solved a Rubik's Cube, and if only Darren tried, he could learn it too.

"The sales data leads to this," Darren said, pointing to the overlapping line on the screen, two snakes weaving back and forth. "And contract data is all in PDFs. We can't incorporate it without hours of manual labor."

"You see. You're using a hammer right now, but you can't see if you're hitting a screw or a nail. Stop and look; otherwise, you'll go around your whole life trying to solve your problems with a hammer. Sometimes, you need a screwdriver!"

Darren closed his eyes, slamming them shut and trying to ignore the platitude. He took a deep breath and opened them again, a sting of pain washing over his eyelids from the unhealed damage.

"You okay?" John asked. "Your eyes are all red and bloodshot."

"Yeah, just a thing over the weekend. DIY project injury, ya know." Darren feigned a smile.

"You should see an eye doctor," John said.

"I have. Gave me some drops."

"Hey, maybe that's the problem with this analysis!" He leaned over and nudged Darren with his elbow. "Now, with proper vision, you can see the right answer."

Darren bit his tongue.

John slapped Darren's shoulder. "Core team in two days, and tomorrow for my review. Thanks!"

"Sure..." Darren mouthed, feeling the weight of a useless conversation.

Moments later, Darren was right back to rhythmically hammering the down arrow as he scrolled through the spreadsheet, hoping for inspiration.

"*Eighteen* more years, and *maybe* I'll see it," Darren said to himself as he looked down at his watch. The time crept slowly, as if the digital arms were stuck in mud.

In the corner of his eye, a long unused icon on his desktop caught his attention. A little flame wrapped around a file. He hadn't used the old file merge program in over a year, but it wasn't the buggy application that stole his thoughts. It was the pixelated little flame.

In his mind, he saw the giant tidal wave-like flame chasing him. Then, the gray eyes staring back at him.

Dr. Abrams said he was in the future with Darren, or rather, Kaden. None of it made sense, but his mind embraced the distraction from the spreadsheet. Swiveling in his chair, he grabbed his phone, his mind now jumping from the tidal wave of fire to thoughts of Kelly.

He frowned when he saw no notifications, but he scrolled to her name and looked at it. He sat in the chair, looking between his phone and the bright grid of data on the monitor in front of him, his thumb hovering over her name.

"You see, you're a hammer looking for a nail," he heard John's overused phrase replay in his mind. "Hopefully, it doesn't take *eighteen more years,* but who knows?"

He came in to work that day with thoughts of over-performing in hopes of being considered for a promotion, but now he was twenty-four hours away from being embarrassed in front of Core Team, the highest ranking leaders from each part of the organization. He could tell a good story around the data. There wasn't enough data to justify continuing the costly program. Another realistic interpretation was that the sales reps weren't adopting the program that they'd sworn would help them sell larger contracts. Over a year of work as the lead analyst on a crucial project, yet all the data pointed to business as usual.

He could recommend a total pivot, and maybe even a few people on the Core Team would respect his recommendation, but his boss, John 'never-wrong' Rondeau, already resisted that line of thought. The hammer searching for a nail.

Darren stood up and stretched, walking through the maze of cubicles toward the break room. When the stale smell of two-hour-old coffee hit his nostrils, he kept walking, opting for fresh air instead of caffeine.

The cool morning was long gone as the sun hung high in the sky. Blurred lines of rising heat surrounded him as he stepped on the black tar of the parking lot. A few paces later, he cut away from the paved sections, moving toward the lake and walking trails at the center of the office park. Overgrown hedges and tall trees shielded the water from view, but there were a few lookout spots and worn down grassy trails that curved behind tall glass buildings. The quiet area shielded by trees that felt miles away from the cubicle had become his favorite place to recharge and get away. He'd be able to put in a consistent effort for ten to twelve hours a day by managing three-hour sessions of deep work, each session bookmarked with breaks at the lake. Along with the occasional mug of stale office coffee, his own little Garden of Eden was exactly what his mind needed to clear the cobwebs and recharge.

As he snaked through the high grass and joined up with the walking trail, his eyes caught someone sitting at his bench. A bit disappointed that his favorite spot was occupied, he decided to keep walking and find the next bench, roughly two hundred yards further down the path as the trail hugged the overgrown shoreline of the lake.

Feeling the humidity in the air, he rolled up the sleeves of his button-up dress shirt. His left sleeve was halfway up when he recognized the person on his bench.

Not a coworker staring back at him.

It was Kelly.

Chapter 6

Entry #1

The lawyer called today. The company is official. My partner insists we all celebrate, but given the health concerns and unknown impact even one glass would have on the drug, there's no way. We settled on sparkling grape juice. I'm blown away at how engaged everyone was as we described our new drug and the animal trials. They were more attentive than most investors and the review board. My partner's distaste at my recommended next steps was obvious, but that isn't a conversation to have when others are around.

We must be aligned when we go to the board. At least a third of them want human trials as soon as possible.

With the state of the nation and economy, I can see why. We haven't communicated the long-term strategy, profit implications, or broader consequences while they eagerly push for our next revenue source. In their words, why spend another few million to reinforce what we already know from animal trials? Spend it on human trials and get one step closer to the trillion-dollar payoff! I will influence their decision.

Others on the board have a concern the public will adopt this treatment too fast and unforeseen issues will arise. The underlying causes must be addressed. The public must trust us.

They want business growth but pause because it can't be too fast of growth, meanwhile metabolic malfunction at the cellular level is growing cancer faster in this generation than any other and it's not an overnight diagnosis. Mutations been growing within us like a germinating seed for decades, now comes a point of inflection. Now it's time for better health and better treatment to push back. We can generate our own step change, but this time in the right direction.

A quick-fix pill is an easy path to a hundred billion, maybe even a trillion if we use our resources right, but I write again: if the underlying causes are not addressed and understood, we'll never fully realize the value of what we've created. This drug supercharges the mitochondria. It's like we are harnessing the power of life itself. A "reverse black hole," so to speak, that pulls in all energy around it and channels it for sustained cellular regeneration.

The media will eat up a good story, adding fuel to the fire of mass adoption, but there will be dissenters. Politics, the economy, and war between the east and west is on the table as the world's resources grow scarcer. The world is ready for a glimmer of hope that unites instead of divides. We need to align the different fractions, give the world a cause they can rally behind, together.

What self-preserving politician will risk their job to stand up to the public when we start public messaging?

Government instability and pending war cover the headlines. America's debt has limited its ability to respond, handcuffing the most powerful nation in the world. A new drug on the horizon that promises to reverse cancer growth. It could be a beacon of light in a dark world.

The first domino will fall.

It is my job to ensure it falls the right way.

CHAPTER 7

The pair sat on the bench, Kelly's arms and legs tucked in close to her body as she looked ahead.

"Why'd you leave?" Darren asked.

She opened her mouth but hesitated, eventually closing it and shaking her head as she looked down at her feet.

"Hey, whatever it is, I'm sorry. We'll work on it. We'll fix–"

"It's not something you can fix," she blurted out.

Darren sat speechless.

"Your voicemail. Do you remember what you said?" she asked, looking him in the eyes for the first time.

Darren's mind raced, searching for a voicemail. What had he said? Did Chris or Kirk use his phone to prank people? It wouldn't have been the first time they used his phone for a cruel joke they thought was hilarious. But she'd known that. She knew his friends well enough to brush off their antics.

She spoke first.

"Visions of monsters and a hooded guy with powers," she said, tears welling up in her eyes. "That's what you said. That's EXACTLY what you said."

The voicemail after leaving Dr. Abrams.

The two sat in silence as the wind rustled the trees behind them.

"So now you want to break up because you think I'm crazy?" Darren said.

"Break up?" She shot up and stepped back. "I never said that." As she stood looking at him, he could see the puffiness around her eyes. This was the first time he'd seen her cry, and he could tell it wasn't the first time she fought back tears on the subject.

"You said we *had to talk*," he said.

"Yeah, but not because I want to break up. Do you want to break up?" she demanded, her sadness inching into fury.

"No!"

"So why'd you say that? We have to talk means break up!" Darren fired back.

"Or maybe it's about something important. It's not always about breaking up! Maybe I DON'T think you're crazy!" she said.

"But you—" he began to fire back but stopped. "You don't?"

"I don't," she said, and her shoulders fell as if releasing a weight she'd been carrying. "Because if you are, then so am I. I've seen it too."

He stood and locked eyes with her.

"The night before you left that message, I had a dream, and every night since, it's the same one, over and over."

He stepped closer to her as he listened.

"I'm running. The entire dream, I'm running," she began.

Darren's eyes widened as she continued.

"There were these men, but they're not men. They're like shadows of someone, an opaque black rock of a human, but not human. They're like *demons*." She cringed. "I think I get away, but there's fire, a wall of fire. I can't outrun the shadows and the fire. It gets closer and I look back. There's a center to the fire, something carrying it and the shadows toward me."

An icy chill went down his spine.

"A man with gray eyes is there. I run behind him and he protects me. He takes all the flames so that it doesn't get me. He stops the person at the center of it all."

"Who's at the center?" he asked.

She stared at him, remaining silent as the tension hung in the air.

"That's why I left your apartment when you started walking out. That's why I haven't returned your calls."

"Kelly, who was at the center?"

"More than the center. It *was* the fire," she said.

"Who?"

"You."

He sat down slowly, silently looking down at his feet.

"What?" she exclaimed. "You don't believe me?"

"No..." He struggled to get the word out. His mouth as dry as a desert. "No, that's not it. I had the same dream last night, but from my point-of-view. I was the fire, and I was trying to catch up to you."

Kelly sat down next to him.

"I went back to the doctor this morning."

"And?" she urged him.

"I don't think you want to know."

She took his hand in hers.

"He said it was real. He said it was the future," he said.

"What kind of future is that?" she said.

"It's crazy, I know. I stormed out of there." He shrugged.

He turned and met her brown eyes. Her auburn hair fell past her shoulders, the long side-cut bangs framing her face.

"We need to go back," she said.

Darren sighed. She squeezed his hand.

"I'm sorry I pulled you into this," he said.

"You didn't pull me into anything. This is bigger than both of us."

They looked out over the lake. The quiet water gently rippled from a passing breeze.

"We need to go back," she said again.

Darren nodded. "We need to go back," he agreed.

He went back to his desk and set an away message to hold incoming emails, then packed his bags. As he turned into the stairwell, the door swung open and nearly hit him.

Jumping back, he looked up to see his boss.

"Working lunch?" he asked, pointing to Darren's laptop bag.

"Yeah..." Darren replied. "Like you said, the answer is out there somewhere. Just have to find it."

"I don't think I said that, but love the initiative. Let me grab my things and I'll join you—"

"No!" he blurted out. "I mean, I need some deep focus if I'm going to crack this nut. You know, it'll be a long haul, but I think I can find synergies between the data and expose the outcome. Gotta find that screwdriver, so I'm not just a hammer." He threw in all the random business sayings he could think of, hoping he sounded genuine as he muttered the nonsense phrases.

John looked at him as if grading Darren's professional career and potential on the spot. Then, a smile broke out.

"Totally agree! Get it to me in the morning. Tonight, if that nut really cracks, eh?" John leaned in and put his hand on Darren's shoulder.

"You'll be the first," Darren reassured.

John nodded and smiled. The silence grew awkward, but he eventually stepped aside, letting Darren slide out.

Kelly was waiting in the parking lot, her stick shift Jetta parked next to Darren's white truck. He waved to her before getting in his truck and pulling away. She followed, both en route to Abrams Eye Health.

A sense of dread came over him as he stepped out of his truck and stood in the gravel parking lot. He sensed something was off with the office, like catching a foul smell on the wind but not yet knowing the source.

Kelly pulled into a spot next to him. There were plenty of open spaces, and that was exactly the problem. There were no other cars. Her confused face matched his expression and he began to recognize what was a bustling office in prior days now appeared more like an abandoned building.

The sign near the road, brightly illuminated during his past visits, was gone, replaced by an ant hill-size pile of dirt in the sunburnt grass.

As he approached the office, his sense of unease intensified. The office looked different, but he didn't initially notice how. Now it smacked him like a speeding truck.

The lettering over the building was replaced by faded paint, the windows boarded up.

Hours ago, the smell of Ms. Barbara's cookies and the sound of her conversation filled the office, but now it was a ghost town, as if twenty desolate years had passed in mere hours.

Darren was at the front door, knocking and peering inside. His knock turned into pounding on the door and shouting hellos for Ms. Barbara and Dr. Abrams.

"This is the office?" Kelly asked.

"Yes," Darren said.

"And you were here recently?" she asked.

"Yes," he replied sharply.

Kelly backed up and took in the building as Darren stepped off the concrete steps of the main entrance, searching for a new spot to peek in between boards and window frames. He tried digging his fingers in, but screws held the corners and midsections down too tight. The wood didn't budge.

"This is the doctor you said could help us understand our dreams?" Kelly asked.

"Yes!" Darren exclaimed. He dropped his fist on the plywood and stepped back, shaking his head.

"I know how this looks, but I'm not crazy. It was open earlier today and last week," he said. Finally, turning from the building, he looked over the lot. "Look, if it were abandoned, would the grass be cut? You don't landscape abandoned lots."

She nodded in agreement.

"How'd you find this place?" she asked.

Darren's eyes shot open as he reached into his pocket and grabbed his phone.

"Google Maps! It had dozens of five stars *and* was the closest to my place," he said, typing away on the screen. "But it's not..." He stopped typing and looked curiously at his phone. "It's not coming up."

Kelly watched as Darren's thumb clicked away on the phone, his confusion turning to frustration as his shoulders sank down.

"The guy's name is Doctor David Abrams. His secretary is Ms. Barbara, and she makes the best cookies. In fact, he told me she sold the recipe to a massive cookie business, something like that, and she's rich beyond belief, but she loves working there, so she still shows up. Would I dream all that up?" he rambled off.

"This just looks..."

"He gave me drops for my eyes. His name is on the prescription, I have them at home. He pulled down the big machine thing where they go 'one or two, two or three,' but–"

"You mean the phoropter?"

"Yes, how do you know that?"

"How do you *not* know that? Have you ever had an eye exam?" she replied.

"Whatever. I didn't see the blurry 'one or two' letter test in the pho-to-raptor. I saw a whole new world. I was *in* a whole new world. Kelly, I didn't just *see* it. I was there, like a living dream. It was so real…"

He trailed off as he saw the doubting expression on Kelly's face.

"You think I'm crazy," he said.

"No. Remember my dream? I went to the bathroom and used a hand mirror to see if the back of my legs were burned. I know the *real* of it."

He saw her confusion flip into determination. Once she set her mind on something, she didn't stop. He saw it happen through her expression and loved her for her decisiveness.

She took out her phone. "My map says nothing is here. Just an address and blurry-looking dirt lot in the satellite image."

Both pulled up their phones and opened their map app.

"These satellite images have a lag, but the building isn't here at all. It's like someone erased it," she said.

"And it had a sign taken out. The dirt mound," he said, walking back to the front of the lot.

"The dreams, now this…" she said as they looked down at the circular dirt spot. She bent down and felt the warm dirt.

"Everything about this place… Erased," Darren said.

"Tell me about the other world, the one from our dreams. How'd you see it?" Kelly asked.

"Through the photo-romper?"

"It's a phoropter," she said.

"Yeah," he nodded. "He pulled down the pho-rapper, and I was there. The place was rough, like the slums of a major city. Bad neighborhood style – garbage stink and humid, stale air."

The wind picked up around them and the silence of the vacant lot turned in a rustling of nearby tall grass beyond the gravel lot.

"I was a kid, and there was a girl with me, Kira."

"That's me," she said. He nodded agreement.

"We were trying to get some food we stashed away. But the city is on some type of lockdown, like a curfew after dark. But there were these... These creatures." He stopped and looked down.

"Agents," Kelly said.

He turned to her and nodded. "They are all black. Not African-American black, but a charcoal, a dead, lifeless black. Their robes are black, but it's more than that. Their skin, their teeth, the whites, or what should be the whites of their eyes, all are lifeless, cracking charcoal of black."

They began walking around the building, looking over the boarded windows.

"You said you were a kid?"

"Yeah, and one of those *things* held us up by the throat. I could feel its claw-like hand around my neck. But then, the hooded man. He saved us, throwing those *things* like leaves in the wind."

"Kira," she said. "What is she to you?"

"My sister, sort of. I think we're adopted, and we were searching for the hidden food together, because our mother–"

"Because our mother doesn't always feed us," Kelly finished.

He silently agreed.

"Your name. Kaden," she said.

"Kaden McCloud," he said.

"How do you know?" she asked.

"I just do. It wasn't a dream to me, at least not the first time. I was there. I was Kaden. Kaden was me."

They stared at each for a long moment before a passing truck broke their concentration. The abandoned building still sat in front of them like a coffin at a wake. Wind picked up dust in the parking lot.

Kelly began walking, looking at the building from new angles as she approached.

"That's his office," Darren said, pointing to the back window.

"That board…" she said, squinting.

The bottom corner of the board had a gap in between it and the white stucco. Darren moved to it and pried it back. The wood creaked, squealing against the other screws, but it yielded enough for Kelly to peek in.

"This morning, there was an exam chair, the photo-opt, and some cabinets," Darren said as he strained to hold the board.

"There's nothing," she said.

"What?"

"Nothing. Totally empty."

"Let me see."

She moved away and he released the board. It snapped back, reverberating against the window with a dull echo that sounded a hollow rattle into the wind.

He found a chunk of concrete near the parking lot and Kelly pulled back the board as much as she could. Darren watched her, impressed at her willingness to help figure out the mystery. She created enough space for him to wedge the chunk in between the board and window frame, giving her relief as she relaxed her pull. He peered inside. The few inches he could see matched what she saw. An empty office sat motionless inside. A blank room stuck in time.

The air left his lungs, falling into a pit where his stomach used to be.

"I feel like I'm taking crazy pills. It was what, four hours ago?"

"You would be insane," she smiled, "if I didn't have the same dream."

He looked back into the slit and looked up at the corners of the room.

"Thank you." He smiled at her. "And geez, if we're both crazy, wouldn't this place be filled with cobwebs? It's empty but clean, just like the landscaping. And there!" he shot back. "There's holes in the ceiling!"

"Holes?"

"From where the photo-doppler thing was!"

"The phoropter?"

"Yes. That thing is huge and was drilled into the ceiling."

They took turns looking into the window and then walked around the building again. All the other boards were tight. Returning back to the exam room window, they peered in again.

"We're still back at square one. Who would scrub this place off the face of the Earth? Online searches, maps, and physically moving everything out in a matter of hours," he said.

Stepping back from the window, he relaxed his grip on the board. The chunk of concrete wedged in between the board and frame slid out and the board snapped back. It slammed repeatedly into the window with a dull rattle in their ears.

Darren sat down, sweat dripping off his forehead in the humid afternoon.

Kelly stared at the window with a curious expression.

"Did you hear that?" she asked.

"Yeah, annoying."

"No, I mean something..." She trailed off as she pulled back the board and reached her hand in between the board and glass.

"What are you doing?" Darren asked.

"There's something else," she said, getting on her tippy toes and reaching up. "I can feel…" She struggled, reaching up as she pulled the board back. "See if you can."

Darren stood up and reached under the board.

"It's a package," he grunted, struggling to grab hold of it. "I can't get a grip." He struggled, pulling on a tiny corner of whatever lay hidden.

On the tips of his toes, he stretched up and gripped the item, but his hand slipped off and again the board snapped back. The thing started to dislodge under the board's vibration. The rattling sound changed distinctly as something shifted behind the board.

Darren now pulled back the board to find a manila-colored packet dropping perfectly into his hand, like candy from a coin machine.

The oversized envelope had a bulge in the middle, hiding something thicker than the envelope intended. Over the center of the packet, in black marker, read:

"Darren and Kelly, this is where you find me."

It was signed "Dr. David Abrams."

Chapter 8

He read the message from the doctor aloud, looked at Kelly, then tipped the large folder.

Two pairs of glasses slid out into his hands.

They looked like standard corrective lenses with basic frames, one a thick black and the other a thinner purple style.

"Cute frames," Kelly said.

Darren shot her a look.

"What?" She laughed. "They are. But I don't get it. The guy's practice gets scrubbed from the Earth, yet he leaves a couple pairs of glasses?"

"Alright, Nancy Drew, let's think this through."

"You know those were my favorite books as a kid?"

"You've mentioned it." He smiled at her. "And you're relentless when there's something you don't understand."

Her brow furrowed.

"That's a compliment!"

Kelly's expression turned into a smile as she tucked a loose strip of auburn hair behind her ear. Darren lost his train of thought and stared at her for a moment. That playful smile set under her large brown eyes.

Meanwhile, she took the purple frames and held them up, letting the light bounce through the clear lenses. She moved to put them on.

"No!" He grabbed her hand. "We don't know what that'll do."

"They may alter my vision..." she said sarcastically. "You know, I have worn glasses before."

"I'm betting you haven't worn glasses like these. We should be somewhere safe when we try them on."

"You think these would act like the phoropter?" she asked.

He nodded and contemplated the glasses. "This is finally making sense. All my life, I've felt like I've been going with the flow. School, college, and now work."

Kelly handed back the purple glasses.

"What are you getting at?"

"Take the last couple of days. Kelly, I care about you more than anyone else."

She couldn't stop the corner of her lip from curling into a smile at his comment.

"I've been planning for so long, but even the thought of us breaking up. It wrecked me."

"What have you been planning?"

He sidestepped her question as the image of an engagement ring, financially out of his reach, floated in his mind.

"It's like I'm riding a river and just hoping to wash up next to a great job or promotion. Like the money will show up and prove my worth, and that I deserve you and a great life together. But it won't just wash up in my lap. Life's not a participation trophy. I need to take control of my life before I expect to control the world around me."

"Darren, I don't want my life to be controlled," she said, her smile fading.

"Neither do I, but you know what I mean. I'm sick of waiting for life to simply show up. It's time we take control of our future."

"What are you really trying to say?" she asked.

"I'm saying that for us to be together forever, I need to get my act together and take accountability for my life."

"Forever?" The smile returned, but it couldn't dethrone the confusion setting in.

His confidence grew as he held the glasses.

"I won't be a man who can't provide for you, and I don't know what our dreams of this other world are about, but I promise you I'm going to find out."

He stuffed the glasses back in the envelope and set off back to their cars.

"Darren?" she called after him.

"There's a whole new world in those glasses!" he called.

"So you *do* think they'll act like the phoropter," she said.

"I do. Both our names on the envelope, two pairs of glasses. He knew we'd be together."

"The eye doctor knew?"

"I don't know how, but he's more than just a doctor. He has million-aire-billionaires circling around him. You should have seen this Thornhill guy, and the customer who came in and hugged him, and Ms. Barbara the cookie millionaire! And once I bring you here, it's all gone. We're going to figure this out."

"Okay, okay." She nodded as she caught his confidence. "Well, if you want someone safe and private, my roommate and her boyfriend are at our place. How about yours? Think Tweedle Dee and Tweedle Dumb will give us privacy?"

"Only if they think we're making out," he said.

"Darren!" She elbowed him.

"What?" He smiled. "But I'm being serious. That's one of the few things they understand, along with Pop Tarts and Xbox."

"Fair enough. Now, let's crack this code." She smiled and squeezed his arm affectionately. She moved to her car so weightlessly and gracefully, she could have been skipping on the moon.

Darren went into his truck and tossed the manila envelope onto the passenger's seat.

"Once you see, you can't unsee," he said aloud to himself, then shook his head. He turned the ignition and the engine roared to life. His hand moved to shift the truck into drive, but he paused, the bulging package catching his eye.

He dumped out the contents, picking up the black pair. Holding them up, he watched the sunlight bend as the road ahead appeared curved and misshaped through the lens of the glasses. He studied the distorted image, moving them closer to his face. Slowly, they inched closer and closer to his face, a fraction of an inch away from resting on his nose. He felt a pull from them to wear them, like a magnetic force constantly tugging on him. Then, a flash of gray eyes flickered in the lenses. Startled, he dropped the pair. The eyes reflected in them were gone as quick as they came.

Looking down, he examined them again, scared to touch the thing that rested on his lap. He moved his head back and forth, trying to catch the light in the lenses, wondering if he'd been scared by his own reflection.

Kelly's four-door Jetta pulled up next to his truck. He snapped back to reality and tossed the glasses back onto the passenger seat. With a wave, he set off down the road as she followed closely behind.

Back in the parking lot of his apartment, his stomach was in knots, like an anchor weighing him down, preventing him from taking another step forward. But as Kelly pulled in and got out of his car, his focus returned. He began to feel more determined. He stuffed the glasses and note back in the envelope and was thankful that Chris's and Kirk's cars weren't in the parking lot.

They went inside and set the glasses on the small circular table. Hours earlier Chris and Kirk spent another morning bickering over the nutritional value of Pop Tarts, but now Darren and Kelly silently studied the glasses. Time seemed to stop. Darren couldn't have said if it was thirty seconds or an hour, but the more he thought, the more the anchor in his stomach returned. He felt the unease and fear weigh him down, pinning him to his chair as his mind raced, unable to overcome the endless thoughts of a future world and the chaos of it all.

"So, who are Kaden and Kira to each other in that place?"

"What?" Darren snapped out of his thoughts as she spoke.

"In this other world, we're brother and sister?"

"I think we're both adopted, given to the same mother. No, scratch that, I know we are," he said.

"I think so too. There was a familiarity with him in my dream. Like I've known Kaden forever," she asked.

He let out a deep breath and finally released the thought that'd been on his mind.

"I don't want you to put them on," he said.

"Oh really? You think Nancy Drew would stop right before entering the dark cave when there's a clue waiting inside?"

"We don't know what they'll do. For all we know, they're just regular glasses."

"All the more reason for me to put 'em on," she said. "How'd it work in the office?"

"Dr. Abrams pulled the photo-bomb down in front of my eyes, and boom, instantaneous. One moment I was Darren, the next I was Kaden."

"My dream was fuzzy, yet so real," she said.

"Same here, but putting that thing on, it wasn't like falling asleep. It was a flipped light switch."

"Only one way to find out if they'll work," Kelly said, holding up her purple glasses.

"No!" He grabbed her wrist. "I'll go first. I've been there. Maybe we're kids again or maybe we're older like the dreams. Either way, we need someone to stay here. If I have a seizure or start foaming at the mouth, whatever craziness happens, you take the glasses off and pull me out."

"Does it work like that?"

"I came out when he took the photo-thingy off my head."

"But didn't you say you got your head bashed in when that monster threw you?"

"That did happen," Darren replied, remembering the splitting pain on the back of his head.

"So it seems like when you die, you come back?" she asked.

"Well, either I died and was pushed out, or he pulled me out," he said.

"And maybe it's like C.S. Lewis's Narnia. Time passes there much differently than here," she replied.

"Only one way to find out," he said, holding up the glasses to his face. She watched as he took a breath, feeling as if the glasses were calling out to him, but they were calling to Kira as well, and she took his pause to flip the script.

"You died last time. I'll test it," she blurted out and snatched the black frames from his hand.

He felt like an astronaut in space without a suit. All the air in his lungs vanished as he watched her slide the glasses over her ears and rest them on the bridge of her nose.

Kelly blinked, returning his stare.

"Sooo..." she said, looking at him through the black frames. She held up her hand and examined it through the lenses. "I don't think there's a prescription on these. They're flat, plane-O."

He finally took in a breath and she took them off, put them back on, then took them off again. Eventually, she set the glasses on the table.

"Well, that was anticlimactic," she said, sliding them back toward Darren. The pair struck his fingertips as if tapping on a door, eager for him to open it.

"Maybe it was just me?" he said, keeping his eyes on the glasses.

"Or maybe they're *just glasses*?" she said.

"Maybe..." he said, still feeling the call of the glasses.

"At least these purple ones are cute," she said, picking up the more feminine pair and raising them to her face. "They seem to speak to me more anyway."

"Speak to..." he thought. "WAIT!" he called out, reaching his hand forward, but he was too late. She slid on the glasses, and instantly, her body went limp.

He leapt forward as she fell from her chair. Reaching out, he saved the brunt of the fall as one arm slid under her, her head in his hand, but her body striking the discolored linoleum floor.

"No, no, no," he repeated as he slid to her side. "It was me who was supposed to go, not you. You can't live in a place like that. You're too... you're too perfect."

He studied her eyelids, but there was no movement underneath. He thanked the Lord when he found a pulse and soft breath, but otherwise, there was no motion. She lay as if in a deep sleep, or maybe more like a coma.

"I can't let you stay there," he said, then he pulled off the glasses. But to his surprise, she didn't wake up. She didn't move at all. Putting them on took her, but taking them off didn't bring her back.

Kelly was right to question the premise of how Darren returned to this life and this world. Maybe it wasn't the phoropter. Maybe it was his death.

She would only return when she died. He rubbed his face with both hands, trying to think. He could call 911 or a friend, or just wait and see if she woke up, but he didn't like any option that would leave her in the future all alone where the charcoal creatures were roaming.

Standing up, he bumped the table and heard the other pair slide. His eyes darted to them. Picking them up, he peered through the lenses just as he had done in his truck. He saw a distorted version of his living room and attached kitchen, but also saw a wisp of fog. Ghost-like movements hovered somewhere deep within the translucence. Then a flicker of gray eyes looked back at him. They held for a breath, then disappeared.

"This is where you find me." He repeated the cryptic message from Dr. Abrams's note, then put the glasses on.

His body fell limp, landing next to Kelly.

CHAPTER 9

T he sound of a door closing hit like a bang, and he shot off the couch. Looking around, he found himself in the living room of a small apartment. Windows surrounded him on three sides and a small kitchen behind. Through the broad windows, a cloudy sky stretched as far as he could see. The distant mountains rested far away on the horizon as clouds hovered above the rising sun. The bright reds and oranges blew him away. But as he looked down, the brilliant natural world of the distant horizon faded into man-made structures. Circular towers, like the one he was in now, were dotted around an enormous central tower. Bright spotlights from the city below, still visible in the darkness, lit up the massive central tower like it was its own sunrise and cared not for the oranges and reds cast across the skies. The illuminated tower stuck up from the city like a sword that came from the center of the earth, stabbing through the crust, left for all the world to see its marvelous display. Even the surrounding circle of high rises didn't dare touch the clouds as the central tower did, as if a thorn stuck into the base of the heavens above.

He noticed the paint on the walls and ceiling, a dirty off-white color. The walls, at one time likely a bright white, were now faded as countless particles of dust and wear stole their vibrance. The floors were a sort of click-together composite of a soft brown, which was also worn heavily in the high-traffic areas. In certain spots, the wear was enough to see the dark gray center of the composite, an open wound of time on the otherwise brown floor.

His eyes returned to the window, and he noticed dirt and grime covering the outside edges of the windows. He leaned forward and looked down, peering in between the buildings. Every street below seemed like an alleyway. There were no white or yellow lines on the roads or traffic lights as dumpster-like metal containers dotted the landscape. One massive metal box like a toddler huddling next to the parent building.

Through the alleys, there appeared to be a motion, like a flow of ants marching on the jungle floor. He squinted, and as the sun rose, finally overpowering The Tower's illumination, he realized it was an overflow of people walking in the morning darkness.

"Morning rush hour," he whispered. Then he realized where he was and who he was.

The alley below could have been the same one he saw on his first visit, where as children, he and Kira desperately tried to escape the charcoal creatures.

The sun rose higher, but the overcast clouds ate up the majority of the light. Scraps fell to the city below and the sun's brief victory over The Tower's lights subsided away. Like a thick blanket over the area, the clouds lingered across the horizon in every direction. The sun's rays trapped behind the blanket.

Scanning the horizon, his apartment building was roughly average height in a series of gradually shorter towers that extended away from the central tower. Each concentric circle of buildings formed ring-like patterns as they took a step-change down in height.

Past the ring of high rise buildings that surrounded the central tower was another steep drop-off. This outer circle was a wasteland compared to the inner structures.

The city seemed to be a show of human architectural evolution. The center tower was an illuminated feat of futuristic engineering and art, the second-tier buildings stepped back to resemble a modern approach to early office and apartment buildings of the mid-nineteen hundreds, but the old box-like structures of traditional office and apartment buildings now re-placed with a circular, tube-like high rise design. Finally, the outer layer was something of a devolution of a common village and scattered households. It reminded him of pictures of abandoned cities after a depression, the concrete version of a modern dust bowl-like event.

Bright dots that reminded him of convenience store and pharmacy signs sparkled across the outer circle like stars in a reverse sky that stretched out like a blanket.

At the edge of the circular city, he saw a wall. It looked strong and tall. Firm-looking construction that was out of place next to the rundown housing within its boundary. The wall enclosed the entire city and held distinct, well-maintained lines in its construction. Bright uplighting, sim-ilar to that of the central tower, gave a bright color to the wall, like a child traced the outer edge of the city with amber highlighter. The wall reminded him of the old Biblical story of Jericho, a wall that must look so imposing and well-constructed from the outside, with the illuminated tower far inside the protected center. But from his point of view, something about the crumbling homes just inside the wall stole away from its impression of strength, as if the strength was only for show and a loud shout could bring it down.

He couldn't see anything beyond the wall. A vast sea of barrenness grew hazy as it stretched into the horizon and eventually the mountainous terrain far off in the distance. From what he could see past the walls, it looked like a desert. There was no green, only a light brown, like dried-out clay. The thick cloud above the city gave a dome-like appearance as the blanket of clouds came down and closed on the barren landscape outside the walls.

Then he caught his reflection in the window and jumped back. He felt a distant memory of putting on the glasses. He knew who he was now, Kaden, and the old life of Darren took a back seat in his mind, like a long-ago daydream that flickered near the base of his subconscious.

He was the same age and general appearance as the flicker of Darren in the back of his mind but with minor differences. In the window's reflection, he saw the biggest difference. Kaden's jet-black straight hair popped out from his head over brown eyes, not the shaggy brown hair of Darren. However, the brown eyes matched perfectly. One thing he would learn was that the eyes always matched.

He brushed his black hair to the side. He studied himself and memories flooded his mind in great detail. First, as a child, the night the charcoal demons threw him to the ground and cracked his head open. But other memories of Kaden's life came to mind, memories he didn't experience through the lens of Dr. Abrams's phoropter. His life growing up, trying to protect Kira. Her craftiness in the face of starvation. Vague memories of a house mother. None of a father.

He turned from the window and looked over the apartment. A purple couch and an orange armchair sat in the middle, an odd pop of color in the otherwise faded white, drab room.

Echoes of doors opening and closing sounded from the hallway. He moved toward the sounds, and as he put his hand on the knob of the door, another memory came to mind. He was late for work.

Sliding into the hallway, a sense of urgency overtook him. He joined a growing line of people that funneled through the dingy hallways and to the stairwell. They marched down flight after flight. Frustratingly, the line slowed as others joined the stairwell from lower floors. In time, he made it out to the road.

The scent of garbage smacked his nose, but he knew it came from the Outer Ring. The direction of the wind didn't matter much, since the Outer Ring encircled the more modern buildings. At best, it was a faint smell, and at the worst, it was like the stench of the Outer Ring hovered on his upper lip.

Kaden kept walking through the wide, street-like alleyways, but a sense of unease crept into his mind. An unnamed stress rose in the back of his mind, but he repressed it, fearful of standing out and making a mistake. He walked with the crowd, trying to blend in yet take the time to look around. However, as he looked up at the unbelievably tall apartment buildings, he bumped the man in front of him. The man grunted but otherwise said nothing, continuing to shuffle with the flow. Kaden kept his head down.

As hundreds of people walked in the morning rush hour, he found it a delicate balance to move without bumping someone next to him. But soon he fell into the harmony of the group. Like a flight of bees, synchronized in their massive movements, people peeled off and moved into their respective workplaces. As the group thinned out, he no longer felt happy to be in sync with the group. The stress in his mind rose, and he recognized it. He felt like one of the herd being mindlessly led. But was it to the slaughter or to greener pastures?

Kaden's feeling of unease stayed with him, now turning his eyes to the remaining people. The crowd contained more men, roughly two-to-one versus women, and everyone wore similar clothes, a mix of blue jean-like pants and either brown or flannel long-sleeve shirts. Some rolled up the sleeves, while others rolled up the cuffs of their pants, a slight tweak to their attire. Overall, the crowd could have been a copy and paste version of itself. Everyone was similar height, weight, and looks. Males had facial stubble and short black hair while females had long black hair. None wore makeup, and only slight variations in hair existed.

He felt more comfortable in the crowd as it thinned, but a moment later, he caught a sight that stopped him cold. Chills ran up his spine. A man slammed into his back. Once again, the collision caused nothing more than a grunt, and the man kept walking. But Kaden remained frozen like a statue to the ground as others walked around him.

Ahead of him, he saw a black figure in a martial arts-style black robe that stretched from neck to toe. It was a charcoal demon from his nightmare, standing thirty yards away. The ashy black skin devoured the light more than reflected it.

Just beyond the creature, he knew his destination. A small sign read *EMR*. His work. Six days a week, ten hours a day. He was allowed in the more modern apartment towers because he was a member of the working class, his time devoted to The Tower's Will, earning him a place in the Inner Ring.

The horrid creature from his dream stood directly in his path. It held its nose up, as if sniffing the air, pacing back and forth like a bored soldier reluctantly giving crisp movements.

Kaden debated turning around and walking backwards, but he'd be swimming upstream. Surely he'd stand out in the crowd. Ahead of him, across from the EMR, was a well-lit food depot, the convenience store-like lights he saw from out his window. He thought of taking a long loop around it, but now it was desolate. The meal lines wouldn't open until lunch.

As he stood still, contemplating his next move, the thing stopped and sniffed the air again.

To his dread, the creature tilted its head and found him. It looked directly at him.

Quickly, he bent and pretended to tie his shoe, but he soon realized his shoes didn't have laces. He rose, continuing to walk a normal pace, telling himself to act naturally and avoid looking into those dead black eyes. Kaden walked this path to work every morning. Why was today any different?

He kept his eyes down, but he felt the sensation like a tractor beam. A gravity in the air pulled on him, tugging him toward the thing as it began stepping to him. Every loud sniff of its black-matte skin pulled him off his path and closer to the creature. He leaned, trying to use his weight, but couldn't avoid it any longer. The beast had his scent and reeled him in like a fish on the hook.

Hunter and hunted were mere feet apart when Kaden finally lifted his eyes to see the dull black stare of the black eyes locked onto him. Like a crossbreed between a man and the ashes of a burnt log, his skin was dead, lifeless. Every inch of his body, even what should have been the whites of his eyes, held the matching lifelessness of used charcoal.

The eyes were not angry, but hungry and determined, like a wolf's piercing expression the moment before its teeth set it to make the kill.

"It's about time!" an older woman's voice called out from behind Kaden.

The creature's eyes left Kaden and moved to the voice.

"Sorry, sorry, but he's needed here. The Twenties are behind. Must operate smoothly," she rattled off.

The beast grunted in disagreement.

"Take him if you wish, but I'm telling you, the Twenties won't run unless we get them serviced. You know what happens when the Twenties don't run?" the woman said boldly to the creature.

Kaden stood frozen, waiting for the creature to relent. He stopped feeling the pull toward it, and the woman tugged on his dingy brown shirt. Jumping at the chance to escape, he followed her. The creature remained silent. He could feel the demon's stare piercing the back of his head, but he refused to look back.

A moment later, she led him into a nearby building, the Empyrean Mechanix Retreat, or EMR. The warehouse-sized facility had forty-foot-high ceilings that housed a rotating fleet of oversized dump trucks. Their wheels, twenty feet in diameter, gave them their name, the Twenty.

As soon as the door closed behind him, the black-robed creature swiftly moved away.

"What is the matter with you?" She pulled him through the first set of bays and into a small office. The walls barely shielded the noises of air pressure torque wrenches and chains clanging. The office resembled a temporary structure, a house of cards in the otherwise stern metal and solid equipment that surrounded them. Regardless of the flimsy walls, her tone gave him the feeling he was being sent to the principal's office.

"Thanks for–" She slapped the side of his head interrupting him. "Ah, what are you–"

"What in the world is a matter with you?" she shouted, interrupting again.

"What do you mean?"

"Don't you '*what do you mean*' me?" she snapped back. "You're late for your shift, and one late person drags down the whole facility's metrics. Would you want your production credits reduced because Enak or Elba decided to monkey around all morning, and especially with an Agent? Huh?" She stabbed at his chest with her index finger.

"Ah." He stepped away from her jab. "An Agent..." he said as he thought. The life and memories of Kaden once again flooded his mind.

"You and her..." She shook her head. "At least she is finding her purpose and doesn't let the wind blow her through every stage of life," she said, turning back and poking him even harder.

"I'm not letting the wind blow me through life," Kaden replied.

"Then prove it. Take control of your shift instead of farting around with Agents!"

"Don't tell me what to control!" he snapped back at her.

She leaned in, hands on her flimsy plastic desk. Her surprise at his talking back pushed her eyebrows almost off her face.

"I need you back in your bay and getting on the Twenties," she said firmly.

Kaden held her gaze.

"You know what happens when you don't work," she said.

Kaden felt a frustration welling up inside of him. The pair stood in defiance of each other, neither backing down.

"I'm serious," she said, her tone now shifting from a commanding shift leader to that of a friend. "You know what happens, don't you?"

Kaden didn't respond.

"No food credits, no rent credits. You hear me, Kaden? I know the food is slop, but don't buck up to an Agent or me. Get in line or you'll be back to the Outer Ring, or worse..." she said.

Kaden cleared his throat and pushed down his anger. Nodding, he left her office.

"And another thing, where's your uniform? You show up in your house clothes?" She called him back. "Like a leaf in the wind. I swear your generation is useless."

She grabbed a set of thick coveralls from a nearby drawer and threw them at him, hitting his chest and falling into his open hands.

"Thanks, Ms. Barbara," he instinctively replied, glancing down and only now noticing he wore a dingy brown crew-neck shirt and gray pants.

"Call me Barb. And if you worry about crossing me, you should be terrified of crossing those devils out there. So get back to–"

"Back to work," he interrupted her. "You got it, boss."

"The first smart thing you've said all morning," she said. "You sure you're okay, young man?" She eyed him curiously, examining him more deeply than before.

Kaden nodded and then stepped out of the office and found his bay. It was next to a feeble-looking old man. He looked up and nodded. Kaden returned the gesture and began sliding on the coveralls. The man turned away, but Kaden stopped with one foot in the uniform as he realized what he just saw.

The man's eyes.

They were a brilliant gray.

The old man slid himself under the belly of an immense vehicle, the eyes a sparkle in the darkness.

Chapter 10

Entry #2

Our goal is to leverage this drug to save all those in need. If I'm going to shepherd this company to fulfill its purpose, I must shift the narrative away from common drug talks and toward the value of human life. We are a caring company, but what happens when people cannot follow simple rules? We show our love by walking hand and hand with them, and in some cases, tables need to be flipped to make them see. Leaders are not impervious to emotions and when the board sees the results, combined with my emotion, the next step will begin.

There was another riot in New York today, along with Paris, London, San Francisco, Berlin, and countless others.

The developed west is tearing itself apart. The people don't feel safe or taken care of. Government spending on health care and welfare are at all-time highs. Obesity and diabetes are continuing to increase, fertility rates are down again, and cancer diagnoses are up. I fear this treatment may be too late to quell the civil unrest, but I must persevere. We can control the narrative and this global health crisis. If it starts with me, then we can enroll two more, then four, and soon, we'll be making great change in the world. Slow and steady.

I must be methodical. I must play the long game.

Chapter 11

Kaden stood looking at the giant wheel in front of him. He felt as tiny as an ant in the shadow of the massive twenty-foot-diameter wheel. The vehicle above the tire was more like a building while the front wheel the ground level's lobby. He was a bug, the wheel the child, and the vehicle the parent. The parent and child looking down at the bug unsympathetically.

Slowly, the process came back to his mind. Darren had never changed a tire larger than his apartment, but Kaden had countless times. Nearly unconsciously, he began to prep the heavy equipment required to lift the truck and service the underside and wheels. Thick chains swayed above him, a safety precaution that would catch the wheel and pull it away should it go off track.

As he prepared the equipment, he found comfort in the instinctual actions, and more memories rose from his unconscious. He knew the two brothers that Barb referred to earlier, Elba and Enak. They were friends of his and stationed a few bays down his row. He remembered the quiet old man with the absurd productivity in the bay next to him. He'd long given up on trying to figure out the tricks of the feeble old-timer. The higher the production output, the happier the entire crew, so the crew welcomed the man.

But the gray eyes of the old man stood out. Visions of Dr. Abrams knocked at the back of Kaden's subconscious. He dismissed the thoughts as he fell into his work, an urge to ensure he caught up to his daily quota.

Reaching up, he hooked the safety chain to the massive wheel and began moving the hefty air-powered wrench to the fist-sized bolts securing it. The high-pitched torque wrench banged against the bolt. A split-second of high-pitched interactions, and the wrench broke the nut free. It spun backwards off the threading, held securely in the socket.

His body felt good as he worked, blood flowing and filling his muscles and mind. A sense of usefulness came upon him. He removed another fifteen-pound nut from the head of the tool and transitioned it onto the last bolt. As he moved the head of the tool onto the next bolt, he didn't see the man in a blue robe enter the EMR, but he felt the two creatures that flanked him. It was like the air in the room took on weight and pressed down on him.

The black-robed creature that pulled at Kaden outside the warehouse was on one side of the blue-robed man. On the other side, a near mirror image of another charcoal demon. The two demons held their heads up, smelling the air as the blue-robed man led them in and scanned the room.

Kaden pulled back, staying behind the massive wheel. He tried to keep working but stole distracted glances away from the Twenty.

"Your bar," a gravelly voice sounded from behind him.

He heard but didn't register the comment, peeking once again from behind the wheel. Other EMR workers were peeking out as well, like meerkats popping their heads above tall grass to look for predators. It seemed everyone in the EMR paused, watching the Agents of Empyrean.

They entered Barb's three-walled office.

"Your bar–" the old man's voice called again, but Kaden caught it off, firing the oversized air wrench. The high-pitched burst of the torque wrench freed the last nut. Kaden leaned over to let the hefty nut slide out of the wrench's head. Above him, the twenty-foot wheel's weight shifted on the bolts' threads. The top of the wheel crept off, like a felled tree's first lean under gravity's pull. The house-sized wheel leaned slowly at first, then accelerated, shooting off as gravity took over.

Kaden looked up in time to see the wheel fall, bearing down on him. Every muscle clenched as he flinched, his eyes closing. He sat, expecting to be crushed, a shoe coming down on a bug, but to his surprise, the blow didn't come. What should have been a fatal, ground-shaking impact was replaced by the screeching sound of the catch bar guiding the wheel on to the overhead chains, counter-balancing the weight of the tire and shifting it safely to the side of the vehicle.

Kaden looked up to see the tire gently rolling into place. He looked in awe at the safety bar, knowing he never put it in place. He thought of seeing the tire come down, and knew it was past the safety bar's catch point. A cold sweat sat across his forehead as his heart pounded.

To his right, he heard the sounds of tools sliding on the concrete floor. He looked over and saw the old man sliding back under an exposed rotor. The old man examined a brake pad larger than his torso, preparing to bleed the brake line.

"They're looking for you," the man said without looking up. His hands moved in firm, methodical motions.

Kaden watched the old man for a second longer and swore he saw a smile flash in the dim light. He turned back to the safety bar, ready to examine it, but a commotion from Barb's office stole his attention. A man's voice snapped in anger. His rage cut through the bays working on the massive vehicles before the sound of air wrenches took back control. A moment later, the two charcoal creatures walked out of the office.

Kaden dropped his head and once again moved behind the immense wheel. He pretended to work on it, his head down, his eyes up, locked on the creatures.

"It's best if you keep working. They enjoy confusing and distracting," the old man said.

"You don't understand, that one was outside and he, it... It was smelling me outside," Kaden said.

"They do that, and I'd say they have your scent now."

"My scent?" Kaden asked.

"It's usually pretty terrible when they have your scent. A trial, or maybe a sorting," the man said. He coughed and cleared his gravelly voice.

"*Usually pretty terrible?*" Kaden repeated.

"Once they have your scent, they either recruit you, kill you, or worse," he said as he came out from behind the rotor and swapped a smaller wrench for one the size of his forearm. His gray eyes came up and Kaden saw a flicker of light in them that didn't match his seemingly weak body.

"What's worse than killing?" Kaden said, now returning to the massive wheel and pretending to push it again.

"Being consumed," he said plainly.

"You mean like recruiting?"

"No, I don't. Recruiting could be metaphorically consuming you, but when I say *consume*, I mean it literally."

Kaden stood in silent terror of the idea.

"Yup. That's how I feel too," the old man said.

Kaden bent down, looking under his vehicle toward the office. He didn't see any blue or black robes swaying. He let out a breath and relaxed. As soon as he did, the voice sounded behind him like a hunter's bullet into the side of a deer.

"You. State your name," the man in the blue robe demanded.

The official had neatly trimmed black hair, in the style of a military cut, and a clean-shaven face. His eyes were a pale, faded color of brown, as if once lively but long ago lost their vibrance. Black boots stuck out from under a full body blue robe tied neatly with a matching belt. The belt's knot created a perfect bow that fell symmetrically off his waist. A memory flashed in Kaden's mind from another life, from Darren's life as a young boy trying out martial arts and craving to get a higher-colored belt.

"Name?" the man demanded again.

"Kaden McCloud," he said, coming out from behind the wheel and standing at attention.

The man eyed him, examining him from top to bottom. Then he turned to the creature at his side, the same one from earlier, outside the EMR. The thing sniffed a deep breath and Kaden felt a pull on his body, as if a flicker of gravity snatching at him.

"And your decision, Elite?" the blue-robed man asked.

The demon gave a confirming grunt as the unnaturally black eyes stayed locked onto Kaden. As the thing examined him, Kaden felt as if he was a main course being studied by a hungry restaurant patron.

"This one does seem... different," the blue-robed man said.

"He sure is," the old man said from behind his vehicle's rotor.

The blue-robed man and one of the creatures shot their gaze toward the speaker, while the one charcoal-like Agent held his gaze locked on Kaden.

"Remain silent," the blue-robed man commanded.

"For only so long," the old man replied. He came out from behind the rotor and looked at Kaden, then toward the man in blue robes. His brilliant gray eyes once again caught Kaden's attention. They seemed to flash like spotlights from the man's weathered face.

"I am a Lead Agent, a blue in Empyrean's core–"

"I see your choice," the old man interrupted. Kaden noticed a slight grin on the man's face, as if he enjoyed ruffling the Agent's feathers. The old feeble man now looked not so feeble. When Kaden first saw him, the coveralls seemed to outweigh him, but now there was a fullness to him. His wrinkled skin also somehow seemed not so wrinkled.

"State your name," the Lead said sternly.

"Who do you say I am?" he asked in response.

"A foolish peasant of the working class who must be mistaken if he is talking to an Agent of Empyrean like he's an equal."

"Equal?" the old man said.

"Far from it," the Agent scoffed.

"But that doesn't mean I can't help you, Ronnoc," the old man said, extending his hand.

Kaden noticed the man in blue's stern expression crack with surprise when the old man said his name. The stern look of enforcement returned, and he looked down at the old man, then traveled to see the man's extended hand in disgust, as if it were a dead animal.

"People see this old feeble body of mine and they think that I won't make it another week. That I'll crumble on the seventh day, like the walls of a once great city," the old man said.

Ronnoc appeared confused. He ignored the man and turned back to his charcoal partners.

"We good here?" Ronnoc asked.

The creature that Kaden engaged earlier slowly shook his head yes, a smile forming on its dull, cracked face.

"A blue robe shows commitment. You're in deep, son," the old man continued.

"Take him away," Ronnoc ordered, and the swift, strong hands of the creature reached out and stuck to Kaden like a magnet.

"Hey, whoa!" Kaden jumped back, but their grasp was too quick, too strong. His upper arms seared with pain, as if a vise grip made from dry ice latched onto him. Fear overtook him and he shouted as he tried to shake away the claw-like grip of the charcoal demons.

As Kaden was dragged away, Ronnoc glanced back at the old man, whose smile now turned to a frown.

"Something wrong?" Ronnoc mocked.

"My heart breaks for you," the old man said.

The Agent laughed and then turned, walking briskly away.

Kaden looked back and saw the old man's gray eyes watching him. He wanted to scream for help, but oddly, just being seen by the man reassured him.

Barb was out of her office, watching the scene unfold, as others peeked their heads out from behind their own Twenties. The crew of the EMR, including those Kaden remembered as friends, Elba and Enak, watched the Elites drag him away. Only the old man, who continued to look not-so-old, made eye contact.

CHAPTER 12

"**S**tand up," Ronnoc's voice boomed as he threw open the door to the holding cell. Bright lights came through and Kaden tried to shield his eyes.

Ronnoc looked down on him, an imposing silhouette in the doorway.

Kaden rubbed his eyes as he sat in the corner of the tiny dark cell. His legs ached as he stretched them after unknown hours on the cold, damp concrete floor.

"Stand up or you will be stood up," Ronnoc demanded, tapping the handle of the mace at his side. Flanking Ronnoc was the pair of charcoal demons.

"I'm up, I'm up," Kaden said in a raspy voice, not wanting the creatures to take hold of him again. The skin where they grabbed him the day before was cracking and dying. They latched on when dragging him into the lower recesses of the giant, illuminated tower and didn't let go. A painful, life-stealing ache resonated deep within his skin and muscles where they held him.

He now followed the trio as they led him to an open room. Dozens of others, each looking a variation of terrified, were being corralled. Many men and women in blue robes, similar to Ronnoc's purple robe, circled the group. Outside of the colorful robes was a circle of the black-robed charcoal creatures. They wore the same black robe and their horrid, dead skin was the same cracking, lifeless rock, but on their heads was a thin, gold crown made from numerous wraps of a gold wire welded together. The gold-crowned creatures stood firm and commanding, like overlords keeping the blue-robed helpers in check, who in turn herded all the sheep-like prisoners to the center of their circle.

Ronnoc led Kaden into the group, then stepped to the front, the only one in purple in between the circle of blue and black.

"You are here to be sorted," Ronnoc said in a raised, firm voice.

A horrified gasp went up from the crowd, but he snapped it back down.

"Some of you are being punished while others rewarded. You each have potential to serve The Tower. If you are dismissed, then you will be summoned again on a future date for your method of serving. All serve Empyrean," he said. On the word "Empyrean," all the blue- and black-robed Agents and Elites snapped to attention.

"It will suit you to stay quiet for an orderly sorting. Pray thanks to Pinnacle for the privilege to be sorted by the Elites."

Kaden followed Ronnoc's eyes as the man looked around the crowd. Some of the people were looking at those in blue robes, some staring at Ronnoc, a few were muttering discontentedly under their breath, all were scared.

"Begin," Ronnoc said.

The ring of Elites stepped forward, the gait of their step not an up and down but a smooth, hovering-like motion.

The crowd shuddered and tried stepping back, but there was nowhere to go. The blue-robed Agents stepped in, tightening the circle, with their hands on the mace-like electrified Spark Clubs at their sides.

The first Elite slowly raised its hands, a cupping motion toward its face, as if moving air to its cracked nostrils. It sniffed in the air and the crowd shifted forward as if pulled by invisible strings. Two other charcoal Elites stepped to the first one's side and motioned their hands. The group shifted as if moving through a funnel. A line formed that led straight toward the first Elite.

Kaden's eyes darted between the Elites, the people in front of him moving toward them, and the many blue-robed Agents behind him. He felt like a sheep being led to slaughter.

Frantically, he searched for a way out. With each thought, the closer he inched to the front of the group and the charcoal Elites.

They began sorting the first of the line. With a flick of his wrist, the Elite in charge moved each person to the left or right, occasionally pausing and sniffing the air around the person.

He kept scanning, looking past the Agents and the Elites, then through the crowd. But nothing. The Agents encircled them.

Then, in the crowd ahead of him, closer to the sorting, he saw her.

Kira.

She was looking around, likely for a way out, just like him. She hadn't seen him yet, and she would get to the Elites first.

He snuck ahead, moving past those in front of him to get closer to the head of the line as the two sorted groups began to move. Moving to the left, one group was being funneled to doors that led outside. Freedom. But to the right, a group of Elites waited.

As Kaden watched, he saw a tall, burly man with curly black hair that covered his ears. His tattered gray clothes resembled someone more likely from the Outer Ring.

"No," he said, stopping cold with a blank stare at the waiting Elites.

The creature at the head of the sorting tilted its head. The cracks in the ashy charcoal showed a curious surprise.

"No, I'm not going with them," he said firmly as he stepped backward.

"You have been chosen," Ronnoc called to the man.

"I watched my Mara get *chosen,* and she never came back! I was too stupid to realize what you were doing," the man said firmly.

The Elite stepped toward the man, and Kaden took the chance to slide up in line next to Kira.

"Hey!" Kira said, lighting up upon seeing him. She gave him a hug that melted his heart, but the commotion quickly stole the reunion.

"Too stupid... But not anymore."

He pulled a dagger from his waistband and turned back to the Elite, thrusting the knife forward.

The Elite raised a hand, and the man stopped. As if the Elite pressed the pause button on the man's life, he stood motionless halfway through his lunging jab.

"No. You dead bastards took my Mara. You'll pay!" he demanded through gritted teeth.

The Elite stepped toward the man, examining him.

"Maybe she is here, waiting for you to join," the Elite said in an unnaturally feminine voice, his muscular, rock-like frame and dead eyes not matching the pleasant, sweet voice that came out of his mouth.

"Issac, is that you, baby? I've been here waiting. Come join me," the female voice called out to him from the charcoal demon.

Issac's head, still held in place, began to shake, like the voice was a worm eating into his brain. Kaden's stomach churned at the scene playing out.

"No!" he screamed back.

"Issac, come to me," the Elite said, its voice like a soft velvet.

"Stop it," he cried out. "Baby, no. It's not you!"

"Oh, but, Issac, it is. I'm in here, and I'm waiting for you," it said as it stepped forward.

"No. You killed her..." He began to sob. "You take children, you take wives..."

Kaden noticed a young girl, six or seven years old, in the crowd. She had slid behind a woman, trying to shield her eyes from the creatures surrounding the group.

"Come to me, baby. My Issac," it said, opening its arms wide and stepping toward him.

The creature released its hold, pressing the play button on the man. Issac lunged forward, the Elite now at his side as he stumbled. The creature was now standing over him, its arms out wide.

Issac's clothes rose, like a wind blowing them toward the creature. Then his curly hair straightened as it stretched toward the being above him.

"No," he said, but the fight in him was dying as his eyes watered.

"Come on, baby. My Issac," the thing repeated in Mara's voice.

Issac was on his hands and knees but began rising off the floor.

"Not here." Ronnoc stepped in behind the Elite. "In your chambers."

Issac stopped rising, held in midair.

A moment ago, a sweet voice had come from the creature, but upon Ronnoc's interruption, a deep, guttural growl echoed from its dead, black mouth. It stared at Ronnoc, then lowered its outstretched arms as Issac fell to the ground.

"Thank you," Ronnoc said, bowing his head and stepping back.

The creature then raised a hand and Issac shot off the ground, his arms and legs outstretched like a starfish. His chest pushed out as his spine arched backward, his tear-soaked face contorted with pain.

"Fine," the demon said from somewhere within the growling depths of its lungs. Then it twisted its extended hand like turning a doorknob. Issac's outstretched arms and legs twisted, his knees and elbows snapped ninety degrees to the side, bones shattered and popped, the end of his limbs now like a circle, matching the motion of the Elite's movement.

The crowd gasped in horror and stepped back.

Kaden noticed Ronnoc roll his eyes at the display.

"We need to get outside," Kaden whispered to Kira and pointed to the large glass walls that looked out over a marble courtyard.

"My lords, forgive me. For the sake of efficiency, shall we proceed," Ronnoc said as the Elites tortured Issac. The crowd stood in awe, watching the black-robed creature as it let Issac's body drop. It then flicked its wrist and Issac's massive frame slid across the floor toward the waiting group as easy as a marble rolling on the hard floor.

Kaden wasted no time, using the distraction to dart to the front of the line and pulling Kira with him.

The creature turned, an emotionless expression on its cracked, ashy black face.

"Go," Kaden whispered, nudging her toward the exit. He could see a growing number of people outside the glass walls watching the commotion within.

"I'm not leaving you," Kira replied.

"Go!" he whispered again, slamming his hip into hers and bumping toward the exit. Kaden used the motion to step toward the Elite. With his head down, he walked toward the terrified group.

The creature stopped and directed its attention toward Kaden. It raised its head, as if smelling the air around him.

A grunt came from the waiting group of Elites and unfortunate souls, Issac a crumpled heap of broken joints. In the group, the demon from outside the EMR. It smiled at Kaden, its black teeth and tongue like a void in space that sucked all life toward it. The lifeless black eyes stuck to him, wide and excited at what they saw.

The lead Elite waved his hand, and Kaden felt an invisible push that hurried him toward the waiting group. The closer he got to them, the more a sense of hopelessness took him. As if all happiness in the world was absorbed by these creatures, but through the corner of his eye, he saw Kira walking through a pair of blue-robed Agents and through the exit.

A small flicker of happiness burned inside him like an undying flame.

"Wait," it said, pointing at Kira, and Kaden's hope extinguished.

She stopped mid-stride, one foot hovering above the floor and her hand mere inches from pushing open the door.

The Elite leading the sorting took in a deep sniff of the air, like a blood-hound searching for scent. The invisible force nearly pulled Kira off her feet, like an invisible rope tugged on her waist. The blood seemed to leave Kaden's face as he imagined what just happened to Issac happening to Kira.

But in the hopelessness of the Elite's presence around him, Kaden felt a warm, calming sensation. Like a small fire warming his heart or a ray of sunshine shooting through the clouds to warm him while the world froze around him.

As Kaden's worries left him, the Elite's body twitched, like its muscles all suffered a brief jolt in unison. The creature quit smelling the air around Kira and waved her away.

The other charcoal demons accepted the decision and returned their attention back to the group.

Ronnoc looked back at Kira as she left, a confused expression on his face. He looked between the group and Kira and found Kaden watching her, then him.

They locked eyes.

Kaden soon dropped his eyes, but Ronnoc now focused on him. The purple-robed man walked over and stood next to Kaden's group.

The Elites sorted the rest of the group. Nearly a third were let free while the other two-thirds were corralled like cattle by the Elites. Ronnoc and the supporting blue-robed Agents oversaw it all, like cowboys getting the herd going and now the shepherd dog-like Elites moved the cows into the slaughterhouse.

The Elites led Kaden and the others out of the immense lobby area and through a dark hallway. Again, he felt a feeling of hopelessness press down on him like a thick humidity coming down from above. A glimmer of hope sat in his heart, like a diamond unable to be crushed by the overwhelming invisible force pressing down on him.

Before entering the dark hallway, he turned behind him to look toward the glass walls that separated the massive ballroom and the outside courtyard. He saw Kira and many others, many looking back in to see their loved ones and friends taken into the dark hallway.

Next to Kira and a step behind her stood a hooded man. His gray eyes flickered as they caught a glint of light. Kaden knew the eyes were trained on him.

Ronnoc interrupted the gaze, shoving Kaden's shoulder to move him back into the herded group as they went deeper into the bowels of Empyrean's tower.

Chapter 13

Entry #3

The trial was a massive success. Human test subject one, who we have affectionately come to call Adam, has shown all signs of reversing their metastasizing cancer. The entire body appears to be in harmony. Not only is it healing prior trauma, but it is actively strengthening itself. Muscle definition is more pronounced, cognitive tests are increasing, and sleep cycles more defined. The success rates in the primate studies were so positive, we came to call this our miracle drug, however, if this one test is any indication of the human response, "miracle" doesn't even begin to describe the benefits. This is purely life-giving. Superhuman may be more appropriate.

I feel like I tiptoed to the Gates of Hell and put a trampoline above Hades. When the departed soul gets right to gates, they are sprung back up into the light!

But alas, my positivity cannot outweigh the coming complications. First is logistical, but easy enough. We must recruit an Eve to go with our Adam. I can already see the ads once our Eve is as strong as Adam; she'll pull a school bus like a strongman competition. Think of the buzz a social ad like that would create.

Finally, I am saddened to say that I sense my partner is letting a false sense of nobility creep into his thoughts. I do not believe his judgment can be trusted anymore. It pains me to write that I have begun filing paperwork to separate. We must protect Adam, and our future Eve. Those are the bedrocks of the coming civilization. If my partner taints them, I'm afraid the Biblical story will play out again.

I must act.

Chapter 14

The Elites herded the group into the maze-like bowels within The Tower of Empyrean. Any time someone slowed their steps, an Elite motioned and threw them forward. Soon, the group fell into a mindless march. The air grew colder, thicker, and more stagnant with each step as the walls seemed to close in around them. Kaden felt like a metallic beast had swallowed the group. With every step, they slithered further down its dank insides. The only sound was the echoing of their footsteps on the hard, ceramic floor, a rhythmic thudding that seemed to mock the pounding of Kaden's heart.

They reached a larger rectangular room that reminded Kaden of a massive steel refrigerator. The walls were sleek and cool to the touch, utterly devoid of any warmth or personality. There was no furniture, no paint, no decor—just a cold, sterile emptiness. Eight doors were set into the walls, four on each of the longer walls. Every door a featureless slab of metal that looked like it could withstand a bomb blast.

The Elites then sorted the group once again. Each Elite chose their desired persons as the larger group quickly divided into smaller contingents of two or three people that were shuffled toward one of the refrigerator-like doors. Kaden found himself face-to-face with the Elite who had singled him out earlier in front of the EMR, its charcoal hand grasping his shoulder with such an excruciatingly tight grip, he winced in pain. The force crunched his shoulder as the dry ice-like burning sensation went through his coveralls, searing his skin. Ronnoc followed close behind the pair, his expression unreadable as he oversaw the room, always with an eye on Kaden.

Each group then entered their smaller room. It was even colder and more austere than the greater room behind them. Like stepping into a freezer, or morgue, the cold air turned the people's anxious breath into a lingering fog. The walls were the same sleek steel as the outer hallways, but the single amazingly bright overhead light gave the impression that the room itself was alive, a compact version of an arctic hideaway with a bright sun high above.

Two others stood beside Kaden, a man and a woman. Both of them showed signs of poverty, ragged living in the Outer Ring. They were filthy, their clothes little more than rags that hung off emaciated frames. The man had a long, unkempt beard that was matted with dirt and grime, and his eyes held a wild, haunted look. The woman might have been younger, perhaps in her early twenties, but she looked like she had aged a lifetime in her few short years. Her hair was a tangled mess, and her face was smudged with soot and dirt.

The Elite that had been eyeing Kaden stood on one side of the room, and in the center, Kaden and the two others. Behind them, Ronnoc stood like an inspector, keeping tabs on the entire event.

For a moment, the three of them stood in the middle of the room, each lost in their own thoughts and fears. Kaden could feel the terror radiating off the man and woman like heat from a furnace, and he knew that his own fear must be just as palpable, but he tried to keep an upright posture. He tried not to let on that his body was beginning to tremble. He told himself it was the cold and not the demon-like black eyes that moved between him and the two others.

Then, without warning, the man let out a strangled gasp. His body jerked forward, as if pulled by an invisible hand. He stumbled toward the Elite like a dog being aggressively pulled on its leash. His feet scraped the ground, his arms flailing helplessly at his sides as he was drawn inexorably toward the Elite.

"No," the man begged, his voice a hoarse, a raspy whisper. "I'll do anything, I swear, please."

The Elite ignored his cries as the man moved toward the creature. Its ashy skin cracked a smile; a horrible, leering grin of black that stole the light around it. The black teeth made Kaden's blood run cold.

As the man came within a foot of the creature, his face contorted in agony, his skin stretching and warping as if it were being pulled from his bones. He screamed. The sound was a raw, primal terror that seemed to tear the air apart as it pierced Kaden's ears.

The Elite opened its robe, exposing its ashy, rock-like chest and stomach. Its midsection was the same charcoal-like black of its hands and face, each a cracked and aged surface.

In a sickening blur of motion, the man was gone. His body pulled into the creature's chest, as if he dissolved into the Elite's body, absorbed like water into a sponge. Only his ragged clothes remained, at first stuck to the creature's body, but soon fluttering to the ground in a pitiful heap.

The Elite licked its lips, a look of deep, savage satisfaction on its face. Kaden saw the ashy rock of its belly seem to lose its dryness, a cracked desert ground now nourished like soil after a rain.

The demon turned its attention to the woman. This time, it didn't pull slowly, but an invisible, aggressive strength ripped at her. She tried stepping back, but didn't have time to move or scream in resistance to the creature's appetite.

One moment, she was trembling with fear, and the next, flying through the air, her body drawn to the Elite like a super magnet. In a split-second that felt like an eternity, Kaden saw her face and body contort, every cell in her body compressed and pulled against the creature's midsection. Her clothes fell to the ground as the remaining ball of flesh disappeared into the stone-like figure.

The creature now seemed even stronger, its once cracking skin now fresher and revitalized. Its body stood taller and more full, like a body-builder ready to go on stage.

Kaden stood, frozen with horror, unable to pull his eyes away from the nightmare unfolding before him. The Elite, more powerful and ferocious than ever, turned to him, its black eyes boring into his soul like twin drills.

"Finally, the unique one. Dessert," it said, its voice a deep, guttural growl that mixed various tones in an unnatural symphony of voices that seemed to rise from the depths of hell. The primary low-baritone sound hid traces of alto and soprano, giving an eerie mixture of voices. It was the verbal equivalent of all the colors in a child's paint set being combined to make a brown-black goo.

Kaden felt the first pull. He steadied himself and the creature flashed a smile. It was toying with him, picking him closer with each nudge. He fought against it with every ounce of his strength, his muscles straining and his heart pounding in his ears like a drum. But his feet dragged across the smooth metallic floor, slowly, inch-by-inch as the creature savored the fight. The Elite's power was too strong, too all-consuming, and Kaden had nothing in the bare room to grab hold of.

Just as Kaden thought he would be devoured, Ronnoc stepped forward.

"He is *unique*, my lord. As you say," Ronnoc said, his voice calm and measured, as if he were discussing the weather rather than the fate of a human life. "As you sense, this one is different, and could be uniquely useful to Pinnacle."

The Elite hesitated, its black eyes narrowed to slits. "You deny me my rightful prey?" the thing snarled.

"Not at all," Ronnoc replied smoothly. "I merely suggest that this one could be more valuable alive than dead. Maybe more satisfying replenishment for you and your kind."

"No," it growled, and Kaden felt the creature's hold wrap around his body. But he didn't move closer to the thing.

"Pinnacle is always searching for new ways to grow, to become more efficient. If the herds below become insufficient for your kind's appetite, we'd need others to support your consumption," Ronnoc said.

Kaden felt his body held in a vise grip from all sides, like a constrictor pulling tighter. His lungs crushed, unable to take another breath.

"May I suggest Pinnacle examine his uniqueness?" Ronnoc said.

The Elite considered this for a long, tense moment, its gaze never leaving Kaden. Ronnoc let the silence hang in the cold, dead air.

Kaden shot back and slammed against the wall, his face blue as he gasped for air to fill his burning lungs.

"If he fails, I'll have you both," the Elite announced in its eerie, demonic tone and then swiftly strode out of the room as if walking on air.

Ronnoc nodded thanks, his head bowed as the creature left, then he turned to Kaden.

"Get up," he demanded.

Kaden looked at him in surprise.

"Or you could stay?" He motioned to the Elite who just left the room.

Kaden scrambled to his feet. There was a lightness in the air as the Elite left, like the thick cloud of oppressive air was rising off the room.

"From now on, you belong to me. You're my trainee. If you survive your trials, you'll be an Agent," Ronnoc said.

Kaden's face now returned to its normal color as he followed Ronnoc out of the room on shaky legs. His mind reeled from the horror he had just witnessed. As they walked through the twisting corridors of The Tower, Ronnoc spoke to him in a low, intense voice.

"You're lucky I was there to vouch for you. The Elites are not known for their mercy. But I see something in you, boy. Traits that could be useful to me, and to Pinnacle."

Kaden said nothing.

They came to a door, and Ronnoc threw it open. It resembled the holding cell he was in earlier that day, except larger, and included a bed, toilet, and desk. Kaden looked into the room, feeling as if he was being upgraded from death row and into a minimum security prison.

"Rest. Tomorrow, I begin to train you, molding you into something greater than you ever thought possible. That is, IF you learn, adapt, and obey. Understand?"

"Yes," Kaden said.

Chapter 15

Kaden stepped into the room and turned back. "Why did you save me?" he asked Ronnoc.

Ronnoc regarded him for a moment, a calculating look in his eyes, and then he slammed the door. The sound of a lock sliding into place came before footsteps walking away from the room.

Kaden settled into his new quarters, the small, sparse room with a simple cot and desk below a flickering light overhead. His mind reeled from the events of the day—the sorting, the horrifying display of the Elites' power, and Ronnoc's cryptic words. He sat on the edge of the small, cot-like bed, his head in his hands, trying to make sense of it all.

His body finally felt the tiredness of the day. He didn't remember falling asleep or any specific dreams, but pieces from his memory swirled around his mind as he slept. The realness of the scenes left him unable to tell if he was awake or in a dream, his mind scrolling through a combination of the brilliant gray eyes from inside the hooded figure. He stood next to Kira outside the glass walls of The Tower as the distorted faces of the man and woman consumed by the Elite danced in and out of vision, reflections in the glass surrounding the gray eyes.

Twice in the night, he shot up from the bed and threw up in the toilet as his body felt the pull of the Elite and he saw its demonic face in his dreams.

Only by focusing on the gray flickering eyes was he able to settle himself and return to sleep.

The next morning, he awoke with an aching body. All the fighting against the Elite's pull left him sore. He paced the room, trying to loosen up. Soon, he found a pencil and paper in the desk. He wrote down his memories of the day before and began feeling better, his body and mind looser than before. Body-weight exercises moved his blood. As he went into his third rotation between push-ups and squats, a thunderous bang came at the door.

The lock slid open and Ronnoc stepped in.

"Rise and shine, boy," he said, his voice cutting through the silence. "Today, your real education begins."

Kaden stood up, beads of sweat on his forehead.

"Good," Ronnoc said as he looked him up and down. Then he motioned for him to follow as he stepped back into the hallway.

As they walked, Ronnoc talked.

"You'll be staying here in The Tower, undergoing a series of lessons and trials designed to mold you into the kind of Agent that Empyrean needs. After individual lessons, you'll be integrated into a group, joining those with similar aspirations of serving Pinnacle at the highest level."

He paused, fixing Kaden with a piercing stare.

"I saw what you did back there, boy. The way you moved that woman aside, putting yourself in the line of fire. That takes guts. Initiative. The kind of qualities The Tower needs. That's why I saved you."

A sense of pride welled up inside him as he remembered how he took control of their situation.

"Tell me about yourself," Ronnoc asked.

"I live in the Inner Ring, we have a great view of the tower–"

"*Thee Tower*," Ronnoc interrupted him. "Respect it."

"Yes, we have a great view of The Tower, and I work at the EMR."

"How long?"

"Sir?"

"How long have you worked at the Empyrean Mechanix Retreat?" Ronnoc asked.

"About eight, nine years," Kaden replied.

"Nine and a half years," Ronnoc stated firmly.

"If you already knew..."

"Without precision, chaos reigns. If we are not *exact* in our duty, then the world begins to unravel. Are you aware that Empyrean is the only known refuge of humanity? Pinnacle created the New Breed and this secure kingdom as every other city in the world crumbled. Empyrean thrived because of his strength and wisdom. It continues to survive because of precise control."

Ronnoc stopped walking and turned to face Kaden.

"Do you understand why we must be exact in our duties?"

"Yes," Kaden replied.

"Good, because failure is death for us all, thus failure of one condemns all others. To be an Agent is to be in service, and if you are not precise, then you are cancerous to Empyrean and must be eliminated. Understood?" Ronnoc's eyes narrowed as if challenging Kaden.

"The city thrives on discipline," he said.

"Yes or no," Ronnoc snapped.

"Yes."

"Good, and not mere discipline. Precision means utter control. We are the ruling class; without us, the world would continuously deprive itself of power by subjugating the labor class. It would churn into an unspeakable hell. We hold that order," Ronnoc said, his eyes firmly locked with Kaden's.

Kaden nodded, unsure if he should respond and forcing himself not to pull his eyes away from Ronnoc. The idea of control spoke to him, as if a deep-seated treasure caught the light in the depths of his soul, urging him to swim down and pull up the glory.

Finally, Ronnoc broke his stare and pivoted forward like a soldier called to attention. He walked down the hallway as he spoke, Kaden following.

"Tell me, how long have you been at the EMR?" he asked.

"Nine years, six months," Kaden replied.

"Good. Now tell me, who are your closest associates at the EMR?"

"Enak and Elba. We started there together at sixteen and have been friends ever since," Kaden replied. The parallel of Enak and Elba in this time and place echoed the memories of Darren's roommates, Chris and Kirk.

"And what of the defiant old man?"

"I... I don't really know him, sir."

"Teacher. You shall call me *teacher*," Ronnoc corrected.

"Okay, teacher, I don't know–"

"I heard you," Ronnoc snapped. "Tell me what you do know. He's been employed there for decades according to our records. And you've been their nearly ten–"

"Nine years, six months," Kaden interrupted with a smirk.

Ronnoc turned, swiftly pulling out his Spark Club and swinging it into Kaden's knee.

Kaden dropped to the ground holding his knee, wincing in pain.

"Do not speak out of turn in the presence of superiors or dare to correct one," Ronnoc said with a stone-cold expression. He watched Kaden for a moment, then resumed walking.

Kaden picked himself off the ground and moved his knee. Nothing felt broken, but it felt like a knot was inside the joint. He knew swelling would follow and likely a bruise covering the area. He hobbled to catch up.

"What do you know of the old man?" Ronnoc asked again.

Visions of the gray eyes flickered in his mind.

"He's great at his job. He keeps the numbers up for the entire EMR and, well, as steady as they come."

"More," Ronnoc said.

"I think he watches out for folks too. Just today, I'm pretty sure he set the safety bar to engage the chain when I missed it. I could be dead. He saved me, but he acts like it's nothing to keep an eye out for everyone."

"More."

Kaden searched his mind, trying to pull memories from the back of his mind.

"Sometimes he seems to be younger than he looks because of how efficient and productive he is. I swear, one morning, he'll look twenty years younger, but the next, he comes in as thin as a rail, but regardless, he always produces. New guys joke how fragile he looks on most days, saying he'll crumble within a week like the walls of Jericho, but he just keeps going. He never engages with that talk, but personally, I think he likes the nickname. I think he likes proving the others wrong," Kaden said.

Ronnoc stopped walking, and they stood outside a door. His eyes jumped back and forth as he thought.

"Say that again," the teacher asked.

"He likes proving others wrong?"

"What do they call him?" Ronnoc said, a rage bubbling under the question.

"Jericho, but–" Kaden said.

"He said his name was David. We have a record for a David at the EMR," Ronnoc said, the bubbling anger now at full boil.

"It's just a nickname, not like the Jericho of myth," Kaden said.

"Do *NOT* speak that name again," Ronnoc demanded, then he turned, his eyes flaring as his mind raced.

Kaden opened his mouth to question but thought better of it. Soon, Ronnoc came away from his thoughts and opened the door.

"Come, meet your cohort. If you survive individual trials, you'll join them full-time," Ronnoc said.

Kaden followed him in the room, the words '*if you survive*' echoing in his mind.

"Agents, I'd like you to meet Kaden McCloud," Ronnoc said as he entered the room. Four students, all roughly Kaden's age, snapped to attention and stood behind neatly arranged chairs.

Kaden remembered he had never told Ronnoc his last name. The blue-robed man had been doing his homework.

"He will embark on the Outer Ring trial tonight. If you see him again, he'll join you."

Two men and two women made up the group. Kaden noticed one man give him a sympathetic look that soon turned back to a stone, soldier-like expression. One of the women seemed to give the same, whereas the other man and woman remained locked on Ronnoc, like expertly trained dogs waiting for their master's command.

All four wore white robes, exactly in style to Ronnoc's blue robe. Kaden felt out of place, still wearing his EMR coveralls above his house clothes.

"Go, sit. You may listen today for a taste of the knowledge you will gain after your trial," Ronnoc said, motioning for Kaden to move to the back of the room, away from the four.

Kaden moved to the back, trying not to limp from the pain in his knee. He looked at the faces of the four. Three remained looking forward, but one man, with black hair in a tight crew cut, eyed him back.

"The alpha of the group," Kaden thought to himself.

Ronnoc began to speak at the front of the classroom.

"The Elites, once Agents and New Breed like us, are not like us anymore," he began.

"You don't say," Kaden whispered to himself.

Ronnoc heard the comment and eyed Kaden with a vicious stare. He sat up straight and decided he would not be speaking again during this class.

"They're improved, gifted by Pinnacle. They're a different breed entirely, given a hint of Pinnacle's power. Minor when compared to the master, but significant when compared to Agents, and god-like when compared to the masses. Yet, not all of the Elites can handle Pinnacle's gifts. Who knows the two responses?"

"Acceptance and ignorance," the alpha replied sharply.

"That's right, Ryon," Ronnoc said and the alpha's straight expression flashed a quick upturn of a grin.

"What is the outcome of each?"

"Those of acceptance become leaders of the kingdom, while ignorance leads to servitude," the stern woman said.

"Wrong, Vala. *Everyone* is in servitude to Pinnacle," Ronnoc said, his eyes looking over the other three. Vala's face remained motionless in her discipline.

"Specific servitude, Teacher," the other woman said, answering a split-second before Ryon.

"Right, Aria. They cannot accept Pinnacle's gift and thus are sentenced to serve all Agents. "*Everyone* serves Pinnacle," he said, eyes darting to Vala. "But failed Elites *specifically* serve all the other Agents."

He scanned each student's face before continuing.

"And how are they denoted? Jace, how about you join the class." Ronnoc looked at the man who hadn't spoken yet.

"A golden crowd for those of acceptance, and nothing for those of ignorance," Jace said.

"Good," Ronnoc said, and Kaden noticed the teacher's varying tones of approval and frustration as Ronnoc interacted with the group. He clearly had favorites.

"The gift grants them each with powers from Pinnacle. It physically changes them from a New Breed into an Elite."

Kaden thought about how referring to the charcoal-like skin as a *physical change* was the understatement of his lifetime.

"Those who fully embrace the power, those who accept it, rise to be one level below Pinnacle, but those who only get a fraction of that power are ignorant of their true capabilities. They are destined to serve the Agents of Empyrean, Agents like us, for their lifetime.

"That is the way of the Empyrean. We shall always serve Pinnacle, the master and savior of the world. The strong rule and control for the greater good, and the weak serve to fill their place. And if we want the New Breed to survive, to thrive in this world, we MUST make ourselves indispensable. We need to become the kind of Agents that are unwaveringly loyal, the kind that serve Pinnacle's true vision. The Elites are the most powerful of all Agents, Golden Elites on top and Ignorant Elites next in line. But Pinnacle's gifts do not come without warning. As Agents, we must balance the Elites. They do not have the intelligence of Pinnacle and are susceptible to their own power and greed. We must be Agents who create order out of chaos, and must be extra diligent to channel the Elites properly."

As the lesson continued, it focused on the history of Empyrean and the role of the Agents. Ronnoc painted a picture of a world in chaos, with the Agents and the Tower's control as the only things standing between life-giving order inside the city walls and sure death outside them. He emphasized the importance of obedience and loyalty to the cause.

"Without us," he said, "Empyrean would descend into madness. The people need structure, they need direction. That's what we provide. That's what you will maintain."

Then, Ronnoc released the students with instructions for the next duties, mainly the day's physical training. The students cleared out and Kaden noticed the students glance back at him, but he couldn't tell if the looks were encouraging for a potential teammate or sympathetic, like those given to an animal before it was to be put down.

Once the four left the room, Ronnoc acknowledged Kaden for the first time since he spoke out of turn.

"Earlier, you mentioned your living quarters," Ronnoc said.

"My apartment?"

"That is what you said. Why do you call it *your* apartment?" Ronnoc asked.

"I've never thought of it another way," Kaden said, unsure.

"Pinnacle is our savior. *Your* apartment does not exist. Pinnacle grants you the gift of a home because of your service to the EMR."

"You're saying it's Pinnacle's apartment, not mine?" Kaden said.

"Yes, there is no private property. There is nothing in the labor class outside of servitude. If they had the choice to buy and sell, and where to live, and how to live, even if Pinnacle returned the freedom to procreate, humanity would crumble. This is the same lesson as your primary lesson today – we control for the greater good."

"We have no rights?"

"You, if you pass your trials and become an Agent, you earn the rights of an Agent. You will also be granted the gift of new living quarters, here in The Tower," Ronnoc said.

"I don't have to move. My, I mean, Pinnacle's building where I reside now is close," Kaden said.

"Don't be a fool," Ronnoc snapped, and Kaden took a half step back, anticipating the Spark Club, but Ronnoc remained firm in his straight posture, his chest pushed out. "Power is gained by proximity to power. I will not let a student of mine destine himself to failure by living outside these walls. You shall live here or nowhere."

Kaden stood silent.

Ronnoc let out a deep breath, seemingly frustrated with having to explain himself. "'Yes, teacher' is the right answer," he finally said. "Now, your trial begins." He reached into a drawer and pulled out a white robe. "Take off that filth and put on your uniform."

Chapter 16

Kaden stood before the mirror in his quarters, adjusting the crisp, white robe of his new uniform that marked him as an entry-level Agent of Empyrean. As he prepared for his first trial in the Outer Ring, a mix of anticipation and trepidation coursed through his veins, but overarching all the *'if'* and *'survive'* talk from Ronnoc, Kaden longed to go find Kira. He wanted to stop by the EMR to see his friends. He'd grown up in the Outer Ring. A few days outside The Tower would be simple, a sort of a homecoming.

The door to his room slid open. Ronnoc entered, the bottom of his blue robes billowing behind him.

"Agent," he said, his voice stern and authoritative.

Kaden bowed his head to welcome his teacher. Ronnoc's eyes narrowed, studying the pupil.

"Three days. The robe must stay on, and you must stay in the Outer Ring. Return and you'll enter your cohort."

With no other instructions, Ronnoc walked him to the exit and dismissed him from The Tower. Kaden stepped out into the familiar Inner Ring of the working class, the sights and smells familiar to him. He decided to head straight to the Outer Ring to get a feel for it; it had, in fact, been years since he'd been out there. Once an Outer Ring person got called into the working class, it was rare they would ever go back, unless they lost their job, or worse.

Once he got a sense of what he'd be living with, he'd go back to Kira and gather more supplies.

The walk through the Inner Ring felt like a Sunday stroll. The evening air was crisp as the sun lowered in the sky and the temperature dropped. However, once he reached the Outer Ring, the contrast was stark. Long gone were the sleek, clean lines of the cylindrical Tower and the surrounding smaller housing towers of the Inner Ring that stood like worshiping children to the one adult in the center.

The Inner Ring's dingy yet stable environment was like insulation between the polished elegance of The Tower and something resembling a sewage system of the Outer Ring. Within a few blocks, crumbling buildings, garbage-strewn streets, and the acrid smell of feces filled his senses. The smells ignited memories from Kaden's childhood, memories of his house mother's absence, and those of him and Kira scavenging for food. Yet, this version of the Outer Ring seemed worse than his childhood, something he didn't think was possible.

The Inner Ring's layout gave way to clear alleys and paths; however, the Outer Ring was more like a city cobbled together from crumbling bricks and weeds. Buildings cracked, houses and paths laid out in a makeshift, unplanned manner, while tall, thorny weeds shot up in the cracks of the uneven brick roads.

As he navigated the narrow, winding alleys, Kaden couldn't help but feel a growing sense of unease. The eyes of the Outer Ring's inhabitants followed him, and for the first time, he realized what the trial was all about. He had lived in the Outer Ring as a child, but looking down at his bright, spotless white robe, he remembered Ronnoc's words.

"The robe must stay on... *If* you survive the trial."

A chill ran up his spine as more gaunt faces watched him from the shadows and corners. Faces peeked out, like moths drawn to the flame of his bright robe.

"You!" a man with a bald head and arms so thin he could have been confused for a skeleton called out, his voice raspy and strained. Wisps of hair stuck out from the side of his head. The angry look on the man's face told Kaden his first interaction back in the Outer Ring wouldn't be an easy one.

Ronnoc's words from the recent lesson rang in his head, that control was everything. If the man disrespected him, he'd have to maintain order, but faced with the obvious suffering before him, he was at a loss for words. But so was the man.

His angry expression and grunts turned to silence as the pair looked at each other. Each appeared ready to fire out words, but each also seemed caught up in the uncertain future of what the other might do first.

Finally, the scraggly man broke the silence. He laughed.

At first, more of a giggle that soon snowballed into hysterics.

The surprise reaction left an unease worse than angry words ever could. Kaden turned and walked. The eerie laugh echoed, as if following him. It rang through the cracked buildings in between coughing fits, the sound of phlegm bubbling through the sounds.

As Kaden walked, he next passed a group of children huddled in a doorway, their clothes ragged and their skin smudged with dirt. One of them, a young girl with puppy-dog brown eyes, approached him cautiously.

"Please, sir," she whispered, her voice trembling. "My brother, he's sick. We need help."

Kaden's heart clenched, the girl's plea striking a chord deep within him. He reached to his side but remembered he had nothing.

"I... I can't, but maybe I could help in another way?" he said, his voice heavy with regret.

"We need medicine or he'll die," the sweet face said as her two hands took his and gently pulled him toward the house.

He felt her calloused hands, wondering how such a young girl could have such thick and rough palms.

"I don't have medicine. Is there something else I can do?"

"Agents have packs, medical kits and food," she said, gently tugging on his hand as her brown eyes looked up at him.

"I'm not yet an Agent. I don't have a kit, but let me see–"

"Then you're worthless," she snapped, her once smooth voice now ragged with harshness. The innocent sadness of giant puppy-dog eyes shifted to a malicious scowl. She squeezed his hand, digging her fingernails into him. He ripped his hand away and she fell back. She'd drawn blood. His hands dotted with half-moon-like cuts from her grimy nails.

She hissed and ran back to the group, disappearing into the shadows of the doorway as other children gave harsh looks.

As Kaden walked away, the image of the girl's face and hissing sound haunted him, but what played on him the most was that the little girl reminded him of a young Kira. He'd spent most of his childhood trying to protect her, and they got out when he got the job at the EMR and her at the Textile Repair Facility. But what if they hadn't been able to survive? What if one of the rotating men that came for their house mother landed one of the blows on him? Some of the men who came calling were docile, beaten men looking for solace; others were filled with rage. These men lashed out when talked back to, usually resulting in Kaden's quick escape out of the apartment and sleeping in a dumpster for a night or two.

Now Kaden wondered if the right blow landed, a broken arm or noticeable limp would have kept him from working in the Inner Ring.

Dr. Abrams. The distant memory of the eye doctor appointment.

He'd sent Darren to first see Kaden as a child on the run. Was this what the doctor wanted him to see? Now Kaden was grown, trying to carve out a place for himself and his family in this world, but his mind returned to the memories of stashing food and running from Agents after curfew.

Suddenly, a commotion erupted further down the street. Shouts and echoes of smashing items filled the air.

He ran toward the disturbance.

As he rounded the corner, he found himself face to face with an Outer Ring mob. They were gathered around a toppled statue of Pinnacle, its once-imposing frame lying broken on the ground. Now he knew what the smashing and shouts were from. But as he watched the rubble, the crowd turned one-by-one to face him, their eyes blazing with fury at his bright white, spotless uniform.

"A new robe," a woman said with disdain.

"And without any lap dogs," a man said with a fiendish delight in his voice.

Kaden raised his hands, trying to project a strong voice and an air of calm authority.

"I grew up out here, and I know what you're going through," he said, his hands extended in front of him in a calm-down type motion.

But his words enraged the crowd further. Some smirked while others stood taller as they walked toward him, emboldened by their numbers. The group surged forward.

"You take everything and leave us to rot in this hellhole!" a woman cried, her face streaked with soot.

"Listen to me, I grew up here!" Kaden called out. "I know what you're going through."

"Yeah, he's one of us," the smirking man quipped. "I left my pretty white robe at home."

"I've scavenged for food just like you," Kaden said.

"Scavenge my family up some warm clothes," another said, eyeing Kaden's robe.

"You're not from here," the woman said, disgust overflowing her words. "You don't scavenge for food here. Out here, you are the food."

She held up a torch, its light flickering in the ruins of the buildings around her as the sun descended on the horizon.

Kaden backed away, wishing he had the same electrified mace that Ronnoc had on his side.

"I'm here for a few days. I don't want any trouble," he said, stepping back again, but the crowd continued to close the gap.

"And then return to your cozy tower?" a man said.

A rock flew from somewhere behind the first row of the mob, striking Kaden's shoulder with a dull thud. The pain was instant and sharp, but it paled in comparison to the realization in front of him. These were not the dangerous rebels he had been warned about, the threats to Empyrean's stability that needed to be put down at all costs. They were people, desperate and hurting, pushed to the brink by the very order he was now trying to join.

At that moment, Kaden made a decision. Slowly, deliberately, he raised his hands even higher and stopped backpedaling. He stood tall, facing the crowd not as an Agent of the Tower, but trying to show them a fellow human being.

"I hear you," he said, his voice steady and clear. "I see your pain, and I understand your anger. I cannot change the world overnight, but I promise you–"

Another rock soared from the front of the crowd, narrowly missing his head, but he held his ground. He was either incredibly foolish or incredibly brave.

"I'm unarmed and with no Elites!" he called out to the crowd and untied the belt of his robe. He opened the white robe to show simple pants and an undershirt underneath.

The act caught many of the group off guard. Some of the mob stopped and watched him. Others continued forward.

He forced eye contact with the closest man, who held a sharp metal rod, broken rebar pulled from busted concrete in one hand. The other held a jagged piece of concrete, likely broken off of the rebar.

The man stopped, stunned by Kaden's actions. For a moment, Kaden feared they would turn on him, reject his olive branch and lash out in their anger. But then, slowly, the tension began to dissipate as the man's posture straightened. The raised fist that clutched the concrete lowered, and the anger in his eyes gave way to confusion, and then sadness.

Moments later, the crowd dispersed, no longer hungry for an easy kill. Kaden stood facing the lead man, his heart racing and his mind reeling as the mob dispersed.

With a deep breath, Kaden nodded to the man as if portraying an apology with his body language, then he turned and walked back toward the Inner Ring. He had a sense of pride as the flickering light of the torches that illuminated the shadows of dusk grew more distant. He felt accomplished, and now, finding Kira was on his mind.

As Kaden left, the man holding the rebar and concrete stood motionless. The rebar was now at his feet, but he still held the jagged concrete with a firm grip. The veins of his forearm bulged as he held the twenty-pound hunk. He picked up the man-made rock, examining it. He was alone again, just him and his crumbling world. The sad eyes twitched and the spark of anger returned. "You won't ignore us," he said through clenched teeth.

Kaden never saw the man's despair flip back to anger. He didn't hear the footsteps running from behind or see the man raise the jagged concrete.

Light flashed and Kaden's vision went black. He hit the ground before his body registered the sharp pain.

A trickle of blood flowed from his head and pooled around his body, his white robe turning red.

Chapter 17

Darren's eyes shot open as he gasped for air, his heart pounding in his chest. He scrambled, unsure of his surroundings, but as his vision cleared, he realized he was back in his apartment, lying on the floor next to Kelly.

He looked at his hands. They were clean. His clothes were jeans and a tee-shirt instead of a white robe. He felt the back of his head. No blood. No wound.

The familiar hum of the air conditioner and the soft glow of his apartment's fluorescent kitchen lights grounded him back in reality. Darren's reality.

He was back.

He still felt like Kaden, the vivid experiences jumping through his mind. He felt the back of his head again, expecting a massive wound, yet the pain was gone, a phantom sensation that lingered just out of reach.

Glancing at Kelly, Darren was surprised to see her still sound asleep, her chest rising and falling in a steady rhythm. Looking out the window to the parking lot, the same cars and same shadows stretched out. A distant fire truck wailed and a car horn sounded from a street nearby.

Darren's hand instinctively reached for the glasses, eager to dive back into the future. But as he held the smooth black frame, he hesitated.

"They killed me," he said, feeling the back of his head once again. Then, he looked at the glasses, unsure if they'd work again.

"I tried to help them. They dispersed, but then... they killed me, and from behind!"

He grew furious, nearly spiking the glasses onto the ground in frustration, but he stopped himself and put them on the table.

"How did it get like this? One small city is all that's left... At least you missed the sorting," he said, looking down at Kelly. He gently scooped her off the ground and brought her to his room, resting her on the bed. He sat at his desk next to the bed, his elbows on his knees hunched over as he watched Kelly and thought about what to do.

"The Outer Ring... It's nothing but chaos," he said. "We survived it, we got out."

He thought of the view he woke up to in Empyrean, the high vantage pointed at The Tower and the surrounding Inner Ring. The Outer Ring seemed like a disease slowly eating away the city as it creeped toward the center.

"The chaos must be controlled," he said.

He stood up and went out to the living room as Chris and Kirk came in through the front door.

"Aye!" Kirk called out.

Darren quickly grabbed the glasses and moved back to his room, hoping a nod of greeting would do.

"Hey, you in for this adventure?" Chris asked him.

"What?" Darren said, stopping a few feet from his door and eyeing his friend.

"It's epic, a whole new future world, and really makes you think what's going on behind the scenes," Chris said.

"What do you say?" Darren said, studying his friend.

"Hey, nice glasses, four-eyes," Kirk called out.

"Yeah... I went to the eye doctor yesterday, remember?" he replied.

"Nope, but let's go!"

"He's not there anymore. His office, well... it vanished..." Darren said.

"What are you talking about?" Chris said.

"Wait, what are *you* talking about?" Darren replied.

Chris pulled a video game up from a small plastic bag.

"The new HALO, crazy future world, bro! And we're doing this," Chris said again.

"Grab your sticks! It's epic!" Kirk said, tossing a controller to Darren. It hit his chest and he instinctively tried to catch it, but the glasses were in his hands. After bobbling it a moment, he finally secured it in one hand and the glasses safe in the other.

"You really wearin' glasses now?" Chris asked.

"I will if they work," Darren said, looking down at them.

"I would imagine they do. I mean, if an eye doctor gave them to you, bro," Kirk said with a laugh.

"Good point," Darren said. He didn't want to bring up how on the other side of the glasses was a man named Kaden, who lay alone on the street in a bloody, dead heap.

"Come on, fire it up," Chris said, elbowing Darren as he walked by.

"No, Kelly's here," Darren said.

"Yo! What up, g–!" Kirk shouted toward Darren's room.

"She's sleeping," Darren snapped.

"Yo, what up, girl?" Kirk whispered, mocking a scream.

"Hmmm, what would the two love birds be doing alone in his room, and now she's sleeping," Chris said.

"I wonnnndeeerrrrr..." Kirk joked.

"It's been a long day. I'll be in my room. Keep it down," Darren said.

"How about you keep it down when you're *sleeping*," Kirk said with air quotes.

Darren rolled his eyes and moved toward his room.

"Okay, we'll need to build our team if we're going to make any progress," Chris said behind him as the game started.

Chris's team comment stuck with Darren. The mobs, the horrid Outer Ring in Empyrean. If Kaden was ever going to improve conditions, he'd need a team as well. Then, another thought struck him: he already had a team waiting. Ronnoc said if he survived the three days in the Outer Ring, he'd join the cohort. But he didn't exactly survive, Kaden's body was lying on the weed-infested cracked brick road, but if it was alive, he'd go back to a team.

He closed the door to his room and sat in the chair. Kelly lay in the bed just as peaceful as before. He hoped she was the same way on the other side, wherever she was in Empyrean. After placing a light blanket over her, he picked up the glasses.

"Any life left in there?" he said aloud, resigning himself to thinking they wouldn't work now that Kaden was dead.

He sat on the bed next to Kelly and lay down, ready for his body to go limp if the glasses worked.

"Let's find a team and clear that ring," he said. Glancing at Kelly, then turning back to the glasses held above him, he put them on, but before he woke up in Empyrean, a vision overtook him.

***

"There's so much here..." a young Doctor Thornhill said as he reviewed a stack of papers. He flipped through the burgeoning manila folder.

Sounds from the surrounding hospital echoed through the walls of the dimly lit office. The converted lab was the largest office in the hospital, but its proximity to the noisy foot traffic and cafeteria kitchen left it as the most undesirable home for practicing physicians.

"David, we'd need a whole other residency to sort through what you've put together," Thomas Thornhill said as he closed the folder and tossed onto the large rectangular black table in the center of the room.

Regardless of the noise, David Abrams jumped at the chance to use the old lab turned office space. Thomas insisted on bringing in two large oak desks, which the orderlies were none-too-happy to help carry into the room.

Wood paneling surrounded the room and a large portrait of Seattle's skyline hung against the longest wall – Thomas's idea after falling in love with the Space Needle as a kid. He mentioned often that one day he'd be in a tower above the rest, and the framed picture gave the sense of being on the top floor, and not crowded away in the bowels of the hospital.

Illuminated X-ray and MRI light boxes hung on one wall, another section housed microscopes, test tubes, and a sub-zero freezer, while the largest section held papers, books, and associated research – David's idea. Large computer towers with a telephone connection to the budding internet collected dust under each of their desks.

"You going to acknowledge me or just keep reading?" Thomas said, impatiently leaning back in his chair.

"How far did you get?" David said, not taking his eyes from the microscope in front of him.

Thomas exhaled an exhausted breath. "Somewhere in between naturally absorbable nutrients versus chemically enhanced ones and the *frequency of all things*. You lost me there."

"Where'd I lose you?" David asked as he picked his head up and scribbled a note on a yellow legal pad.

"I've heard of Nikola Tesla, but Walter Russel and John Neely? I don't understand how these guys have anything to do with our cancer research," Thomas said.

"Did you get to harmonic resonance?"

"Yes! I know those principles. Tacoma Narrows bridge shook itself apart because of an improper assessment of its natural frequency. But, David, you didn't answer my question. What do those guys have to do with cancer research?"

"It's all coming together, but there's still the time component," David said, sticking his head back onto the microscope.

"Time component? Please tell me you're referring to drug trials. I can't take another year of eighty-hour weeks in a hospital with your cryptic studies. You know there's only a hundred and eighty-six hours in a week, right?" Thomas said, standing up and admiring the skyline of Seattle as if they were in a top floor penthouse and not in the basement of a hospital, where every toilet flush from the floor above sent the sound of rushing water around their room.

"Two things." David pulled up his head and rubbed his eyes. "Two things we must always remember. First, this world is slowly killing us, and it's not the world, and it is us humans, our decisions. Those are the root cause of our slow death. Second—"

"Wait, that's already two things," Thornhill interrupted.

Abrams kept going. "Second, time and space can be unlocked. It's all here, like a puzzle dumped out on the table. All the pieces were spread out, but I finally have them flipped over. We can start looking for the outer edges and major shapes! It's all here in front of us!"

"David, I'm the smartest person I know, yet I'll admit you're the better researcher and medical student. No way I make it through medical school without you. But you're losing me more and more every day. I thought we were developing a drug to fight cancer. You're talking Einstein and Theory of Relativity here. If you keep writing new rules and new lines of thinking, or whatever it is you fill those legal pads with, then you cannot expect progress to follow. New, effective drugs must have deliberate, focused research. That research must be challenged and iterated against. If I can't follow you, how in the world will a peer-review panel?"

"And anything trying to be perfect without direct and constant intervention isn't viable," David said.

"Yes! But, wait, slow down. We need a way to push this to its limits. Something to go in and push the literal activation path within the mitochondria. We throw all sorts of controlled situations at it, through official, documented trials, and the cream will rise. Come on, were you the one who said good science is like a good prosecutor? You have to make an accusation of every motive to find what fits. Now let's make that accusation our hypothesis and go to trials! Quit talking about time and space, and start talking about published research."

"We shouldn't publish," David said.

Thomas looked at him, wild disbelief spread across his face.

"What?" Thomas said softly, anger in his voice. "If there's no publication, there's no peer-reviewed studies. Without a peer-reviewed study, we say good-bye to FDA approvals–"

"Not yet," David replied.

"You understand that's like telling an entrepreneur that his company can't go public, right?" Thomas said. "I'm trying to scale us. How can we help the world if the world doesn't know?"

"Play this out, Thomas," Dr. Abrams said, finally pulling his head up from his work and giving Thomas his full attention. "Our treatment cures cancer, I'm sure of it, but it's not what the establishment wants, or the stock market, for that matter, wants to hear. We're blocking inflammatory effects of unnatural nutrients and enabling the individual cells to operate on a frequency harmonious with the Earth. We're dialing the clock back on evolutionary biology but without sacrificing modern society."

"And not only will we save millions, that sounds like the first TRIL-LION-DOLLAR drug to me. What's the holdup?" Thomas interjected.

"Put yourself in the shoes of our competitors. Better yet, name our competitors," David asked.

"All the major drug companies. The system is ripe for an overhaul any-way," Thomas said.

"Yup, and?"

"And..." Thomas looked at him curiously.

"We're taking Big Pharma on head first, but we're also taking on Big Sugar and all the major players in the food world," David said.

"No, we're not," Thomas replied.

"We're announcing to the world that our drug stops the negative effects of unnatural nutrients. We're telling the world we solved the problem with cancer and it's the junk we're eating."

"Everybody knows you have to eat in moderation. That's nothing new," Thomas said.

"Exactly. Modern medicine treats nutrition like an unwanted stepchild. It locks it away in the tower like Cinderella. How many classes did we take on it in medical school?"

"Uuhh—"

"One. Exactly *one*. And if you were listening during biology, you know that adding things like sawdust to a recipe or more seed oils than a person could consume in a year likely isn't the way to optimize nutrient absorption. I read a label the other day saying that a pea protein had thirty grams of protein–"

"Mostly nitrogen and not protein we can absorb," Thomas interjected.

"Exactly. We publish this, we show the world our activation method, but we must do it at the right time."

"We'll never get the world ready for the *right time*," Thomas said.

"I'm not talking about getting the world ready. I'm saying we get ready. When we're ready, if I survive, then we show them *my* case."

"I'm in for that," Dr. Thornhill said with a smile.

Chapter 18

Kira

Kira slipped out of bed and made her way to the living room. She sat on her purple couch in the faded white living room as the bright light from The Tower forced its way into and all around the space, like a spotlight focused on her, reminding her of the brother The Tower stole.

Kira went to the exit while Kaden walked with the Elites into the depths of The Tower, and he didn't come out.

She had to move away from the light of The Tower. She already couldn't sleep, and now this bright sword that stabbed the landscape burned her mind's eye. Desperate for fresh air and a distraction, she got dressed and went outside for a walk. The cool night breeze caressed her skin as she stepped onto the empty streets of Empyrean, her short, black hair moving back and forth, showing her ears and then covering them up as she moved. The city's eerie silence was broken only by the distant hum of the lights in and around the tower.

She was lost in thought when a flicker of movement caught her eye. There, in the shadows of a nearby alley, stood the same man that saved her and Kaden when they were kids. The same figure that stood outside The Tower when Kaden helped her escape the sorting. The mysterious man with the piercing gray eyes who kept showing up in near-death moments.

Kira's heart skipped a beat as she watched him, his tall, muscular frame barely concealed by the tattered cloak he wore. He met her gaze for a moment, then slid into the shadows of a nearby alley.

Without hesitation, Kira followed, her curiosity and desperation for answers never giving caution a say. She trailed behind him, keeping a safe distance as he navigated the winding streets and narrow passages of Empyrean. His pace was purposeful, his strides long and confident, as if he knew exactly where he was going, but slow enough to allow Kira to stay just within sight.

Before long, Kira realized they had crossed the invisible boundary that separated the Inner Ring from the Outer Ring. The stark contrast was immediately apparent, the tall apartment buildings and tradesman shops giving way to crumbling ruins and makeshift shelters. The air here was thick with the stench of poverty and despair, a reminder of the harsh realities that lay beyond The Tower's pristine facade.

The man stopped below a tree in a small courtyard. Various plants shot up, more than overgrown weeds, alluding to the remnants of a long-forgotten garden flourishing amidst the rubble. He turned to face Kira, his expression unreadable in the dim moonlight.

"Kaden has chosen his path, now you will choose yours," he said.

"What path? Who are you?" Kira asked, her brow furrowed.

He stepped closer, his piercing gray eyes seeming to see straight into her soul. He remained silent as Kira's heart raced. Finally, he spoke.

"You've heard of the Lighthouse Remnant?"

"I... yes, but they're just kids' stories, aren't they? Something to distract from the Elites," she said.

He placed a hand on her shoulder, his touch warm and reassuring.

"Your brother has been given a glimpse of the past, a chance to understand the events that led us to this moment. But you, Kira, your role is to shape the future."

"He never came out of The Tower," she said, looking down.

He picked her chin up and motioned toward the bright light of Empyrean's center structure. Its brightness and shadows cut through the streets as if the light and dark sections were soldiers in the midst of battle.

"When The Tower falls, it will be up to you to unite the people," he said.

"How can I possibly do that?" She laughed.

He smiled, a knowing glint in his eye.

"You are so much more than you know, Kira, and Kaden needs you, now more than ever."

"The Elites are superhuman and they say Pinnacle controls the world with mere thoughts–" She stopped and turned back to him. "Kaden needs me? He's alive?"

He nodded a yes.

"Who are you?" She moved closer to him.

"Who do you say I am?" he asked.

"You're Him, aren't you? You're the one who saved us, who keeps saving us. Why?"

"That's the reason I'm here," he replied.

"They call you Jericho, but it can't be. He died in the lighthouse."

"So the myth goes." He stepped back and smiled.

"The Elites will kill you if they find you!" she said in hushed tones.

"The Lighthouse Remnant is your path," he said.

"They're a joke of a group. I grew up in the Outer Ring. It's a mess, but you, you already know that, don't you?"

"You were made for this, and he needs you now. Right now," he said, looking across the garden and into the cracked cobblestone streets ahead. She followed his gaze and then, like a breeze, he was gone, disappearing in the mix of light and shadows. She turned around and looked in and out of the surrounding alleyways, unable to find him.

"*He* needs me? Well, where is–" She stopped cold as she saw a figure lying in the middle of the road ahead. It was right where Jericho was looking before he left. A light from The Tower stretched out, covering the body. Like a spotlit, the light lit him up and darkness held the broken bricks around him.

She stepped slowly, looking for signs of life. It was a man with short dark hair in a white robe and a pool of blood.

"Agent?" she said, wondering why Jericho would lead her to an Agent.

She stepped closer, seeing the white robe was red along his entire upper section, but something about the man's face held her. He was chest down, with one side of his face pressed hard against the broken cobblestones.

"No!" she gasped. "No..." she said again, a whisper as she held back tears.

Darting forward, she stopped a foot away, looking at her brother Kaden's lifeless body. An enormous gash, outlined in dried blood, split the back of his head. His eyes were half closed, exposing the whites of his eyes.

"Kaden..." she said.

She bent down to touch him, slowly extending her arm as she looked over the fatal wound.

She reached out... Gently, she touched his shoulder, and then shot back as Kaden rolled over, his head shooting off the ground and his mouth opening wide, gasping for air. Like a deep-sea diver breaking the surface and sucking in air, his eyes bulged open as he pulled in one desperate breath after another.

"Kaden," she said, now kneeling at his side.

His lungs heaved as he blinked and looked around, finding her. "Kira," he said.

Chapter 19

Kaden woke up, stomach down on the purple couch as red pillows supported his head. He groaned as the lingering pain from the back of his head radiated down his neck and into his back.

"Hey," Kira said from the kitchen. She came over and gave him a cup of water.

"How you feeling?" she asked.

"Like death..." Kaden said. She raised her eyebrows and couldn't help but smile. Her smile ignited laughter in Kaden until he winced and reached to feel the back of his head.

"Better not. I stitched it, but..." She stood over him, looking down on his wound. "It's holding. I think you'll be okay in a while. Probably a nasty scar."

"Think I'll have a line in my hair forever?"

"You mean improvement?"

"Funny," he said as he stood up. Blood-soaked towels dotted the red pillows. "A good thing you chose red."

"I would have grabbed orange to match the chair, but orange pillows are far more rare than red," she said.

"At least we have a choice in something here," Kaden said.

Everything in Empyrean was controlled by either Agents or administrative staff that lived in The Tower or in the closest buildings within the Inner Ring. Everything from laundry service to food delivery had a specific schedule and quantity based on the age, gender, and occupation. Kira and Kaden officially submitted a request to live together when they both had jobs, and to their surprise, The Tower approved. They'd lived together in the middle of the working class section of the Inner Ring ever since. It was rare for two orphans in the Outer Ring to stay together. Their friends Elba and Enak were the only other pair they knew of.

Once a month, they were each granted a steak; otherwise, fabricated fruits, vegetables, breads, and pastas followed a strict seasonal rotation. Food production and textiles drove the majority of jobs in Empyrean. Dozens of factories produced the foods, where the highest-ranking of Tower administration chose new flavors and compounds. New clothing followed a similar pattern as occupation-specific clothes were distributed upon job approval, while house clothes followed an annual basis.

"New" stretched the use of the term. Kira was a seamstress in a nearby textile mill. She knew most new clothing were simply repairs of worn out materials. Just as Kaden worked six days a week to pay The Tower for his lodging and food, Kira worked similar hours repairing used clothing to make it like new. Her fingertips were callused from adjusting the fine needles and metal components of the heavy duty sewing machines. Everything received a double stitch and textile managers would rip clothing apart and throw it back at the seamstress if they noticed loose threads.

Furniture was a different story. The Tower's lack of staffing to provide replacement furniture gave way to an underground barter system. Through the decades, bright colors and artistic pieces became extremely desired, as they provided the only color pop in the otherwise dingy apartments. Once, the walls were a bright white, but generations passed and building materials, including paint, were strictly controlled. However, scraps of old clothes and pieces of wood became beautiful pieces of brightly colored furniture.

In the past few years, Kira managed to obtain a patchwork orange armchair, a pair of red pillows, and her pride and joy, a purple loveseat-style couch made of mostly one fabric.

As Kaden leaned his head back and forth, stretching his neck, Kira came and sat on the purple couch looking up at him.

"How'd I get here?" Kaden asked.

"I found you out there, face down, and the brothers helped carry you up," she said.

"But how'd you find me in the Outer Ring?"

"How'd you get out?" she asked, her expression shifting to serious.

"The stories are true. The Elites don't just consume all the meat in Empyrean, they take in people."

Kira's face went into disgust.

"They took me into a room, one Elite, two others like me, and an Agent. The Elites pulled them in, I mean literally in. It was... unspeakable," he said.

"And you?"

"The Agent stopped them. He saved me and offered me a job."

"You can't seriously be... I saw the robe but figured you'd grabbed it during an escape, or... or something," she said.

"I'm an Agent, or at least could be if I make it through. I never thought I'd be one either, but when you get the chance of being an Elite's dinner or joining, well... But now, I see the need. The Outer Ring is a mess. It's not safe out there for anyone."

"See the need? We grew up out there. You didn't *see the need* then?"

"Kira, I was in the Outer Ring for a few hours, at most. Those people were rioting and then they turned on me. I thought I made it out, but apparently not," he said, moving his hand to the back of head but not wanting to touch the sensitive wound.

"They get nothing from The Tower. You know what it was like growing up out there, and it's worse now," she said.

"I think I do, but it's all a blur. It's mixed with... another life. I remember Darren's childhood. I think I remember mine. And I remember Kelly," he said, catching her eyes.

Kira looked down and rubbed her hands together.

"It's hard to blame them when they have to fend for themselves," Kira finally said.

"They'd be more like the Inner Ring if they found jobs. If they contributed. There's no control out there! Rolling mobs regularly burn buildings and rip down statues of Pinnacle," he exclaimed.

"To those people, it's a protest. They want a better life. Don't you remember it out there? It's hell," she replied.

Kaden remembered hiding food to ensure they could eat. He remembered fighting off a group of men who had eyes for Kira. And he also remembered the sharp pain of the rioter who cracked his head open.

"It'll never improve out there without order," he said, looking around. "Where's my robe?"

"What kind of *order*? You think sending Elites out there to devour more souls will help them?" she said.

"Maybe it would," he commented.

"Who are you?" Kira stood up and shouted. "My brother and I ran from Agents, knowing if we got caught with extra rations, *we could die*. Now you're on their side?"

"Look around, Kira. What's beyond the wall? Sure looks like a lot of nothing to me," he snapped back.

"There used to be a lighthouse out there," she said.

"And now it's dead. Without control, this place dies, you die!" he screamed.

She paused and stepped back.

"I think there's still something out there. And I'm not a child who needs your protection anymore," she said firmly.

He scoffed and turned away, looking out the window.

"No, and neither am I," he said bitterly.

She went to the kitchen and pulled out his robe.

"Here," she said, throwing the robe at his back.

"You cleaned it?" he said, examining it. She'd managed to get most of the blood stain out of it. A thin ring of pink ran around the upper collar and back.

"Yeah."

"Even though you knew you wouldn't want me to put it back on?"

"Yeah, well, I learned from my brother that family supports each other."

Kaden's mind raced back to all the times they had helped each other growing up. He moved to put on the robe, but paused and looked at her.

"This *is* how I support you now," he said.

"By going alone, nearly getting yourself killed?" she said, her eyebrows raised and one hand on her hips.

"It's just a trial, to see if I can survive–"

"Fail," she interrupted, giving him a blank stare to challenge his statement.

He bit his tongue, wanting to scream back at her, but knew she was agitating him because she cared.

"Fair enough." He took a deep breath, swallowing his frustration. "But how can we make change without participating? How long until the chaos of the Outer Ring makes it to us here?"

"And how long until the Elites decide we're expendable?" she fired back.

They stared at each other from across the room, neither breaking the gaze as tension filled the room.

The silence was cut as the door burst open.

"The McClouds!" Enak said as the two brothers barreled into the room.

"Not a good time, fellas," Kaden said.

"I knew they couldn't hold my boy!" Elba said, bounding to Kaden and patting him on the back.

"What was it like in there? Do they really chop people up and do tests on them?"

Kaden slid his arm into the white sleeve as he put the robe on.

"Stealing a robe to sneak out, look at our boy!" Enak said eagerly, jumping up and down.

"Good to have you here. Barb's been concerned. She wasn't sure how we'd hit quota without you but thankful, all good now that you're back," Elba said.

"I'm not coming back," Kaden said as he put on the robe.

"Whoa," Elba said, the situation dawning on him. "You didn't steal that robe; it's how you got out. You joined…"

"Wait, what?" Enak said, his youthful energy finally coming to an end as he stepped back from Kaden.

"New job, fellas, and it's time I get back to it. Another day in the Outer Ring and then, hopefully, I'm on a team and can make some impact on this world," he said, his eyes darting to Kira. She didn't respond, her arms now folded at her chest as a thin strand of black hair fell over her face.

The three were silent as Kaden left the apartment and made his way back to the Outer Ring.

"We're not a team, then, huh?" Elba said, but Kaden closed the door behind him without answering.

"Whose team? What's he doing?" Enak said, but Kaden didn't hear. He was already down the hall.

He pointed himself at the outer wall and walked for hours to get there. All the way to the wall and through the worst of the Outer Ring, moving past pockets of tents in between crumbling buildings, thin buildings made of scrap metal that looked like they would blow over with a hard sneeze, and larger brick housing. The brick buildings were a mix of livable and broken down. Both held more people than they were designed for.

The outer wall was an engineering marvel compared to the slums it housed. It stretched forty-feet high. The first twenty were smoothed to prevent climbing, while the top half was a mix of concrete and stones, a hardened tapestry of smooth and jagged stones of all shapes, sizes, and colors. The smooth bottom portion of the wall was a polished-like finish, but chips and cuts over the years dug into the hard surface. The gashes were like scars from giant clawing hands, the city trying to break free from its cement coffin. Kaden remembered people chiseling away, trying to make footholds to climb over the wall or a group of men with homemade pickaxes and scaffolding. They'd whale away on the wall for weeks and get a few feet into it, until an Agent came by on patrol. The men in the group were rarely seen again and the hole would be covered with new cement and polished over.

As Kaden walked the inner perimeter of the wall, small village-like sections of living places scattered the outer areas, as if they were trying to get as far from The Tower as possible. Most put their heads down when Kaden walked by. They saw the robe and wanted no part of it, even if it was the white of a new recruit. He wished he had a Spark Club; he thought how the rioter who smashed his head would have thought differently if he'd seen the electrified mace at Kaden's side.

As the day grew hotter, most people stayed inside and the streets were bare. The outskirts of the Outer Ring seemed to be an exhausted dog, lying in whatever shade it could.

Midway through the day, he came up to a smoldering barrel, the dying embers from the overnight fire giving off the wisp of smoke that weaved through the air and up, out of the city into the atmosphere.

Two men sat near the barrel under a large overhang, the remnant of a long abandoned building. The roof and three walls held strong and created a wide, cavern-like space. The pair argued, their voices growing louder and echoing from the covering and bouncing off the giant wall.

As Kaden approached, he watched the men. Once they saw him, they scoffed and dismissed him. Instinctively, Kaden put his hand to his side, as if grabbing an imaginary Spark Club. The men took notice, and immediately, their faces went pale. They scrambled to their feet and disappeared in the shadows.

Kaden was surprised, but as it dawned on him why they ran, he smiled, proud of dispersing the rising tension between the two.

The gentle slope of the outer wall made an enormous circle around Empyrean. Kaden may have walked one-fifth of it by the time the sun was falling in the sky. His stomach rumbled and feet ached. It was time to head back to The Tower. Another couple of hours and he'd pass the first trial, albeit with a near-death experience and one day asleep. He put that in the back of his mind, thinking it more a battle scar proving his worth than a failure of Ronnoc's instructions.

The first hour of the walk back passed uneventfully as he approached the end of the Outer Ring. Then, with the taller buildings of the Inner Ring within sight, a commotion nearby stole his attention, a young girl's scream.

He dashed over to see a trio of men dragging a girl into the shadows. The girl wore the same seamstress uniform as Kira. She was working in the Inner Ring but still living out here, and walking alone as darkness fell. Kaden guessed she was twelve, maybe a couple years older at most, but no way fifteen. Yet somehow she had landed a full-time job, like due to family debts or begging for a way to buy food, or both.

Kaden ran toward the group as the girl kicked at one man, but the other two had her arms and were pulling her into an open doorway. He sprinted, trying to reach the door before they pulled her in. She reached out, grabbing the door frame, but with a quick jerk from the pair behind her, her hands broke free and they pulled her into the dark of the room.

The trailing man stepped in, then turned as he entered, seeing Kaden. His face was blank, emotionless as he saw Kaden's white robes. Then he slammed the door closed, the sound of a bolt sliding into place hitting a split-second before Kaden lowered his shoulder and slammed into the door.

He fell back in pain, his shoulder screaming. The door hardly moved.

Standing up, his hand tingled and his shoulder pulsed as he tried to shake the pain out of his arm. He stepped back and then lunged forward, sending his foot crashing into the spot right above the handle. The door rattled, but the frame held. Again he kicked, again, again. He heard a slight splinter, a cracking of wood, and he stepped back to get more of a running start.

"Shut her up!" a voice boomed from inside the home, and a slapping sound curdled his blood.

Kaden quickly scanned the side of the building. There were no other doors or windows. He exploded forward three steps, and his foot went up, but before it landed, the back of a man shot into the door from the inside. The reinforced wooden door cracked down the middle, the midsection of a man exposed in the opening, then it fell with a thud. Kaden tried pulling up from his kick, but his momentum was too much. His foot glanced off the now slanted door and he smashed into the wall with his other shoulder. He rolled off it and fell back to the ground, now both shoulders in pain.

He looked up to hear more chaos from inside the little building. Shouts from the men went silent as dull impacts shook the house. Kaden got up and yanked on the broken door. As he pulled on it, the hinges and remaining lock scraped against the door frame. He heard voices from inside the room. The girl was talking with someone.

He finally pulled the door back to find all three men scattered in the room, as if thrown away from the girl by an invisible explosion. The girl sat in the center, on the only chair that remained standing from a small four-chair set. The other three were up against the wall with a plastic square table on its side, two legs broken.

Kaden was surprised. She wasn't on a bed and all her clothes were intact. She sat as if she was in the eye of a storm, the surrounding area and three men ravaged by the storm.

She never looked up to see him. Her hands covered her face and she cried uncontrollably.

"What happened here?" Kaden asked, stepping over the man whose back broke the door that he could hardly budge.

"Her uncles." A voice came out from behind Kaden, startling him. He turned to see a hooded man, gray eyes shining from under a hood.

"Wha..." Kaden tried saying as he looked around and back at the man.

The hooded man took off his hood and stepped forward.

Multiple figures from Kaden's memories and dreams converged.

"You," Kaden said.

"Her uncles were discipling her," he said, looking around the room at the unconscious men.

"You mean beating her?"

He nodded.

"Is life that bad out here? She is trying to get home from work," Kaden said.

"Not for working. She promised her little sister to save herself."

"From what?"

"From her father promising her in exchange for work," he said.

"To who?" Kaden asked.

"To the rulers of this world. They like to be called the Elites," he said.

Kaden stood watching the man he'd seen in both of his lifetimes.

"Who is Pinnacle?" Kaden asked.

"The leader of the Elites, and of all the Agents. Agents like you." He pointed to Kaden's robe. "And he was an old friend," the man said.

"Did you kill them?"

"No, they'll live, but they won't be the same."

"Who are you?" Kaden asked.

"Who do you say I am?" he asked, a slight grin coming on his face.

"You're a figure from my past, from my dreams... You're the old man from the bay next to me at the EMR, you're the hooded figure that saved Kira and me as kids... And you're..." he hesitated to say it, but it eventually came out. "You're Doctor David Abrams."

He nodded calmly.

"And you're who they call Jericho. The keeper of the lighthouse, out in the desert. You're supposed to be a myth. A dead myth."

"I am alive and well," he said, his grin flashing a smile but fading as he looked back at the crying girl.

"What about her?" Kaden asked.

The man didn't answer. His gray eyes locked on her like an arrow ready to be released. The girl looked up and caught his eyes.

"I'm sorry, I'm so sorry," she said through her tears.

Jericho walked to her and placed one hand on her head. He then bowed his head and she did in unison. She stopped crying. He took his hand off and left the house through a back door. Kaden looked at the girl, who wiped her eyes. Her breath seemed to be settling.

He ran after Jericho, but once he turned the corner from the house, the man was gone. He ran into the nearby alley. Nothing. The street out front, empty. He ran around the building, looking in windows of other houses and in between buildings. Nothing.

Finally, he looked back in the house. The girl had stood up the broken furniture and was trying to make the men comfortable. She was caring for the men who had just taken their anger out on her. Her nose was now swollen from one of their strikes. Kaden heard her sniffle, a remnant of her prior tears being told to quit, as he slipped back out of the house.

He felt inspired to help others the way Jericho had. He didn't have the same powers, but he could join a team. He could work to control the chaos around him.

Looking up, he saw The Tower between the rising apartments and workspaces of the Inner Ring. He went to it.

CHAPTER 20

"**N**ame and rank, Agent," a guard in blue robes outside The Tower demanded as Kaden approached.

"Kaden McCloud," he said, then looked down at his white robe, part of the collar still pink from the blood stain. "I believe I'm a white?" he asked more than stated.

The guard turned to study him. Kaden felt smaller as the man looked him up and down, distaste written all over his face, as if Kaden was the roadkill a pet dragged to the house.

"Teacher?"

"Ronnoc, Purple," Kaden replied.

"Three days in the Outer, eh?" he asked, the sharpness in his voice dulling.

Kaden nodded.

The guard smiled, his expression now of a friend as he slapped Kaden on the shoulder, the same shoulder that took the brunt of the door when Kaden charged it. He winced, but the guard didn't seem to notice.

"Ronnoc was my brother's teacher; put 'em right through hell. Nearly died on his three days," he said.

"Similar," Kaden turned, showing the crusty scab on the back of his head.

"Nice. Wash that out before you get around any Elites. They love the smell of blood, pick it up like dogs, they do. I'm Jay," he said, extending his hand.

"Nice to meet you, Jay. Any tips for studying under Ronnoc?" Kaden asked as he shook it.

"Yeah, he's a prick. Never wants to look bad in front of seniority."

Kaden bobbed his head in understanding.

"I can see that. How's your brother faring?"

"Not good."

"A terrible assignment?" Kaden asked.

"Nope, he's dead."

"I'm, I'm sorry to hear that," Kaden said.

"I'm not. He was a prick too. Had it coming," he said. His face hardened and looked forward, a glint of sadness hidden behind the rough expression.

"Can I ask how?"

"You can ask anything you want. I'm not one of those demons. Riot, Outer Ring. I saw the whole thing," Jay said.

"That's where this came from. I thought I settled 'em, but one guy and one big rock." Kaden pointed to his head wound that still throbbed in pain.

"No, wasn't a man. Those bastard Elites," he said, his lip curling.

"Elites killed an Agent?"

"You really are green," Jay said.

"I'm white, not green," Kaden replied.

"You're either an idiot or a smart Alec," Jay scoffed. "But wise up. Elites turn on us every chance they get."

"They turned on your brother?"

"Yeah, my brother the prick, he was smacking some fool around. You know, one of the loud ones in the group who runs their mouth? Well,

Jarrell decides he ain't going to take the man spitting and screaming in his face, so he slaps the taste out of this bastard's mouth. The other Outer Ring folks get all fussy and start throwing rocks and sticks and all that. There were a few of us whites and blues nearby, but Jarrell was a purple, he was up in the ranks and had a couple Elites with him on patrol. When they don't get crowned, they become our personal bodyguards. They go with you on every patrol."

"Sounds like we're their punishment," Kaden said.

"Exactly. All Elites are powerful and selfish, but some are monsters. As the crowd got all fussy pants on them, Jarrell the prick decides to enforce his will. He never liked using his club, so he starts punching the fools, and he's got a jab that'll knock teeth out. See, this spot right here was from when I was twelve and stole his monthly steak." He opened his mouth and pulled back his lips on one side where his canine tooth was gone.

"So, Jarrell puts a few of 'em down, but now the Outer Ring folks start swarmin' 'em, and more Agents come from nearby. That's where I get involved. I see Jarrell doing his thing, putting the fools on their backs. He's smiling, he's got it under control, but the Elites don't think so. Dem bastards act like they don't like a fight, but really, they love it. They get to feed in the chaos of it all. We would of made quick work of that rabble, but Jarrell's Elites shut it all down. They went outright consumption on the lot, ripping off their robes and pulling in a dozen of the men. They don't give two craps, the pricks, about who they eat. The bastards pulled in my brother with the troublemakers, didn't even blink. They lick their lips, puff up like some muscle head, and move on."

"The Tower can't be losing good Agents like that, though. I can't imagine," Kaden said.

"Get over yourself, kid. The Tower cares 'bout The Tower. Elites run the show, and they are on Pinnacle's puppet string, but he don't ever care enough to snap 'em back up. He lets 'em run wild. The pastures below were made to feed 'em, but it ain't 'nough," he said with a scoff.

"The pastures?" Kaden asked.

"You got a ripe lot to learn, kid. Ronnoc, the prick, is going to have fun with you." He laughed, then turned away, pacing in front of the entrance.

"But what about–"

"Go on!" he called out, shooing Kaden into the monstrous building. As Jay walked away, the massive spotlights of The Tower turned him into a black silhouette. Kaden turned toward the entrance.

Once inside, exhaustion began to set in. He felt tired and his stomach rumbled an angry, hollow roar. As he approached his quarters, he found a small note attached to the door with a floor and room number on it. The room was halfway up The Tower. Thinking of the flights of stairs he'd have to climb, he tried the door. Locked. Unhappy but accepting, he went to the stairs.

His feet ached as marched up the many flights. His body was ready to shut down, but his mind was growing curious to what waited ahead.

Overhead lights lit the long, cold hallway as he looked at the numbers of each room. The hard ceramic floor of large, white tiles stretched forward against a stainless steel siding of the walls. Large metal door handles dotted white, freshly painted doors. The apartments in the Inner Ring started out this color, but over time became an entirely different shade of white as wear and tear set in without upkeep.

Kaden found the door and opened it. Inside, Ronnoc was speaking to the small four-person cohort. Class was in session.

"He made it." Jace looked up at Kaden with a welcoming smile. Aria, next to him in the second row, appeared to be pleasantly surprised.

Ryon and Vala both looked at him, bowing their heads slightly. A respectful gesture, yet their eyes showed how unimpressed they were.

"Welcome back, Agent McCloud," Ronnoc said. "Please take your seat." He motioned Kaden to the back chair once again.

For the next hour, Kaden tried to keep his head up, but his eyelids drooped every few seconds. His blinks became long, drawn-out mini-naps. Eventually, he started biting his tongue and pinching himself to stay awake. He knew outside the sun was set, but inside The Tower, the bright white lights gave a feeling of high noon.

Ronnoc's lesson rolled past Kaden like a breeze slipping through his fingers. As soon as he heard a word, it was soon gone and drifting further away. He didn't notice Ronnoc dismiss the class until Jace gave an exaggerated cough before leaving the classroom. Kaden snapped to attention and stood up as Jace chuckled. Kaden gave him a thankful nod, but soon Jace was gone and Kaden left alone with Ronnoc.

The teacher approached him, examining him up and down as he walked in a circle around him. The pink-stained portions of the robe met a disapproving grunt while the dried blood and stitches led to a curious, dismissing grunt.

"Okay, well, good job by you for not dying. Your reward is in your room. And tomorrow, you join the class full-time. Congratulations," Ronnoc said in a monotone, unimpressed voice before abruptly leaving the room.

Kaden sat back down, contemplating lying on the floor and falling asleep right there, but he forced himself back up and trudged down the numerous flights back to his basement quarters. The idea of lying on his cot pulled him like a magnet, his eyelids heavier with each step.

Back at his room, the note was gone and the door unlocked. He swung it open to find a lavish meal on the desk, a steak with a hefty dollop of melting butter, a side of bacon, and a glass of milk. Steam rose off the meat and the smell filled the small room. His eyes lit up.

He jumped more than stepped to the desk and devoured the plate, only slowing when he noticed most of the steak was gone. The last few bites went slow as he savored the juicy meat. With the steak gone, he enjoyed the bacon; bite by bite, he chewed and felt his energy return. Polishing the meal off with the milk, he stood up and felt satisfied. With a deep breath, he took one step and then fell onto his bed. Over the covers and still in his robe, he slept.

He awoke to a thundering knock at his door.

Chapter 21

"**S**tand up and tell the class what you learned about your trial," Ronnoc said as class started the next day.

Kaden stood up slowly, looking around at the others, and finally back to Ronnoc. He didn't expect to be called on, especially to start the day. He decided to start from the beginning.

"I went straight to the Outer Ring and quickly found a riot. They were defacing a statue and I sought to disperse it," he said.

"Oh?" Ronnoc seemed to perk up.

"I talked to the crowd, explaining how I grew up out there as well and how I understood what they were going through."

"Did they help you find the pink coloring?" Ryon said. His face was straight, but Vala struggled to hold back her laughter.

"Sort of. The crowd did disperse, but one of the men came up from behind me with a block of concrete and, well, see for yourself." He turned around and pulled up his short, black hair, exposing the stitches and redness of his wound.

"Oh my..." Aria said, leaning forward.

"You should be dead, mate!" Jace called out.

"I would have been, but my sister was close. She found me, fixed me up, and then I went back out. I walked the wall, but it was pretty uneventful compared to the first day."

"I'm not sure that counts. Your *sister helped*?" Ryon asked, his eyes moving to Ronnoc. The teacher didn't acknowledge him.

"Who cares? He didn't give up or die. That's the important part," Aria said.

Ronnoc raised his hand, silencing the group.

"We don't need a history lesson. I asked what you learned," Ronnoc said.

"I learned not to turn your back on the people out there. They cannot be trusted in their current state," Kaden said.

"Current state?" Ronnoc followed up.

"Like I said, I grew up out there before landing a job at the EMR. Been there nine point six years until The Tower pulled me out." His eyes went to Ronnoc, but the man's stern face didn't crack a smile at the exactness.

"You didn't seem like you wanted to be pulled out. What changed?" the teacher asked.

"I've always felt aimless, Teacher. I have a best friend, who is like a sister to me. We were in the same home, and friends we've met through work and whatnot over the years. All of us were lucky to get out of the Outer Ring alive, and I'm not going to let the filth out there pull anyone back in. The Tower can control it, we can control the chaos of filth and make Empyrean a better place for our loved ones. I'd be dead without my loved ones. It's time we make the world a better place for them."

The entire group sat up in their seats as Kaden spoke with confidence and hope.

"Okay," Ronnoc said as he moved to the front of the classroom. "Sit down."

The next hour and a half consisted of lessons on the various occupations within Empyrean. Kaden knew the mechanic's duty from his own experience and had enough info on the seamstresses from Kira. The construction and waste roles kept him engaged in the lesson, especially those which used the massive trucks called Twenties, that Kaden worked on at the EMR. He learned they were originally designed to clear a roadway, matching nearly the exact width in between buildings. The problem now, though, was there were many more back alleys, yet the Twenties were used in many versatile ways. Moving rubble from a crumbling building, bringing in an entire troop of Agents or Elites to squash an uprising, or merely block an entire roadway. And with every deployment, they de facto cleared the roadway it traveled with its low-hanging front bumper that acted like a bulldozer.

After the classroom lesson, the group walked through the winding inner hallways of The Tower. Up a few floors, and into an open area, they came into a room like nothing Kaden had ever seen.

Visions from deep in his subconscious, memories from his alternate life of Darren came to mind. Memories of elaborate outdoor obstacle courses from his high school ROTC days, thick black forty-five-pound plates and Olympic barbells of gyms, open floors with various shapes, padding, and chain-link walls from martial arts studios.

He looked up now as Kaden. The gigantic space went up hundreds of feet, like a cavern etched out within The Tower and completely undetectable from the outside. Various groups of white-, blue-, and purple-robed Agents were scattered across the training grounds. A pair in purple robes rolled around on one of the open mats to his left. They wrestled from a crouched position and then went to the ground, grasping for each other's robes and limbs, seeking a submission hold. A group of Blue Agents were swinging from ropes that connected to high-level platforms. Kaden felt pain in his shoulder just looking at the acrobatic one-handed swings the group made from various handles. A row of monkey bars started the overhead path, then the monkey bars were free-swinging in the next section, like that of a trapeze artist. One man in blue dangled back and forth, his hands hanging from the free-swinging bar as he waited for the next bar's swing to come into range. But he lost his grip and fell twenty feet onto a semi-padded surface before the next bar ever lined up with his swing. Kaden saw him wince as he tried bouncing back up and head back to the start. The floor seemed to have enough padding to avoid serious damage but little enough to still feel the pain. As the course went on, single ropes with handles made from irregular and oblong shapes forced awkward one-handed grip. One female in a brown robe was swinging from one of the last ropes before the ending platform. She appeared shorter than average, but her lean body and agility gave the appearance of a lemur, swinging naturally in the air. She appeared as if she would suffer the same fate as the man behind her, as she waited for the next rope to come into reach.

The entire group looked up at her as she swung her legs, generating more swing. Her motion accelerated and she extended her hand, but the other rope was still too far.

"No chance," Ryon said as the group watched her.

But amazingly, the other rope didn't keep swinging away; it seemed drawn to her hand like a magnet as she released her rope and then, incredibly, she seemed to float through the air as the next rope waited for her. Like the entire system was magnetized and she understood how to levitate across the gap. With another smooth movement, she released the last rope and planted her feet on the circular finishing pad.

"Show off," Ronnoc shouted as they walked toward the open mats.

The woman turned, and to Kaden's surprise, she appeared much older than he imagined. He could see a worn face, a familiar face he couldn't place.

"Jealous!" she called back down to Ronnoc, who threw his hand out and brushed her off.

"Who is that?" Kaden asked Jace.

"Beth-ell, the most experienced Brown," Jace said.

"I thought Brown was the highest rank?" Kaden responded.

Jace shook his head.

"Elite." Ryon bumped his shoulder into Kaden, a little harder than a mere accident. "Elite is ultimate."

"How does someone go from a Brown to an Elite?" Kaden said.

"You don't want to know," Jace said.

"And you don't have to know, because you'll never make it that far," Ryon said.

"Oh, cram it, Ryon. You're the tough one who will?" Vala shoved him, catching him off guard.

His face went red and he leapt back at her. She smiled in delight watching his reaction. He shot back at her, raising his fist. Kaden thought he was going to throw a punch, but Ryon faked the punch and grabbed her arm, twisting it behind her back. Vala winced in pain but then her smile only widened, both of them enjoying the fight.

"Mats, twelve rounds. Three minutes on, one off," Ronnoc ordered. "Aria, set it up."

"Got it. Twenty seconds to get into positions," she called as she ran to the side of the mats and began setting a timer. The small black box with large black numbers started a countdown.

"What are we doing?" Kaden asked Jace.

"You haven't been prepped for physical training?" Jace looked at him in surprise.

"Jace, you're with me. Your mount is pitiful," Ronnoc called to him and he lay on his back so Jace could take a mounted Jiu Jitsu-style position.

"Great..." Jace whispered before jogging over to Ronnoc. He stepped over him and sat on the teacher's lower stomach. Ronnoc raised his hands and Jace extended his. With each of their left hands, they rolled the long sleeve of their opponent's robe, gaining control over that arm but losing their dominant hand.

"I'll help you out, newbie. Goal is to submit the other. Anything goes. We start on the beep and we break on the beep," Ryon said, eyeing Kaden with a snicker to his expression.

"Guess that's you and me?" Aria said to Vala. "Always the girls paired up."

"Can't wait to pop your arm off," Vala said, a little too seriously for it to be sarcastic.

"Just like last time, eh?" Aria nodded.

"You didn't submit me either," Vala exclaimed.

"But you've never submitted me," Aria said with a laugh. Vala let out a snort as she threw a punch, her long black hair now in a ponytail flying up behind her.

Aria narrowly slid her head away. She pivoted, grabbing the extended arm and taking Vala to the mat. Aria quickly scrambled to gain position and soon was on top as Vala grunted in frustration.

"Striking before the bell, eh?" Aria said as she maneuvered.

"Must always be ready," Vala said in a deeper than normal voice. She threw her hips up and Aria fell forward, giving her enough space to escape the hold as she slid back through Aria's legs.

"Nice," Aria said.

Vala didn't respond as she sized up her opponent.

"So, how much training have you had?" Ryon asked, pulling Kaden's attention back to him.

"Oh, ummm, none, I guess, a few years of wrestling when I was a kid," Kaden said.

"Okay," Ryon said as his lips clamped together. The corners of his mouth curled up in a smile, but his front teeth bit down, keeping his smile at bay.

"So what exactly are we training for?" Kaden asked.

"Survival," Ryon said.

The starting timer beeped.

Kaden noticed Ronnoc and Jace begin. Aria and Vala continued as they were, and Ryon shot at him like a snake striking its prey.

He went low, like a professional linebacker making a complete wrap-up tackle. He dropped his shoulders and rammed into Kaden's waist. Ryon's hands wrapped behind Kaden's knees and pulled his legs out. Kaden flew more than fell, slamming into the lightly padded ground as the wind ran out of his lungs and the partially healed wound on the back of his head screamed in pain.

Before Kaden could respond, Ryon was on top of him. His forearms shot at Kaden's neck, one swiftly wrapping behind and the other digging into Kaden's throat with the outer bone. Ryon's wrists curled and latched together, forming a vise grip with his forearms around Kaden's throat. He squeezed and Kaden gasped for air, squirming like a live wire, but Ryon's weight positioned perfectly on Kaden's center of mass.

He couldn't breathe and he couldn't move. Soon, his vision began to fade as oxygen was cut off.

"Submit?" Ryon said in Kaden's ear. Kaden tried to cry out surrender, whatever he could to escape the chokehold, but he couldn't speak.

"Just submit and I'll let go," Ryon said again, an enjoyment in his voice. Darkness crept further from the outer edges of Kaden's sight.

"No? Suit yourself," Ryon said, then he tightened the grip and Kaden thought his throat collapsed. Kaden continued to squirm, his arms grabbing at Ryon's robe, desperately trying to get the man off of him. Ryon was the largest in the group, and with his perfect placement, Kaden felt like a car was on top of him, locking him to the ground.

His arms flailed, smacking Ryon's side and back.

"He's tapping," Aria called out.

Ryon didn't change his grip and Kaden's consciousness faded.

"He's tapping!" Aria now screamed.

"Yeah, yeah, sure." Ryon released his grip and Kaden gasped for air.

The red block numbers continued to count down. Two-oh-two, two-oh-one, two minutes, one-fifty-nine. To Kaden's horror, only one minute had passed.

"Clock's ticking, let's go," Ryon said, coming back at him.

He lunged for Kaden's arm. Kaden raised his arm, trying to defend himself but not realizing he was giving the limb up. As Ryon took it, he began to spin, starting an armbar-like grip. Kaden instinctively reacted, using his momentum to twist his hips. He caught Ryon off-balance and pulled him a step forward. Continuing his spin, Kaden slammed into Ryon's back and drove him to the ground.

Ryon's surprise prevented him from immediately countering. The bigger man scrambled as Kaden fell onto him. With the added weight on his back, Ryon went into a turtle-like position, but Kaden had an arm under his chin, and fresh knowledge of how to make a vise grip around someone's neck.

Kaden pulled up on his chin, jerking Ryon's head back as he put his weight on the other man's back. Ryon pancaked and Kaden executed the vise grip from behind. He put his other arm on the back of Ryon's neck and curled his wrists, locking them, his knees under Ryon's shoulders, pinching his upper body. Ryon's legs kicked like a beginning swimmer awkwardly trying to freestyle with only his legs.

Kaden tightened his grip, but Ryon didn't seem to be running out of air as Kaden did. He tightened again, but Ryon only continued to squirm, gradually creating space before Kaden re-centered his weight and turned him back into a pancake with his head held uncomfortably back.

The timer beeped, but Ronnoc shouted for them to hold their positions. "HOLD!"

Ryon jerked back, but instinctively, Kaden kept the tight grip.

Ronnoc walked over them and bent down. He shifted Kaden's forearm that pressed up into Ryon's throat.

"Use your bone to cut off his air; the meat of your arm will only pad him," he said.

Kaden shifted his hand, tightened his grip from the new position, and he felt the side of his wrist dig into Ryon's throat. Kaden felt Ryon's body react, shaking more forcefully. He was now the live wire.

"Tighter. When you have it, you use it until the end," Ronnoc said coldly as he stood over the pair.

Kaden hesitated, but feeling the fierce shaking of Ryon's body, he tightened again. He felt his opponent's windpipe against his wrist. It felt good to physically control the man who just subjected him to such punishment.

"He's tapping!" Aria called out.

Kaden only then noticed Ryon's hand repeatedly slapping his arm. He released his grip and stood back.

"Good," Ronnoc said. Then he looked down at Ryon, who was holding his throat and gasping for air. The disappointed look said more than words could.

"Agent McCloud, you're with me now. Jace, join Ryon," Ronnoc said.

Jace slid down next to Ryon and couldn't hold back his laughter. Ryon shoved him as he caught his breath.

"No training, eh?" Ryon said, staring darts with his eyes at Kaden. But Ronnoc pulled Kaden to an open area on the mat before he explained it was merely a reaction.

"No training? Ever?" Ronnoc asked him.

"I got into a lot of fights as a kid. Outer Ring, ya know?" Kaden said.

Ronnoc nodded knowingly.

"Let's channel that, starting on the mat. Put me in the same position you put him," Ronnoc said.

Kaden stepped onto his teacher but hesitated as he tried to remember how he got in the position. Ronnoc reached back and yanked Kaden down, setting the position.

"Slide one arm under, then lock them to take my neck." He pulled Kaden's arm and slid it under his chin. "When you have the chance, take it, because you won't get another."

The beep of the next round started and Ronnoc slid his hand in between his neck and Kaden's arm. When Kaden tried tightening his grip, he ensured his bone was positioned right and his wrist was on his teacher's windpipe, but no matter how hard he tightened, he couldn't secure the choke with Ronnoc's hand in between.

Ronnoc waited patiently, his body as relaxed as if he were lying on a couch. He subtly shifted his weight as Kaden tried to grip tighter, but once his weight shifted off Ronnoc's center of gravity, the teacher reached down and grabbed one of his knees. The teacher hooked the leg as he spun out from underneath and soon was on top of Kaden, executing his own chokehold, using the collar of Kaden's robe around his neck.

The thick material seared like a rug burn as it pinched the side of his neck and cut off blood flow. Once Ronnoc executed the move and Kaden felt the pain, the hold was released and they restarted.

"If my hand is in the way, you lose the choke, so you must adapt. But if you're under attack, protect and be patient. You can wait forever, regaining your strength, biding your time if your opponent cannot finish you."

"But I had your face in the mat?" Kaden replied.

"It's not comfortable, but I knew I'd get you. Time only refreshed me; it was my friend."

Ronnoc transitioned them to a different starting position and told him to start again. In each instance, it took Ronnoc little time to reverse his holds and secure his own dominant position. And each time, the teacher made him feel the pain before letting up. Occasionally, Ronnoc called out instructions to one of the other pairs as they tangled each other up. Sometimes demanding they switch partners and sometimes scolding one for not properly executing a move when they had the chance to submit their opponent. Kaden felt like a young child who struggled harder and harder to beat the adult, but his strength and knowledge of the game was light years away. Ronnoc smoothly and swiftly deflected his advances, then made him pay.

The final beep sounded and the cohort sat on the mat, everyone breathing heavy except for Ronnoc. Kaden felt his skin burn from the countless times Ronnoc used Kaden's robe against him. The thick robe was an unforgiving weapon when tightened against his skin. It left numerous red spots, mini rug burns that dotted his face and neck.

Kaden was the first to stand up, but he soon sat back down. Certain joints felt like the bone was replaced with a wounded jellyfish after Ronnoc bent them in unnatural ways.

"Clean yourselves up. Tomorrow's lesson begins at sunrise," Ronnoc said coldly and walked away.

The group smiled, and Aria bounced to her feet.

"I'm off, folks," she said with renewed vigor.

"Why is she so happy?" Kaden asked Jace as they lay on the mat next to each other.

"Tonight's an out of Tower night," Jace said with his own smile, but he paused when he saw Kaden's confusion. "You really do know nothing." He elbowed his new friend and then stood up, extending a hand, but Ryon smacked Jace's hand away and looked down at Kaden.

"Next time, you and me," he demanded.

Kaden looked up at the six-foot-four frame with broad, muscular shoulders.

"Bring it on," he replied.

Ryon scoffed and walked away with a confident smile.

"Or how about I twist you up again instead of you picking on the newb," Jace said, shoving Ryon.

"You wish," Ryon played it off.

As they got to their feet and dispersed, their robes still moist from sweat, Jace showed Kaden the laundry and shower area. They cleaned up and exchanged their sweat-soaked garments for clean ones.

"What's an out of Tower night?" Kaden asked.

"Just like it sounds. You're allowed to leave The Tower for the night, but make sure you're back before sunrise. Most Whites get two or three days a week, but not us. Ronnoc keeps a tight leash and we only get one a week," Jace said.

"Where do you go?"

"Home. My apartment is on the thirtieth floor and looks north, toward the mountains. I love it," Jace said.

They walked through a series of halls and staircases, Kaden beginning to get a sense of the labyrinth within The Tower's walls.

"You?" Jace asked.

"Mine looks at this. I can see a little of the mountains; they look peaceful," he said as his mind went to Kira for the first time in hours.

"They are peaceful, and you know what legend says, the Lighthouse was up there somewhere."

"The myths?" Kaden said.

"The myths," Jace confirmed. "Jericho lived far off on the horizon. He was a beacon of hope, showing how life can flourish despite the desert. But as all the other cities fell, the Lighthouse became the only thing visible outside our walls. Most nights, you can't see the stars through the clouds, so folks locked on to that light."

"And what happened to it?"

"Eventually, it faded, or so I've heard. The legend says Jericho, an old man with powers even greater than Pinnacle, kept the light burning. But over time, I think people just stopped looking at it, they were caught up in trying to impress The Tower, or escape it. Really, that's all life is in my opinion. You're either with it or against it."

Kaden wished there was a window nearby. He longed to look toward the Lighthouse.

"It's gone now, right?" Kaden asked, vaguely remembering stories from his youth as Kaden. He regretted having a house mother who kicked him out more than welcomed him.

"Yup. Rumor has it that Jericho died, and eventually, it faded away. Or at least that's what they tell kids to scare 'em from going outside the walls. Not even the most powerful person in history could survive out there."

"Careful with that." Vala turned a corner and came up from behind them, her long black hair still wet from the showers. She wore the customary blue pants and white shirt of an off-duty Agent. "Pinnacle is the most powerful person in history. His power is undeniable. Only his status as a *person* is questionable."

She sounded as if she was reciting a textbook, her firm look holding no hint of joking.

Jace put up his hands and bowed his head, mockingly surrendering to her correction.

"See you in the morning, Vala. Hope you're as bright and cheery as ever," Jace said with a smirk.

"Don't be late again. Ten lashes," she said as she turned the corner.

"Lashes?" Kaden asked.

"You don't want to know." He shook his head. "Don't be late."

Kaden left The Tower and walked back to his apartment in the Inner Ring. His body was sore and his mind overwhelmed with new knowledge, but he couldn't wait to see Kira.

Chapter 22

Entry #4

I've done it. She'll live on forever in the research.

Eve.

The first two attempts failed, but we learned. The epidermis failure was traced back to an inability to process UVB light into Vitamin D; it created a hard, black structure. The dead skin flaked off like an onion peeled away, exposing muscle and organ in an agonizing death. It was painful to watch, yet progress continued. By activating the subcutaneous layer of fat under the epidermis, the epidermis can fail, yet the body is protected, skirting the Vitamin D failure.

In true science, there is no loss without knowledge gained. Bypassing the epidermis failure and exciting the subcutaneous layer of fat has increased the strength and recovery markers tenfold. This is Adam all over again, but a stronger Eve. Additionally, she is more compliant, the perfect subject. She is exactly what the world needs at a terrible time like this.

Scarcity of farmland has driven the global powers mad. Russia and China, once thought to be in a war that would rip Asia apart, are now in allegiance and mobilizing toward Europe. The US isn't much better off. I fear the steady decline of raw material production and inflation of the US dollar has reached a cliff. If we don't solve the problem now, World War 3 is around the corner.

Times like these reveal true character, and all our preparation has led to this. I laugh when I think of the serendipity, or shall I call it providence: I switched our cash reserves from USD to cryptocurrency last year, and with the global crisis and USD inflation, crypto has exploded. Our fifty million was once paltry compared to the pharmaceutical giants, but now their cash on hand is de minimis and ours tens of billions, and climbing with every news story about the rising cost of goods. That doesn't even consider the revenue from our new miracle drug. Tack on a trillion in revenue and exponentially rising cash reserves, and we'll have a hundred trillion evaluation. If projections are accurate, there will be only a few dozen companies left standing if war breaks out. A true winner-take-all model in every sector of a global economy that we're positioned to lead. Countries will fall but in their place, corporations that control the flow of goods and services. And what more vital service to humanity than healthcare? Our discovery will heal the underlying health epidemic of the population.

The nations will fight it out, but they'll run out of money and come to us. The problems we face as a global society: a fertility epidemic, a global health crisis, a shortage of arid farmland, and a pending world war.

The next steps are therefore simple.

Our new drug solves the health crisis, adding cash and building a loyal, healthy following. The war will destabilize nations and currencies. With our incredible reserves, we can influence all nations on Earth. We funnel that cash into synthetic food production to alleviate scarcity and starvation. With health, food, and farmland scarcity out of the picture, military aggression will subside. The pieces all fall into place, except one.

My partner.

He still refuses early expansion of the drug. He'd taint Eve before getting FDA approval for drug sales.

I feel as if he is trying to undermine me every chance he gets. Does he not see where the world is going? His refusal will only strengthen my resolve.

He claims that things are changing inside of him, that he sees and understands more, that the learnings from the first two Eves need more research. I fear the long-term effects are not manifesting in measurable medical ways. I think he's mentally unstable.

He claims there's a subtle vibration, like a frequency emission, inside of himself. He's even gone so far to claim it can be channeled and that it can move, shift, and change things.

I should have seen this coming. Like a snake in the garden, he's plotting to steal Eve.

I fear his common sense is gone, just like the general public as we face this pending war. The masses are growing more impatient and rash. Thomas Jefferson said, 'Educate and inform the whole mass of the people... They are the only sure reliance for the perseverance of our liberty.' But what would Jefferson say if he knew the path before us? What if he knew what I know?

No one on Earth can do what I do.

Chapter 23

"So that settles it!" Enak called out.

"Settles what?" Kaden asked as he entered the apartment.

Kira, Elba, and Enak sat on the colored furniture around the worn wooden coffee table at the center. They each looked up, surprised to see him.

"Nothing, nothing," Enak called out with exaggerated arm motions.

"What are you doing here? I thought you were an Agent now," Kira said coldly.

"I am. The rest of the time in the Outer Ring went easy, and this morning, I joined my cohort. Four of 'em. This guy Jace is nice, and so is Aria, but the other two are a bit uptight."

"Enjoy your new family," Kira said dismissively.

"After class today, we went to this training center. You wouldn't believe the stuff they have in there, but ugh." He bent his neck and rolled his shoulders. "I am beat." He sat on the couch. The other three stood up as soon as he sat.

"What are you all talking about?" he asked.

"Nothing, we were just leaving," Elba said.

Kaden didn't notice Elba's questioning look as he laid his head back on the purple couch.

"We get one night out of The Tower each week, maybe more if our teacher eases up. We should plan something for next week, if I'm not so tired," he said.

"We have plans," Elba said. And without waiting for a response, he motioned to Enak. The pair left with a quick wave to Kira.

"They okay?" he asked.

"We didn't expect you," Kira answered.

"I thought you'd be excited to see me," Kaden said.

Kira crossed her arms. From the small kitchen, she stared daggers into him.

"This is best for us. I promise," he said.

"Sure... Is this from you?" She slid out a green container on the counter.

"Oh yeah!" He rose and went to the kitchen. "No more meat only once a month. You'll get it weekly now that I work in The Tower."

"Get rid of it," she said firmly.

"What? You're crazy. You'd rather eat the fake stuff?"

"Yes, I would. You know there is only so much and three more boxes a month for us means three less for those not in The Tower," Kira said.

"How can we help them if we're not strong ourselves?"

"If you don't take that box out, I will," Kira said as she grabbed an off-white jacket and gracefully slid her arms into it as she pivoted toward the door.

"Why are you acting like I'm some sort of pariah because I want a better life for us?"

"We didn't expect–"

"Yeah, yeah, you didn't expect me!" he shouted. "But why should it matter? We've never had secrets before!"

Kira stopped at the door, watching his outburst.

"We didn't expect you *to become an Agent*," she said, then closed the door.

"I'm doing this for you!" Kaden screamed as he picked up the top of the container and threw it at the door.

Moments later, he picked up the container's top. Walking back to the crate, he took out an aged piece of meat that resembled a slice of jerky and put the rest of the container in a cabinet. He took a bite of the meat and stared at his room. Turning from the apartment, he went back to The Tower for the night.

A loud banging on his door woke him from a deep sleep.

"Don't be late, newb!" he heard Jace call out from the other side. Kaden shot up, already dressed in his robe. Kaden followed Jace to the classroom as they playfully tried to outrun each other in the maze of halls and staircases.

Jace squeezed in right before Kaden. The others were all in their seats at attention.

"Close," Ronnoc said to him with a stone-cold stare.

"You said sunrise, but there are no windows here or in our quarters?" Kaden wondered aloud.

"You'll figure it out," Ronnoc said. "We're talking Elites again today, particularly the crucial step of promotion, from Brown to Elite. Who knows who the first Elite was?"

"Trick question," Vala snapped. "The first Elite didn't get promoted. Her body resisted."

"Good. Explain," Ronnoc said.

"We saw her yesterday. Beth-ell is considered a Forever Brown. Her body resisted the upgrade, but still she serves Pinnacle loyally."

"Did she get nothing from the process?"

"No, she was granted extended life by Pinnacle for her loyalty. She is the oldest known Agent," Vala replied again.

Kaden thought of the woman he saw, the only one who completed the high-top ropes course. Her skin looked aged, but her body still moved as strong, swift, and agile as anyone Kaden had seen.

"Why do you say *known*?" Ronnoc followed up.

"Because no one can know the age of the Elites unless their promotion is recorded. They don't age like us New Breeds."

"Very good," Ronnoc replied.

"She really knows her Elites," Kaden whispered to Jace.

"She worships them," he replied.

"Aria," Ronnoc snapped, and she sat up in her chair. Her black hair was cut to a similar length as Vala's, similar to all women Agents, but it was bushier and typically in a loose ponytail versus Vala's thin, tightly pinned-back hair that let one long strand fall. It framed the side of her face and gave a streamlined, serious look.

"Yes, Teacher," Aria replied.

"Describe the promotion of an Elite," Ronnoc asked.

"A reward for life-long service of Empyrean," she answered.

Vala shot her hand up, but it went ignored.

"Service to whom?" Ronnoc followed up.

"To Pinnacle," she corrected herself. "Pinnacle's gift, a reward, to Brown Agents for a life of service."

Vala's hand went up again, and once again, Ronnoc ignored it and locked on to Aria. Her forehead began to show signs of perspiration.

"Ummm," she thought. Ronnoc's face didn't budge, stone-cold as he watched her.

"Brown Agents. A life of service," Aria said without much confidence.

"Neverending life for service," Vala burst out.

Ronnoc rewarded Vala's correct answer with a look of bitter disappointment. Aria let out a breath.

"Unimaginable power and endless life for dedicated loyalty, a trade of life for loyalty. That is the promotion Pinnacle offers," Ronnoc said.

"What's the catch?" Kaden asked. "I mean, dedicating your life, a never-ending life, is pretty big. Does that explain the consumption, is that rejuvenation?"

"Think of it as fuel," Ronnoc said plainly.

"Consumption of fuel?" Kaden repeated, and those around him seemed to shift uncomfortably in their chairs.

"The consumption is about fuel. The power of the Elites, even that of Pinnacle must be replenished," Ronnoc said. "Now, moving on to ring containment and occupations."

"But those are people," Kaden interrupted. "They consume *people* to refuel their power?"

Ronnoc slowly turned to Kaden. He stared, as if studying the younger man and anticipating the next question.

"Yes," he eventually said.

Kaden unconsciously leaned back in his chair. Jace, next to him, bowed his head, and the others avoided Ronnoc's gaze.

"Oh..." Kaden said.

"Now, moving on. The occupational structure of the Inner Ring and how it supports containment," he continued.

Kaden listened in and out of the rest of the lesson. The faces of the consumed man and woman ran through his mind like ghosts haunting his thoughts. He tried to put them away, but the stretched faces, full of horror as they disappeared into the Elite's chest, stayed with him.

Daily, he saw their faces.

Chapter 24

The next weekend, Kaden left The Tower and walked back to his Inner Ring apartment. He knew so much more about the workings of Empyrean: the role and criticality of each job sponsored by The Tower, the hierarchy of robe colors (white, blue, purple, brown, and finally, the Elite black), and even an introduction to Empyrean's food system. He'd never thought about it as a boy, but Ronnoc's lesson on the underground pastures where herds roamed and natural life was protected perked Kaden's interest.

Still, as he approached his apartment's door, he wondered what Kira was doing. How would she respond to his continued involvement as an Agent, especially now that he was enjoying it? He pushed aside guilty thoughts that his desires were causing a rift between him and his best friend as he opened the door to their apartment.

To his surprise, it was empty. He walked through, the silence unnatural after living in The Tower, where hums of machinery and training cohorts constantly echoed through the walls.

He looked out the wide window that viewed The Tower, where he looked out the first time he came to Empyrean as an adult. The great spire erupted from the earth like a bright, shining sword. The sun was setting and the massive spotlights illuminated a brilliant haze, giving The Tower a glow that illuminated the city. Kaden studied it, trying to find where his quarters would be inside the enormous structure. He felt confident he picked out the physical training area that covered multiple floors, but there was no way of really knowing. The only windows were so high, clouds enveloped them most days. He imagined seeing the world from those windows on a clear day.

His eyes turned to the base of The Tower, and he pondered the underground pastures. How much space must be carved out for roaming herds? What kind of animals and plants were down there?

The sound of the opening door pulled him away from his thoughts.

Kira, Elba, and Enak came into the room. Their smiling faces turned cautious as they saw Kaden.

"Hey!" Kaden said cheerfully. "I'm off again; what are you all up to?"

The three exchanged glances.

"Just going for some walks, not much," Kira said, and the group remained quiet.

"Hey, I understand this is weird, but I'm doing it for the right reasons," Kaden said.

"Doubt that," Enak quipped.

Kaden's eyes tightened and he felt a hint of anger, but he dismissed the comment and continued.

"We all might as well be family. I know we all came from the Outer Ring, but it's been trying to kill us since we were kids. Agents can get control and make a better life for everyone here and out there, but they can't make lasting change alone. We need people like you to also enforce the policies that will maintain peace in the city."

Kira started laughing.

"Peace?" she said in between her laughter.

"I'm not saying it's going to be easy, but you know how dangerous it is out there. We can't let kids grow up in that chaos like we did. We enforce the law, and that opens new grounds for new jobs. That leads to more goods, services, and most importantly, *food* for everyone in Empyrean. Can't you see how those dots connect?"

"How could *you* think they do?" Kira fired back, the other two watching the pair go back and forth like watching the ball in a tennis match.

"You know what I'm learning next week?" Kaden said, his volume growing.

"Propaganda?" Kira said, and Kaden's face twitched, but he ignored it.

"I'm learning about the underground pastures. I'll find out how the most nutrient-rich food source we have in the city goes from free range to your mouth, unless you want synthetic crap the rest of your lives," he said, a hint of bitterness coming out.

"You're going to see the pastures?" Kira quipped.

Enak and Elba tensed up. Kira shot them an angry look as if they were concealing a secret about to spill over.

"I hope you see it one day too. You wouldn't imagine the great stuff that goes on inside The Tower," Kaden said.

"*Great* stuff, huh..." Kira's face turned solemn. "Tell me about your first day, the consumption. Great?"

Kaden opened his mouth to speak but stopped.

"Yeah, that's what I thought. A great pasture, a great dream of control, but you ignore what it's built on, the lives of everyone not granted admittance into your Pinnacle worship club," she said.

"Kira, I'm on a team. It's not just me and you against the world anymore," Kaden said.

"Hey, we're still here," Enak interjected.

Kaden continued, "I'm in a cohort. It's a good group. We're learning so much. It's a team inside The Tower, but I need *you* still on my team, because I'm doing this FOR YOU!"

"You're doing it for yourself!" she snapped back, disgusted.

Kaden stood in disbelief, shaking his head.

"You want to control the Outer Ring for the sake of its people? Why not go see why they plan uprisings? You want to talk about the pastures and where food comes from? Why not follow that food and see where it winds up?"

"The Tower must take care of itself if it's going to keep the order–"

"YOU WANT TO KEEP THE ORDER SO YOU FEEL STRONG!" Kira screamed.

The pair stood, both breathing heavily.

"Kaden, I love you. I'm sorry, but... you were caught up with keeping us alive so much as kids that you're blinded to the fact that you're still searching for control. You want to be stronger because you feel weak," she said, and Kaden felt the words like an arrow through his heart.

"I'm not weak," Kaden said through gritted teeth, his face red.

"I didn't say you were," Kira said, standing tall and confident in her words.

Kaden looked at Enak and Elba.

"You know this ain't right," Elba said.

Kaden threw up his hands.

"None of you understand." He shook his head.

"I'm sorry, brother. You say you're on a new team, but you've always had one right here," Kira said.

His shoulders dropped, and she looked at him sympathetically for the first time in weeks.

Kaden turned his head. The bright Tower outside the window beckoned to him.

"Being strong doesn't always mean using force," Kira said.

Kaden turned to her, her comment sparking his curiosity.

"Where'd you hear that?" he asked.

Kira pulled her shoulders back and brushed a strand of black hair behind her ear.

"Jericho," she said. "You should talk to him. He's in the Outer Ring most days."

"He's talking like a threat to The Tower," Kaden replied.

"We're not joining your team," she said firmly.

He locked eyes on her, noticing her eyes beginning to water, but she stood tall. He left without another word.

Chapter 25

The introductory rope course provided little challenge to the cohort. Kaden was even getting the hang of it. The soreness in his muscles after all the prior workouts was slowly fading. Each day brought another lesson in the classroom for the mind and an entirely new lesson for the body in the gym. Rope courses, submission-based wrestling, hand-to-hand combat, and weights and plyometrics filled their training afternoons.

But this week was flipped: the mornings were physical training and the afternoons were lessons.

"Why are we training in the morning?" Kaden asked Jace.

"We're going down," Jace said with a wink.

The idea of lush green grasslands filled his mind. He'd lived within the concrete walls of the Outer Ring most of his life. Any weed that sprouted was quickly killed due to lack of sunlight, air, or enough soil underneath. It was a hard life where even plants struggled to survive. Memories of his past life as Darren, now feeling so distant they were more like dreams, of deer and racoons, otters and birds, ran through Kaden's like a ghost slowly vanishing. The life of Darren fell into a haze, his mind packed with knowledge of Empyrean, Agents, Elites, and all the inner workings of the city. His motivation shifted with his ambition.

He was also learning to fight. A few weeks in, and he was able to submit Aria and Vala, mostly due to his size and much to Vala's competitive dismay. He was behind Jace, but felt he was closing the gap. However, the worst part of their mat exercise and sparring was Ryon. His bitterness from Kaden's reflexive submission from day one still seemed to drive the man. He punished Kaden every chance he got.

"You and me," Ryon said as Jace set up the timer.

"Fine, bring it on," Kaden said, trying to hype himself up and not let Ryon know how he really felt.

"All thirteen," Ryon repeated.

"No, Ronnoc will join us later, so we only have five. We rotate, with someone always getting a round break," Jace called out.

"Not a freaking chance!" Ryon shouted back, louder than anyone expected.

"Hey, you want someone, take me on," Jace said. Ryon still got the best of Jace, but he was far closer to a match than a beginner.

"I got this," Kaden said.

"Okay," Jace dismissed, and he sent piercing eyes at Ryon. "Okay, ladies, let's start on the ground and rotate through chokes and arms."

Both women nodded, but Ryon snapped back, "Ronnoc wants them to work on takedowns."

"Who put you in charge?" Vala pushed back.

"Teacher did when we spoke this morning. Takedowns or you can take it up with him," Ryon said, looking at each of the three.

"Did he also tell you to pick on the new guy?" Aria said.

Ryon ignored it as the first beep went off. He shot at Kaden, who knew this move and skipped back, but the bigger man reached out and hooked his leg. Ryon held the leg tight and spun, twisting him to the ground and quickly scrambling on top of him. Kaden resisted, but Ryon went for the position advantage, getting in a mounted position. All his weight pushed on Kaden's chest. He threw his hips up trying to get space, but the bigger man leaned back with him and kept his weight on top. Ryon slid his knees up, tightening them under Kaden's armpits as he went for the neck. But Kaden kept his elbows tucked as close to his body and slid his hand in between Ryon's forearms. After a moment of ineffectiveness, Ryon pivoted and attempted to use Kaden's robe collar to choke him. The aggressor leaned over him and Kaden felt like he was in a cave of human sweat. Ryon slid his hands into Kaden's robe, grabbing the collar and pulling it the opposite direction. Kaden felt the robe burn against his skin, but again, he was able to slide his hand in between his throat and the tightening collar to protect his neck.

Frustrated, Ryon shifted tactics a third time. Noticing the hand protecting the neck, Ryon grabbed at Kaden's elbow, ripping his arm up. Kaden's forearm muscles felt as if they were going to be cut in two, but once again, with a little shift, he was able to avoid the submission.

Ryon snorted a breath of frustration, and it encouraged Kaden. He was being dominated in position but surviving. Ryon couldn't close him out.

Again, Ryon pivoted, now giving up his mount position as he tried to tear Kaden's arm up and out of the socket. He swung his hips and pulled Kaden's arm in between Ryon's legs, locking his wrist toward his waist. Kaden's inner elbow was facing straight up. One of Ryon's legs went over Kaden's chest and the other wrapped over his face. With a slight raise in his hips, Ryon could hyperextend Kaden's elbow.

Kaden jerked his elbow down, gaining only an inch of leverage that created a gap in between his shoulder and Ryon. The tiny gap was enough to shift the position of his elbow, saving it as Ryon aggressively shot his hips up. Ryon's frustration led to an extreme force, way more than sparring warranted. If not for the shift of positioning, Kaden's elbow would have been snapped backwards.

Even in a safer position, Kaden's elbow screamed in pain, but nothing near a full armbar. Kaden survived this hold just like the others.

As Ryon went to regrip his hand and pull Kaden closer, attempting the same move again, Kaden twisted his arm and freed himself.

The beep sounded, ending the round.

Ryon sat, sweat dripping down his face as his shoulders rose and fell. Kaden took his rest and noticed he wasn't as tired as his attacking competitor.

"Only a matter of time," Ryon said coldly.

"Maybe," Kaden said with a smile.

The timer went off, ending their rest, and again, Ryon shot at him like a bolt of lightning. The second round was similar to the first, with Ryon exerting more effort and inflicting plenty of pain as he searched for the right submission, but Kaden survived. Then, the third and fourth rounds followed suit. By the fifth round, Ryon was so tired that Kaden was able to get the dominant position. Ryon's defensive skill still prevented him from locking in a submission, but the larger man's fatigue evened the playing field.

When the beep sounded on the thirteenth and final round, the pair fell apart from each other. They lay side-by-side, their chests heaving up and down as a pool of sweat formed under them. They now noticed the other three sitting to the side, watching their stalemate.

"Very nice," Jace said.

"Congrats, you're both equally pathetic," Vala said.

Ryon rolled to his side, eyeing Kaden. Both were still catching their breath.

"Come on. To the ropes," Ryon said with an exhausted breath.

Kaden wanted to roll his eyes, to lie there as long as it took to gain back his energy. But now that he was keeping up with the best, he wasn't going to stand down.

"Bring it," Kaden said with a long exhale and subsequent deep breath.

Ryon stood and walked to the intermediate course, the first time the group had approached it.

"Maybe you two should start with the old course," Aria said, pointing to the beginner start line.

Ryon shot a look of disdain then continued on his path.

"First across," Ryon said before climbing the ladder to the start position.

"Agreed." Kaden shouldered him aside and scaled the ladder first.

He reached out and grabbed the first set of monkey bars, quickly going through them, but he hadn't thought of his sweat-soaked hands or his wet robe. The sweat from their match weighed him down, and combined with his wet hands, he could feel his grip sliding.

"You are off course!" Ronnoc shouted.

The distraction mixed with his wet hands left Kaden to gravity. He fell, landing hard on the minimal padding ten feet below.

The teacher went straight for Ryon, who now bowed his head and began to climb back down the ladder before starting, his face white.

"I put you in charge, and this?" Ronnoc said. "Have you even done the mats or are you showing the team to swing gleefully from the WRONG course!"

"We've done the mats, Teacher," Jace spoke up.

"Looks like the mats did you," Ronnoc snapped without shifting his gaze. He stared down the larger man and walked swiftly to him, with a fierceness of a general ready to wage war. He came millimeters from Ryon's nose.

"Explain," Ronnoc demanded.

"We were going... going..." he stuttered.

"They were trying to stop me," Kaden called out from behind.

Ronnoc still didn't turn from Ryon.

"I wanted the intermediate course after we finished mats. I ran over here and he came after me, the team followed," Kaden said.

"You allowed a team member to directly disobey instructions?" Ronnoc said.

Ryon stood firm, ready to take his punishment.

"Disobedience is NOT tolerated in The Tower. Have you not learned the Elites are the disciplinary board? How long would you last if *they* had you?" Ronnoc moved closer, touching noses as a spray of spit exploded with every word.

Ryon remained silent. Finally, Ronnoc turned to Kaden, who was now dreading his punishment. A vision of being put back in the room with the Elite that wanted to consume him flooded his mind. But Ronnoc didn't storm after Kaden; the teacher eyed the student with a curious expression. Then he turned back to Ryon.

"A leader reels in disobedience," he said to Ryon and then walked to the center of the group. Ryon's shoulders only went down a centimeter or two, but it appeared the weight of the world was lifted off them when Ronnoc turned away

"Clean up; we go down in one hour," Ronnoc said.

The group smiled and began moving away before Ronnoc shouted, "Not you, Kaden. You're with me."

Ryon stood next to Jace, and both gave sympathetic looks back to Kaden. Ryon held for a moment longer, his face stern, but it held a look that Kaden had only seen in friends. Ryon, for the first time, didn't look bitterly toward him.

As the others showered and rested, Kaden sat in a small chair in the center of an interrogation-style room.

"How much of that was true?" Ronnoc asked as he paced around him.

"All of it, Teach–"

He couldn't get the words out before Ronnoc smacked the back of his head.

"You were covering for Ryon's frustration and competitiveness. Do you think I'd believe the new guy in class would pull the entire group to that course right after mats?"

"No, but yes, I–"

Another smack to the side of his head interrupted him.

"We are a team, Teacher," Kaden said.

"Maybe..." he said. A long moment of silence passed as Ronnoc walked circles around him. He felt like a prisoner, held hostage as the interrogator waited for him to spill the information. But Kaden resolved himself to not say the next word, no matter how awful the silence felt as Ronnoc's boots rhythmically struck the floor.

"What is it about you?" Ronnoc wondered aloud before leaving more silence hanging.

Kaden didn't respond.

"The Elites noticed something about you. You had a *smell* they caught... And that man in the EMR, he was defiant to me, as if on your behalf. Why?" he said.

Again, Kaden remained silent.

"Maybe we should bring in everyone from the EMR and see if the Elites smell anything on them?"

Kaden resisted the urge to speak.

"Or should we find your living records, bring in your sister to give them another chance to sort–"

"No!" Kaden couldn't hold back.

"It was quite odd seeing one family member move aside and another one taken in. I was curious to find out who she was after seeing you move her aside," Ronnoc said.

Another uncomfortable silence passed. The teacher stopped pacing and stood in front of Kaden, looking down on him. Kaden readied himself with the idea of being punished, he imagined an Elite walking the room behind Ronnoc and the teacher walking out, leaving them alone with each other. He imagined the dead, charcoal eyes staring at him and the black hole-like mouth licking its lips as it opened its robe, ready to suck the life out of him.

"To be a good Agent, we must protect our team. I've seen you protect your living partner and a member of your cohort. That is valued. On behalf of Pinnacle, thank you," Ronnoc said.

"You're... welcome, Teacher," Kaden said, taken aback.

"I only thank you through him. *Pinnacle* thanks you, not me," Ronnoc snapped.

Ronnoc moved to the door and opened it.

"You have twenty minutes, then we go under," the teacher said, then he looked back at Kaden's confused expression. "*He* has taken notice of you."

CHAPTER 26

K aden cleaned up, put on fresh robes, and sprinted to the meeting point. Weeks ago, he wouldn't have known the maze-like inner halls of The Tower, but now he ran through the labyrinth with confidence. The group was already there and Kaden stepped only a moment before Ronnoc.

"I trust you all know what this is?" Ronnoc asked as he entered and looked toward the door in the center structure.

The group nodded, except for Kaden.

"Good. We'll ride down and view the pastures from the crow's nest. Tomorrow, we'll go deeper." He studied the group and then hit a button on the center column and a curved down slide opened, revealing an inner room.

"An elevator," Kaden said under his breath.

"A what?" Jace whispered back.

"An elevator, I mean, it just... reminds me of something."

"This is The Tower's vertical transport," Ronnoc called to him.

"I like 'elevator' better," Jace said.

"Yeah, that does have a nice, fancy ring to it," Aria said.

"It's a vertical transport!" Ronnoc insisted, and the cohort tried to hide their smiles.

Jace silently mouthed *elevator* to Kaden as he followed Ronnoc into the room.

Ryon held back, and quickly grabbed Kaden's elbow, holding him back as the women entered.

"Hey," he said, sneaking in close to Kaden, who felt like Ryon wanted to go another thirteen rounds.

But to Kaden's surprise, Ryon said, "Thank you. You didn't do that earlier." Then he quickly slid into the vertical transport.

"Coming?" Ronnoc said as Kaden stood outside.

Kaden hopped in and took a place behind Ronnoc, who stood at the front, with his face nearest the sliding door. Kaden tried not to laugh as Jace once again mouthed *elevator* from behind Ronnoc's back and the entire cohort smiled.

After a brief ride down, the doors opened, and Kaden had to shield his eyes from the intense lights. They walked out onto a circular, steel mesh-like structure that wrapped around the vertical transport and saw lush, green fields run in all directions.

"This is the crow's nest. It's the center of the pastures, and the stairs from here lead to labs, classrooms, and the various animal facilities," Ronnoc said.

"It's amazing," Aria said.

"Whoa..." Vala said, walking to Aria's side. The two held the handrails of the crow's nest and looked out over the green fields.

"Is it *real* grass?" Jace asked.

"Yes, Pinnacle's salvation of the natural world, built right underneath us," Ronnoc said.

The group stood in silent reverence of the green ocean stretched out before them, none having seen anything more than a scattered tree or weed in their lifetimes.

"I've heard the stories, but to see it..." Aria said.

"Never realized this much was down here," Ryon said.

"Most in the world above will never know the extent of life that Pinnacle breeds below The Tower," Ronnoc said, looking out on the pastures.

They all took in the vast green landscape and the bright overhead lights that resembled a sky filled with numerous suns. They dotted the ceiling of the cavernous kingdom below ground, and were in stark contrast to the relentless haze of overcast skies in the world above.

"Are those trails?" Vala asked.

"Yes. Your new running trails," Ronnoc said and the group looked like kids on Christmas morning.

"We can go down there?" Aria asked.

"Soon, but today, we explore the labs and you learn the processes," Ronnoc said.

He led the team across a catwalk and up a series of white wire mesh stairs. Most of the cohort were looking down through the mesh at the green grass, but Kaden began looking up. He studied the underside of The Tower, marveling at the physical structure. The Tower above was like a modern castle built from cold metal and steel-like designs that gave a cool and calculated feel. But down here, Kaden got a sense of technology. There were lights, and not just the bright, fabricated suns; there were smaller lights dotting the walkways. And as Ronnoc led them into the laboratories and other facilities, there were screens, digital locks, and more tiny lights signaling something like a security or maintenance system governing the underbelly of The Tower.

"This is where the meat, harvested from the herds below, is tested for quality. The best goes up to The Tower, and the masses get the rest based on their occupation and living quarters," Ronnoc said.

"Why different quality to different people?" Kaden asked.

The group remained quiet, as if stunned by the question.

"What?" Kaden added.

"Are you serious?" Vala asked, then her eyes moved to Ronnoc, who nodded, giving her approval to answer.

"The Agents need the best nutrients to stay smart and healthy, so we can lead Empyrean. If our food supply was in jeopardy, well, what do you think a hungry, and angry, Elite would be like?" Vala said.

Kira's voice screamed in his mind and memories of nights without supper ran through his mind. His stomach growled at the thought, but he remained quiet, not voicing what he felt like his inner Kira.

Soon they moved from the laboratory and down a long, white hall. The lab they went through was empty, but numerous other labs were filled with blue-robed Agents, busily moving samples of meats.

"Over eighty percent is beef, with the rest a mix of venison, bison, or wolf," Ronnoc said.

"Wolf?" Jace asked.

"Wolves are less than one percent of the population. But necessary," Ronnoc said.

"Wolves are down here?" Ryon voiced what the rest of the group was thinking.

Ronnoc gave a confirming nod as he began explaining, "Over the decades, Pinnacle discovered the herds grow weak. They don't move as much to find new grass and as they stay more localized, they devour what's under them. The systems here regenerate the grasses, but their birth rates were impacted. Less offspring and each generation weaker than the last, and the meat leaner. An inferior product that was dwindling. However, Pinnacle added wolves. Once they were put into the population, it forced movement in the herds. Their grazing patterns stretched further, requiring less intervention for the grass to regenerate, and the animals grew strong as they sought survival. Quality of meat and production volume rose."

"Wow, great intervention," Jace said.

"It was, until the wolves began over-eating, over-populating."

"Wait, so there are wolves down there on our new running paths?" Vala asked, and Ronnoc gave a confirming nod. "Oooookay," Vala added.

"How'd you keep the wolves in check?" Kaden asked.

"Pinnacle expanded this area, giving every breed more space to escape. But the wolves continued to form new packs and spread," he said, now coming to a great white door. He slid it open and a downward staircase waited in front of them. A smell of blood and heat came from the tunnel.

"Below are the processing facilities; we'll tour it and then head back up," Ronnoc said.

"And what of the growing wolves?" Kaden asked.

"They hunt the herds, and we hunt them, of course," Ronnoc said.

The group moved into the processing facility, a massive slaughterhouse. Various cattle carcasses hung on chains and hooks larger than a hand. They moved around on paths built into the ceiling, an efficient processing system that killed the cow, drained its blood, and then broke it down piece-by-piece. Nothing went to waste. The smell of the dried blood along with some of the more gruesome parts of the process filled Kaden's nostrils.

"So this is where our monthly supply comes from?" he said to Jace as they walked through.

"This is where all the meat in Empyrean comes from," Jace responded.

The group looped back around using another catwalk structure to one of the countless columns that shot up unnaturally from the grasslands to support the weight of The Tower above. Ronnoc pressed a button and a door in the column opened, exposing another vertical lift.

"Ah yes, another el–" Jace said with a smirk as Ronnoc's eyes shot at him. "Another *vertical lift*," he exaggerated, and the group tried not to laugh.

They all stepped into the lift and the door slid closed. Before it moved, a distant rumble shook through them, as if the Earth itself moved.

The bright lights in the small tube-like lift went out, replaced by flashing red lights and sounding alarms. Ronnoc moved, punching the button to open the door. Nothing. He hit it again, and again, but nothing. Then he put his fingers to the sliding door, trying to dig into the side where the large curved door closed. He couldn't get to it.

The group was trapped, and more rumbles broke out, like an earthquake overtaking them as it vibrated the structure. It grew louder, stronger... closer.

Chapter 27

Another explosion and the entire vertical lift shook. Ronnoc pried at the door but to no avail. Kaden soon jumped on it, digging his fingers into the crack where the door slid into the base structure. The room shook again as a roar sounded just outside and the impact shifted the door. Kaden screamed in pain as his fingers were pinched. He couldn't feel the tips of at least half his fingers, but with the others, he could feel the edge of the door.

"I got it," he said through a clenched jaw.

The door shifted, maybe only a centimeter, but it was enough for the group to rush toward Ronnoc and push on the door.

The sound of metal scraping metal rang in the tight quarters, but the door was moving.

"Aaahhhh!" Kaden screamed as he pulled. His fingers left a red trail that crept out of the crack.

After a few more inches of exerted effort, the door caught its path and flew open.

Kaden looked at the mangled tips of fingers. They pulsed in pain as they dripped.

"Good work." Jace slapped his back and Kaden turned to see Ronnoc giving him an approving nod.

But no sooner than the door opened did smoke begin to fill the room. They rushed out to find the steel mesh catwalk a tangled mess. Fires roared near the labs and black smoke rose around them and began blocking the overhead lights. Suddenly, Kaden felt the realization like a weight dropped on his head; they were underground, in a confined space, with raging fires all around them.

"Where's the stairs?" Kaden shouted.

"Past the labs, near the center elevator!" Ronnoc called back over the chaos around him.

The group took off running.

"He just said elevator!" Jace shouted with a smile. Ryon sent a punch to his arm in response.

The group ran through the inner hallway, seeing the destruction of the labs around them. They bent low, with a slow, jogging motion to keep their heads out of the smoke.

The ground under them shook and fell. It was only a six-inch drop but felt like six hundred as Kaden's stomach threatened to jump out of his throat.

Aria lost her balance, but Vala reached out and quickly helped her to her feet.

"Watch your footing!" Kaden called out, nearly stepping on an up-turned piece that mesh ready to impale a falling Agent.

"Just ahead, the other side of the crow's nest," Ronnoc called out.

The path ahead was torn apart. Jace, Ryon, and Ronnoc all stopped to investigate.

Kaden saw the gap and hollered for them to step aside, turning his crouched run into a sprint. He leaped over the break and took the lead. He turned back to see Ryon make the jump.

"You got it!" Kaden called back as Aria went next.

Another explosion went off in the labs and Kaden saw a blue-robed body fly from a window in a far-off lab. It soared down to the pastures below.

"Ronnoc!" Kaden called out, but the body was limp before it hit the ground with a thud, smoke coming off it like a mushroom cloud.

Vala, then Jace; each punched through the black cloud and made it across the gap.

"Ronnoc!" Kaden called again, but then from the black cloud, jumping the gap, the teacher shot out. His entire left arm was on fire as he dropped to the catwalk to smother the flames. Jace took off his white robe and beat it down on Ronnoc. Ryon quickly followed, and a moment later, the fire was out, but Ronnoc's skin was bubbling with a severe burn up his neck and past his ear.

"I thought you were..." Kaden started, but Ronnoc stood up and the group centered around him.

"Not yet. Come on." Ronnoc began moving again as flames ripped around them.

They were close to the crow's nest now. Kaden found the door and swung it open. Flames ripped around them as fresh oxygen entered the area, but the staircase looked in good order. He turned back and called to the group as a small secondary explosion ripped through the labs. The sound of shattering glass rang out and water jets began shooting from the ceiling. The fire suppression system finally engaged, and Kaden wondered if it had ever been used.

As the group got to the door, Kaden caught motion out of the corner of his eye. He turned to look at another catwalk. He froze at what he saw.

She stood looking back at him.

Kira.

She held a food container as their eyes met, fire and billowing smoke raging around them.

The group was now past him, four of the five in the staircase.

"Come on!" Jace called back to Kaden, but his gaze was locked on his sister and the rest of the world went silent.

Kaden opened his mouth to scream her name, but another explosion ripped through their area. Jace was thrown into the side of the staircase as a ball of fire enveloped the column. Ronnoc, Ryon, Aria, and Vala disappeared behind the wall of fire. Jace was thrown into the side of the staircase column and fell in a crumpled heap. Kaden was shot backward, off the catwalk. In his last moments, he envisioned himself like the blue robe he saw moments ago, falling lifelessly like a sinking stone, to the ground fifty feet below.

His body smacked the earth, and to him, everything went black. Life flew out of him.

CHAPTER 28

Kira

"I'm excited," Enak whispered to Elba and Kira.

"I can't believe we're doing this," Elba responded.

"We must," Kira said. Then turning to the pair, she met their eyes with a determined look before leaving the building. They quickly followed.

Multiple groups of three dispersed from the back of the textile factory, each with the same mission, but following a different course.

"Okay, let's go over this one more time," Kira said as the plan replayed in her head. "We find the hidden staircase, we break through and go down, and then..."

"Then we grab what we can inside and set these off," Elba said, holding up a pack filled with bulky explosives.

"How many of the groups do you think will make it down?" Enak asked.

"Not all of 'em, that's for sure," Elba replied.

"Tip of the day, don't die," Enak said.

"Shut it," Kira said as she held out her arm, stopping them as she looked around the corner. The coast clear, they continued toward the Outer Ring.

The trio moved swiftly, following less-known paths through the shadows. Soon it would be daylight and they needed to be making their way down the staircases when the sun came up. Moments later, they came to a door. Kira put her hand on it, testing it. Locked.

"I can pick it," Elba said.

"We don't have time for that. We smash it," Enak said as he pulled out a small mallet.

"It's going to be loud," Elba whispered.

"Loud? There's either a group of Elites on the other side of this door or an unguarded staircase–" Enak said.

"Or they're at the bottom and come up to meet us in the shaft," Elba interrupted.

"It can't be *unguarded* if they're at the bottom," Enak said.

"Let's pick it," Elba said again.

"I'm smashing it," Enak retorted.

"Will you two just do it?" Kira urged.

The trio held their breath, knowing a pair of Elites could be on the other side of the door. Enak looked back to Elba, he nodded. They both looked to Kira, then Enak swung the mallet, knocking the knob clean off the door. Elba stepped forward, kicking in the door. The door knob rattled on the cement as the door flew open. A dimly lit staircase waited for them. An empty staircase.

They ran in and Kira shoved the door closed behind them, its bent frame not completely lining up after Elba's kick.

They moved down flights of stairs for what felt like eternity, occasionally pausing and listening for steps above or below them. The metal stairs clanged with every step, a rhythmic ping that followed them and echoed up and down the hollowed out concrete column. Eventually, they came to another door. This time, when Kira tried it, the knob turned, and they quickly slid out of the tunnel.

"I can't believe it. One door and a staircase and we're here," Kira said in disbelief.

"They've never been under attack before. No need to guard it," Elba said

Each shielded their eyes as they transitioned from the dim staircase to a blinding light. They felt the grass before they saw it. The grass brushed against their shins and calves as their eyes adjusted, a feeling they never felt before.

"I can't believe it," Kira said again.

"It's real." Enak laughed. "Even with all the planning and all they told us, I still wasn't sure I believed it, but here it is..."

The mission left their minds for a split second as they looked out onto an endless sea of green that rolled with the wind.

"It really exists..." Elba said, staring off in wonder.

"But it's all fake," Kira said, forcing herself to remember why they broke into the pastures. "The light is man-made, the winds come from air vents. A facade of real life."

"Sure is a pretty good facade," Enak said, still looking on in amazement.

"She's right, let's do this," Elba said, ensuring his pack was still secure.

"There's our mark," Kira said, pointing to a circular steel structure about a quarter mile ahead of them. "The crow's nest."

Kira took off, jogging through the grass. Elba started, then saw Enak still struck in awe. He tugged on his brother, pulling him as the pair caught up.

"I don't see anyone else," Kira said, looking side to side. "We should see *someone.*"

"Neither do... whoa!" Enak pulled back as the ground gently sloped and dozens of cattle stood grazing in front of them. Enak stepped forward, and a few of the larger ones raised their head, studying him while still chewing a mouthful of green.

"Hold up, hold up!" Enak called to his brother, noticing a long-horned steer snort as it stepped closer.

"We should go around. Far around," Kira said.

The bull bobbed its head up and down as it snorted, its two long horns bouncing in the air.

"I've never seen one, especially so close." Elba watched the steer, now going from a walk to a trot.

"And we shouldn't get any closer," Enak said, this time taking his turn to pull his brother away.

They began running, and as they grew further away, the steer slowed, content with protecting its ground and herd as it snorted back to its place.

"I can't believe this place!" Enak said as he and Elba were all smiles.

"Remember why we're here," Kira said as they approached a staircase. "There's still no one else..." she said, looking back at the fields from an elevated view.

"Come on, let's get these things off my back and on some tower," Elba said.

They moved low and swift through a series of catwalks and came to a large white door.

"It's not locked," Enak said.

"Good," Kira said, motioning for him to go inside.

Quietly, they opened the door then stopped. Voices sounded from near-by and then froze like statues. The voices passed and they tip-toed along.

"These are the labs. There should be no Elites this time of day," Kira said.

"How do you know?" Enak replied.

"That's our information, just trust it," she said, trying to keep her voice down.

They squatted in silence, listening for the voices.

"We each get a container, then set off the charges," she said.

She looked up at doors, watching for men and women in blue robes.

"We get in and get out," she said and the pair nodded. "Elba." She nodded toward a series of doors that led to another catwalk and another column. A group of white-robed Agents and a blue were waiting outside the column.

She stopped, watching the group. A door opened down the hall and Enak rushed her into the nearest door, narrowly escaping the view of a Blue Agent coming out from a nearby lab.

Inside the room, they found a stack of containers, each packed with meat. They quietly grinned, elated, and then ducked as more doors nearby opened and closed.

They held their position for a moment longer, then they left the containers and each planted multiple charges, positioned to knock out the catwalk behind them and shield their escape.

"Ready?" Elba said.

Kira lifted her head up, checking for anyone in the nearby hallway. She gave a confirming thumbs-up and Elba hit the button.

The countdown began.

They sprinted back through the room, grabbing a container each and then took off down the hall to the catwalk. Elba stopped and put down his container, planting more explosives as the first few went off.

Explosions ripped through the labs, dropping the catwalk down to the green pastures below. The few blue-robed Agents in various lab rooms rushed out to find more explosions near them. They went off and the Agents flew backward from the concussion.

"Come on!" Enak shouted.

Elba placed the last charges, meant to knock down the crow's nest and secure their escape. He set the charges and picked up his container, now running toward Kira, who looked out at the staircase. She looked back, seeing down the hall to the smoke billowing up from the labs. It rose and clouded the overhead suns, casting an overcast haze on the green fields below. The green appeared more gray as dark smoke filled the high ceilings.

Through a break in the columns of smoke, Kira caught sight of a man standing and staring at her. They met eyes and stared.

Kaden.

Another explosion went off behind Kaden, and she saw him shake as the platform under him gave way, flames and smoke roaring upward.

"It's set!" Elba said, grabbing her arm and pulling her down the steps, breaking her stare with the smoke that billowed where Kaden once stood.

They ran as fast as they could through the grasses, past the spot of the herd who had stampeded away at the sounds of the explosions, and toward the hidden staircase. Once inside, they slammed the door behind them and began the long trek back up the staircase, holding containers packed with food.

Chapter 29

Entry #5

The facts: The world is at war and Empyrean Enterprises is fully funded with private and public funding. My valuation metrics were accurate. We are now acting on behalf of the US government's health department to install the 'The Hope Drug' within the American people.

Public perception is so positive, riots in other first world countries have broken out from their desire to be the next country to get the Hope Drug.

More facts: Ninety-nine percent of patients show extremely positive short-term benefits. The remaining one percent die within twelve months of injection. The cost of health innovation.

To think, only years ago, the modern west was driving itself mad with social issues such as DEI activism and ignoring real issues such as the painkiller crisis that was killing its people. The media drove the mainstream narrative, keeping eyes off what lobbyists didn't want you to see. But now, the death toll is on screen and shown to be stable at one percent. Those that die are being martyred by the survivors. We've gone from ignoring preventable death to embracing it. A world where the public willingly accepts sacrificing one of every hundred people, and the world is protesting to expand the drug.

The world knows they cannot solve their own problems and they've turned to the Hope Drug. We went from freedom and liberty of the founding fathers to a population that demands someone else solve their problems. I write that and it sounds like a bad thing, but it is not. The world has evolved into another level of specialization. I once heard that to make a toaster from scratch, it took over nine months and cost two hundred and fifty times more than simply walking into a store and buying it. What is different now? We've commoditized optimal health. First, with those who need it most, those who are at death's doorstep. A terminal patient on the Hope Drug sees their health do a complete one-eighty. For those not terminal, instead of fighting your hunger cravings or forcing yourself into hours at the gym, the Hope Drug optimizes health at every stage.

Trillion-dollar evaluations are not enough. This is like fluoride in the water; it'll be everywhere, and Empyrean is the spigot.

I have moved my thoughts toward the future. War and protests still ravage the landscape, but they will be a thing of the past because the people of the world have hope. Finally, they have hope.

Chapter 30

D arren jolted up from the bed and slid off the edge. His elbow smacked the arm of his desk chair, sending it crashing into his desk. He cringed, holding his elbow as he sat up.

"Yo?" Chris called from the other room.

Darren looked around, confused at the small room he was in and the old shag carpet beneath him. He was just in wonderfully green pastures, before they... Before the explosions went off and turned their small portion of the pastures into a hellish inferno.

The last thing he remembered was the catwalk below him falling away. Kaden dropped through the smoke, down to the hard ground below, and woke up here, now, as Darren.

Back on the bed, Kelly rested, still as peaceful-looking as ever.

"Yooo, you good?" Chris shouted from the living room.

"Good. Just fell," Darren said.

He heard the brothers laugh as they went back to playing video games.

"Kira. Kelly, what did you do?" Darren asked her as thoughts of seeing Kira across the catwalk flashed back in his mind.

"They're going to find you, and they're going to kill you. But then again," he said, looking over his hands and becoming comfortable as Darren once again. "Maybe when you die, you simply come back here."

His mind went to the punishment that The Tower and Elites would enforce. Kira would be tortured. She might even be consumed by an Elite. The vision of the sorting when the Elite spoke in the feminine voice to voice's husband. It was like the woman was inside the Elite, speaking from a deep pit that locked her soul away.

"Would you come back here if they consumed you? Would I?" He watched her heart beat through the subtle pulse on her neck.

"I can't stop them from finding you. They'll sniff you out, along with Elba and Enak. Nobody is more powerful than–" But he stopped himself mid-thought as a vision of gray eyes came to mind.

He grabbed the glasses and held them up. Doctor Abrams sent him to Empyrean. He'd also given them these glasses. The stories of Jericho, of the old man in the EMR. All of them were Dr. David Abrams.

He set the glasses down and opened his laptop, searching for Dr. David Abrams. Time didn't seem to be linked in the two worlds. Nearly no time here had passed, yet it was months in Empyrean. Last time he was sent back, he'd spent a couple hours here, and it seemed to be a couple hours in Empyrean.

"I have time to search. Only one man can stop the Elites," he whispered to himself then began scrolling the search results. Just like the office disappeared from all internet searches, all online records of Dr. Abrams seemed to be scrubbed too. He searched for a few moments, frustration growing, but then an idea hit: medical professional records. All eye doctors were board approved; they must have records stating their approval to practice medicine. He began combing federal and state websites for links to locations that verified the medical status of doctors.

He found it: Medical board certification in his state for David Jacob Abrams.

But his heart sank when there were no contact details. Other than his medical certification ID number, there was no private information. Frustrated with the website, he continued with the idea of public records and began searching real estate records in his and neighboring counties. He knew the doctor had a family; the pictures were in the office and he had overheard as much. There were only two counties within reasonable driving distance of the office.

He found him in the second county he searched. The property was a ranch-style home bought fifteen years ago by David and Sarah Abrams. He copied the address into his maps app and hit the directions button. It was only twenty-five minutes away.

He took in the info and turned to Kelly, still peaceful and secure in his bed, then left a note for her to call him if she woke before he slid out of the room.

"Hey, I have to check on something. Kelly is sleeping. Tell her I'll be back ASAP if she wakes up?" Darren asked as Kirk's character on the screen shot an opponent, the head flying off and the game ending. The two erupted in celebration.

"You got it," Chris said, still smiling.

"And keep it down," Darren said.

"Sure, sure." Chris's face straightened as he whispered.

"No promises," Kirk called out as he started the next game.

"We got you," Chris said, then he sat down. "Hey, where you heading?"

Darren froze, not wanting to answer truthfully.

"Going to see a doctor. My eye doctor," he replied.

"Yeah? Hope it helps," Chris said as their next game started up.

"Me too..." Darren said, leaving the room.

His GPS started at twenty-five minutes, but he made it in twenty as he sped whenever the road opened up. As he pulled up to the address, he looked down, double checking. He had to be at the wrong place.

There wasn't a house at seven-six-five Mount Zion Drive; it was more like a warzone.

He parked on the side of the road and walked up to the yellow crime tape wrapped around the red brick mailbox, looking at the crater and debris where a house once stood. Darren remembered the satellite image of the house when he looked up directions. It was white with gray trim. It appeared to be two stories, but he couldn't tell from the overhead shot. There was a front porch that extended across the front side of the house and wrapped around one side. Darren imagined it connected to the kitchen, a convenient way for the Abramses to bring out the lemonade as they sat on the rocking chairs in the shade. Behind the house about a hundred yards back was a pond. It looked like just the right size for a kid to learn how to fish. Darren imagined Dr. Abrams and his son and daughter from the office pictures casting lines into the circular pond as frogs croaked in the early morning light.

But in front of him were the charred remains of wood and brick, like a missile came down from the heavens. It could have been Sodom or Gomorrah, wiped from the Earth.

"You know 'em?" an elderly woman said behind him.

Darren broke his daydreaming about what the property used to be and turned to the woman. She was short, just over five feet with a face full of wrinkles. Yet, they were the kind of wrinkles from an enjoyable life, decades of smiling and laughing worn into her skin as she gracefully aged.

"I did," Darren said. "But not well. I was hoping to talk to the doctor. Do you know what happened?"

"I spent two hours with a man in blue last night, explaining that I don't," she said.

"Oh, well, is everyone alright?" Darren asked.

"Child, you hadn't heard?"

Darren shook his head.

"Only yesterday, right at sunset, that whole house blew up," she said and then exhaled a sorrowful breath. "And took the sweetest little family we ever knew with it." Her eyes sparkled as they watered.

"What? Yesterday? Exploded?"

She nodded, still looking at the crater.

"What happened?"

"It exploded, boy. You seem to have a listening problem, remind me of my grandson," she said, but then she smiled a sympathetic smile and patted his arm.

"But, I don't understand... I saw him at his office yesterday morning," Darren said.

"If you figure it out, please clue the police in on it. They're just as baffled as you, although they won't admit it."

She smiled at him again and rubbed his upper arm. "I'm sorry, son," she said and then turned, slowly moving back up her driveway and up her steps. She turned and waved, the white envelopes she held from her mailbox waving back at him.

Darren turned back to the wreckage. He stared at it, still in dismay, and said a prayer for Dr. Abrams and his family. Then he went back to his truck and thought. Ideas of how to find out more information went through his mind, police, local hospitals, relatives, or other neighbors. Meanwhile, Kelly was still living Empyrean as Kira and the full force of The Tower coming after her.

He couldn't stay here forever, but he needed more. His cohort in Empyrean might be dead. The Elites waited.

"God!" he shouted as he smacked the steering wheel of his truck.

After a deep breath, he started the engine and let the truck roll forward, looping around the cul de sac. He looked through his mirror to the crater where the house once stood.

There was a man in the reflection, standing at the center of the debris.

Darren slammed on the brakes and threw the truck in park. It jolted, rocking back and forth as he jumped out and looked back at the house.

But no one was there.

The confusion didn't stop him. He moved back to the line of tape, then pushing up the yellow tape, he ran up what was left of the driveway. No one was around.

His heart sank, wondering if his mind was being torn apart by living in two different worlds, but as doubt crept into his mind, he saw something from the corner of his eye. Out by the pond, far behind the place where the house stood, something moved.

Darren followed it.

A set of trees on the other side of the pond shielded the sun. Through the brightness of the day, he couldn't make out what was under the canopy, but as he rounded the pond and moved closer, he found him.

A man in a hooded cloak sat bent over.

He looked up at Darren.

It was him, Dr. Abrams, and he wore the same cloak as the man from Empyrean. The same cloak as Jericho.

His eyes as gray as ever and his cheeks fresh with the moisture from tears.

"Hello, Mr. McArthur," he said.

"Dr. Abrams, what happened here?" he asked.

"It's begun," he replied.

"Your family. Doctor, what happened to your house? Are they okay, are you okay?" Darren asked.

"I will be," he said, taking in a breath and straightening his back. His frame looked fragile a moment ago, but as his posture changed, his shoulders and chest looked more muscular than Darren remembered the doctor being. Darren watched the doctor as he looked back at the house. His physical form seemed to strengthen with every breath.

The doctor met his eyes and gave a reassuring smile, like that of a parent to a sick child, and Darren's anxiety melted.

"Doctor, what happened here?" Darren asked.

"The beginning of the end," he said, and there was a look of sadness on his face. "Darren, it's time you go back."

"To Empyrean? The cloaked man who saved Kira and me as kids, Jericho, David in the EMR... it's all you?"

The doctor looked at him. He gave a confirming nod.

"How?"

The doctor shook his head. "You'll see."

"Why is this happening?" Darren asked.

"Think of it like this: the world is a wheat field and the owner of the field planted good seeds in proper lines, but in the night, someone came to sow weeds. Quickly, the weeds are sprouting amongst the wheat."

"So remove the weeds," Darren said.

"No," he answered, "you can't uproot the weeds without taking the wheat with them. They both grow together, until harvest."

"And harvest marks the end of the growing season?" Darren said.

The doctor nodded his agreement. "At harvest, the weeds will be collected and burned, then the wheat will be brought into the barn."

"You sent me and Kelly to see the harvest. Is that what this is all about?" Darren said.

"You both have a part to play," the doctor said.

"I'm not sure about that, because I think she just killed me," Darren retorted.

"It's not always easy to see which are weeds and which are wheat."

"Knock off the comparisons and get real," Darren said, frustration bubbling up.

"You're seeing behind the veil now. Nothing is *more real*."

"And where does all this go?"

"Right now, you go forward." He extended his hand, placing it on Darren's head.

Before he could object, the world around him changed. He was no longer under the trees with Dr. Abrams but back at his apartment, standing next to the bed. Kelly was gently lying on the bed and noise from the video game in the living room came muffled through the wall. Darren opened his door and looked out. Chris and Kirk were playing their game.

"Hey, you back already?" Chris said.

"Yeah..." Darren said, then he noticed his truck in the parking lot through the window. He stared at it, confusion taking him over.

He shut the door and stared at the glasses on his desk. He picked up his desk chair and slid it away from the bed. He sat back on the bed next to Kelly and held up the glasses.

"Harvest time... Time to bundle up the weeds," he said, putting them on.

Chapter 31

Kaden opened his eyes to smoke spreading across the sky above him. His body moved slowly, his joints grinding, like the Tin Man needing oil. His vision went in and out as the sky above became a blur.

"He's alive!" a voice called out in the distance. Soon, he felt himself moving, sliding across the grass. He coughed and tried to get up, but his head barely moved, a weight too heavy for his neck to bear.

"Get 'em up there," another said, but it seemed farther away than the first. Everything went black.

The next time he opened his eyes, he looked up at a smooth, white ceiling. Beeping noises sounded around him like insects on a summer night.

He tried moving, but again, his body resisted. Muscles and joints screamed in pain as if moving for the first time. His fingers twitched as he tried to close his fist.

"Hold up," Ronnoc's familiar voice came from his side.

The man came into focus. He wasn't in his normal blue robe but his house clothes. They were the same as Kaden's, the standard issue light blue pants and a white shirt of the Inner Ring working class.

"Hold still," he said as he came closer. Kaden saw a patch of white gauze running from Ronnoc's shoulder up his neck and to the side of his head.

White medical tape crossed his side like a spider web holding the cloth in place. Severe burns.

Kaden tried to speak, but it came out like a puff of sand through a dry pipe. He coughed and another hand held up a cup of water.

"Here," Jace said.

He picked up his head enough so that Jace could put the cup to his lips. Jace wasn't covered in burns like Ronnoc, but his arm was in a sling and a deep purple ran under both eyes. A pair of black eyes from a broken nose.

"Thank you," Kaden finally said with a cough. "How long?"

"About three days," Ronnoc said.

"I thought you were dead. You flew off the crow's nest like a bird, a bird that couldn't fly," Jace said.

Kaden smiled. "What happened?"

"The Lighthouse Remnant. They attacked the labs," Ronnoc said.

"For the food?" Kaden said, and Ronnoc's expression changed.

"Why do you say that?" the teacher asked.

"Because I saw..." Kaden stopped himself. In his mind, he saw Kira holding a food container. "I saw something before the explosion. In the labs. The containers were all shifted."

Ronnoc eyed him, then Jace spoke.

"Seems like we got 'em all, though." Jace nodded to Ronnoc.

"Intelligence is coming out now. Elites stationed around Empyrean captured nine groups, over two dozen people claiming to be in the Lighthouse Remnant, but it seems they didn't get them fast enough."

"Some got through?" Kaden asked.

"Our superiors claim they got 'em all, but I don't agree," Ronnoc said.

Kaden remained quiet.

"If anyone is left, we'll snuff 'em out. The fools just declared war on The Tower," Ryon said as he approached the group. Vala and Aria came in behind him. Each of them had various patches covering burns and injuries, similar to Ronnoc, and Kaden remembered the fireball that shot into the stairwell before he was blown off the catwalk.

"They're like weeds," Vala said with disdain.

"No, more like cockroaches," Aria added.

"Hey, Kaden, nice job down there," Jace interjected.

"Yeah, we could still be in the elev– I mean vertical lift, if you hadn't jammed your fingers in there," Aria said.

"Yup," Ronnoc said reluctantly. "Now all you rest up and be ready for tomorrow. It's our turn."

The group steeled a look of determination on their faces.

"Our turn?" Kaden asked.

"We're going after them, going to stomp out those cockroaches!" Aria said.

"Pull the weeds," Vala said, elbowing her. The pair smiled.

"Tomorrow morning, in the lower hall. We have a send-off," Ronnoc said.

"A send-off? I've never heard of that," Ryon said.

"What you don't know could fill The Tower," Ronnoc snapped. "But yes, it's rare."

"Has The Tower ever been attacked, I mean *in* The Tower?" Jace asked.

"No. The Elites have always captured them. They have a sense for those things," Ronnoc said.

"They got nine groups; there can't be much more than that out there. We all know the Outer Ring, either from growing up there or our trials. How foolish could a person be to believe in those old Remnant stories?" Jace said.

"Misguided cockroaches," Aria said.

"Dead souls awaiting their consumption. They'll be begging to be killed before the Elites get them," Ryon added.

"How's all your Spark Club progress?" Ronnoc said and the group once again lit up.

"Great!" Vala said eagerly.

"Teacher, are you saying..." Aria began asking.

"You four are all trained up, and I suspect this one will be okay." He motioned to Kaden. "He's always a step ahead of death." Ronnoc's eyes narrowed on Kaden. "Tomorrow morning, the lower hall," he said and then left the infirmary.

"We're getting promoted," Ryon said.

"Don't jinx it," Jace said.

"I bet Ronnoc will be a Purple. He's been a Blue for ages," Aria said.

"We'll need a group lead. All Blue groups have a leader, their Purple," Vala said.

Kaden looked at Ryon; he'd been the de facto leader, if even an overly forceful one since Kaden's arrival. But as he looked at Ryon, he saw Ryon, and the others were looking back at him.

"No?" Kaden asked. "Ryon, it's you."

"No. We'd be dead in the pastures right now without you." He paused and looked over the group. "I can admit it now, it's you," he said with an approving look.

Jace put his hand on Ryon's shoulder, reassuring the bigger man, and then looked back at Kaden.

"Come on, Captain. What do you say?" Vala said.

Aria reached down and squeezed Kaden's hand.

"If a promotion comes and we need a formal leader," Kaden began as he looked across the eager faces, "then I'd be honored."

Kaden slept most of the day and awoke after dinner time. A full-course meal was brought out by a blue-robed staff member of the infirmary. He thanked the man, then watched the blue robe swing behind him. He noticed the infirmary was like the labs, numerous blue-robed workers but none with a Spark Club.

"Hey," Kaden called to the man. "Excuse me, mind if I ask how your promotion to Blue went?"

"Of course," the man said. His voice was low, a deep baritone that matched his wide-set jaw, deep eyes, and short black hair. "I started out just like you all. We didn't have as close of a group, though. I'll tell you, a group like yours is rare."

"What was it like for you?"

"Most cohorts are groups of individuals, and once you get promoted, you get more choices. I didn't fare so well on my trials. I wanted to heal more than fight. But my lead was strict, our time as Whites was tough, especially on the mats and gym," he said.

"Tell me about it," Kaden said, remembering the constant beatdowns at the hands of Ryon.

"Once we were promoted, we all went our separate ways. You get more choices when you're a Blue, but as long as you serve The Tower, you'll find a home. Just keep your head down."

"Head down?"

"Yeah." He leaned in and talked lower. "These walls talk, brother. Any word that could be construed as treason eventually will be."

"What does that mean?" Kaden asked.

"It means the Elites sniff you out. Someone is always talking, always trying to get a leg up to get closer to Pinnacle."

"What happens when–"

"We're done with this conversation," he interrupted, looking over his shoulders.

Kaden reluctantly nodded but asked one more question as the man began leaving.

"You don't wear a Spark Club," he said.

"I heal, and I keep my head down. If you get a club, you should still do the same. Those things change a man. You think you're more powerful than you really are," he said.

"Have you–" Kaden began asking, but the man left mid-conversation.

Chapter 32

Kaden ate his dinner and got up, walking around and stretching. His body was healing faster than he expected, a sign of minor injuries and the extra care given by the infirmary. The new injuries felt more like muscle soreness, no major breaks or muscle tears. Twenty-four hours ago, his body could hardly move, but now he felt energized and unable to sleep. His energy finally back, he felt like he just drank three cups of coffee. Checking himself out of the infirmary, he went to his quarters, taking long walks through The Tower's inner halls on the way. After eventually getting a few hours of restless sleep, he awoke to Jace pounding on his door. Soon, they were entering the same grand entrance area where Kaden had been sorted for Elite consumption months before.

As they walked into the room, a group of Agents were in a large circle, their different ranks showing off in an array of colorful blue, purple, and brown patterns. Ronnoc and the cohort gathered together and then motioned into the center of the grand circle.

"So, this is a promotion ceremony..." Jace whispered to Kaden.

"Wow," Aria said quietly behind them.

Ronnoc and Ryon held stoic faces, standing tall as they walked. Aria and Jace kept their eyes straight, like soldiers marching in beat.

Vala struggled, trying to keep her typically perfect posture, but a limp from her injuries prevented it. Kaden could see she was tightening her jaw, trying not to wince in pain as she kept up with the group.

The Circle of Agents was the most formal ceremony within The Tower that Kaden had seen. The sorting was like herding cattle but now, the silence in the room gave an ambience of formality. At least fifty Agents stood, forming the gigantic circle. As Kaden and the group followed Ronnoc to the center, they all kept silent. The lack of noise felt eerie, like a funeral, as the click of their black Tower-issued boots struck the floor. They stood in the center, a picture of wounded, yet unyielding warriors.

Once inside the circle, Kaden scanned the circle around them. A woman in brown robes stepped in, toward the center of the circle. He recognized her, the Brown Agent from the advanced ropes course.

She was the only person Kaden had seen in Empyrean without jet black hair. There was an underlying black, but it lay below streaks of white, giving the appearance of gray from afar. It was braided and then pulled back and wrapped in a circular fashion, a crown of white and black hair braids atop her head.

"Ronnoc, you have led and taught this group," she called out, turning and meeting eyes with various other Agents in the circle. Seeing from closer up, Kaden saw a wrinkled face, but it was bright, full of life.

"Examinations passed and physical foundations have been met, and the recent survival of your cohort amidst the horrendous attacks proves their resourcefulness. You have built a valuable group for Pinnacle and The Tower. I, Beth-ell, Brown Agent of Empyrean and servant of Pinnacle, offer you this promotion," she said, raising her hands.

As her hands went up, other Agents near her walked forward with a series of robes, five blue and one purple. Ronnoc took the purple robe first and then each member took their respective blue robe.

"Thank you," Kaden said softly as he took the robe. He recognized the man, Jay, who gave the blue robe. He was the man on patrol outside The Tower, the one who called Ronnoc a prick and whose brother died at the hands of an Elite. Jay responded to Kaden's thanks with a cold stare.

Beth-ell walked forward and the other Agents walked back to their position in the circle.

"Commence your promotion," she called out.

Ronnoc was the only one who moved. He took off his blue robe, quickly stripping down to his Tower-issued, skintight underwear, a thin piece of white cloth. The tightness made them nearly transparent against skin. Ronnoc didn't seem to mind, exposing his body in front of the entire crowd as if he were alone in his quarters. Bandages from his injuries covered his upper body and the thin undergarments the lower.

As their teacher changed robes, Kaden noticed more than just the gauze that still covered Ronnoc's neck and ear. There were bruises going up his back, but also many old scars across his arms and shoulders.

Ryon was the first to follow Ronnoc's lead, removing his robe. Kaden caught Jace's eye, unsure and uncomfortable at stripping down in front of the group, but soon Jace followed Ryon. Both removed their arms from their white robes and let them fall.

As the men complied, Kaden caught a glance of Aria and Vala. They still hadn't removed their robes, but as Kaden noticed them, so did Ronnoc. The teacher stood, showing his body to the group of onlookers and then pulled up the new robe, his bare upper body still exposed. Before the purple robe was pulled over his shoulders, he tilted his head back and whispered to the group.

"Do it," Ronnoc said to them.

Vala swallowed and closed her eyes, then she began to remove her robe, the standard garments hardly shielding her from the onlooking eyes.

Aria didn't move as quickly and drew the attention of Beth-ell. The older woman turned and looked at her, squinting her eyes, narrowing her gaze on Aria like she was drilling into her mind.

Aria soon complied, her eyes watering and a silent tear dropping down her cheek as she quickly changed robes in front of all the other Agents.

Kaden tried not to watch the others, keeping his eyes from them. He closed his eyes tight as he changed. The group finished their change and stood, once again in a deafening silence that Beth-ell broke.

"Ronnoc is dead!" she screamed out. "Welcome Ron-ell, Purple Agent and fellow protector of Empyrean!" she called out, and the crowd erupted in thunderous applause. As the noise died down, another group of Agents stepped forward and handed the group their very own Spark Club. Their new blue robes had a small loop ready to holster the weapon.

Kaden held the device and the group all looked around at each other. Ryon and Jace matched Kaden's sense of satisfaction while Vala held a look of great triumph, as if awarded a lifelong achievement award. Aria feigned delight, but her eyes still held a sadness from the changing portion of the ceremony.

"Please, IGNITE! And claim your ranks in service of Pinnacle," Beth-ell said.

Kaden heard the first crack of electricity from Ryon. Like a mini-lightning bolt, a flash of electricity snapped around the metal ball at the end of the mace-like club. Others in the group soon followed, even Aria, whose sadness temporarily dissipated as she wielded the electrified club. Kaden was the last. He looked over at the others, seeing the wave of lightning rush over the metal ball. Then he looked at his hand and squeezed, and the end of his mace ignited. He felt like Zeus in control of the Heavens. The heat from the tiny bolts emanated in the air all around his hand. He kept his grip tight, the mace crackling and flashing a bright light on the faces of all those watching.

He shot his hand up, pointing the Spark Club to the sky, and screamed in triumph. The others in the group followed suit, even the newly named Ron-ell. The entire circle followed, the great hall a cacophony of celebration.

As the fervent cries eventually died down, Beth-ell stood before the group.

"Go forth with your mission. Find and eliminate the Remnant. The Elites will follow behind to clean up," she said in a scornful tone that the expression of every other Agent in the room seemed to echo as faces tightened and lips curled.

Chapter 33

The next day, the group patrolled the Outer Ring together in their new uniforms as their new rank. The people of the Outer Ring avoided them as they tried gathering information about the attack, scattering like insects when the light turned on for every alleyway and building they approached.

"This is useless. Where are the Elites?" Ryon said in frustration as he smacked his Spark Club against a nearby dumpster. A resounding echo thumped through the air, like a haunting drum beat.

"They have been absent, that's for sure," Jace replied.

"Ronnoc, I mean Ron-ell, wasn't too thrilled to see no Elites at our promotion," Ryon said.

"They attend *all* promotions, except ours," Vala said with a bitterness in her voice, as if they were speaking of someone that stood her up.

"What are they up to if they're not doing their normal duties?" Kaden asked.

"Normal duties?" Vala laughed. "No one except Pinnacle tells them what to do. Only the lower-ranking Elites, the non-goldens, join patrols, but even they think Agents are worthless."

"Didn't they used to be Agents?" Kaden asked. He glanced at Aria, but she hadn't spoken much since the promotion ceremony.

"Yes, but no Elite is the same person after *THE* promotion. They aren't even *people*," Ryon said.

"I heard they're devouring people. Consuming them to learn their secrets and then moving to the next person until they get anyone a part of the attack," Jace said.

"Where'd you hear that?" Ryon snapped.

Jace shook his head then added, "They're killing people left and right. A genocide of the Outer Ring."

"Good riddance. Without order, what do we have? Look past the walls; it's a whole lot of nothing," Ryon said.

"I'm not disagreeing, but I mean, come on, can't they learn something without trying to consume everyone?" Jace said.

"You go tell the Elites how to interrogate," Vala said, a sharpness to her voice.

"Come on, let's do another lap and then back to The Tower. Split up and meet back here," Kaden directed, and the group nodded, each of them ready to end their patrol.

Kaden turned a corner and found an empty alleyway off the main walkway. He kept going and turned again, another empty area. Everyone seemed to be hiding since the Rings found out about the attack on The Tower.

He turned again, ready to move back to the group, but paused when he saw a man disappear behind a door. He caught the outline of a long jacket and hood.

"Hey!" he called out, but the door kept slowly swinging closed. Kaden ran after it, catching it before it closed. "Hey!" he called again, the man now a floor or two down on metal stairs that spiraled down into darkness.

Kaden turned back, looking for someone in his group, but then went into the stairwell, his hand clutching his Spark Club as he trotted down the stairs.

Numerous times, he struck his head, elbow, or foot on the iron structure of the stairs. His club clanged against the center pole. He slowed, fighting the dizziness as he chased the man who always seemed to be just out of reach. The unforgiving iron and concrete felt to him like a mocking fighter, throwing jabs and cheap shots in the darkness when he least expected, slowing his progress as he worked his way down. When he hit the bottom, he once again slid his fingers into the closing door at the last moment. To his amazement, it opened up to the pasture. He wondered how far he went down, but then it dawned on him how Kira escaped after the attacks. Seeing her was a secret he still kept.

Looking around, he saw there was nothing but grass. He searched for the hooded man. There were no places to hide, but nobody to be found. The green pastures flowed in the artificial winds, and in the distance, he could see the wreckage of the labs.

He turned back to the long staircase, and back toward the team, but brilliant gray eyes were in front of the door, waiting for him.

Jericho.

Before Kaden could react, Jericho grabbed his forehead with his palm, and in a flash of light, Kaden's consciousness left Empyrean.

He opened his eyes to see two men. Like a camera watching a scene play out, he was invisible in the room. Before him was Dr. Abrams, an IV attached to one wrist, and Dr. Thornhill nearby reading a monitor.

"I can't believe it. It's working!" Dr. Thomas Thornhill exclaimed.

"It is... Well, we have a sample size of one!" Dr. Abrams joked.

"It doesn't matter. This proves it. It works!" Dr. Thornhill leapt as he pulled away from the monitor.

"But why not in all the other subjects? We need truth here," Dr. Abrams said.

"David, stop it. We had successful primate trials and yes, there's been a few setbacks, but what great achievement in history hasn't had bumps along the road?"

"It radically increased cancerous cell growth in a minority of the participants. If we don't understand that, then we can't go forward."

"Agreed. Yes, of course!" Thomas shouted reluctantly, turning around and rubbing his eyes. "Look, we're saying the same thing here. I'm not saying we mass market this tomorrow, but we must keep moving forward. David, we have the cure for cancer! This is every scientist's dream! Every prayer that goes up for healing, we have it, right here! What if when man discovered fire, they decided to test it until they fully understood it? We'd never have a hot meal let alone have survived extreme winters. If we don't move forward, we are saying we want people to remain in pain when we have a cure. We are sitting on value here, and not just monetary. I mean real human-life value!"

Thomas sat back down, giving an exaggerated plea by clasping his hands together toward David Abrams.

"You created this compound. It's yours. Can you tell me NOT to go save the world with it?" Thomas said.

"Thomas, since this treatment began, I've been seeing things..." Thomas looked at his friend skeptically. "And lately, they've been clear as day. At first, it was like a dream, then more like a memory, but now, it's like I can choose where and when to view, as if time and space are merely a canvas I'm standing on."

"David, we're talking about the cure for cancer. Don't get philosophical on me when we have a trillion-dollar, humanity-changing drug in our grasp."

"This isn't philosophical. It's real, Thomas, and I know you doubt, but I've seen what will happen when we unleash this drug on the world."

"You can't project anymore. It's time for action!" Thomas exclaimed.

"No, I don't mean project. I mean this didn't just alter my cancer cells – I'm stronger now than I was in my twenties – and my brain, it processes differently. I fundamentally see the world, time, and space differently. I can see the past and present in a different way. And not just behind us. Like I said, it's like I'm on the canvas of space and time, with one side-step to hundreds of years in the future. To the time of my death," he said. Thomas stood up, a solemn expression taking over his previously pleading face.

"At my death, you stand above me pronouncing yourself as the Pinnacle of Evolution. I'm not the only one in your wake. I've seen the billions who died along the way."

Thomas was silent, staring at his friend.

"I understand that is a lot, my friend," Dr. Abrams said.

"A lot? A LOT?" Thomas broke his solemn expression and began laughing uncontrollably. "Okay, we're not doing this. I know we've discussed the merits of pleading insanity on the witness stand, but you can't talk nonsense and blame it on the drug just because you don't want the trials to move forward."

"That's not the case," David replied.

"Then what is the case?" Thomas said sharply, throwing up his hands and stopping his laughter. "You've always taken the high ground. Here's the facts: A TRILLION-dollar drug of your creation is staring us in the face and you're scared to move forward because of bad dreams. Money isn't a bad thing, David! I've ignored this far too long. You could have been anything you wanted—a neurosurgeon, a top researcher—but NO, you went the route of optometrist. Are you kidding? Sure, great hours, I get that, but the eyes? Saying no to this drug is you self-sabotaging yourself all over again!"

"And I see now why I chose my path," David said.

"I can't even tell if you're joking anymore. David, help me here, because I don't want to take the next step without you."

"But, Thomas, you already have," he replied.

"What's that supposed to mean?"

"I've seen it, when you enact the clause that removes me from this venture. I know the contacts, Thomas."

"How dare you..." Thomas's frustration boiled as his face turned rad. "How dare you..."

"You've already written the contracts. You have the votes, and it'll paint a better picture in the media once I'm out of it. Then, you'll use your influence to wipe out my office and family completely. Internet records, school records; you'll ensure that my name is stricken from history."

Thomas stood straight up. With his chest out, he leaned over and closed the gap to David, challenging him.

"So why not stop me, then? Huh? If you're so smart and see it all now, stop me. Prevent it all."

"The world is confused." David stood his ground and matched Thomas's posture. "And unfortunately, they want the death you bring. Who am I if I take away their choice? Who am I if I force them to act as they should? Ruthless oversight is not the way."

The two stood, staring into each other's eyes. It would be the last time they met face-to-face for over four hundred years.

"Your walls are so high, so mighty. You think you're better than everyone, but you're not. Your high and mighty walls will crumble, and like the walls of Jericho, you'll come crumbling down," Thomas said.

"And you will be the one to kill me," David said as a tear trickled down his steeled face as Thomas scoffed.

"Good-bye, old friend," David said. He pulled out the IV and left the lab.

Thomas Thornhill picked up his phone.

"Do it. Remove him," he said. "Yes. I'm sure," he confirmed.

As he lowered the phone and ended the call, he looked back at the door that David Abrams recently left, then his face turned red as it scrunched up with rage. He slammed his fist onto a nearby table. The thick slab of wood snapped in two under Thomas's extraordinary strength.

Kaden heard the wood rattle on the smooth tile floor. It gradually faded away as Jericho took his hand off of his head. They were back in the pastures.

Chapter 34

Kira

Her heart pounded as she crouched in the narrow passageway, her ears straining for any sound of pursuit. The damp air clung to her skin, carrying the musty scent of earth and decay. She'd been in these tunnels countless times before, but never with such urgency, never with the weight of so many lives on her shoulders.

She allowed herself a moment to catch her breath, leaning against the rough wall. The cool stone grounded her, reminding her of why she had joined. The Lighthouse Remnant might be hunted, and reeling from nearly thirty of their best members now missing, likely dead or worse, consumed, but they were far from broken. Only her trio made it through to raid the pastures, yet thankfully, the charges were more than enough to cause extensive damage to The Tower.

A faint scratching sound echoed through the tunnel, and Kira tensed. Three quick taps, then two slow ones. The signal. She responded with the counter-rhythm: two quick, one slow, three quick. A figure emerged from the shadows, and Kira relaxed as she recognized Elba's familiar silhouette.

"We need to move," he whispered, his voice barely audible. "The patrols are getting closer to the eastern entrance."

Kira nodded, falling into step behind him as they navigated the maze-like passages. The tunnels were a marvel, a hidden network of old sewers that honeycombed the foundation of Empyrean. Some were ancient, remnants of the city's early days. Others were more recent, painstakingly carved out by the Remnant over years of secret work.

As they moved deeper into the network, the air grew warmer, tinged with the scent of bodies and cooking fires. They were approaching one of the larger caverns, a makeshift refuge for those fleeing The Tower's increasingly brutal crackdowns.

The narrow passage opened up into a vast underground chamber. Kira blinked, her eyes adjusting to the warm glow of strategically placed lanterns. The cavern buzzed with quiet activity. In one corner, a group huddled around a map, their hushed voices barely carrying across the space. Children played a silent game with pebbles, their faces a mix of concentration and suppressed excitement. They were brought up to never shout with enjoyment. Talking was allowed, as long as it was controlled.

Elba moved forward, looking over the groups.

"Kira," a voice called out, and she turned to see Riggs, a burly man with a bushy black beard and broad upper body, waving her over. His usual aggressive demeanor was tempered by exhaustion, dark circles prominent under his eyes.

"What's the situation?" Kira asked as she approached.

Riggs ran a hand through his unkempt hair. It was nearly as bushy as his beard, but it turned wavy with length. "It's dung. The 'lites are back in the Outer Ring, along with daily 'gents. They're..." He swallowed. "...consuming our folks left 'n right, trying to find us."

Her stomach churned at the thought. She'd seen the aftermath of Elite "interrogations" before, a pile of empty clothes left behind, drained of body, soul, and knowledge with shattered families and friends in the wake.

"How many have we lost?"

"Too many," Riggs growled. "And ain't over. More 'gents promoted every day. They've filled the Rings with dem bloody electric poppers. And one of them…" He hesitated, his eyes finding hers.

"What?" Kira pressed, though she already knew, deep down, what he was going to say.

"Kaden's a Blue now. He's on patrol," he said.

The words hit Kira like a physical blow. She'd known Kaden had joined The Tower, and had seen him during the attack on the pastures. But to hear he was actively hunting them, hunting her… It made it all too real.

"The council, at least those left, are talking about moving the group," Elba said as he jogged back to her, his voice low and urgent. "The Agents are getting close to the eastern entrance. Each day, there's more."

"We just moved," Kira said.

"Because they ate most o' leadership," Riggs said. "Only a matter of time before they eat the smarts on this place."

Kira nodded, pushing her personal turmoil aside. "Yeah… How quickly can we evacuate?"

"An hour, bit less," Riggs replied. "But we're runnin' out of safety. Our folks they *took*…" He cringed, thinking of his friends consumed. "Our folks knew where we'd go. Dem 'lites will piece it together."

"I heard of a northern chamber," Elba said.

"And I heard the walls there are as weak as a 'gents' morals," Riggs snapped.

The two looked at Kira as her mind raced, considering and discarding options. Then, an idea surfaced.

"We're in the old sewers, what about the new ones?" she said, the plan forming as she spoke. "Near the western wall, not far from here, is a pump station. Remember, we used to stash food there as kids. The tunnels there run deep."

Elba's eyes widened in recognition. "That could work. The depth would make it harder for the Elites to smell us, plus, well, the other smells would cover it up."

"I'd rather not go down the giant toilet tubes, brah," Enak interjected as he walked up behind Elba and slapped his shoulder.

Riggs ignored Enak's entrance as he thought. Then he nodded slowly, a glimmer of hope in his eyes. "We ain't been there, it's still maintained. A risk, but... I like it. Our best shot."

"You think the council will go for it?" Kira asked.

"Lady, you're the only survivor of the raid. Your idea, dey be in," Riggs said. "I'll spread the word."

Kira let out a deep breath. Everyone in the Remnant looked at her differently when hers was the only group that returned.

"Hey, we brought containers back too," Enak said.

"Good for you." Riggs patted his shoulder like a father encouraging a toddler.

As Riggs moved away, barking quiet orders to the gathered refugees, Kira turned to Elba. "We need to secure the route. Can you gather a small team? We'll scout ahead, make sure the path is clear."

Elba nodded, disappearing into the crowd. Kira took a moment to survey the cavern, watching as people hurriedly packed what few possessions they had. Her heart ached for them – for the children who should be playing in the sun, for the elderly who deserved peace in their final days.

Within minutes, Elba returned with a small group – Alister, a council member and fellow EMR worker, and two others Kira recognized. They were all grim-faced but determined.

"Alister, it's an honor," Kira said.

"No, the honor is all mine, young lady," the older man said. His balding head reflected the light of a nearby fire. "Please, lead the way."

She nodded. "Let's move," she said, leading them toward one of the smaller tunnels branching off from the main cavern. As they entered the passageway, the sounds of the refugees faded, replaced by the soft echo of their footsteps and the occasional drip of water.

They moved swiftly but cautiously, every sense alert for signs of danger. The tunnels twisted and turned, occasionally opening into smaller chambers or intersecting with other passages. Her mental map from years of hiding in the sewers with Kaden as kids was as clear as if it were etched behind her eyelids. She moved efficiently and graceful, like a spider up a dry spout.

As they approached a junction, Alister held up a hand, signaling for silence. They froze, straining to hear. For a moment, there was nothing but the sound of their own breathing. Then, faintly, the echo of voices.

Kira's blood ran cold. She recognized one of the voices.

She gestured frantically, urging the group back the way they had come. They retreated silently, ducking into a small alcove just as the voices grew louder.

"Good riddance. That's what we're here for, to keep this place in line; otherwise, we have what? Look past the walls," a male voice sounded up.

"I'm not disagreeing, but I mean, come on, can't they learn something without having to kill the person?" a different male said.

"You go tell the Elites how to interrogate," a female said.

The group crouched silently with slow, steady breathing.

"Come on, let's do a quick lap and then back to The Tower. Split up and meet back here," one more male said.

Kira's heart jumped. She knew that voice. Instinctively, she looked toward Elba and Enak. Based on their wide eyes, they recognized the person too.

A moment later, they heard footsteps shuffle away. Alister looked out and then quickly flicked his hand, the group followed, rushing out of the tunnel and through a broken down brick building. They sprinted across the street and around a corner where Kira pulled up a manhole cover. The group slid through, scurrying down and out of sight.

"Hey!" she heard from behind. It was him. He'd seen her.

Dread filled her body and she slowly turned, unsure if she could face Kaden. But to her surprise, he wasn't looking at her; he was at a doorway a mere ten feet away, peering inside.

"Hey!" he called into the doorway again.

She was a statue, holding the manhole cover and trying not to breathe, praying her muscles didn't twitch under the ninety-pound load. A moment later, Kaden ran into the door and Kira slowly let down the cover. The group continued on through the darkness.

Chapter 35

K aden stammered, nearly falling backward as the vision from Jericho ended. He felt like the past and present were intertwining in a dizzying dance. Yet, Jericho's gray eyes held a mixture of compassion and wisdom, steadying Kaden when he looked at the man. He smiled gently, reminiscent of a teacher about to impart an important lesson. "Tell me, Mr. McCloud, have you seen a farmer sow his field?"

Kaden blinked, caught off guard by the seemingly unrelated question. "I... Well, no. There are no farms in Empyrean, just these pastures."

Jericho nodded, his expression thoughtful. "Imagine a man who goes out to sow his seed. As he scatters it across the field, some fall on the path and are quickly eaten by birds. Some fall on rocky ground, where it springs up quickly but withers under the hot sun because of shallow roots. Other seeds fell among thorns, which choke the plants as they grow. Finally, some seed falls on good soil, where it produces a crop a hundred times what was sown."

Kaden's brow furrowed. "What does this have to do with what I saw? With Dr. Thornhill and Dr. Abrams?"

"The seed, Kaden, is knowledge – truth. The vision you saw is like that seed, scattered across the field of your mind," Jericho explained patiently. "Some of it may be lost, some may take root briefly, only to wither away, and some may be choked out by doubts and fears. But if you nurture the truth that falls on good soil within you, it will grow and flourish, yielding a harvest of understanding beyond measure."

Kaden pondered this for a moment, trying to grasp the deeper meaning. "And Dr. Thornhill... is he the bird? The thorns?"

Jericho's eyes sparkled with approval. "Even thorns were once seeds themselves. The question is, what kind of soil will you be, Kaden?"

Before Kaden could respond, Jericho held up a hand and his eyes looked past Kaden. "You have a choice, Kaden. Will you speak truth or keep it hidden?"

Kaden's mind went to Kira as the explosions raged around him. Protecting her was the most natural thing he could do, that felt like "truth." However, lying to his teacher, that certainly wasn't speaking the truth.

Then, as if on cue, voices behind him rose up. Kaden's heart raced as he recognized Ron-ell's authoritative tone, accompanied by the low, menacing growls of a pair of Elites. A depressive sense permeated through the air around them.

Kaden turned back to Jericho, a question on his lips, but he'd vanished. One moment, he was there, solid and real; the next, he was simply... gone. Kaden blinked in disbelief, wondering if he had imagined the entire encounter.

"Agent Kaden!" Ron-ell's voice boomed across the pasture. "WHAT are you doing down here?"

Kaden spun around to face his superior, his mind scrambling for an explanation. Ron-ell stood at the edge of the clearing, flanked by two imposing Elites. Their charcoal skin seemed to absorb the artificial light, their deep black eyes gleaming with predatory intensity.

"Teacher." Kaden snapped to attention, forcing his voice to remain steady. "I was investigating a disturbance. I thought I saw movement in a doorway, then a staircase. It led me here."

Ron-ell's eyes narrowed suspiciously. "And how exactly did you get down here? These areas are restricted, the entrances barred and sealed since the recent attack."

Kaden's mind raced, Jericho's parable echoing in his thoughts. What kind of soil would he be? "This chamber and staircase, totally unlocked. We were about to report back when I followed this path. It was suspicious."

"Yes, it certainly is," Ron-ell commented.

One of the Elites stepped forward, its nostrils flaring as it sniffed the air. A look of confusion, and something that Kaden hadn't ever seen on an Elite. A sort of look that resembled fear passed across the charred face. The deep growl slid into a hiss.

The other Elite moved closer to Kaden, its black eyes boring into him. The demon remained silent as its sniffs invisibly pulled on his chest.

Kaden's heart hammered away like a jackhammer, but he forced himself to meet the Elite's gaze.

Ron-ell looked between Kaden and the Elites, his expression a mixture of suspicion and frustration. "You say you saw movement? Describe it."

Kaden hesitated for a moment, Jericho's words about truth and seeds echoing in his mind. He made a split-second decision. "I think it was just a shadow, Teacher. I found nothing."

"Hmmm," Ron-ell sounded.

"The lighting in those stairwells play tricks on your eyes. Nothing like a nice bright elevator," Kaden tried to joke.

Ron-ell stared at him blankly, then studied him for a long moment, unsatisfied with the attempted humor. Finally, he spoke, his voice tight with barely contained anger. "Return to your post immediately, Agent

Kaden. A good leader doesn't abandon his team. If your group is still on patrol, then they still need their captain."

"Yes, Teacher," Kaden replied, relief washing over him. He turned to leave, but Ron-ell's voice stopped him.

"And, Kaden? It's a vertical lift!"

Kaden forced himself to hold a straight face, but underneath, relief washed over him. As he made his way back to the maintenance shaft, he could feel the Elites' eyes on him, their unsettling gaze seeming to pierce his soul.

Once he was out of sight, Kaden leaned against the cool concrete wall of the shaft, his mind whirling. The vision Jericho had shown him, the strange parable, the Elites' reaction to the lingering scent – it all swirled together in his mind.

He thought back to Jericho's words about the farmer sowing seeds. What kind of soil would he be?

CHAPTER 36

Entry #6

As the war escalates and the world finds out how many nuclear weapons are actually housed across the globe, winds
will pull the clouds toward the equator and the globe will
warm. Desert landscapes will grow, taking over all the arid
land of modern society, but there is a silver lining. The
higher levels of carbon dioxide will ignite an explosion of
plant life, which in turn will clean the atmosphere. It will
still be centuries before humans can safely venture south,
but until then, we'll have the great Northern territories
and clean air, well, relatively clean air.

We've found the locations, and they all have geothermal
potential. Whether springs or caverns or just pockets of

warmth, the locations will have incredible potential underground. The subterrain will provide the foundation to new life and society above.

We've scouted many locations already. Crews are en route to start excavation, but first, the Lighthouse. He's there, planning his own version of survival. I'll use it as an example to unite our people. We all must live in harmony, but only I know the extent to which he cannot be trusted. He sees the lighthouse as a beacon of hope to all the surrounding cities. He knows that all global communications are likely to fail. If the warheads go off and cover the globe, we'll be sent back to a technological dark age. We'll save what we can and make our own beacon of hope. A tower to rise into the heavens. A symbol of hope, of remembrance, that will unite the people as we rebuild a fallen world.

Chapter 37

Kaden trudged back up, the dark, metal staircase taking him twice as long as it did for him to descend. The unforgiving metal and concrete of the confined stairwell caught his head twice. He felt lumps forming on the top of his head when he finally reached the top. The streets were empty as he retraced his steps back to the last spot where the group met. No one.

He did one more loop, wondering how much time the vision and climbing the staircase spent. The overcast clouds seemed exactly the same during daylight hours, but the air was growing crisper and days shorter in the recent weeks. Winter was approaching, and based on the location of the sun, Kaden supposed Empyrean was someone high in the Northern Hemisphere.

Kaden walked through the Outer Ring and back into the Inner Ring section, taking wide swaths through the alleyways, hoping to find someone from his group.

Soon, he caught the glimpse of a blue robe and ran to catch up.

He turned the corner and ran into the back of the Agent.

The man spun, snapping his Spark Club to the ready and holding it inches from Kaden's face. Kaden reacted by pulling his club, but the other man's draw was quicker. The electrified ball popped as strings of white hot electrons rolled across the surface, like a plasma ball waiting for a human's touch to focus its power. The mace pointed at Kaden's face, six inches away, while his own club was barely out of its sheath.

"Jay?" Kaden asked, recognizing the man.

Jay lowered his club. "What are you doing out here?"

"Got separated from my group. Keeping an eye out as I head back," Kaden said.

"You're hours overdue. Halfway through our patrol," Jay replied.

Kaden nodded, resolving to head straight back to The Tower.

"Aren't you the group lead?" Jay asked.

"Yes."

"Yeah, you've been here a whole five minutes, makes sense. Now it's moving too fast for you. Who would have thought," Jay said, his voice laced with sarcasm.

"Have *you* ever seen the outer stairwells that lead to the pastures?" Kaden fired back.

"They don't exist," Jay scoffed.

"I just went down one. So, I'm pretty sure they do," Kaden fired back.

"Your shift's over." Jay turned away. Kaden watched him leave and then turned back and continued his walk back to The Tower.

He walked through most of the Inner Ring and then stopped as the same depressive feeling he felt when the Elites were around overtook him. It was like a thick humidity that pressed down on him, stealing all feelings of joy.

Then, something hit him. It simultaneously grabbed his throat and midsection and slammed him against a wall.

He felt like he had been hit by a truck. He tried moving, but was pinned against the wall. His limbs stretched out, his feet off the ground.

The body came from the corner of his eye, moving so smoothly that it levitated more than walked. The charcoal dead face slid right in front of him. Its cracked, rock-like skin like dry ice, he could feel the lifeless cold emanate off it as the thing studied him from only inches away.

It sniffed and Kaden felt his skin pull, like it was being stretched away from his body.

"You," it growled, and Kaden recognized the thing, the same Elite who first found him outside the EMR.

"Me," Kaden replied, gritting his teeth.

"The smell is on you," it said, sniffing again.

Kaden felt his rib cage bend unnaturally toward the creature. His throat and waist were pinned against the concrete wall as his chest was being pulled out. Like a pencil being bent, ready to snap, he thought his sternum would break out of his body at any moment.

"Hold," a female's voice rang out. Beth-ell came into view, a second Elite at her side.

"Smell of lighthouse," the thing growled.

"Hmm." She turned her head to Kaden, interested.

The Elite at her side sniffed, and Kaden's neck wrenched as his head jerked toward the demon.

"Different," it growled, a rasp of a sound.

"Different, eh? He did rise up quickly," she said, her wrinkled face now next to the original Elite who still invisibly pinned Kaden to the wall.

Beth-ell's eyes narrowed as she studied Kaden, her wrinkled face a mask of calm authority that exuded confidence. "Release him," she commanded the Elite.

The creature hesitated, its black eyes boring into Kaden with predatory intensity.

"I said–" Beth-ell began to repeat, when the Elite relented.

Kaden felt the invisible force dissipate, and he slumped against the wall, gasping for air. His ribs ached where they had been unnaturally bent.

Beth-ell turned to the Elites. "Leave us. Patrol the Outer Ring."

The creatures backed away, their movements unnaturally fluid. Beth-ell watched them go, her stern expression an unmoving rock.

"Walk with me, Agent," she said, not waiting for a response as she strode down the alley.

Kaden fell into step beside her, still flexing his chest from the unnatural bending.

"You've risen quickly through the ranks," Beth-ell remarked, her tone neutral. "Ron-ell speaks highly of your potential."

"Thank you," Kaden replied cautiously. "I'm just trying to do what's right for Empyrean."

Beth-ell's laugh was dry and humorless. "Are you? Tell me, young Agent, what do you think of our Elites?"

Kaden hesitated, weighing his words carefully. "They're... formidable, and certainly maintain order."

"A diplomatic answer," Beth-ell said. "But not honest."

They turned a corner, entering a small courtyard. Beth-ell sat on a crumbling stone bench, gesturing for Kaden to join her.

"Do you know why I never became an Elite, Kaden?" she asked.

He shook his head, not admitting what he'd heard from his group and surprised by the personal nature of the question.

"I have served Pinnacle longer than I can believe, and when I took the promotion, something happened. My body took it, but not my mind." Her eyes took on a distant look. "Now, long after, I can see what the transformation does. It doesn't just change the body; it warps the mind, the very soul. Did you know that half of all Brown Agents who accept the promotion for Elite status don't make it?"

Kaden remained silent, sensing there was more to come.

"But the power is too much to ignore. I can see it in other Agents' eyes; they crave it. Your teacher, he'd sell each of you, no questions asked, for a chance at Elite."

She turned and studied him. "But you. You have a different, what did they say, *smell* about you. The Elites are tools, Kaden. Powerful tools, yes, but tools nonetheless. And tools can be... unreliable." She turned to face him directly. "Pinnacle's vision for Empyrean is grand, yet still functional. He's as practical as I've seen 'em come. The Elites... they're a means to an end, not the end itself."

"Then why work with them at all? I'm sure you've heard of their *tactics*."

"I've more than heard. I've commanded it." She smiled a sinister smile. "But Pinnacle wills it. And Pinnacle's will is absolute." She leaned in closer. "But loyalty to Pinnacle doesn't mean blind obedience to every aspect of The Tower's structure. Do you understand?"

Kaden nodded slowly, but had no idea where she was going.

"Good," Beth-ell said. "Now, let me pose a scenario to you, Agent Kaden. Say you discovered a group of citizens in the Outer Ring hoarding food and resources. You have on good information that they stole it, directly violating The Tower's laws. What do you do?"

Kaden's thoughts immediately went to Kira, and he forced himself to keep his expression neutral. "I would discuss it with my teacher," he said carefully.

Beth-ell's eyes glinted. "A safe answer. But what if I told you that group included children? Starving children? And that you must act now or they'll move and be lost."

Kaden felt a cold sweat break out on his forehead. "Hoarding resources leads to chaos. We are trying to instill control for the betterment of all. Stealing... is a threat to all of Empyrean," he said with a voice that lacked confidence.

"Indeed it is," Beth-ell agreed. "But can't an Agent enforce laws at their discretion?"

She stood abruptly, not giving him a chance to answer, and began pacing the small courtyard. "The Outer Ring is seething with discontent, Kaden. The recent attack on the pastures is just the beginning. Every generation, similar actions play out, yet the Elites would have us purge entire sections, root out any hint of rebellion with brute force and consume them to gather intelligence."

"And you disagree?" Kaden asked.

"I disagree with their shortsightedness," Beth-ell snapped. "Pinnacle's vision is for a stable, prosperous Empyrean. That can't be achieved if we slaughter half the population. If the Elites are so strong, then why do they react so swiftly? It's like their actions are out of paranoia." She turned back to Kaden, her gaze intense. "We need Agents who can *think*, Agent Kaden, who can see the bigger picture, who understand that true loyalty sometimes requires creative interpretations of orders."

Kaden's mind raced. Was this a test? A trap? Or was Beth-ell genuinely confiding in him?

"Are you asking me to do something?" he asked.

Beth-ell's smile was enigmatic. "For now? No. Continue your duties. But watch. Listen. Difficult choices are a sign of greatness, Agent."

Chapter 38

Kira

Kira's fingers twitched as she made her way through the winding tunnels. The acrid smell of smoke still clung to her clothes, a slowly fading reminder of the recent raid on the pastures. Days had passed and the common pleasantries she'd cherished from her apartment, like running water and a warm bed, raised doubts of her commitment like a seed germinating.

She put the smell, and doubt, out of her mind as she approached the main cavern. Her keen eyes darted around, taking in every detail. The low murmur of voices, the makeshift shelters, the worried faces.

The crowd parted as she neared the center, where Elba and Enak were distributing food from the last of the stolen containers.

"Kira." Elba nodded, his usually cheerful face etched with concern. "We're trying to make it all stretch, but..."

"What about the northern tunnels? We haven't fully explored them yet. There could be more resources, maybe even a way to grow our own food. The pastures were growing real plants," she said.

Elba blinked, caught off guard by her sudden shift. "Kira, we can barely keep everyone fed as it is. We don't have the manpower for exploration right now. And we have to return to our Inner Ring work soon too. Barb can't cover for us indefinitely."

She opened her mouth to argue, but a commotion erupted nearby. Two men were shouting, their voices echoing off the cavern walls.

"There's others starving up there!" one man shouting while pointing toward the ceiling.

"We did what we had to do!" the other man shot back. "Or would you rather we all die down here?"

Kira moved swiftly, inserting herself between the two men. "This isn't helping anyone. We can't bring it up. The Elites are seeing to that, so ration it here," she said as her eyes went to the ground.

The first man, Tomas, glared at her. "People in the Outer Ring are suffering even more now because of what we did! That's not why I joined."

Kira felt a sinking feeling run through her. "They are..." she said softly and walked out of the center of the two men.

Before anyone could respond, an older woman stepped forward. Barb, one of the few remaining council members and the manager of the Empyrean Mechanix Retreat, placed a scarred hand on Tomas' arm. "Come," she said firmly, giving his arm a pull.

The woman's eyes caught Kira's. "Council meeting, now," the elder said.

Within the hour, Kira found herself seated in a small chamber, surrounded by the remaining members of the Lighthouse Remnant's leadership: Barb, Riggs, and Alister.

Enak, Elba, and Tomas stood around the center three, next to Kira.

"We should never have attacked the pastures," Barb growled.

Kira leaned forward, her eyes bright with determination. "No, it was exactly what we needed to do. We can't control how they'll respond, but we showed they're not invincible. That's our advantage now."

"Advantage?" Barb replied, with more gravel in her voice. "We're barely surviving, Kira. We've lost more than half of the council and three containers only go so far. We needed twenty to make this work. Twenty!"

She felt a flare of frustration, but pushed it down. "We can't back down now. The Remnant is all that stands between The Tower and total control. We need to act, and act quickly."

Barb raised her hands and leaned forward as if clearing the air of the prior conversation. "Perhaps it's time we remember why we fight. The young ones – they don't know the true history of the Lighthouse. They don't know of Jericho."

Kira's ears perked up at the mention of Jericho. Here was a mystery she'd been itching to unravel since childhood.

As Barb recounted the tale of Jericho's creation of the Lighthouse, Kira's mind whirred with possibilities. When the story concluded, she stood abruptly, unable to contain her excitement.

"Don't you see? This is exactly what we need! They believed He died out there with all those Elites they sent for him. He was the one light in the darkness of a barren world, but HE defeated the Elites, to undermine The Tower's control and show us what is possible. And now, he's here. He walks among us! I've seen him."

"Kira," Elba said gently, "I'm sorry, but no one else has."

She spun to face him, her eyes blazing. "Kaden has."

"And Kaden made his choice!" Enak snapped from his brother's side.

The council members exchanged wary glances, but Kira's mind raced.

"We use what we have – knowledge. We start teaching people, helping them become self-sufficient. And while we're doing that, we search for Jericho's secrets," Kira said.

"I like the optimism, but what of the Elites, and the Agents? They patrol more now than ever?" Alister asked.

"Exactly!" Kira grinned, the thrill of the challenge evident in her voice. "Every successful conversation will give more hope than we could have ever dreamed."

Alister smiled, but he remained silent. Meanwhile, Barb scowled.

"And how do you suggest we start?" Barb asked her.

"We could begin by asking anyone who appears to be suffering if they'd be interested in a new way, a new hope in Jericho?" Kira said.

"Everyone is suffering," Barb replied, unimpressed.

Kira smiled in agreement, and Barb didn't appreciate it.

"I must get back," Barb said, "and I suggest you two do the same. Tomorrow's quota waits for no one."

As the meeting concluded, Barb walked up next to Kira.

"He's out there. You can tell the world, or what's left of it, but we've tried that before. They miss him every time. He's right in their face, and they miss him, every... single... time."

Barb left, with Enak and Elba saying good-bye to Kira and following Barb. Kira watched them go, fading into the dark of the old sewer system's tunnel.

"Miss Kira! Miss Kira!" a small voice called out, interrupting her thoughts.

She turned to see Celia, a young girl, running toward her with wide eyes.

"Hey, baby girl, what is it?" Kira asked, kneeling down.

"I heard noises. Down in the lower tunnels. Like... like singing, but not like any singing I've ever heard before," Celia said.

Kira looked at her, confused. "Singing?"

"Yeah!" She jumped with exuberance.

"Show me," she said, and took the young girl's hand.

They walked through the area Celia was playing in, away from the adults, and they descended deeper into the tunnel system. The air grew colder, damper, but she barely noticed, her mind focused solely on the mystery ahead. Meanwhile, Celia rubbed her own arms as the cold set in.

When they reached the dead end, Kira's eyes narrowed, studying every inch of the wall. She noticed the faint shimmer almost immediately. Like two gray eyes peering back at her, a reflection of herself, but not her.

"Celia, go find Alister. Tell him to come here right away," she said, her voice distracted as she reached out to touch the wall.

The moment Celia was out of sight, Kira stepped closer to the wall. The barrier shifted away and a chamber beyond revealed itself. It was unlike anything she'd ever seen, filled with swirling lights. In the center, He stood.

Their eyes met and Empyrean's past, The Tower's rise, and Jericho's stand against the Elites in the darkness of the desert, the myth of the Lighthouse Remnant all flooded her mind. When it ended, she found herself kneeling and staring up at Him from across the room.

She barely registered Alister's voice calling her name from beyond the wall. She called to him, but he didn't seem to hear, as if she were miles away.

She stood up and stepped back, Kira's eyes gleamed with determination and excitement. She had no idea what power she saw or what consequences it might bring. But one thing was certain – the real investigation, the true fight for Empyrean's future, was only just beginning. She'd seen the past, through Jericho's eyes, and now she was more confident than ever.

She stepped back, and turned to see Alister. He jumped as if she came from thin air.

"Let me tell you what He showed me," she said.

Alister's eyes widened.

Chapter 39

Kaden

The class entered their weekly review with Ron-ell. The once daily classroom lectures were now weekly given their promotions, and each new Blue Agent would soon be given a series of recruits to train.

"What better way to learn of leadership and The Tower's glory than to teach it," Ron-ell told them.

Their classroom material ended and each Agent was to go find their new Whites, but Ron-ell held Kaden back.

"Teacher?" Kaden asked.

"Not you. You're being requested elsewhere." Ron-ell eyes went to the ceiling.

"No?" Kaden asked.

The man nodded. "The senior council has asked for your presence." Ron-ell led him up the stairs until his legs burned, and still they climbed.

At the top, Ron-ell's stern face tried to hide his fatigue, but the deep breaths through his nostrils gave him away.

"What is this all about?" Kaden asked.

"Your first question might be better phrased as thankfulness," Ron-ell snapped.

"Have you ever been asked to see them?" Kaden asked.

Ron-ell ignored him, a bitter look on his face, and Kaden understood the impatient snap in his teacher's tone. Ron-ell was jealous.

"I'll keep you updated," Kaden said as he turned toward the large archway that was carved into the hallway.

"Be sure you do," Ron-ell said.

They came to the door and the depressed feeling he'd come to associate with the Elites overwhelmed him. Ron-ell eyed him, motioning to the doors. He tried to shake the feeling, but he stumbled, dragging his feet under the invisible weight around him. He was used to the feeling of two Elites, but this felt like hundreds, like the weight of the world was on his shoulders and pressing down, anxious to see him crumble. Then all of a sudden, it was gone. He shook off the weird sensation as Ron-ell impatiently waited.

He moved toward the large archway and pushed open the doors, expecting to see a long table filled with the highest-ranking Agents, but instead, he saw only one person sitting in the corner of a massive, and beautifully designed, ballroom space. The walls and ceilings were an incredible work of art. The carved marble columns that rose around the circular room extended up to meet at the center of a huge dome structure. Colorful flowers of marble adorned the walls and the dome ceiling was painted with branches and vines. The greenery gave a warm and vibrant feeling to the otherwise cold, yet exquisite marble structure. The whole grand ballroom was like a garden, redesigned by a master artist of the renaissance and carved from a mountain of marble. Even leaves on the flowers were carved into the walls.

"Hello, McCloud," Beth-ell said from across the ballroom. "I'm sorry to remove you from meeting your recruits, but we felt the time was right."

"It didn't take long for you to call on me," Kaden said.

"Your usefulness is becoming apparent, and He insisted," she said.

"He?" Kaden asked and the room immediately felt smaller. Once again, he could feel the pressure of the air around him similar to the depressive sense the Elites gave off but magnified immensely. Each molecule of air was like an invisible weight that compressed Kaden's physical being and stole energy from him.

"Agent McCloud, I'd like you to meet the ruler of the world and the most powerful being to ever exist, Pinnacle." She raised her arm and a door in the back of the ballroom smoothly opened.

"Hello, Mr. McCloud," he said as he seemed to glide across the floor. His wideset jaw and light brown hair were like a magnet for Kaden's eyes. Every other person in Empyrean had jet-black hair, but his was soft, brown, and wavy. His eyes were gray and bright, similar to Jericho's, but with more of a sparkle to them, like flecks of blue dotted them somewhere in the endless pools of gray ocean.

"I've heard so much about you," he said. His voice was firm and calm, yet powerful. It resonated through the air smoothly yet undeniably, like a slow motion sonic boom toned down for all to hear with ease.

"Hello, sir," Kaden said, bowing his head.

"Please, we built this place to help mankind, not to intimidate. Call me Pinnacle." He was now standing next to Beth-ell and Kaden wondered how he covered the length of the ballroom so quickly.

Pinnacle lifted his head, ever so slightly, and smelled the air. Kaden felt a gentle tug, like a flicker of magnetism toward the man. Pinnacle smiled as he looked down on Kaden, who was just above average height, but the ruler was at least six-six, maybe taller, with broad shoulders and a shiny black robe that wrapped a thick, muscular base.

Pinnacle was the only person he'd ever seen wear the black robe of an Elite, yet his skin was an olive Mediterranean tan-like tone.

"Tell me your story?" Pinnacle asked.

"The Outer Ring. Grew up to join the EMR, and this past year was set to be sorted, but Ronnoc, now Ron-ell, pulled me out and trained me," Kaden replied.

"Hmmm," Pinnacle hummed. "Why?"

"I don't know why, other than he said he saw greater things for me," Kaden said.

"Why do you persist? I mean, what is your purpose?" Pinnacle asked.

"I want to save my sister from poverty and corruption of the Outer Ring. I want a better life for my family," Kaden replied, speaking from the heart.

Pinnacle laughed. "It always amazes me the family ties that come from living quarters, even when bred from my blood."

"Bred?" Kaden's confused expression caught Pinnacle's eye.

"You're a rising Agent in The Tower. It's about time you know some secrets for how we maintain a just society. The first is population control. We control all births. Did you know that, centuries ago, women bore children? I know, weird. But now, we breed in vitro and ensure a healthy New Breed every generation. So in a way, no one is brother and sister as they imagine, but in a better, more enlightened way, all are brothers and sisters. My children."

Kaden remained silent, his past world as Darren smashing into this new world's reality like a comet the size of Texas.

"Your sister isn't really your sister any more than Beth-ell here is your sister, but regardless, you can think of me as your father." He smiled at him.

Pinnacle's smile faded, replaced by a look of stern contemplation. He began to pace the grand ballroom, his black robe flowing behind him like a shadow given form. Each step echoed off the marble walls, creating a rhythmic backdrop to his words. Beth-ell calmly watched the conversation.

"You've heard of Jericho, I assume," Pinnacle said, his gray eyes fixing on Kaden.

Kaden nodded, careful to keep his expression neutral. "Yes, the stories are told in the Outer Ring. A figure of hope, they say."

Pinnacle's laughter cut through the room. "Hope? Is that what they call it now? Let me tell you about the common man's precious *Jericho*. There's a truth that the whispers of the dark alleys conveniently forget."

He stopped pacing, turning to face Kaden fully. The weight of his gaze was almost physical, pressing down on Kaden like a tangible force.

"He's a coward who couldn't face the realities of our world. He spoke of rainbows and lollipops, of a perfect society where everyone held hands and sang songs. But do you know what happens to people who believe in fairy tales, Kaden? They die. They starve. They freeze in the wasteland beyond the walls and structure that keep us safe. Worst of all, they doom those foolish enough to follow them."

Pinnacle's voice grew louder, filling the vast space of the ballroom. "We were once colleagues, long ago, but he defected. He thought he could get around reality, and he eventually led his followers into the desert, promising them salvation. He steered them away from rock-solid foundations of medical practice as if their *belief alone* would make flowers bloom in the sand and water spring from barren rock. According to him, faith would heal all their troubles. But do you know what happened?"

He paused, letting the question hang in the air. Kaden felt compelled to answer, "They died?"

"Not just died but suffered immensely, and for what? They withered away under the merciless sun, their bodies consuming themselves as they waited for a miracle that never came. Mothers watched the light from their children's eyes fade with hunger. Fathers dug shallow graves in the unyielding earth with their bare hands. And where was Jericho? Where was their savior?"

Pinnacle's eyes flashed, a storm of emotion behind the gray pupils. "We sent envoys, countless groups of Elites who were built to withstand such devastating conditions, but nope, they wanted no part of salvation. He confused them, then abandoned them. Left them to rot in the wasteland while he ran back to the comfort of his lighthouse. I imagine his conscience finally caught up to him, couldn't bear to watch the consequences of his foolishness, so he turned his back on those who trusted him most."

Kaden felt a chill run down his spine. The story conflicted with everything he'd heard about Jericho, everything he'd seen and felt in the man's presence. But Pinnacle's words carried the weight of absolute conviction.

"But I..." Pinnacle continued, his voice softening, taking on an almost paternal tone. "I couldn't stand by and watch. I sent out search parties, more than Elites. We sent Agents. People risking their own lives, my own people, to save those misguided souls. We brought the survivors back, tragically not many, but some were not yet stepping on death's doorstep. And do you know what they told us?"

He stepped closer to Kaden, close enough that Kaden could see the flecks of silver in his eyes. "They told us of Jericho's lies. He filled their heads with dreams of a paradise that could never exist, and when those dreams crumbled to dust, he left them to face the consequences alone."

Pinnacle turned away, walking toward one of the ornate pillars that lined the ballroom. He ran his hand along the carved flowers, a gesture that seemed almost tender.

"This is the reality we live in, Kaden. A world where beauty must be carved from stone, where life must be protected by walls and rules. Jericho would have us tear down those walls, expose ourselves to the horrors beyond. He claims to fight for freedom, but his is a freedom leading to chaos, to death."

He turned back to Kaden, his expression grave. "The Lighthouse Remnant, those fools who still cling to Jericho's teachings, they're nothing but bitter ghosts. They rage against the very system that keeps them alive, all because they can't accept that their prophet was a fraud. They plant bombs, steal food, sow discontent among the people. And for what? For a dream that died in the desert along with Jericho's first followers. Like an adolescent eager to prove their worth, to show the world all they know, but tell me, were they there when this city was built? Were they there when the bodies of the envoys were lost? Or were they there to care for the stragglers on the brink of death we pulled from the desert?"

Kaden found himself nodding along, swept up in the tide of Pinnacle's words. But a small voice in the back of his mind whispered doubts, reminding him of the suffering he'd seen in the Outer Ring, of the brutal tactics of the Elites.

"Have you seen Jericho? Have you heard him call out?" Pinnacle eyed him with a sideways glance and Kaden's heart seemed to fall in his stomach. He didn't answer.

"Exactly, he's gone. He died out there running away from his mistake."

Blood seemed to flow back into his body as Pinnacle didn't force the question. Yet, the ruler of Empyrean seemed to sense his inner conflict. He approached Kaden again, placing a hand on his shoulder. The touch was warm, almost comforting, and Kaden felt the immense power contained within it like an electrical charge powering him up.

"I know it's not perfect, Kaden. I know there's suffering, inequalities, hardships. But we're fighting against the very entropy of our world. Every day, we hold back the tide of destruction, every child that grows up safe within our walls, every meal we put on a table – these are victories. Small, perhaps, but real. Tangible. And if we need to exert a little forcible control to avoid the death he caused in the desert, well..."

He squeezed Kaden's shoulder, his voice taking on an almost pleading tone. "Jericho offers pretty little lies. I offer harsh truths but give the strength to face them. He promises a paradise he can never deliver. I promise a future we can build together, brick by brick, sacrifice by sacrifice."

Pinnacle released Kaden and stepped back, his demeanor shifting once more to that of the ruler of Empyrean. "You've risen quickly through our ranks, Kaden. You've shown an aptitude, a strength that sets you apart. But you've also shown compassion, a desire to help others that reminds me of myself when I was younger."

He glanced at Beth-ell, who had remained silent throughout his speech. She nodded, a slight smile on her lined face.

"We believe you could be instrumental in rooting out the Lighthouse Remnant once and for all," Pinnacle continued. "Your background, your understanding of the Outer Ring, your relationships – these are invaluable to the average Agent. But more than that, your ability to empathize, to connect with people, could be the key to exposing the truth of Jericho and his false promises. We may need to crack a few eggs in order to save the entire batch, but we'll save them from repeating history's mistakes."

Kaden felt a sense of pride at this private conversation. His agreement came out before his mind had time to think. "How can I help?"

Pinnacle's smile returned, warm and encouraging. "For now? To listen. To learn. To see Empyrean for what it truly is – not a perfect utopia, but practical survival in a world that would see us extinct. And when the time comes, to stand with us against those who would tear down everything we've built."

He turned, gesturing toward the grand doors of the ballroom. "Go now. Return to your duties. Beth-ell will remain in contact when needed. Remember what I've told you. The next time you hear Jericho's name whispered like a prayer, remember the bodies in the desert. Remember the price of blind faith and empty promises."

As Kaden moved toward the exit, still reeling from the encounter, Pinnacle called out one last time. "And, Kaden, be mindful. The Remnant can poison even the strongest minds with their toxic, false hope. Don't let yourself be swayed by pretty little lies and impossible dreams. The Tower of Empyrean and its warriors must be rooted in truth. If we hold in truth, then the world will be for the common man, and the sounds of happiness will reach the deepest depths of the earth!" He glanced at Beth-ell and flashed a broad smile as he pumped his fists. "Oh, how can you not be roused by such a thought!"

The doors closed behind Kaden with a thud, leaving him alone in the corridor. His mind raced, trying to reconcile Pinnacle's words with everything he thought he knew about Jericho and the Lighthouse Remnant.

As he made his way back down through the levels of The Tower, Kaden replayed Pinnacle's speech in his mind. The vivid descriptions of suffering in the desert, the passion in Pinnacle's voice as he spoke of protecting humanity – it all felt so real, so convincing.

But then he thought of Kira, of the determination in her eyes when she spoke of the Remnant's cause. He remembered the harsh conditions in the Outer Ring, the brutal tactics of the Elites.

Chapter 40

Entry #7

Why did they think this would be a traditional war? Ground, sea, and air combat are like tribes throwing sticks to the technology we've created in the last fifty years. Biological warfare and AI-based attacks have remade the landscape of civilization, but still, we cannot forget about nuclear warheads. It was over before the first red button was pushed and sent the warhead filled rocket out of the surfaced submarine and into the most populated cities around the world.

Biological weapons poisoned natural resources, a scare tactic that only escalated each side. AI attacks destroyed servers across the globe, rendering communications and the internet useless. My contacts tell me that it was meant to seek out and eliminate private military servers. Eventually, the tech did its job, but it took too long infiltrating the separated servers that control the warhead launch.

I journal now on my own local network. There must be thousands of local networks around the world, but soon, nuclear winds will eliminate rural populations. Only a small portion of land will have a chance and we're on our way. The once frigid tundra of Northern Canada is now a moderate climate in the aftermath of our destruction of the Earth. My partner is rumored to be there already, providing safe haven to his followers.

The whole global catastrophe is rather unfortunate. The Hope Drug's rollout was a massive success before politicians and militaries got in the way, but nonetheless, the world begins anew near the Arctic Circle. I've learned so much and have refined the process and governing structure that it will effectively run itself. A perpetual motion machine of life, where the New Breed will usher in a new future. A future that won't allow such corruption and death. A future we control at all costs.

Chapter 41

"The Elites are slowing their interrogations," Ron-ell told Kaden before the next team patrol. "That means they've found what they've wanted... or are being called off. Only Pinnacle can call them off."

To Kaden's surprise, Ron-ell never asked him about his meeting with Pinnacle.

"Move to the Outer Ring, patrol the wall and look for any suspicious activity. The culprits of the lab attacks are still out there. Bring back intel, something freaking useful," Ron-ell said bitterly, anxious to please leadership.

Kaden and the team approached the Outer Ring without much discussion. But as soon as they crossed over, past the generally maintained buildings and into the crumbing decay, Jace erupted.

"Spill it! You met him!" Jace asked.

"I did," Kaden said softly.

"And?" Ryon insisted.

"He told me about Jericho," Kaden replied, and the group seemed to step back in their confusion.

"What? Why waste time on that?" Ryon added.

"What exactly did he ask of you?" Vala said in a direct and bitter tone. Ever since the promotion ceremony, she hadn't been the same, as if an anger boiled below the surface.

"He didn't ask anything," Kaden replied.

"He ALWAYS asks something," Vala snapped back.

Kaden shrugged.

"So, what about Jericho? Did he bring up the Lighthouse?" Jace asked.

"Yup, said Jericho led his people into the desert to die. He thinks Jericho abandoned them and died himself," Kaden said.

"I'm not sure I believe that," Aria said.

"And why not? Who's going to survive a GROUP OF ELITES coming for them?" Ryon fired back.

"It's just... it doesn't feel right. No way he's gone. Kaden, do you think he's gone?" Aria asked.

"I..." Kaden exhaled as he decided whether to speak the truth or not. "I don't think he's gone either," Kaden said as images of Jericho flooded his mind. From saving him as a child, the EMR, and recently, in the pastures.

"Good riddance to bad rubbish," Ryon said. "Everyone knows it's death outside of the walls."

"You don't know what it was like when this place was founded," Jace shot back.

"It was, what, hundreds of years ago? Nobody *really knows*," Ryon replied.

"Some might," Kaden said softly and the words hung in the air, stopping Jace and Ryon's back and forth.

"Outside of Pinnacle, who?" Ryon asked.

"Jericho. If he's more than a myth, then he's been here since the beginning," Kaden said.

"But he's dead, soooo there's that..." Vala said.

"Is he?" Kaden said, and the group could have all stepped back at once.

"Okay, we've had enough of special talk in our little family here, but let's get real. Aria, Kaden, don't talk like that anymore," Jace said.

Aria looked at him with a confused expression while Vala's angry expression shot at her.

"He's right. You better be careful what you say, Agent," Ryon said.

"Why is that so–" Kaden tried to get out.

"Kaden, shut it. I'm serious," Jace interrupted, shoving Kaden and staring him down.

"Fine," Kaden said, throwing his hands up. "Just thinking out loud here."

"Leaders don't talk, they lead," Ryon said firmly, then he walked past Kaden, knocking his shoulder into Kaden's. He felt like, in a split second, he went from leading the group to being a first-day recruit again.

Thirty minutes of silence and they still all walked toward the Outer Ring's walls. Jace fell back, keeping pace with Kaden.

"Do you know why our cohort had an opening?" Jace asked him, his voice low.

Kaden shook his head.

"Because the guy before you asked a lot of questions. Questions that Ron-ell didn't like answering. Like how was food rationed, where was it stored, and what happens to extra rations if they aren't used in The Tower. He was sent to the Outer Ring, a lone assignment we all get, but this was his second. He never came back."

"You think someone...?"

"What happened to you when you went out there wearing the white robe, without training or a club? Doesn't have to be plotted if you line up the situation. But regardless, look at the facts, all those questions about food and rations, and then a few months later, an attack on the labs?"

"Yeah," Kaden acknowledged his point.

"Jericho is dead. That's how The Tower sees it, and that's the way they want it to stay. So, that's how we see it."

Kaden nodded.

"He's dead. Keep it that way," Jace said, his expression as serious as Kaden had ever seen it.

The sun was high behind the overcast skies when they finally reached the wall.

"Three together on the wall, two more patrol a block in with a check-in every ten blocks," Kaden ordered. The group nodded and spread out.

Aria remained the closest to Kaden, both furthest from the wall, so they paired up and took the inner block. Jace, Ryon, and Vala quickly set off.

After they walked a while, Kaden struck up a conversation with Aria.

"You're from the Outer Ring, right?" he began.

"I am," she said, not continuing the conversation.

"Did you know your parents?"

"Does anyone?" she replied coldly, and Pinnacle's comments about breeding the next generation flared in his mind.

"Do you know what's up with Vala? She's been, well, she'd been extra Vala lately," Kaden asked.

"You were at the promotion. You tell me," Aria said, and he heard the same bitterness in her voice that made its home in Vala.

"What..." He thought back to the horribly uncomfortable changing portion of the ceremony. "The changing?" Kaden asked.

She lifted an eyebrow in response.

A few minutes later, she finally spoke up.

"Having to change in front of a room of people is one thing; as a woman, it's freaking awful. The undergarments are see-through and every single person in that room knows it. Yet, the ritual insists that promoted Agents face the group and change robes."

"I've never thought about it like—"

"And that's not the worst part. See, you men in The Tower take it for granted, until you get high enough. Then, it becomes your advantage," Aria said.

"Advantage? I've talked with Beth-ell; seems like she commands everyone around her outside of Pinnacle, male or female," Kaden asked.

"She's different, the exception that proves the rule, and look closer, she's as bad as any of the males. She only answers to Pinnacle and throws scraps to the others."

"So, what are you saying? After the promotion, women have it different?"

"I'm saying we're the scraps! Every Purple and Brown Agent in that place now has their eyes set on us. Thankfully, the Elites consume men and women alike. Never thought I'd say that, but here we are. You think Agents cooped up in The Tower aren't going to have urges?"

"I've never even thought about it. I'm sorry, Ar—"

"Yeah, no one has, unless you're a female. And Vala is so bitter because she knows they're coming for her first. We're both from the Outer Ring. Different parts, but same story. Cute girls in the slums are tradable goods, Kaden. If you don't get out..." She exhaled like she was done with the conversation but then kept going. "There's a reason she works so hard to rise up. She wants to wield the power before others use it on her. She'll get there. I promise you that. She's a lot stronger than I am..."

"I'm not so sure—"

"Don't patronize me. She's stronger and more driven. But if you saw the way they looked at her..." She shook her head. "They will go after her until they break her, until she submits, and everyone knows it. Even Beth-ell approves. She does it to keep the men in check, to keep control," Aria said.

"I won't allow it. Not to anyone on my team," Kaden said.

Aria laughed sarcastically. "Like you have a choice. What will happen when Ron-ell's superiors ask for a private session? Huh? Will you be there to stop it?"

"If I can, yes!" Kaden fired back.

"Sure." Aria dismissed it and the two walked in silence through the quiet streets.

The Elites interrogating and consuming swaths of people from the Outer Ring had taken its toll. The normally broken people were even more rundown, afraid to show their face to anyone from The Tower. It was like everyone knew their patrol was coming and had run away.

"Why don't you leave?" Kaden eventually asked.

"And go where? The Outer Ring? Try to become some job-holder in the Inner Ring? Leaving The Tower is just as much of a death sentence. At least I get a shot at a better life in The Tower."

"What about outside the walls? Has anyone ever gone out there besides the parties Pinnacles sent?" Kaden asked.

"No, and this is why nobody wanted to patrol with you."

"What? Why?"

"Because you talked earlier like you know HIM, when we all know he's dead. Look, I know it's a great story, and I'll admit hopeful, but it's a fairy tale. Those parties into the desert were generations ago, and who knows how exaggerated. Jericho is dead, he's a myth for all you care, so knock it off."

They patrolled in silence, every ten blocks moving toward the wall and waving to their three teammates, then coming back.

"I'm not sure what we'll expect to find out here," Aria said, kicking a piece of brick. It bounced toward an alleyway and settled, but a rumbling noise echoed through the walls. They stood, listening, and as the sound grew from a murmur, they heard the unmistakable sound of a chanting crowd.

"Rioters," Kaden said. A hand went to their Spark Clubs at their side as they moved toward the commotion.

Turning the corner, they didn't see a determined group of rioters, but two different factions at each other's throat. The chanting group was calling for the other, smaller group, to leave. And it seemed they were winning, but one woman was at the front of the group, holding a book, and preaching over the crowd.

"Go! Go! Go!" the crowd chanted in unison, but it bled into "No! No! No!" as the agitation grew.

"If you read it, if you thought about it, you'd know the truth," she called back.

Kaden and Aria approached, but he stopped in his tracks when he saw the frustrated woman turn from the crowd.

Kira.

She didn't see him. When Aria moved toward the group, he quickly followed. A few of the group caught a glimpse of them and quickly informed the others. Soon the chanting and arguments were over, with both sides skeptically watching the Agents, ready to retreat.

"What's going on here?" Aria called out, but it only accelerated their departure. She exhaled. "Like bugs when the light comes on," she said. But Kaden didn't hear her. He was watching Kira and she was watching him. They locked eyes just like back on the pastures as explosions ripped through the labs and walkways.

Soon, a man tugged at Kira's arm and she disappeared behind the re-treating parties. Kaden sprinted after them, but he turned a corner into an empty lot. He couldn't see Kira eye him from the shadows of the sewer drain across the alley.

Chapter 42

Admitting to himself he'd lost her, Kaden turned back to where the crowd previously stood. Aria stood face-to-face with Beth-ell and two Elites. The charcoal demon sniffed the air as their ashy, rock-like skin seemed to absorb all the light from the sun.

"Ah, Agent McCloud. You remember my entourage, of course," Beth-ell said as the pair of Elites shot their cold, black eyes toward him.

"Agent Beth-ell," he nodded with respect, "how could I forget." The pain in his midsection came to mind. "Can we help you?"

"We've tracked members of the Remnant here. What did you find?" she said in a commanding voice. Her wrinkled yet determined face shot back and forth, reading both Aria's and Kaden's faces.

"A common riot. We dispersed it," Aria said.

"No riots are common, especially now when enemies of freedom plot against The Tower," Beth-ell snapped back. "Agent McCloud, we've spoken of you seeking out the Remnant. State your progress," she demanded.

"We haven't found anything yet. Just this disagreement, but when we approached, everyone scattered," Kaden said.

"And anything special? I heard from my companions," she motioned to the Elites, "they smelled like... well, like you," she said as she watched him, tilting her head and studying him extra close.

A piece of him wanted to point down the alley where he just lost Kira, but he couldn't. The look in Beth-ell's eyes told him that she knew he wasn't giving all his information. With the fear of being labeled a traitor, but unable to give up his family, a new thought dawned on him. He flipped the line of questioning back on them.

"I'm not sure what they're smelling, but since I was recruited, they've been on me. Maybe your dogs should find another scent to hound after," Kaden said as firmly and commanding as he could.

"Oh?" Beth-ell feigned surprise and the two Elites snarled. "What a great offer. I think you should direct them to a new scent."

"I wasn't–" Kaden tried to say.

"Oh yes, I agree wholeheartedly," she interrupted. "Your partner and I will search the perimeter, while you practice leading Elites."

Aria looked increasingly uncomfortable as Beth-ell moved closer to her, putting her arm around her.

"Please, show us how it's done," Beth-ell said as she led Aria away. Aria's eyes tracked to Kaden, a pleading look.

Before he spoke up, an Elite swiftly approached.

"Where," it growled, its face within inches of his. The other Elite lifted its head, sniffing the air and turning toward the direction Kira went moments before.

Kaden remained silent, his eyes on the one that moved toward the alley to his right. It cocked its head, looking toward the sewer, and it dawned on Kaden how she had escaped so quickly.

"What have you found out from the dozens you've devoured so far?" Kaden said in as confident of a tone he could muster.

Both Elites turned to him. The one nearest smiled as it picked up its hand and turned it, as if opening a door knob. Kaden's stomach felt like a bomb went off.

His jaws clenched as he tried not to scream, a horrible pain exploding as the monster twisted his internal organs.

"Kill me and see what it gets you," Kaden sneered, moving closer to the Elite.

The creature snarled as its cold, black eyes stared back at Kaden. Somewhere deep inside those hideous black eyes that hid all signs of a pupil, he caught a fleck of gray somewhere deep within the dead black.

The thing twisted its hand again, and Kaden clenched his jaw so hard, he thought his teeth might crack as he fought the urge to scream.

The demon stepped closer and backhanded him. It felt like a stone baseball bat struck him, sending him backward, rolling to a stop against a heap of bricks. Glancing up, he saw the other Elite watching the action and no longer pursuing Kira.

His bluff worked. They left her trail.

"Mission accomplished," he thought. "But now what?"

The two beings closed in on him. A stone-like hand moved and his body followed, picking him off the ground without touching him. But Kaden's quick wrist pulled the Spark Club out. He held it directly in front of the Elite, squeezing the handle and causing a crackle of electricity to sweep over the smooth metal ball at the end.

The Elite's stone face showed no expression as it continued to stare past the electricity and into Kaden's eyes. It stepped closer, raising its hand and locking Kaden's arm and the club in place. Kaden tried moving his hand, but it felt like half his body was caked in invisible cement.

To his shock, the Elite stepped into the hot white ball of electricity, pressing its chest against Spark Club. Small muscles in the face twitched, but its body remained firm. Its shoulders rose, as if the charge set off an internal laughter. The creature smiled. The charge burned the black robe, but the Elite seemed to enjoy the sensation, as if the electricity charged it to full capacity.

Finally, it released Kaden's hand and the club pulled back. The Elite exhaled, breathing comfortably, like it woke up refreshed on a bright morning. The thing seemed bigger, stronger, as if its charcoal muscles grew during the electrocution.

"Where," the thing said, and its raspy voice rose from its throat as if escaping the pits of hell.

"Do your job. I'll do mine," Kaden refuted, and he swung his club as fast and hard as he could, right at the creature's head.

But an inch before contact, the club stopped, frozen in time. The thing turned its head and looked at the club, then back at Kaden.

From the corner of Kaden's eye, he saw the second Elite come closer, its hand up and invisibly holding Kaden's club to protect its partner. The Elite directly in front of Kaden now opened its burnt robe, exposing the charcoal skin of its chest and stomach. It was like a Venetian statue or a Roman god, its body perfectly chiseled with bulging shoulder and chest muscles above defined abs. It flexed its hands and opened its mouth, as if licking its lips, then it moved its hands wide. Kaden felt a pull so strong, it was like a black hole opening up in front of him.

He shot at the demon's chest. The horrible faces of others consumed flashed in his mind. The demon had waited, but now he finally got his feast as Kaden flew toward him.

Then a rock struck the thing's head. Then another. Kaden fell to the ground and heard the sound of bricks striking the ground like a wave of falling rain. He looked up to see the Elite take another brick thrown by a group of men and women.

The arguing groups. They were back, and now they were fighting against the Elites, hurling whatever they had at the demons. The group was smaller, but more furious in their actions against the creatures.

The Elite near Kaden turned and waved his hand. Across the broken brick courtyard, two men shot back like they were hit by an invisible bus. The other Elite threw up his hand and three bricks in mid-air shattered into tiny pieces like clay pigeons.

Kaden scrambled to his feet and picked up his Spark Club. The Elite that was about to consume him now turned his back to him. With the Elite distracted, Kaden might be able to swing the club and knock its head off. He could end the one Elite who constantly found him. But just as Kaden took hold of his club, a brick struck his shoulder, knocking him back.

The two Elites made quick work of the group, throwing people aside left and right as if casually cleaning a hallway, shooing the dust bunnies aside.

The last of the small group were rolling in pain, but a noise echoed from below the earth. The sound crystallized as it grew, roaring from the alleyway where Kira had escaped. It culminated as the wave of people shot out of the sewers screaming a war cry and wielding common tools and broken sticks sharpened to a point. They threw their weapons and picked up bricks and stones, hurling them at the Elites.

The charcoal demons wiped away the first wave, but the sheer numbers in the crowd overwhelmed them as the flood continued out of the sewers. Gradually, more and more rocks and bricks or sharpened rods made their way through the chaos, striking the creatures. At first, Kaden thought the demons were impervious to the damage, but as more projectiles hit their mark, he saw the rock-like charcoal skin being chipped away. The Elites didn't seem so muscular anymore, their bulging and menacing figures cracked as they gradually fought off the crowd.

One Elite soon fell to its knees and the crowd erupted in celebration. The invigorated rioters raised their level and threw all they had at the thing. But as Kaden watched the situation unfold, surprisingly, the crowd didn't pounce on the creature. They kept their distance. He thought they would jump on it, like a fighter trying to end its opponent, but in this deadly fight, the menacing crowd stayed five to ten yards away, continuing to hurl deadly objects.

Then, the second Elite fell. Kaden was away from it now and caught its emotionless eyes staring back at him. The crowd ignited to an even higher level of intensity. Like rainfall, deadly objects rained on both Elites.

The fallen Elite, the creature who first connected with Kaden since his first walk to the EMR, the one who continually showed up like a wolf stalking its prey, now peered back at him as if a fallen soldier looking back at his comrade. There was no pleading in its dead eyes but a look closer to confusion, as if it wondered why Kaden wasn't joining the fight.

But Kaden made no move to help the fallen creatures.

Their stare was broken when another brick struck the rock-hard charcoal head, splitting a chunk of its cheekbone off its face.

The group was so focused on the Elites, they hadn't noticed Kaden, but now as the tide of the battle was fully in their favor, many noticed where the Elite was looking.

Now they saw him.

Without hesitation, they moved to him like he was a third Elite.

Kaden backpedaled, seeing the aggression in their eyes, holding up his hands to separate himself, but the mob came harder as they sensed another victory. A small stone thrown like a baseball hit his midsection.

He wasn't running or talking his way out of this one.

Another rock. Then the head of a tool, something like a makeshift hammer, flew toward him. He swung his Spark Club, knocking the projectile away. Unlike the Elites, the mob had no problem getting closer to Kaden. One man pulled a knife that resembled more of a short sword. He lunged at Kaden, but using the club like a hockey stick, he cross-checked the man back into the crowd. Another shot forward, swinging a thin iron rod like a bat. It struck Kaden's back and he fell to one knee.

"Get back. I'm not your fight!" Kaden screamed. The assertion only fueled the mob's emotion.

From the corner of his eye, he saw the Elites. One was down on one knee, objects still raining on it, chipping away at the rock-like body. The other was on its back, one arm moving as if a flicker of life escaping through its fingers.

The mob continued to stone them both from a distance.

More unintelligible cries of battle rose up as the bulk of the crowd shot at Kaden. One rage-filled man with tattered clothes and a long beard that resembled a bird's nest shot at him with the corner of a brick in his hand. Kaden squeezed the grip of his club as he swung it at the man. The electric pop dazed him while the force of the club knocked him back, the concrete piece falling from his hand. He fell back, knocking into a screaming woman who wielded a sharp, spear-like object. Both fell within a foot of the Elite, the Elite who a moment peered at Kaden and seemed to wonder when the Agent would engage.

A tiny crack of a smile came to the corner of the Elite's mouth. The dead black eyes shot to Kaden like a thankful flash and now he knew why the crowd didn't come too close. The robe opened and its chest was exposed. It rolled over, pointing itself toward the fallen. Kaden saw the horror in their eyes as their bodies contorted. He'd seen this horror before. A split second later and the pair were gone, only their clothes and makeshift weapons left in front of the Elite. The creature rose to its feet, energized, and once again looking like a charcoal statue of a Greek god. The damage from the fight sealed over, leaving a divot where the damage broke pieces away, but now the cracking stopped, leaving scars in the rock-like skin.

The demon now fought with renewed vigor and used its powers to send two unfortunate souls to the feet of his partner. Its downed Elite took longer to pull the two into itself as it struggled for strength, but it was like two objects circling a black hole. The gravity had them, and the outcome was inevitable.

The creature pulled them in, consuming the two. Its body became fuller, stronger, and soon it was back on its feet, appearing more powerful than ever.

Much of the mob was now focused on Kaden. He desperately fought them off, catching a stray rock or pole to his side. His adrenaline kept him on his feet, all the conditioning from The Tower's exercises coming to fruition. Every round that Ryon tried suffocating him or breaking a limb, it prepared Kaden for the continual fighting ahead of him. Yet, every minute, he gave the furious group another inch. The electric pop of the club kept one person at bay and fended off an iron spike, but then a broken brick would catch his leg or his side, causing him to wince. Like a boxer pounded with body blows, his arms began to drop. His head was open.

With most of the group converging on Kaden, the newly refreshed Elites quickly eliminated the part of the mob nearest them. Soon, they mowed down the group, now more viciously throwing their attackers high into the air and letting them crash down, smashing into the hard, cracked brick streets. Spatters of blood began covering the open square as the crunching of bones echoed in the streets. Where makeshift weapons and stones once rained on the Elites, wearing them down, now the Outer Ring fighters fell like hellacious hail from the clouded skies.

The groups shifted positions as the Elites carved into the group. Soon Kaden found himself fighting alongside the same Elite who would have consumed him moments ago. He pushed off a trio of attackers, playing them toward the Elites' path. The creatures consumed one person that came too close, refueling mid-fight, and sent the others sky high, allowing them to crash down and crack their skulls on the concrete. The Elite nodded to Kaden as a thankful teammate would.

As the melee continued, Kaden sensed an attack from behind. He spun without thought, swinging his Spark Club, crashing down on the would-be attacker's shoulder. A bone-crunching sound shot up against the force of the Spark Club. But then Kaden saw the man wasn't coming at him, but was shielding Kaden from another who was trying to drive a javelin-type spear into Kaden's back.

The protector now crumpled to the road, his shoulder and collarbone dented unnaturally into his upper body. His head fell back and Kaden caught his face.

"Enak!" Kaden screamed as a sense of dread filled his stomach. Enak saved him from a spike running through his back and out of his chest, and was met with the Spark Club in return. Enak fell to his knees, and the javelin attacker gathered himself, now focusing on Enak. He looked to execute the traitor who defended the Agent. His hate-filled eyes flocked on his new target.

"No!" Kaden tried to jump in front of Enak, but he was too late. The sharpened iron shot forward, aiming at Enak's heart.

It hit his skin right as the soot-covered man was sent flying, crashing into the crowd and turning another pair into bowling pins. The iron ripped at Enak's skin, tearing a gash in the skin but only ripping the surface skin and not bone or organs.

Kaden turned, catching the Elite's eyes as they both pivoted to face a new set of foes. The new wave overtook Kaden before he could get to Enak. He was sent back as Elba scooped his brother up. The pair fell behind the fight as the attacking group clawed and scratched at Kaden's eyes and mouth, trying to damage whatever parts of him they could. With three men on him, one was putting his knee to Kaden's wrist and prying the club from his hand. The man lifted his knee and dropped it, sending it crashing into Kaden's wrist against the hard brick underneath. His hand lost feeling and the club rolled out. The man picked it up and raised it above his head. He screamed as he began swinging it down, like an ax to split Kaden's head like a block of wood.

Before it struck, the man flew away, crashing into a nearby wall, and the club fell. It landed inches away from Kaden's skull and cracked the brick beneath him. A second later, the two men on top of Kaden were lifted off and sent away as if following a giant arch. Two thuds sounded down the alley as Kaden scrambled to his feet.

The two Elites stepped up next to him as the mob retreated. The pair of charcoal monsters looked at Kaden, then to the dispersing crowd. Bodies littered the battlefield.

Without a word, the Elites swiftly moved to find Beth-ell.

Kaden fell to his knees, bloodied and battered. Moments later, Aria and the rest of their team ran to meet him.

Chapter 43

Kira

"That's wrong. He's alive and can help us in this fight!" Kira replied back as the group in front of her mocked and chided her. She tried showing them the manuscript she'd found in the mysterious portion of the tunnels. She tried telling them that Jericho had saved her and had spoken directly to her. However, the conversation quickly turned from disbelief into an argument, only escalating further as she pressed her case.

Alister moved forward, urging them to listen to Kira, but the group thrust forward and someone shoved him. The group wanted none of their supposed hope. Their frustration turned into the urge to fight more than any speech or desire to listen.

The group's murmuring halted as two blue-robed Agents turned the corner. The alley grew quiet as instinctively. Both groups quickly dissipated through the inner working of the buildings.

Kira examined the two Agents and caught his eyes.

Kaden. Promoted to a Blue, and patrolling the Outer Ring with a partner.

They locked eyes, but Alister pulled her arm, bringing her around a corner. A split-second later, and they quickly slid through a manhole cover. Elba gently closed it.

"Was that?" Enak whispered to Kira as the small group crowded shifted to the four-inch drainage slit on a nearby curb, eagerly watching the Agents.

"It was," Elba said for her as he looked into her eyes. She shifted the corner and found a place near the drainage slit. A figure in blue moved, looking across the alleyway, then a moment later, it was gone. They stayed hushed as a conversation came from around the corner.

"Come on, he's made his choice," Enak whispered, and the group moved with him, silently escaping through the rank-smelling sewer system. Alister followed while Elba watched Kira, a sympathetic expression on his face, but soon, he also walked away. They moved down the tunnel where light grew ever dimmer, yet Kira stayed, watching between buildings and trying to hear as her brother talked to someone just out of sight.

The others' faint footsteps faded entirely as the distance between them and Kira grew. Her ears tuned in, adjusting to the quiet tunnel. She leaned in, putting her ear toward Kaden's conversation.

She saw Kaden step back as she watched intently. An Elite stepped into the frame and twisted his hand toward Kaden's stomach. She gasped, putting her hands to her mouth to stay quiet. Her brother didn't scream as his face grimaced. She could tell he was holding in the intense pain.

Another second passed and her eyes grew wide as a second Elite came into view. It sniffed the air and moved toward the drainage slit she peered out of.

She stepped back, covering herself in shadows. The creature looked around, taking steps side-to-side, but now it stopped. Its charcoal head and dark, empty eyes turned toward her. She froze, unsure it saw her through the small opening and to the shadows below.

It stepped closer, tilting its head as it focused on her. The thing sniffed and felt a tug toward it as it crept closer. If it found her, it'd have a track to find the Remnants' new hideout.

That couldn't happen.

She could run, hoping to get far enough down the tunnel so the thing didn't have her scent, but it was mere feet away, and peering toward her still.

Then it turned as a commotion broke out behind it.

"No," she silently mouthed as she saw Kaden trying to fight off the first Elite.

She watched him swing his weapon as the Elite stepped forward. It took the Spark Club to its chest and grew strong, as if recharging its batteries. A sickening smell loomed in the air as its robe burnt and its hard, cracked skin grew white-hot from the electricity.

The demon smacked Kaden and he flew back. The pair moved closer to him, abandoning her pursuit, and ready to stomp out his dissent. She bent down and took off running as fast as she could through the low-ceiling tunnels.

"They're going to kill him, or worse," she called out as she finally caught up.

"What? Who?" Alister turned to meet her, Enak and Elba at his side.

"Kaden, my brother; he's an Agent and there are two Elites. They're going to kill him, or worse, consume... We have to help!" she pleaded.

"Two Elites?" Enak said.

"Kira, he's a part of The Tower; they're on the same side," Elba said.

"Not these two. You'd know if you saw what I saw. They're going after him," she said.

The trio stood speechless.

"Fine, help me or get out of the way," she said, running back down the tunnel.

"Wait, we need more than just us," Alister said, others from behind them now coming back to the discussion.

Kira stopped and quickly thought. "You're right. We need them too."

She dashed away before they could argue, taking a quick turn in the tunnel system then coming to a patch of sunlight. She shot up inside a smaller courtyard.

She smiled in delight as she came out of the manhole and found way more than she'd hoped for. Dozens of families made their home in this small alcove away from the main alleyways, including all those who dismissed her to the point of anger a moment before.

"What are you–" one of the disgruntled and protective men said as she shot toward them.

"There's Elites, two of them, we need help. They're killing!"

The man stopped and looked at her, at first confused by the request for help, but then he turned and looked at a woman behind him. She had two kids on her lap, and both were scared, burying their faces in their mother's chest.

"We can't move forever," the woman said. Kira could hear the tiredness in her voice.

The man turned back to Kira. His sympathetic face transformed into an angry, battle-ready scowl.

"Two of 'em?" he asked.

"Two," Kira confirmed.

"Remember to keep your distance, men. Let's show these bastards a real Outer Ring welcome," he said.

Dozens of men and women stood up, giving an affirming grunt. They grabbed whatever weapon they could. Some kicked portions of a nearby wall to gather more jagged rocks and lumps of brick, piling it into their clothes.

Kira shot back into the tunnels and led the mob to the fight. She shot out of the manhole, ready to save her brother. She threw the first stone, striking the Elite as it sought to consume Kaden. The other Elite threw her to the side. Before she struck the wall, she saw a barrage of weapons overwhelm the demons. They turned away from him.

CHAPTER 44

A knock at his door woke him from his dreams. He'd been having the same fire dream each night. It raged behind him as he tried to catch Kira, then Jericho stepped out and took the fire from him.

"You're the fire," Jericho said before leaning back to expose his neck, allowing the flames to engulf him.

Five days ago, Kaden was carried back to The Tower. They praised him for fighting alongside Elites to repel the Outer Ring rioters. He'd hardly moved as his body recovered.

The knocking repeated, this time louder.

His body creaked as he stood. He opened the door to see his teacher standing, clutching the lapels of his purple robe. It looked freshly cleaned, not a crease in the perfectly pressed purple.

"I see you're able to walk. Good. Get your robe. You've been summoned *again*," Ron-ell said bitterly. Jealousy echoed in his voice.

Kaden dressed, his joints aching and muscles stiff, but soon he was walking beside Ron-ell. It felt good to stretch his legs, but he could feel his strength not fully recovered.

Ron-ell led him up numerous flights of stairs. The first trek up the stairs left him winded; now his legs twitched and burned. His teacher stayed a few steps ahead of him as if urging him to go faster and keep up.

Just like the first meeting with Pinnacle, Ron-ell brought Kaden to a gigantic archway filled with two huge doors that opened up in a grand domed ballroom. He walked in as Ron-ell waited outside.

Beth-ell waited inside.

"Congratulations on your victory. You will be recognized for your support of The Tower, an example of Agent and Elite, fighting side-by-side in the name of Pinnacle," she said in a flowery voice.

"I don't need to be recognized. I was just trying to–"

"Shut up and play the part," Beth-ell interrupted, her voice now stern and commanding. She leaned in, putting her mouth close to his ear. "And if you talk back to my Elites again, we'll find you when you sleep and consume you slow enough for you to feel your flesh pull off your body."

She stepped back, still facing Kaden and a smile on her weathered face, then she pivoted and walked to the other side of the room.

"You may enter, Ron," Beth-ell called back. Kaden turned back to the doorway and saw Ron-ell sneak in, as if he were caught eavesdropping. He shot a look of disdain toward Beth-ell.

"It's Ron-ell now, Beth..." He let a syllable of silence hang in the air, as if he was ending, before letting the rest of her name drop. "...-ell."

The three stood for an uncomfortable moment, only Beth-ell seemingly contented with the lack of action.

Then a thunderous clap shot out from across the grand ballroom. Kaden flinched in response, his eyes wide and alert. It seemed like a clap of thunder erupted inside his head and he felt a blanket-like oppression set on his shoulders, the air heavy and pressing down on him.

From underneath the painting of a rising sun that came down from the top of the massive dome ceiling and slid down to center over a dark hallway stood Pinnacle. He wore a black robe and his face was clean shaven and handsome. He began clapping repeatedly as he walked in the room, looking at Kaden as he praised the young Agent. Beth-ell and Ron-ell both knelt, and it took Kaden a moment, but he followed suit and soon put his knee to the ground.

"Congratulations, my son!" he said in a booming voice, his smile all charm. "Please rise, all of you rise. It's time to celebrate!"

"My lord," Beth-ell said and bowed her head, now back to her friendly, flowery voice.

"The Elites should be rewarded and our Agent McCloud here will be seen front and center of the ceremony."

"The Elites have already met their consumption quota. We could simply wait–"

"Nonsense!" Pinnacle replied. "I've already made the preparations, my daughter."

"My lord, my great teacher, it was by your command that we should never over-consume. Recently, in the Outer–"

He flicked his wrist and Beth-ell snapped to attention, her mouth slamming shut.

"I have arranged for a special Inner Ring event." A hint of impatience crept into his voice, but it soon went back to a proud voice of celebration. "My daughter, this is a momentous occasion. Not every day does a new Agent get promoted so quickly and show such promise as to be recognized by the Elites."

Kaden noticed Beth-ell's surprise at the mention of Inner Ring, but she dared not speak out again.

"I will set up the sorting, my lord," Ron-ell said as he stood up, his head still bowed.

"No. No, not this time, my son. This is a true celebration and I cannot have you steal it from your great pupil," Pinnacle said. He walked to Kaden and grabbed his shoulder like a proud father. "I think one day we'll be calling you Ka-ell. Maybe more influential than your teacher here." He nodded back to Ron-ell, who was noticeably perturbed but quickly set back into a stoic expression.

"Sir," Kaden said, and he nodded out of reflex.

"You earn your first badge of honor today. You'll be at the front of the line, seen by the highest Elites, and it is really quite an easy duty. In fact, you've observed one already, but now you're on the *right* side of it."

"Sir?"

"My lord!" Ron-ell shouted.

"Apologies, *my lord*," Kaden said.

"Ron-ell is one of the best in formal arrangements – he's done many sortings – although I suspect you will surpass him in most, if not all, ways," Pinnacle said.

Kaden fought the urge to look at Ron-ell's expression after Pinnacle's undercutting comment.

"Are you ready?" Pinnacle said as he squeezed Kaden's shoulder. He tried not to wince in pain, but an ounce more force, and Kaden suspected his bone would shatter under Pinnacle's grip. Yet, the charming smile on the leader's face gave the sense he was as casual as ever.

"Yes, my–"

"Of course you're ready!" He cut Kaden off. "You wouldn't have been promoted if you weren't!" Pinnacle cheered. He released his grip and led them out of the ballroom and through a series of hallways, always a half step ahead of Kaden, subtly guiding him.

"A celebration sorting!" Pinnacle said, then he leaned into Kaden's ear. "You get to guide this one," he said with a smile and grabbing his shoulder once again. "And feel free to give them extra. This celebration feast is for you *and* them. They tend to remember and reward."

Pinnacle nudged him forward. A pack of eager Elites stood waiting, while a group of civilians waited in a circular group across the room. Kaden remembered the fear he experienced when he was in the middle of his large group. The horrifying vision of an Elite feasting on the two people in the back room ran through his mind.

"Do your duty," Ron-ell snapped from behind him as Pinnacle took a seat in a shadowy throne across the room.

Kaden stood up straighter, deciding he must do what it took to maintain order. He stepped toward his position, but soon paused. He recognized two from within the group. His friends, Elba and Enak, stood in the middle of the group. Enak's arm was in a sling and his shoulder wrapped where Kaden's Spark Club had made contact. He knew there must be a patch of gauze under his shirt where the spike ripped at his skin.

Kaden, in his blue robe, stood before the assembled group, his heart pounding in his chest as he tried to maintain an air of authority and composure. The weight of his new blue robe seemed to press down on his shoulders, a physical reminder of the responsibility and power that had been thrust upon him.

The Elites loomed nearby, their charcoal-like skin and empty black eyes filled with a hunger that made Kaden's stomach churn. He could feel their eagerness, their desire to feed, and he knew that the slightest misstep on his part would unleash their fury at him as well as the doomed civilians.

"We are here to celebrate an achievement between Elites and Agents. A sign of The Tower working together for the people of Empyrean!" Beth-ell announced, her arms raised wide.

As he scanned the faces of the people before him, Kaden's breath caught in his throat as he found them again, Elba and Enak, their expressions a mix of fear and confusion. Elba caught Kaden's eye, as if silently pleading for answers, for reassurance that everything would be alright. Elba tried to portray a sense of confidence with their old friend at the helm, but Enak looked at him with a sense of disgust.

But Kaden couldn't give them the comfort they yearned for. Not with Ron-ell, Beth-ell, and Pinnacle watching him from the sidelines, their gazes sharp and assessing. He sensed they were waiting for him to prove his loyalty, to demonstrate that he was worthy of the power and position he had been granted. Ron-ell knew Kaden's history at the EMR. He must have known Enak and Elba worked there, and he likely plucked them from their shift himself.

Kaden looked at the closest Elite, who returned his gaze with a mix of impatience and hunger. The Elite looked away from Kaden and into the shadows across the room, where Pinnacle sat. Their leader didn't move, and soon the Elite looked back at Kaden as if sending a signal of readiness.

"Begin," Kaden said, mustering up as firm of a voice as he could, but inside, his heart sank. From that point forward, the Elites ran the show. They invisibly forced the crowd into a line, just as they did when Kaden was in it, and began pulling unsuspecting civilians forward, one-by-one.

He searched the line and let out a breath, thankful that Elba and Enak were toward the back. He had time to think. But the Elites were swift in their sorting, their hunger driving them as the line shrank faster than anticipated. Like a marching band filing out to the field, each person moved forward and efficiently moved left or right as the first Elite smelled the air and flicked his wrist, shifting the entire weight of the person one way or another. Kaden now recognized the sniff and sort. It was appetite-based.

There was no scenario in his mind where he could save his friends' lives. His mind reeled trying to find realistic ways. He could try a distraction, like he did with Kira when they switched spots, but Ron-ell's eyes were on him. He could try to influence or even bump the first Elite aside, but he knew challenging the highest-ranking Agent within Empyrean was a death sentence. His mind raced as his hands twitched. The consumption rooms in the bowels of The Tower waited for Elba and Enak.

Then a thought crossed his mind, slithering in and giving him a sense of joy: What if they weren't chosen? He could still oversee the event without losing his position or his friends' lives. If he did nothing, there was a chance that everything would be okay. But he knew the odds, and it wasn't likely both made it out alive. But it wasn't just their two lives; he knew his life was being judged as Ron-ell and Beth-ell walked the edges of the room.

Kaden caught Elba's eye. The older brother raised his eyebrows and clenched his jaw, silently urging Kaden to help, but Kaden could only stare into his eyes and then look away as a stranger interrupted his thoughts.

"Say, my boy in blue, what is all this about?" a man with greasy hands and overalls asked as he passed by. He seemed vaguely familiar and Kaden stepped back, ignoring the man.

The line continued to march forward and the man again came up to Kaden, catching his eye. He recognized the uniform and the grease.

"You work at the EMR?" Kaden asked.

"I do." He nodded.

"Who brought you here?" Kaden replied.

"I'm not concerned about how I got here, but more how I leave here." The man pointed up to the Elites.

"And you should be. They control gravity itself, only Pinnacle is stronger."

"I heard they're dead Agents," the man retorted.

"What?" Kaden reacted.

"Yup, resurrected by Pinnacle and given new life, but forever in servitude."

"No, they were promoted," Kaden said.

The repairman scoffed as if batting Kaden's comment back at him.

Kaden took another look at the man. His pot belly and long mustache gave a friendly vibe. The rosy cheeks made Kaden think of long ago memories from his life as Darren. The man looked jolly. A jolly repairman, who was somehow light on his feet and freely questioning a blue-robed Agent on his way to a coin flip decision for his life or death.

Kaden stood back, bewildered by the man.

"Who brought you here?" Kaden asked again.

The jolly man laughed. "Oh, He said you might ask me that. He said resist when appropriate, but that ultimately, I won't be able to. He said that I'll need Him to save me. How about that for trust, eh?" he said, laughing.

Kaden was at a loss at the man's cheerful attitude.

"How can you be happy right now?" Kaden said.

"Seriously?" he asked back, as if the question was a joke, then he saw Kaden's seriousness. "Because I trust Him. He's never let me down before, so if He says He'll save me, well, I'll do what I can while I'm here, but you know... it comes down to Him. And when He comes, I'll be ready."

Kaden remained silent, more confused by explanation. The man moved forward and waved. Kaden was astounded. The man acted as if he was on a stroll around the park and not to his death.

"You fool, you have no idea," Kaden whispered under his breath. He kept his eyes on the man as he came to his sort. The Elite forcefully flicked his wrist and threw the jolly repairman into the consumption group. Kaden's shoulders slumped, knowing the jolly man's life was soon over. Even in his joy, he couldn't be saved from the horrific death that waited.

"Hey!" Elba whispered as his part of the line came near Kaden. "You gotta get us out of here."

"I'm trying, but..." Kaden whispered back through gritted teeth.

"You're a blue; just freaking tell them!" Enak whispered harshly under his breath.

"If I stop it, *everyone* will die. Guys, I'm sorry, you're going to be sorted."

"Kaden, don't do this. You can stop it," Elba said in a calmer tone than Kaden would have expected..

"I... I..." Kaden's voice trailed off into hopelessness.

Elba's hopeful face shifted to solemn. He took in Kaden's response and clenched his jaw, then turned toward the Elites. "Then we'll face what lies ahead," he said softly.

Enak didn't take the solemn path like his brother.

"Traitor!" Enak screamed and the crowd picked their heads up. Everyone's eyes shot back to Enak and Kaden as their eyes locked.

"Your shoulder was in the heat of battle; it was an accident," Kaden said in a low tone, his hand reflexively going to the Spark Club at his side.

"You were our friend! She said we could trust you!" Enak stepped out of line and moved to Kaden.

"Brother," Elba said, reaching out, trying to stop him.

"We went back to save him. We saved him! Now this and that?" Enak motioned toward his shoulder, then the Elites, who were now taking notice. "You're a traitor and a liar!"

"Don't do this," Kaden said again, trying to keep his voice low.

But it all happened in a flash, too quick for any of them to stop what happened next. The entire room seemed to be sorted at once.

The group being set free slid toward the exit as the group set for consumption slid closer to the hallways that led to the depths of The Tower.

The remaining line divided into two, with Elba being pushed toward the exit and Enak picked off the ground, moving toward the consumption tunnels with half of the others in the line.

Kaden pulled out his club and readied himself for whatever might come. He thought of the riot of the previous week and expected either an Elite to throw him down or a person to try and rip his eyes out, but the event was over before it started. There was no commotion as the numerous Elites shifted everyone, like picking up a child's toy set and placing them all nicely back in their place.

Beth-ell and Ron-ell watched Kaden. No motion or sound came from the shadows where Pinnacle sat. "Traitor!" Enak screamed. His cries bounced through the halls and echoed in Kaden's mind.

Kaden stood there, motionless as the crowd around him was now an empty ballroom. His hands trembled and his heart heavy with the weight of his inaction. A small consolation prize was that he knew he had passed Pinnacle's test. He had proven his loyalty, had shown that he was willing to do whatever it took to maintain his place within the Tower. But the cost of hearing his friend's scream weighed on his heart.

"Traitor!" echoed in his mind.

He stood watching the halls that led to certain death. The faces of those he'd seen consumed stretched in his mind. He imagined Enak and the times they laughed together. The sounds of screaming, the hollow, dead sound of when a scream ended, the person consumed and lost to the world.

Moments later, he didn't have to imagine anymore.

Screams sounded from the halls.

Chapter 45

Kaden stepped into the training room, his blue robe billowing behind him as he walked. The prior week weighed on him, the battle alongside the Elites, attacking Enak, and the sorting where he saw his friend taken by the charcoal demons. Thoughts of his friend's eyes flashed in his mind, the sense of betrayal and confusion as he held his broken shoulder. Those looks turned to rage during the sorting, Kaden's betrayal outweighing the pending death in front of him.

"There he is!" Jace exclaimed, his eyes wide with excitement as Kaden came in. "The Agent the Outer Ring can't kill."

"Those fools should be glad they only caught *you* and not all of us," Ryon said, clapping Kaden on the back. Kaden tried not to wince from the remaining bruises. "We always knew you had resiliency, bro."

He forced a smile, the praise feeling hollow as he thought about fighting alongside Elites that consumed the people of the Outer Ring to regain their strength. He had helped those creatures kill, more than once.

The others exchanged glances, their expressions a mix of surprise and confusion as they saw Kaden's bleak expression.

"You okay?" Aria asked. "Kaden, we heard Beth-ell talking you up like you were Pinnacle's prize pupil."

"Fighting alongside Elites AND seeing Pinnacle?" Vala exclaimed.

Kaden shrugged, trying to downplay the significance of the event. "It was just a formality, really."

The others shook their heads, disbelief etched on their faces.

"No, that's a BIG deal," Vala said, a hint of anger in her voice that Kaden wasn't as excited as she thought he should be.

"I can't imagine being in the presence of such greatness," Ryon added, his voice hushed with reverence. "To think, the creator of the New Breed, the savior of Empyrean, right there in front of you."

"You could feel his power, that's for sure," Kaden said, remembering the overwhelming weight of Pinnacle in the air when they met. "But come on," he said, eager to change the subject. "I've been in bed for seven days and aching to get out. Let's run today."

"You got it," Ryon said.

The others followed, changing into their athletic attire and setting off toward the lifts. The debris and construction from the attack on the labs forced detours within The Tower, but soon they were at a working vertical lift and jogging toward trails on the green pastures that lay hidden beneath the city. A new world open to them as a higher rank.

As they ran, the conversation once again turned to recent events. Kaden ignored the small talk as he searched the horizon for roaming herds, a welcome distraction.

"I heard there was a sorting yesterday," Jace said, his voice low and conspiratorial. "One of the biggest in recent memory."

Kaden's stomach churned at the mention of the sorting, the screams of the condemned still echoing in his ears.

"I heard it was a special occasion," Ryon chimed in, his eyes gleaming with a kind of morbid curiosity. "A celebration of sorts, for an Agent fighting alongside Elites," he said, nudging Kaden.

All eyes turned to Kaden, who felt the weight of their gaze like a physical burden.

"You *led* a sorting?" Jace exclaimed.

"It was just a standard sorting," he lied, his voice tight. "Nothing out of the ordinary."

The image of Elba and Enak being led away by the Elites, their faces contorted with fear and betrayal, was seared into his memory.

"I bet it was amazing to see the Elites in action," Vala said, her voice tinged with awe. "To witness the power of The Tower firsthand." She waved her hands back and forth, mimicking the Elites.

"They pulled people from the Inner Ring this time," Kaden said. He could feel his stomach in throat as the words came out.

"Whoa," Jace said. The group paused for a moment.

"A necessary evil," Vala said, her tone matter-of-fact. "The sorting ensures the survival of the New Breed, the continuation of Pinnacle's grand vision. The vision that built Empyrean; the vision that keeps us safe."

Kaden's blood ran cold at the casual cruelty of her words, and the way the group accepted it. He thought of the jolly repairman, of his unwavering faith that everything would be okay.

"And what about the people who are sorted? What of the consumed?" Kaden asked the group.

The others looked at him, their expressions a mix of confusion, and then a few smiles broke out as if Kaden was kidding.

"They serve a higher purpose. Come on, that's day one material," Jace said. "Their sacrifice ensures the strength and prosperity of Empyrean."

The group began walking again, but Kaden didn't let it go, calling them back as he continued.

"Have any of you seen a sorting or witnessed what happens in the tunnels of the Elites?" Kaden fired back, his face emotionless as he looked at the path ahead and jogged forward.

The group was silent as their feet struck the gravel trail that cut through the high grass.

Kaden shook his head, unable to contain his disgust any longer. "No? Then you don't know what you're talking about," he said, his voice rising with each word. "You didn't see what I saw, the faces as the Elites... they absorb people. They literally consume them."

The group looked at each other and then back at Kaden.

"That's exactly right. The cost to keep the tower running," Vala said, and all bowed their heads in a sign of respect. Even Kaden reflexively nodded before catching himself. The group began again, turning their warmup walk into a run. Small gaps emerged between the individuals as Kaden poured it on, his unused muscles now feeling good as he ran ahead of the group.

"Kaden," Ryon said after catching up to Kaden, his voice low as if an off-the-record conversation. "You are testing us, right? Because otherwise, you're treading on dangerous ground here. The sorting is the will of Pinnacle, the foundation upon which the Tower stands. It will NOT be questioned."

The weight of what he had witnessed, of his own complicity in the atrocities of the Tower, felt too much to bear, but Kaden held it inside. He imagined swinging the Spark Club at the Elites and shattering them as he stood tall, saving the people and bringing down the monsters trying to devour them.

"Kaden?" Ryon said again as their feet padded the gravel in unison.

Kaden turned his head to Ryon and forced a slight grin, a subtle lie to help end the conversation.

Ryon laughed and then dropped his shoulder, running into Kaden playfully.

"Hey, who thinks they can beat out our leader for the last mile!" Ryon belted out.

"Woo!" Aria screamed as the others picked up their pace.

They began sprinting as the group laughed. Kaden cracked a smile as the physical test stole his attention. They all dashed forward. For those few minutes, the thoughts of Elites, the Outer Ring, Enak, and the faces of those consumed left his mind. He enjoyed running with his friends.

Then, from the corner of his eye, Kaden saw him.

A hooded figure stood twenty yards out in the grass as it swayed from the central air of the great underground pastures. Kaden couldn't see his face, but the brilliant gray eyes stood out from the shadows under his hood.

Kaden stopped and turned back, searching to get a better look at the man. But as quick as the figure was there, he was now gone.

The entire group stopped and turned back to him.

"You okay, boss?" Ryon said before he turned to look at Jace, both giving each other questioning looks.

"Yeah, I thought I just saw... I saw..." Kaden trailed off.

"He knows he can't beat us! Come on!" Vala shouted before taking off in a sprint. But like a roaring thunder came from the grasslands, a stampeding herd of cattle, led by massive steer, shot across their path. The gigantic horns of the leading bull caught Vala's cheekbone as she ran forward, gashing open the side of her face. She flew backwards, nearly being trampled as the herd flooded past them. They scrambled to pull her back as more steer shot across the trail.

The entire group watched in awe as the Earth reverberated below their feet.

Kaden looked at the herd and then back toward the spot where he saw him, but Jericho was gone.

A moment later, the herd passed by, leaving a cloud of dust and flattened grass.

"What spooked 'em?" Jace said.

"No idea, but once I get my Spark Club, I'm coming back and knocking off that horn," Vala said as Aria bent down to pick her up. "Get off," Vala pushed Aria back.

"Whoa," Aria said, lifting her hands. "Just trying to help, girl."

"I'm not your girl or anybody else's," Vala snapped back.

The group stood in awkward silence as Vala felt the blood on her cheek and sheepishly looked down, avoiding eye contact. Her face was red with rage and embarrassment to match the bloody gash.

"Let's keep our heads up," Kaden said, taking the focus off of Vala. "And you suckers can try to keep up!" he added as he took off sprinting.

Jace and Ryon took off after him.

"See you at the finish line," Aria said, slapping Vala's arm and flashing a smile.

Vala wiped her cheek, smearing red across her skin, a morbid decoration to her scowl.

The entire group was running after Kaden.

Chapter 46

K aden and his group rode the vertical lift back up to the lower recesses of the tower. Tiny smiles broke out as they caught their breath, except for Vala. She required stitches, the skin now separating further where the horn struck the side of her cheekbone, but her expressionless, stoic face stayed firm. The others couldn't hide their happiness from the difficult yet playful run together through the grassy fields. The joy was infectious between them.

As the door of the vertical lift opened, Ron-ell stood, his arms crossed and face tightened.

"Explain yourselves," he demanded.

Kaden stepped forward and stood at attention, a bit confused as the others poured out of the lift.

"Our daily physical training, Teacher. Scheduled," Kaden said.

"Scheduled?" He pointed to Vala's cheek. A thin line of blood ran down as the rest of the gash was hardening. She dropped her head toward Ron-ell's questioning gaze.

"A stampede, but Vala is tough and quick enough to only get brushed. She finished the run with us," Kaden said. Vala raised her head with confidence at his comments.

"Your run is the last thing on my mind, and stampedes can happen," Ron-ell said.

"You warned me they could happen when we are in the pastures," Kaden said in agreement.

Ron-ell exhaled a quick burst from his nostrils as his jaws clenched, blowing off the explanation as if it didn't matter. He paced back and forth, examining the group. Stopping at Vala, he looked at her wound, but then went about his pacing and examination of the entire group.

"Get it stitched. Now," he commanded.

Vala instantly responded, leaving the hallway in a brisk, military-like march.

"The rest of you, go clean up. I'll be leading your classes today," he said. Then he turned to Kaden. "Not you."

The group looked back sympathetically, but Kaden reassured them with a glance.

"Good luck, boss," Ryon whispered.

Ron-ell silently watched Kaden as the others left.

"Follow me," he finally said, not explaining as he led Kaden down the halls and into an interrogation room.

"Another exercise?" Kaden asked.

"No. Sit," Ron-ell responded, motioning for Kaden to sit in the center chair.

"Teacher?" Kaden asked questioningly.

"I said sit."

Kaden decided not to argue and he sat in the chair

Ron-ell didn't make eye contact but instead walked the outer edges of the room, shifting his gaze as he thought and spoke.

"Why the stampede?"

"I don't know. They came out of nowhere, and thankfully, we weren't trampled," Kaden said.

"There are two things that I don't understand. First, why the herd started running. It's been months since the last recorded stampede," Ron-ell said.

"I can't say. We were on the running path and they came from the grasslands, but as you first taught me, stampedes can ha–"

"I know what I taught you," Ron-ell snapped. "The second thing I don't understand is why you stopped."

"Stopped? We finished our run, Teacher. You taught us that Agents never qu–"

"I KNOW WHAT I TAUGHT YOU!" Ron-ell jumped at Kaden, taking fistfuls of his athletic shirt in his hands and driving them up into Kaden's throat.

His teacher's knuckles compressed his throat, closing it as the two men locked eyes, Ron-ell's burning with rage and Kaden's bulging with shock.

Ron-ell held the grip and pushed up into Kaden's lower jaw to ensure he felt it before letting go. He returned to methodical pacing around the room, staring at the walls and floor, as if the outburst never happened.

Kaden swallowed and regained his breath, feeling the soreness of his throat.

"One thing I didn't teach you is to lie," Ron-ell said.

"Lie?" Kaden said, his voice scratchy, before coughing to clear it.

"What did you see in the fields?" Ron-ell demanded.

"I was... distracted," Kaden said as he saw the figure of Jericho in his mind.

"There's footage. You stopped," Ron-ell said, bending down and staring at him, his breathing like an angry metronome that sounded in time with Kaden's thoughts.

"Only one weird incident, and I'd believe you," Ron-ell said.

"More than one?"

"You were quite clever. I'm still working it out myself, but the pieces are there."

"Teacher?"

"At the sorting yesterday, who did you speak with?"

Kaden's stomach dropped as he thought about Enak's outburst before going back to the consumption room.

"The *happy* man," Ron-ell mocked as he started pacing again. "And then, the angry child."

"Enak was his name," Kaden said firmly and Ron-ell stopped, looking at Kaden with surprise.

"Was?" Ron-ell added as he resumed to pace, his boots striking the ground and echoing in the small interrogation room. "Both men that *you* spoke with disappeared," he added.

"Consumed," Kaden corrected.

"I mean what I said. They disappeared, vanished, *before* being consumed. Almost like whatever it was you were looking at in the pastures. Nothing, just a ghost, eh? I have reports of them going back into the tunnels. And you just admitted to stopping to look back before the stampede, but there is something in both cases that seems to be just off camera, just out of our system's reach."

Kaden thought, his heart wanting to leap at the hint of Enak avoiding their dreaded fate. But he tempered his emotions. The Elites could have consumed them early, on the way down the tunnels.

"The next footage is of them leaving the tower. It seems rather odd, almost like they knew someone on the inside that helped them avoid detection..." Ron-ell trailed off as he swiftly turned away from his pacing and stared down at Kaden.

Confusion, yet a hopeful feeling welled in Kaden's stomach.

"I couldn't take an Elite's meal away from them," Kaden said.

Ron-ell nodded and let out a deep breath. "I agree, even in your new-found camaraderie with the Elites... Yet you know more than you're telling me. You have a smell that excites the Elites, Pinnacle is showing you uncommon interest, and from where you get these privileges, I don't know."

The door slammed open, striking the wall in a deafening metal-on-metal noise that boomed through the room.

In the doorway, standing confidently in her brown robe, was Beth-ell.

"Get him out of here," she demanded.

"I'll be done soon enough," Ron-ell replied.

"No, now. And not back to his quarters, outside The Tower," she said as she entered the room. Her tone was more than a direct command; it was furious. "Three days in the Outer Ring, boy," she ordered as she looked down her nose.

Kaden opened his mouth to respond, but he waited. Then he nodded and stood up.

"Get out, and *if* you return, then you will resume training," she said.

"That's for new recruits, not a blu–" Ron-ell began.

"Do NOT assume you know the ways of Pinnacle!" she shouted.

Ron-ell straightened his posture and clenched his jaw. She turned to Kaden.

"Get out," Beth-ell demanded.

He stood up and left the room, turning right to head to his quarters.

"Wrong way," Beth-ell sounded from the room and out to the hallway.

Kaden stopped mid-stride and turned around, leaving The Tower in only his athletic clothes, his Spark Club back in his quarters.

He stepped out of The Tower as a crack of lightning broke out from the sky and a sheet of rain fell from the gloomy clouds.

Chapter 47

Kaden left The Tower as the cold rain drops struck him like little angry pinpricks. The Tower's lights shone through alleyways as if mocking him, darting out for blocks and casting deep shadows in between its man-made light.

He squatted down under an overhang in a desolate corner.

"Three days…" He shook his head. "I did it once, I can do it again," he said to himself.

He turned to find his old apartment, Kira's apartment, and looked up at the corner of the building. An uneasy feeling sat in his stomach. What would Kira say if she knew his duty was to oversee a consumption sorting? What would Elba say if he were there?

Then a thought dawned on him that he tried not to grow too hopeful. What if Enak did make it out? Ron-ell said there was an unexplained escape. But the idea of someone escaping an Elite was unfathomable. Kaden had done it, but only with Ron-ell's sponsorship, and the disgruntled Elite still had a nose for him.

"Maybe someone was sponsoring Enak and the jolly repairman," he wondered aloud as the rain beat down around him. "But if so, why would Ron-ell not know?"

He turned his head away from his old apartment building and walked the other way, his mind lost in thought. He soon found himself near his old workplace, the Empyrean Mechanix Retreat. The large red letters, EMR, painted on the corner of the building hung like dried, unwashed blood. The 'Retreat' portion of the name stuck out to him like it never had before. What retreat is characterized by six days a week, ten hours a day? *Retreat...* he thought. An obvious mischaracterization. Like an evil clown, pretending joyful laughing as it killed, he stared at the red painted letters.

Moments later, the rain picked up and he pushed open the side door to escape what felt like a waterfall. He shook off the water, but his thin short-sleeve shirt and shorts were still dripping. His dark hair matted to his forehead and around his ears. Leaving a trail of water, he ventured into the main hangar-like area.

A clanging of metal on metal rattled through the empty building, but even in the off-hours, someone was always at work to help hit Barb's quota. Kaden's heart leapt, thinking that Jericho could be inside. He imagined the old man at the bay next to his, cranking away on whatever massive tire or brake line that needed repairs. But he found empty bays where he had hoped for much more. He looked at the empty bays, disappointed as a puddle from the dripping rain formed under him.

"I thought you had a new job?" a deep voice called out from behind him.

He recognized the voice and slowly turned to find him. The jolly repairman.

"You... How? How'd you get out?" Kaden asked.

"You better get some towels. Barb will throw a fit," he said, smiling as he threw Kaden two oil-stained rags. He dropped one into the puddle, and its color instantly darkened as it soaked up water. Kaden wiped his face off with the other.

"How'd you get out? And who told you that you would be safe?" Kaden asked as he trotted over to the man's bay.

"Whoa, slow down," he said as he looked at the massive vehicle next to him and then back at the tools spread out at his workstation. "I'm Alister, by the way."

"Alister, how'd you get out, and who told you that you would be safe?"

"You just don't stop, eh?" Alister laughed. "Listen, I think you already know the answer to both of those questions."

The man picked his eyes up from his tools and locked them onto Kaden.

"Jericho," Kaden whispered.

"Ding ding!" Alister boomed. He shook his index finger toward the sky as a smile erupted.

"But why are you here, working?"

"I have a quota to hit," Alister responded.

"You were moments away from an Elite consuming you. You escaped from The Tower, and I bet they're out looking for you, but you're here..."

"Yup," he announced loudly, and its echo bounced off the oversized machinery and high ceiling.

Kaden stepped back and put up his hands, like a child trying to stop his sibling from waking their parents.

"It's my shift, young man. He didn't save me so I could go hide under a rock somewhere. I have a job to do, and I'm going to do it. No reason the grunt work shouldn't be done with any less effort," he said.

"You're not concerned with the Elites?" Kaden asked.

"Those demons?" He chuckled. "I'd be stupid not to be, but what can they do?"

"They can literally devour you," Kaden replied.

"Sure, they could. And I won't be dumb enough to cross their path unnecessarily, but he already saved me. Those things cower when he's around."

Kaden pulled back, confusion on his face.

"Don't believe me?" Alister said.

"It's just that simple for you? You escape the Tower and go right back to work?"

"Well, gosh, no. It's not simple at all, but that's no reason to complicate it further. Besides, I know he's stronger than them. So, I trust him and that makes it easier, or *simple*, as you put it," Alister said.

"Where is he–" Kaden started.

"WHAT IN THE WORLD?" a voice shot out over them.

"I told you she'd lose it," Alister laughed.

"You have to tell me where he is." Kaden rushed as he heard Barb's shoes click against the concrete floor.

"Kaden?" she called out. "You are the dead man leaving a river in my shop?"

"Sorry, Barb. I'll clean it up, I swear, I just need to find–"

"NO! You do NOT need to *just find* anything except some towels. Wait..." She looked over his athletic clothing. "Where's your robe? Agents don't go anywhere without..." she said as her voice dropped to near whisper.

Kaden rolled his eyes like a child being forced to admit a white lie.

"I got in trouble, but it's just three days out and then I'm back in. While I'm out, I need to find–"

"Get out," Barb demanded.

"Barb? Come on."

"Get out!" she demanded.

"Wh..." Kaden's mouth hung open.

"I've seen what happens to those who cross The Tower, and it won't happen here."

"Don't you know he was just in The Tower?" Kaden pointed to Alister.

"He's doing his job, and they know where to find him. *You*, however, do NOT belong here, so get out."

"Barb? I need to find Jeri–"

"I WON'T ask again!" she shouted, her arms crossed, staring him down.

"You won't find him here," Alister said, nodding toward the exit. For the first time, Alister wasn't smiling, but there was a glimmer in his eye as his head motioned to the exit door. "...out there," Alister mouthed.

Kaden slowly stepped back.

"Sorry for the water, Barb," he said.

She didn't reply as her eyes stuck to him like a magnet.

"Did Enak come back into work?" Kaden called back.

"He's not scheduled. Keep walking," Barb called back.

Kaden left the EMR and ventured back into the rain. His body was finally feeling dry, but the cold rain soaked him once again. He looked up to the skyline that brushed against the angry clouds. The mist of the clouds traveled around the buildings like a rising tide overtaking the shore.

He once again looked up to his old apartment building but couldn't step toward it. Turning away, he began moving to the Outer Ring as the storm intensified.

Walking on the streets, he seemed to be the only one foolish enough to be outside in the strong winds that whipped through the alleys. The one man he was searching for certainly wasn't in these winds. Kaden went through the streets as the wind blew him back and forth. Each time he turned past a building or crept into an alley, a gust of wind tried to knock him over. Every shadow was either an Elite or Jericho in the dim light as his imagination played with reality.

The wind roared between the buildings and filled his ears as it pressed against his body. The sound was deafening, and Kaden looked up, seeing the tall buildings scattered around the center tower. The tops of them all seemed to shake in the breeze as the noise of the wind made Kaden feel as if the Earth itself was shaking. And yet, no Jericho as Kaden left the Inner Ring and ventured into the outer edges of Empyrean. He felt foolish for thinking Jericho would pop up again. The hope of him appearing suddenly, like he did in the pastures, slowly faded as his hope dwindled.

He made his way into the Outer Ring and saw the remnants of a fire flicker above the edges of the barrel housing the flame. The flame had survived the rain, but a gust of wind roared and the barrel toppled, ashes erupting as flaming embers scattered, the rain sizzling against the flames finally winning the battle to put out the flickers of light. Kaden felt an unexpected kinship with the flame, both beaten down by the storm.

As the fire came and went, Kaden resumed his search for Jericho.

Finally, he decided to quit fighting the storm and found a quiet corner away from the winds. Now shivering from his soaking clothes and dripping hair, he pulled his knees in close to his chest and held tight. Burying his head between his knees, he couldn't stop his body from trembling. Cold and alone in the Outer Ring, he braved the storm as the bitter winds took turns splashing him with another spray of rain and chilling rush of air.

He shivered in the storm and closed his eyes.

Soon, he began to feel warmer. The storm still blew, but it seemed further away, as if a blanket were laid on him, like a protective, warm bubble that the rains couldn't penetrate. The downpour danced side-to-side like millions of synchronized swimmers in mid-air, each trying to find a way in, but a calmness came down on him.

"I'm not out there," a gentle whisper sounded in his ear. He would have jumped if it weren't such a pleasing, smooth tone. "I'm right here," he added.

Kaden turned to see Jericho sitting in the alley, directly next to him in the middle of the storm as it raged around them.

Chapter 48

Kaden watched Jericho. The man who once looked old and feeble in the EMR months ago now appeared to be decades younger and noticeably fit.

Jericho remained silent, smiling politely.

"How's Kira?" Kaden eventually asked.

"You've been walking through storms all night to find me and the first thing you ask is something you could have found out yourself?" Jericho replied, his eyes moving up to the taller apartment buildings toward the Inner Ring.

Kaden looked down.

"She's fine, and so are the others. They're still learning, just like you," Jericho said.

"Learning?"

Jericho nodded an agreement, then he stood up and began walking away. Kaden looked up in disbelief, but Jericho paused, looking back at Kaden and showing a desire for him to follow. Kaden hopped to his feet and quickly caught up.

"I'm learning about The Tower, about Empyrean, and the people of its rings. What are they learning?"

"The same thing," Jericho replied.

"How? From who?"

"They're outside The Tower, but they're not that different. There are leaders and structures within the Remnant, just like in The Tower."

"And Kira is officially in the Remnant now?"

Jericho shook his head yes. "She's been wanting, wishing to tell you all along."

Kaden felt a twist of shame at the divide between him and Kira, but his curiosity moved past the feeling.

"Why do you keep showing up? In my dreams, in the past or future, I forget which, but I know you're everywhere."

"I am," Jericho answered.

"You show up below in the pastures, and during my sorting, you were outside with Kira, both within The Tower boundaries. What are you telling them about The Tower, about Pinnacle?"

"Not much. The Tower's actions say enough."

"Wait, if you're not going into The Tower for the Remnant, then whose side are you on, The Tower's or the Remnant's?" Kaden demanded.

"Neither."

Kaden took a deep breath and threw it out with his frustration. The rain started letting up.

"You chose the life of an Agent, so what's your opinion of the Remnant?" Jericho asked as he turned a corner and continued leading their walk.

"I think they're misguided to say the least," Kaden responded.

"And?"

"And they're likely to get themselves killed. I'm sure you've seen the Elites and have heard about what happens after the sorting."

He nodded.

"So, you know nothing can go against them. Plus, their tactics aren't exactly warm and cuddly, but you have to admit it keeps this place in order."

"Does it?"

"Yes! If this is all that's left of civilization, think about how fragile humanity is. If this city falls, then our entire species goes extinct. You have to give Pinnacle credit for that."

"No."

Kaden stopped in surprise and looked at Jericho, who kept walking. Quickly, he caught up.

"How can you say that?"

"Humanity is already extinct, at least the version you're familiar with, what Darren knew. It died hundreds of years ago," Jericho said.

"No..."

"Have you heard of the New Breed?" Jericho asked.

Kaden slowly nodded, the term creeping up in his mind.

"In Thomas Thornhill's eyes, it was the result of decades of cancer research. The medical breakthrough that evolved humanity into something greater."

"And it worked. We're here." Kaden lifted his hands up, pointing to his chest.

"Did *he* bring you here?" Jericho asked.

Kaden's face went pale.

"No... you did, Dr. Abrams did. You showed me all this..."

"Thomas's story has been refined for generations upon generations. He and his Elites have taken control of the world. They overthrew what was built here, and their roots go deep under this city, but more importantly, they go deep into the hearts of its people."

"But if he saved the world, from all those carcinogens and war, then shouldn't we be grateful for what we have?"

Jericho stopped walking and turned to face Kaden. "We can be grateful for what's left of life, but he didn't save humanity. He killed it."

"What?" Kadden gasped.

Jericho turned and walked up a set of rickety stairs that led up a side of an old building. Kaden followed.

"What do you mean killed it?" Kaden called out.

"Glyphosate or Agent Orange, whatever name it takes, is one of many carcinogens that will always be present in a fallen world. Declining fertility rates were more a sign of wealth and low childhood mortality. Poverty-stricken areas rely on child labor, children must work instead of go to school. If children can grow and thrive with medical care, parents have less children and invest more in them. Survival rates go up."

"Okay..." Kaden said, taking it in.

"To your other point, war over fertile lands has been happening since Kane was expelled for killing his brother. It's important, but not new. None of that would have ended humanity."

"What happened?"

"Greed, then control."

Kaden leapt up a few stairs at a time to get closer to Jericho, who seemed to glide on the stairs with ease, as if his legs levitated more than walked.

"The chance at a trillion-dollar drug didn't start when you met Thomas in my office. It started years earlier. Thomas Thornhill was the first to anchor his future into what *could be*. HIS version of what could be."

Jericho reached the top and walked out onto a roof. The skyline of Empyrean stood before them. The clouds lightened and the thick rain cloud split. Kaden squinted as the brightness hit his eyes. The never-ending overcast skies parted, something he'd never imagined could happen in

Empyrean. Only a silhouette of Jericho remained in the blinding light before him.

Jericho looked back as Kaden's eyes adjusted.

"This is *his* version of what could be," Kaden said.

"His version, but he ignored the truth."

"What's the truth?" Kaden asked.

"I am the truth. My blood in those medical trials all those years ago were the way, the only way, and he ignored it to define the truth for himself," Jericho said.

"But a portion survived. He helped lead and save everyone left, right? This is a good thing," Kaden said, his conviction wavering.

"The New Breed is an abomination, a twist of the power revealed in my blood during the trials. Ninety-nine percent of the population died as a result, and then ninety-nine percent of those survivors perished in the aftermath. The remaining one-thousandth are forever changed by the so-called miracle drug. Those left are the New Breed, and the ancestors of the current population under his dominion."

"Of eight billion, that's only eight hundred thousand survivors, meaning over seven billion dead..." Kaden said, his jaw hanging open in disbelief.

Jericho nodded, his eyes watering.

"But there's not eight hundred thousand in Empyrean, maybe ten thousand, or less."

"Twelve thousand, five hundred and forty-two," Jericho said.

"How do you..." Kaden asked, but his voice trailed off as he saw the seriousness in Jericho's eyes.

The two remained silent as the distant sounds of the waking city began to ring out.

Kaden's mind darted through all he knew: his past as Darren, meeting Dr. Abrams and putting the phoropter on and first traveling to Empyrean to become a young Kaden. Then Kelly's involvement, becoming Kira in this future, and fighting in opposition to The Tower and Kaden's new life here. All of them were in grave danger as Pinnacle and the Elites ruled with an iron fist.

But as Kaden thought, Alister came to mind. His relentless confidence in Jericho still stood out like a budding flower in this desperate, dying landscape.

"You've been showing me what you want me to see, but I don't understand what you want me to learn. Why didn't we have this conversation years ago? I was in your office. Then, I was outside your home, your home where your family... They died, didn't they?" Kaden's mind raced. "But your powers. You had them then, you could have saved them."

"No," Jericho replied so plainly that it sparked confusion and anger in Kaden.

"How can you say 'no' like that? From what I've seen, you control space and time. Gravity itself bends to you, yet you let your family die. And by that same mark, you could have stopped Thornhill all those years ago. Seven billion people, and for what? *You* could have prevented this, YOU COULD HAVE SAVED EVERYONE!" Kaden screamed.

Jericho watched Kaden, patiently ensuring the younger man was finished.

"How could you... ?" He stepped back. "I can't follow you. At least the rest of the world is trying something. You say your the truth, but you wait AND WATCH as millions, billions, of people suffer and die. How many generations did it take for all those billions? And where were you? I tried to find you back then, we went to your office. You moved, you shifted, you hid from me. Why? Why all these years of death?"

Kaden turned away from him, stepping backwards toward the stairs.

"I can't follow someone who hides when we need them most."

To Kaden's surprise, Jericho didn't protest, but remained patiently watching him. The older man's eyes gave off a forgiving and welcoming look, but his body stood firm and tall.

"You shouldn't run away. They're waiting for you."

"You let this evil happen."

Jericho remained on the rooftop, but Kaden didn't give him another chance to speak, running down the stairs.

By the time he hit the ground, the storm clouds returned.

Chapter 49

Entry #8

In Homer's Iliad, Empyrean was a land of perfect happiness where men lived like gods. In the ruins of this world, there will rise a greater glory out of the catastrophes that man brought upon himself. The Hope Drug is showing cracks, just like this world saw and what led to the global epidemics and war that is destroying ninety-nine percent of life on the planet.

This is my declaration.

I will insert the controls required to fix the drug and I will rebuild the world. I will create a new breed of humans, an evolution of the species, that will be more resilient than ever before. The neanderthal and other sapiens died out as homo sapiens' brains grew, eventually conquering the entire earth. No, there is a cellular evolution. Our bodies are catching up to our brains.

My intellect and learning have prepared me for this one thing. I am the last remaining light in a broken world and the perfect person to lead us out of the latest mass extinction event. I know the drug, maybe even better than patient Adam. He is still missing, but my Eve is here and helping unite the world.

We shall go north, to reclaim the northern territories into our Empyrean, where the new breed of men and women shall live like gods.

I can see the benefits of the Hope Drug's evolution even as we still manage testing. Each version is getting more stable, and more powerful.

The activation path is similar to the original drug; however, I found a flaw that is turning out to be more of a feature than a bug. I can supercharge the mitochondria, putting the body in a sort-of extreme ketosis — it uses an incredible amount of energy, but it's not driven by ketones alone. In this state, energy is unlocked from any type of cell. Let me write that again to celebrate the discovery once more, an energy that is more powerful and more stable than ketones can be derived from ANY cell type.

Fat cells still appear to be the preferred power source, just as in ketosis, but muscle, organs, and even skin cells get pulled into the stronger cells. The weaker cells get decomposed; they are effectively consumed by the stronger cells to leverage energy production. The body is consuming itself, like a hyper-drive version of autophagy, the older, less functioning cells are cleaned out.

The typical human body holds enough fat for ketosis to burn ketones for days, weeks, even months, but this condition is burning energy at an alarming rate. The energy is transformed into a new type of strength. It's incredible.

I'm feeling it myself.

Why should I rely on our test subject, Adam? It's time for a new Adam to take control of this world.

Chapter 50

Kira

Her footsteps echoed through the dimly lit tunnels. The air was thick with the scent of dampness and despair, mingling with the smell of blood and tears of the wounded. As she moved from one makeshift infirmary to another, the faces of the injured blurred together, a tapestry of pain woven along the dark floors.

She paused at the bedside of a young woman, only a few years younger than Kira but barely more than a girl. Her arm had been shattered after an Elite threw her fifteen feet in the air. The girl's eyes fluttered open, unfocused at first, then sharpening as they locked onto Kira.

"You," the girl whispered, her voice hoarse. "You convinced us to go."

Kira's throat tightened. "I'm sorry," she managed, the words feeling hollow even as they left her lips. "We're doing everything we can to—"

"To what?" the girl interrupted, her voice gaining strength. "To fight more Elites or to get more of us killed?"

Before Kira could respond, a hand gripped her shoulder. She turned to see Riggs, his bushy beard unable to hide the concern etched on his face.

"Kira," he said softly, "the main chamber. Come."

She nodded, casting one last glance at the injured girl, who scowled back. As they walked, the whispers of doubt that plagued her mind for days were coming to life from the lips of the injured. They were louder, more insistent than her fears.

"...shouldn't have risked so much..."

"...and for an Agent..."

"...how many more will die..."

Kira straightened her back, trying to project a confidence she no longer felt. As they entered the main chamber, the furious discussion quieted and a hush fell over the gathered crowd. Faces turned toward her, some hopeful, others accusing, and many were tired and afraid.

Riggs cleared his throat. "Kira has words for us, about the recent... losses."

She stepped forward, her mind racing. What could she possibly say to ease their pain, to justify the lost lives? But before she could speak, the chamber erupted back into a louder chaos than before.

The source of the commotion soon became clear as the crowd parted, revealing Enak. His arm was still in a sling, a testament to his encounter with Kaden, but his eyes blazed with the fire of a warrior going into battle.

"You knew he made his choice. You knew," he said with disdain.

"Enak!" she reacted. "We thought you were–"

"Dead?" Enak scoffed. "Thank the light, but no thanks to you or your Agent brother."

The crowd pressed closer, squeezing in for the unfolding drama. Kira could see Elba trying to push his way to the front, concern written across his features.

Enak's voice rose, filling the chamber. "The Elites came back. They showed up at the EMR," he said and the crowd drew back in surprise.

"They took from the Inner Ring! They took me, my brother, even Alister. We were sorted, right smack in the middle of The Tower, and guess who presided over that sorting?"

He turned to Kira. She didn't respond.

"Your brother. The same one you were trying to save when you lied about them coming for us. We should go fight two Elites? For what? It was to save your brother who did this to my arm and then watched as the Elites pulled me into their death chambers. And who saved me? Our former childhood friend? NO!"

Kira was shaking her head.

"Jericho saved us, while you led us to fight the enemy!"

Gasps and exclamations rippled through the gathering. Kira felt as if the ground was shifting beneath her feet. She was elated to hear Jericho's name, but there wasn't any joy growing in the crowd.

"Jericho himself pulled me from the jaws of death," Enak continued. "Are you working with Kaden? Are you feeding us to them so he can get another colored robe?"

"That's not true!" Kira protested, but her voice was drowned out by the growing clamor.

"How many died in that fight?" someone shouted from the back.

"My sister is still missing!" cried another.

"We trusted you!"

The accusations flew like arrows, each one finding its mark. Kira felt herself backing away, overwhelmed by the tide of anger and betrayal.

Suddenly, Riggs' voice boomed out, silencing the crowd. "ENOUGH!" He moved to stand beside Kira, his bulk a reassuring presence. "Have we forgotten everything we stand for? Everything we've fought for?"

Elba joined them, his quiet voice carrying surprising strength. "Let's not forget what happened to our leadership. How many died in the attack on the labs? Twenty-seven never made it back, but Kira led us out. We brought back food that all of you and all your children ate. Yes, we've suffered losses, but we've also struck blows against The Tower that we never thought possible. I think she's earned the right to make these decisions."

The crowd's mood wavered, uncertain. Kira seized the moment, stepping forward. "I understand your anger, your pain. I feel it too; with every life we lose, I feel it. But we can't turn on each other now. The Tower, the Elites – they're the real enemy."

She took a deep breath, steeling herself. "Yes, I tried to save my brother. And I would do it again. Not just because he's my brother, but because every life we save from The Tower's grip is a victory. Every person we bring back to the light is one less soldier in their army of darkness."

A tense silence fell over the chamber. Kira could see the conflict playing out on the faces before her – their anger warring with hope.

Then, from the back of the crowd, a familiar figure came forward and the crowd watched one of the few senior members still alive. Kira's heart rose in her chest as Barb, her mentor and friend, stood out from the crowd.

"We have rules. Don't mess with Elites. You shouldn't have gone out there," Barb said.

Kira felt her heart sink as Barb's eyes were filled with disappointment.

"Barb," Kira began, but the older woman cut her off.

"No, you listen. I've seen what happens when people cross The Tower. I warned you, didn't I? But you didn't stop and think." Barb's voice dropped as her face lowered to the ground. For the first time in Kira's life, her mentor seemed to be losing her faith. "Now we're all paying the price."

The words hit Kira like physical blows. She opened her mouth to respond, but found she had no defense.

Barb continued, her voice softening slightly. "It was too risky, too costly. And look where we are now – broken, hunted, turning on each other. I suppose it's not your fault; you haven't been prepared for leadership. None of you have."

The chamber fell silent once more, the weight of Barb's words settling over them. Kira could feel the eyes of the Remnant upon her, waiting for a response, a solution, anything. But for the first time since she'd been thrust into leadership, Kira found herself utterly lost for words.

"I..." she began, her voice faltering. But she never finished her sentence. She turned and left the chamber, ignoring the calls of Riggs and Elba behind her. Her walk turned into a run through the twisting tunnels, past startled Remnant members, until she reached the hidden sewer exit that led to the surface.

The cool night air hit her like a shock as she emerged into an abandoned alleyway. She leaned against the rough brick wall, gulping in deep breaths, trying to clear her head.

Chapter 51

Kaden sat up as the rain finally broke. He managed to get a few hours of sleep, curled up under an overhang of an abandoned building. The Outer Ring had changed from when he was a boy, running from Agents and rioters, but he still knew of a few spots where he could be safe and mostly out of the weather.

"Two more days," he said as he stood up and looked at the looming Tower as it shot high above all the other buildings around it, like an overly strict mother watching all her children and demanding their compliance under her watchful eye.

The sun was yet to rise. The cold night air chilled his skin. He rubbed his arms and moved around to get his blood flowing. As he ventured out from his makeshift shelter, the streets were eerily quiet, as if the night cast a depression over even the most resilient of Empyrean's residents.

As he turned a corner, a familiar figure caught his eye.

"No..." he whispered in surprise.

Kira stood at the end of the alley, her eyes scanning the horizon as if searching for something – or someone. When she spotted Kaden, she lit up.

"Kaden!" she called out, her voice barely above a whisper, her eyes scanning around him.

He approached cautiously, still unsure of where they stood after everything that had happened. "Kira? What are you doing out here? It's not safe."

She smiled with a sarcastic laugh. "Is anywhere safe?"

As they drew closer, Kaden could see the toll recent events had taken on his sister. Dark circles rimmed her eyes, and her usual confident posture was slightly slumped.

"Are you alone?" she asked.

Kaden hesitated a moment, then nodded.

"You?" he asked in response.

She confirmed.

"I've been searching for Jericho," she admitted. "I thought... I thought he might be out here, might have some answers."

Kaden felt a surge of anger at the mention of Jericho's name, remembering their last conversation on the rooftop. But something in Kira's voice made him hold his tongue.

"I just left him, but no idea where he'd disappeared to this time," he said, unable to hold back a bitter tone. Kira picked up on it and eyed him, but he brushed it off. "Come on," he said instead, gesturing to a nearby doorway that offered some shelter. "Let's get out of the wind."

Once they were settled, Kira tentatively spoke as if thinking of every syllable. "How's... how's your training going? And congrats... on the Blue, I mean."

"Well, that ordeal with the Elites out there got me kicked out for three days. So there's that..." he said.

"Kaden." Her face grew grim. "Did you oversee a Sorting?"

His face went pale. He wanted to lie, to run, but he was tired of trying to convince himself.

"I did. I should have stood up to them, but the Elites, my leaders, even Pinnacle was there," he said. He let out a breath, his body slumping over. "I was weak... Scared to do anything real. Enak caused a commotion, and this jolly Alister guy was talking with me... Both set off alarm bells, and I was too weak to do anything. I stood there and watched..." His eyes grew watery and Jericho's face came into mind. The saddened face that watched Kaden storm away, off the rooftop. It was how Kaden felt in that moment, a broken heart over watching a horrible thing happen to someone he loved.

Kira reached out and put an arm around him.

Kaden continued, "And then it was made worse when Enak and Alister disappeared. Fighting with Elites was seen as a good thing, but with their disappearance, it all flips. I'm being accused of being a traitor now. That doesn't go over well."

"Sorry to hear." She rubbed his shoulder. "Well, don't tell your people, but I'm a high-ranking member now," Kira said. "Enak accused me of working with you, for The Tower. I suppose we're just two traitors consorting with each other."

"Congrats on the promotion, I guess." He laughed, feeling his heart uplifted by being with her. "Knew that was only a matter of time with your conviction."

"That, or when the two dozen or so highest-ranking members get devoured by Elites, it's easy to climb the ladder." She forced a smile, but a wave of sadness took it away.

"The lab?"

Kira nodded, still looking away.

"Why'd you have to blow it up? I was there, my whole team down there," Kaden said.

"Kaden, let's not do this. You know the food situation, we lived it, and I didn't know who would be there. We prayed for no casualties, but had to force The Tower to rethink its food testing and distribution."

Kaden thought about how he went to be Darren when he died, but he was so much Kaden in this world that the past felt like a childhood fantasy.

"Do you remember being Kelly?" Kaden asked.

Kira's eyes widened as if reminded of a dear, long-forgotten friend. "I do," she confirmed, but then concern washed over her face. "At least I think I do. She's like a version of me that I once dreamt I could be, but then turned out like this."

"I think I died down there. In the explosion you all set off, then the fall. It all killed me, and I returned to Darren. It's hard to explain," he said.

Kira watched him for a moment as they sat in silence.

"I have dreams of her, or me, whatever. And I always know I'm madly in love with my boyfriend," she said, elbowing him. Both smiled yet looked away.

"Want to know something I learned since being on the inside?" he said, his eyebrows raised.

"Shoot. Unless you're done consorting with the enemy?"

"Only just begun." He smiled. "In our dreams, the past world, people reproduce together. It's a decision between two people. But here, it's The Tower that breeds everyone. They control all births and then distribute the children to a place in the Inner or Outer Ring to control the population."

"Of course The Tower controls it. That's nothing new," she said.

"How'd you know that?" he said, holding up his hands in surprise.

"You really notice nothing. Why all the orphans in the Outer Ring, with parents who can't even take care of themselves?" She shook her head at him. "The Tower breeds children and gives benefits to people who take 'em in. That's nothing new, at least to the women out here." She looked down then laughed sarcastically.

"Should I still call you sister, or maybe call everyone else brother and sister? I mean, if we're all test tubes..." Kaden asked.

"I don't know anymore." Kira exhaled, and it looked like she slumped down six inches, as if she released a backpack full of bricks. "Kaden, I don't know what I'm doing anymore. The Lighthouse Remnant... we're losing. Not just to the Elites, but to fear and doubt. They look to me for answers, and I don't have any."

Kaden listened, surprised by her candor. This wasn't the fiery, determined Kira he was used to.

"I believe in what we're fighting for," she continued. "I believe in the Lighthouse Remnant. But..." Her voice broke slightly. "I'm starting to think we can't do this alone. We need Jericho."

Kaden felt a conflicting surge of emotions – sympathy for Kira's struggle, but frustration at the mention of Jericho, and a gnawing doubt about his own role in all of this.

"Kira," he said gently, "how can you still have faith in Jericho? After everything that's happened? He could have prevented all of this. Where is he when we need him most?"

She looked at him, her eyes shining with a mixture of tears and determination. "Because I've seen what he can do, Kaden. He freed Enak and Alister from right under the Elites' noses. He's been guiding us, protecting us, even when we couldn't see it. Who do you think was in that alley when we were kids?"

Kaden shook his head. "But what about all the people who've died? All the suffering in Empyrean? Where was Jericho for them?"

Kira was quiet for a moment, considering his words. When she spoke again, her voice was thoughtful. "I used to ask myself the same thing. I'd rush into every fight, every decision, thinking I had all the answers. But now... now I'm learning to step back. To see the bigger picture. Even now, I don't know if I made the right move to go after those Elites and try to save you."

"That was you?" Kaden gasped.

"Didn't work out too well in the end. You shoulda heard Barb," she said.

"Oh, Barb is as grumpy as they come. You should have seen her face when I was standing in the middle of the EMR, soaking wet and a puddle underneath me," he said.

"Wow, she must have..."

"Oh yeah, she was livid." Kaden smiled. "But, Kira, thank you. Those Elites would have killed me, and maybe I would have returned to being Darren. But who knows how all this swapping really works, or what would happen if they consumed me."

"I can name one person who does." She leaned forward, her gaze intense. "Kaden, I don't understand everything Jericho does or doesn't do. But I've realized that faith isn't about having all the answers. It's about trusting even when you don't understand."

Kaden's anger only boiled hotter.

"The world Jericho is fighting for," Kira continued, "it's bigger than just Empyrean. It's about the very nature of humanity. You should read the manuscript he's left for us! And I mean sometimes... Well, sometimes that means not intervening in every little thing. It means letting people make choices, even if those choices lead to pain. What kind of savior would he be if he used his powers to force everyone to do exactly what he wanted?"

A thought ignited in Kaden, his eyes lighting up. "He'd be Pinnacle..." he said, his own words striking him like a revelation.

The pair remained silent as Kaden pondered her words, remembering his own struggles with the moral complexities of life in The Tower. "How do we live in this world?"

Kira gave a small, sad smile. "That's the hard part, isn't it? But I know that doing nothing isn't an option. We have to keep moving forward, keep fighting for what's right, even if we don't always know the best way to do it."

She hopped up to her feet.

"I suppose that settles it, then," she said.

The sky began to lighten, the first rays of dawn creeping over the horizon. Kaden found himself seeing Kira in a new light – not just as his impulsive sister, or whatever relation they were to each other, but as a leader grappling with impossible choices. Just like himself.

"Kaden," Kira said suddenly, her voice filled with a new urgency. "Come back with me. Join the Lighthouse Remnant. We could really use someone like you. I think it'll be good for you as well."

For a moment, Kaden was tempted. He looked at her outstretched hand. The thought of leaving The Tower, of fighting alongside Kira was alluring. But then he thought of his team, of the complexities within The Tower itself. He remembered Pinnacle's words about the fragility of their last bastion of humanity.

"You think they'd take an Agent?" He laughed and looked up through a hole in the pitiful roof above them, peering at the overcast sky. An urge inside him wished to see the stars as he grew somber. "I can't, Kira," he said softly. "I'm an Agent."

Disappointment flashed across Kira's face, but it was quickly replaced by understanding. "I get it, but you're welcome. You know that, right?" she said.

Kaden didn't answer.

"Be careful, bro," she said.

Kaden stood, and for a moment, they were just each other, not leaders within opposing factions. Kira stepped forward and hugged Kaden tightly. He returned the embrace, feeling how much he had missed her.

As they parted ways, Kaden found that his anger toward Jericho subsided, replaced by a curious need to understand. Why had Jericho acted as he did? What was the bigger picture that Kaden couldn't yet see?

He watched Kira disappear into the awakening city, her faith having planted a seed of doubt in his own convictions. As he turned back toward The Tower, Kaden realized that his path forward was no longer as clear as he had once thought. Control, freewill; they were not absolute.

The sun finally crested the horizon, casting long shadows across Empyrean as the sky lit up on the horizon. In that moment, caught between light and darkness, Kaden felt the weight of choice pressing down on him. He took a deep breath, squaring his shoulders.

"Less than two days," he said to himself.

As Kaden made his way back through the waking streets of the Outer Ring, his mind was a whirlwind of conflicting thoughts and emotions. Kira's words echoed in his head, challenging everything he thought he knew about Jericho, about The Tower, about the very nature of their world.

He found himself paying closer attention to the people around him as the Outer Ring came to life. A woman struggled to carry a heavy bucket of water, her face etched with lines of exhaustion. Two children darted between buildings, their laughter a rare sound in the somber atmosphere. An old man sat in a doorway, his eyes vacant, as if he had seen too much in his long life.

These were the people Kira was fighting for, Kaden realized. Not just against The Tower's oppression, but for a chance at a real life, at hope. And yet, wasn't The Tower also trying to protect humanity in its own way? The complexity of it all made his head spin.

As he neared the border between the Outer and Inner Rings, Kaden spotted a familiar face – Alister, the jolly repairman who had escaped the sorting. The older man was whistling as he tinkered with a piece of machinery, seemingly oblivious to the world around him.

Curiosity got the better of Kaden, and he approached. "Alister?"

The man looked up, his face breaking into a wide grin. "Well, if it isn't the blue-robed wonder himself! Still without your robe, though, eh?"

Kaden shrugged, now used to wearing only his damp athletic clothes.

"Come to drag me back to the sorting?" Alister said.

Kaden winced at the reminder. "No, I... I just wanted to talk. Could you tell me how you escaped?"

Alister's eyes twinkled. "Didn't I tell you? He said He'd save me, and He did. Simple as that."

"But how?" Kaden pressed. "The Elites, the consumption rooms... how did you get out?"

Alister set down his tools, his expression growing serious. "Son, some things you just have to experience to understand. But I'll tell you this – when Jericho showed up, it was like... like the very air changed. Those Elites, they just froze. And then we were outside, free as birds."

Kaden shook his head, struggling to reconcile this with what he knew of The Tower's security.

"That's impossible. The Tower's defenses–"

"Are nothing compared to His power," Alister finished. "You've seen it yourself, haven't you? Out there in the pastures?"

Kaden remembered the strange occurrences, the way Jericho seemed to appear and disappear at will. "I... I don't know what I've seen anymore."

Alister laid a hand on Kaden's shoulder, his touch surprisingly gentle for hands that spent a life in manual labor. "That's a good place to start, son. Admitting you don't know everything. It's the first step toward real understanding."

As Kaden mulled over these words, a commotion further down the street caught his attention. An Agent and two Elites were approaching. Above the purple robe was a familiar face. Ron-ell.

Alister followed Kaden's gaze and quickly stepped back. "Looks like that's my cue."

With that, the jolly repairman melted into the crowd, leaving Kaden to face his former teacher alone.

Ron-ell's eyes narrowed as he spotted Kaden. "Agent McCloud. I see you've decided to fraternize with the locals during your exile."

Kaden straightened, forcing his face into a neutral expression. "I'd say gathering intelligence. As any good Agent would be doing," he fired back.

A flicker of something crossed Ron-ell's face, but Kaden couldn't read if it was approval or annoyance. "Indeed. Well, your time out here is halfway over. I expect to see you back at The Tower tomorrow evening, ready to resume your duties."

As Ron-ell and the two Elites at his side continued their patrol, Kaden felt a chill run down his spine. The encounter was a stark reminder of the world he would be returning to, a world of rigid hierarchies and unquestioning obedience.

And yet, as he watched Ron-ell disappear around a corner, Kaden couldn't shake the feeling that something had fundamentally shifted within him. Kira's unwavering faith, Alister's quiet confidence, even Jericho's cryptic words on the rooftop – all of it was coming together to form a picture he couldn't quite make out yet.

As the sun climbed higher in the sky, casting its light over the patchwork of hope and despair that was Empyrean, Kaden made a silent vow. He would return to The Tower, yes. But this time, he would do so with open eyes and an open mind, ready to seek out the truth no matter where it might lead him.

CHAPTER 52

Entry #9

He's abandoned us once again. Coming out of an aggressive cancer to be a symbol of life, survival, and power yet stepping away is one thing. He had a family and it was a big change; we all did what we had to do. Now the world is a nuclear wasteland and he builds a lighthouse away from the city. He's mocking us, claiming to be there for more survivors, the travelers who have heard and come to seek life. Fool.

I'll build a tower that will make his lighthouse look like a toothpick. We need to pull together. I have the New Breed and the source material for the Hope Drug. The latest version is the most powerful. The small side effect of losing

one's epidermis to a layer of rock is a fair trade to be able
to control physical matter. We bend gravity to our will and
society follows.

His abandonment will not go unseen. We had it. For a
hundred years, we survived, we two and our model of Eve,
as the world slowly killed itself, yet the finger hovering over
the button finally went down.

Once that button was pushed, it was all over. We could have
reunited our partnership. We could have built the New
Breed together, but no.

He goes into the desert.

He goes to his death.

CHAPTER 53

Two days later, Kaden was back in his quarters and devouring the first full meal since he'd been sent out of The Tower. He picked up his freshly cleaned robe and went to class, eager to rejoin his cohort, but as he walked into the room, the figures before him stopped him cold. The air seemed to leave the room as a pressure came down on him.

Four Elites stood around the room. Each of their dead eyes shot to him as he entered. Ron-ell stood at the front of the room, unperturbed by Kaden's entrance.

"What is this?" Kaden asked.

"A lot has happened since your disappearance," Ron-ell said as he nodded to the class. They stood up and left. Jace's and Aria's eyes looked at Kaden with sorrow, speaking sympathetic words that Kaden couldn't interpret, while Ryon and Vala were stone-faced, never meeting his eyes as they followed two of the Elites out of the classroom.

Ron-ell and two Elites remained, surrounding Kaden. Behind Ron-ell were diagrams of tunnels, three areas highlighted.

"What's that?" Kaden asked.

"No longer for you to know. Mr. McCloud, there has–"

"Agent McCloud. I'm an Agent," Kaden interjected to Ron-ell's chagrin. "Why do I feel like I'm coming back to a different Tower?"

"Your speech patterns of late have detected something. How shall I say this? You've been sympathetic to the Remnant. And given the prior anomalies on your record, I'd say it adds up," Ron-ell said.

"My speech patterns?" Kaden said, bewildered.

"Do you not think everything in this great Tower is not recorded? Pinnacle sees all, and believe me, he has granted more mercy than you deserve. Even your own cohort has expressed their concerns."

"My cohort?"

"NOTHING goes unheard in these walls, or is your weak Outer Ring mind unable to comprehend how The Tower operates? You're a fool, Kaden. I've wasted my time with you and you've complicated my ability to serve Pinnacle. Your disloyalty impacts your cohort as well."

Visions of Ryon's and Vala's confused or angry expressions shot into his mind like a bomb going off. Had they ratted him out to Ron-ell for ill speech about The Tower? Ron-ell was only too quick to jump on it, already furious with Pinnacle's taking a liking to Kaden.

"Anything else, *Teacher*?" Kaden said, bitterness rising to the surface as he became acutely aware of the two Elites that eyed him like their next meal.

"I accuse you of treason," Ron-ell snapped. "I saved you. I brought you in!" His anger sent spittle off his lips as he spoke. "And this is how you repay me? By consorting with a rebellion, by undermining Pinnacle? He gave you a sorting in your first year and you don't even realize the honor!"

Kaden remained firm in the face of Ron-ell tirade.

"Fine, kick me out," Kaden rebutted, but he knew the hammer was yet to drop. The Elites were too eager.

"No more trials. You will be brought before the council, judged, and the sentence carried out immediately."

"Sounds like not much of a trial," Kaden replied.

"You can join your traitor sister as the Elites decide your fate."

"No," Kaden refuted in disbelief.

"We know who you speak with, we know who was in the pastures setting off explosives. Elites consumed their leadership and know what they know. It wasn't weird the only party we didn't catch was your former roommate and friends? Hmmm, put those pieces together, *Agent*." He moved.

"You can't–"

"The matter is over!" He waved his hand and the Elites finally jumped into action, moving to secure Kaden and pushing him with an invisible force outside the classroom and down the hall.

"No–" Kaden began, but he felt a force constricting his chest. It was nearly impossible to breathe let alone speak. They held him ahead like he was a carrot on a stick dangling before themselves. His chest felt like a gigantic snake constricted him as he struggled for short breaths.

As they left the staircase and stood before the grand, domed ballroom, Beth-ell cut off the Elites. She stood before Kaden, her weathered face of countless years showing no emotion as she studied him, looking into his eyes. Kaden took tiny breaths, sucking in what air he could as he looked back into her eyes. Then, suddenly, she revealed her disappointment.

"I thought you'd be so much more..." she said, shaking her head. She stepped back as the Elites pushed him into the room.

His third time in the great room with the exquisite marble-carved artwork covering the walls, running up the doomed ceiling. The first two meetings here were with Pinnacle, the empty room echoing their conversation. But now, the entire edge of the circular room was filled with Agents and Elites. They stood in a repeating pattern, one Agent then two Elites.

Kaden's eyes widened at how many surrounded the room, thinking there must be nearly a hundred Elites alone, and another fifty Agents. His awe turned into two thoughts. He'd never contemplated how many Agents and Elites were in Empyrean. But he also had another thought, that there were only hundreds of Agents and Elites, but tens of thousands of people living in the Inner and Outer Rings, an order of magnitude more bodies under the rule of a vicious minority.

The Elites released him, throwing him to the center of the room. He skidded on the stone floor, his hands squeaking against the smooth polish and echoing off the cavernous roof.

Kaden stood up, his heart pounding as over a hundred of the most powerful beings all silently watched him. All their attention shifted from him to the dark hallway across the ballroom.

First, she flew out, sliding across the floor like a child kicked a toy. The room remained silent and the air escaped Kaden's lungs as he saw Kira slowly stand up, covered in bruises and cuts from a torturous night.

As she stood, she turned to see the circle of Agents and Elites around her. An expression of horror seemed to lurk right under the surface of her battered face. She straightened her posture and the flicker of a fearful expression turned to determination. Kaden's heart burned for her, so proud of her resilience and her faith to encourage whatever hell they forced upon her.

She spun, meeting Kaden's eyes, and he ran to her. They embraced, then pulled back, silently looking into each other's eyes.

"I'm sorry I got you into this," Kaden whispered.

"It was a team effort," she replied.

The brief moment of joy held their hearts, rejuvenating their spirits, but it was fleeting. A moment later, the oppressive weight of the air fell on them like rocks from the sky. Never had Kaden felt the very hope in his soul being pushed down, like an ant trying to hold up a human's shoe. The weight crippled them both and they dropped to one knee, as if they were forced to bow.

Then, footsteps echoed from the dark hallway, like a timer counting down their fate.

Click... click... click... click...

Kaden squeezed her hand and forced himself to stand up. His back screamed as it pushed against the invisible force, but he stood.

Click... click... click... click...

Pinnacle's face came out of the tunnel. It flashed a terrible expression, and a wave of black washed across his olive skin. He scowled, and Kaden was smashed to the ground, the shoe stepping on the ant.

Kaden felt like the weight of the world was pressing the life out of him. Squirming, he tried getting up, but his body couldn't move. A moment later, he and Kira were ripped apart, separated from the center of the room. Then, Pinnacle's scowl turned into a smile as he raised his hands and lifted both up, each feeling like a string puppet jerked from the floor to now their toes barely scraping the surface of the stone floor.

"Welcome, my children," Pinnacle said, smiling with his pearly white, perfect teeth. "The two before you are charged with treason against Empyrean. We've built a perfect paradise in this world, one where the common man can rise to unbelievable powers and long life, yet as anything in the world, there are those who seek to tear our great society to the ground."

He spun, raising his hands as he made a spectacle of the situation. Beth-ell and a pair of Elites stood looking back. Ron-ell, in his fresh purple robe, stood obediently in between another pair of the charcoal demons.

"We once celebrated this young man for fighting next to Elites, but it shows us that we must root out evil even in our own midst. What is the saying, my children, take the plank out of your own eye before that of your brothers? We cannot give life to the world if we are divided against ourselves."

His arms dropped and his eyes went to Kaden and Kira.

"They are deemed guilty and their punishment set. Yet, in the sadness of treason, we find the light. We will use this for a special ceremony. You see, our Elites picked up on something special in this pair, the smell of the forbidden one," he said and the room seemed to growl in unison like attack dogs now primed with a trigger command.

"His stench is infectious and must be rooted out!" he said, shooting out his hand and pointing at the pair. The room shook with his emotion, the surrounding crowd cheered, and a dull black, charcoal-like coloring rippled over Pinnacle's perfect features.

"Therefore, I will execute their judgment. I shall consume them," he said and stepped toward them. His rage instantly flipped to a grin. "Who first?" he said softly, his eyes going back and forth between them. The gray eyes stopped on Kira, and he began opening his black robe. His bare chest was chiseled with muscle. As he stepped toward her, his smile grew more sinister and Kaden noticed another wave of black flutter over Pinnacle's skin. The charcoal of the Elites flashed through him like a swarm of worms freely crawling under his skin.

"You won't," Kaden said, trying to move toward Pinnacle, but his toes merely brushed the ground as he levitated about the floor, unable to gain traction.

Kira's face remained steeled as Pinnacle approached, and Kaden could see he was toying with her. Her hair began to raise, pointing toward Pinnacle's exposed chest, then her clothes stood as if being blown by the wind. Finally, Kaden's heart sank as her face contorted in pain as if her insides were being pulled forward by a medieval torture device. He knew the feeling after his standoff with the Elites. Slowly and methodically, Pinnacle increased the pull on her, his smile showing constant enjoyment.

"Stop it!" Kaden shouted. "Leave her, you want me!" All of his cries fell on deaf ears.

Pinnacle was focused on Kira and now her arms and legs raised as she smashed her eyes closed. He seemed to hold her up by a string as he toyed with her, pulling her body, tenderizing her before consuming her.

"He's more powerful than you'll ever be!" Kaden found himself scream-ing and he caught a flicker of Pinnacle's eye as it twitched toward Kaden and then back to Kira. He stopped toying with her and raised his hand. Curling his fingers, he called her toward him. She shot at him like an iron filling pulled by a magnet.

Anguish filled Kaden's heart as he saw her fly toward him. The world seemed to be in slow motion as she accelerated toward him.

But she never reached him.

She stopped midair and then gently lowered to the floor. The pain on her face subsided and color returned to her flushed cheeks.

Pinnacle's eyes widened, and his bulging shoulders shot back as he flexed his chest, but to his dismay, Kira didn't move. He tried again, and again, but still, she remained safe and looking healthier than before, the bruises and scrapes all healing in front of the entire crowd.

"You will not–" Pinnacle screamed, but then an invisible force threw him back. The surrounding Agents and Elites gasped at their master.

The room trembled, as if the whole Tower shook, and the sound of cracking rock began. Pebbles from the dome above them began to fall intermittently as the floor shook. Then the pebbles turned to boulders larger than a man. One of the massive crumbling objects fell, landing on an Agent and smashing the life out of him instantly as an opening in the dome showed a mist-filled light.

"YOU WILL NOT!" Pinnacle demanded, but the room shifted despite his pleas. Two circles, diagonal from each other – one on the wall and floor and the other on the opposite wall and dome ceiling – ripped open. Like an invisible cylinder was pulled from the room, Kira and Kaden saw the room around them lift away. They were being removed from The Tower. Surrounding Agents and Elites were crushed by falling stone or fell through the openings, falling outside The Tower hundreds of feet to their deaths below.

Pinnacle stood up, his body now nearly all black, matching the charcoal skin of the Elites as only a piece of olive skin danced around him. Fury washed over his face.

"I built this! I made it great when you failed!" he screamed and it carried through Empyrean like an erupting volcano.

Kaden and Kira were carried away from The Tower and toward a smaller apartment building nearby. Kaden looked up at The Tower as Pinnacle screamed in protest. An entire chunk was pulled out from the monstrous structure that scraped the heavens. Cracks were forming on the outer walls around the grand ballroom. The once mighty Tower now stood in the daylight like a dead tree, wavering in a windstorm.

The windows shot out of the apartment behind Kira and Kaden, and the marble floor below their feet rested gently in the room. There was a purple couch and orange chair. They both saw it and they caught each others' eyes.

They were home.

They ran back to the opening in the window, looking to The Tower. Now thousands of others gathered against their windows and in the alleys below, watching the carnage play out. In The Tower, Kaden could see Elites smashed against the ground far below, breaking into countless pieces like shattered opaque rocks. The courtyard surrounding The Tower was littered with clumps of black and a colorful sprinkling of Agents in their various robes. Lines of red connected them all, appearing from high above like a red spiderweb.

Everything seemed to fall from The Tower, the crumbling walls, Agents, and Elites, but there, still standing where he tried to consume Kira, was Pinnacle. Fury was written across his face as his eyes watered, continuing to scream into the roaring winds.

Then, something rose off the ground, like a car going against rush hour or salmon swimming upstream; one man rose while all others fell.

Kaden already knew in his heart when he heard Kira whisper, "It's... Him."

Jericho rose through the air and into the hole in the side of The Tower. All Empyrean saw him levitate up. Then he calmly walked to confront Pinnacle.

Kaden heard their conversation as if they were standing right next to him.

"You left, and I did what you couldn't," Pinnacle said.

"The end begins now," Jericho replied.

The pair locked eyes and Kaden braced for an explosive battle that would likely send The Tower falling, killing everyone in and around it. But to his surprise, Jericho didn't make a move. He stood, his chest out as Pinnacle reacted.

"It is!" Pinnacle said, his body turning black like charcoal as he shot his hand at Jericho.

Kaden imagined Jericho batting it away and striking Pinnacle down. He imagined Pinnacle being tortured, getting everything he deserved for leading the world with an iron fist. An unimaginable punishment to fit the unbearable and countless crimes of death, pain, and sorrow he'd caused through the centuries.

But Jericho didn't stop the death blow that came at him. Instead, he leaned forward, moving his chest into the perfect position for Pinnacle's piercing hand.

Pinnacle stabbed Jericho's chest, his hand rupturing skin and breaking ribs apart. Jericho's body shook like a twitching muscle, then Pinnacle ripped out his hand and held a still beating heart. The blood dripped down his arm and spattered the floor around him.

Jericho swayed, all of Empyrean watching him, then he fell to the ground.

Pinnacle watched him fall, a flicker of surprise that erupted into exuberance. His tower crumbled around him as his warriors fell to their death, but Pinnacle held up Jericho's heart in victory, screaming a war cry that rang through all of Empyrean.

Chapter 54

Entry #10

I've named them Elites for obvious reasons. They are a perfected humanity. Within five generations, we've eradicated the weaker genres in the surviving human race. Eve was pushing for it to be within one generation, a swift genocide and replacement. However, she does not see the bigger picture. The dying out species provided the perfect labor required to advance the foundational needs of Empyrean while the first generations of the New Breed honed the technology required for total surveillance and sustainability of this new world. No longer will human error be the guiding force of our future. I have set the course properly for the common man to survive adequately in a series of living arrangements. It is the perfect harmony where they worship the centralized tower, all efforts focused on the greater good, and those special Agents and Elites enforce the rule of law. The structure is nearly perfect, and if there is dissent, as there will inevitably be, we control births, education, day-to-day work, the financial system, and housing. Any dissent will be quietly and quickly eradicated. Which brings me to the main thought I journal about today... He is still out there. The one remaining citizen of the world who carries the original human genetic code.

His lighthouse is not dying, but burning brighter. I built a tower to the heavens, yet he mocks me every day with that pale light in the distance. It provides a false hope, luring my New Breed out into the desert and to what? Their sure death.

I cannot control this world if his light shines to even a spark.

The time of waiting for his own death is over.

I will kill him.

CHAPTER 55

"**N**o..." Kira whispered in disbelief as she saw Jericho's body fall.

Kaden clenched his fists so hard, his nails dug into his palm. They watched Pinnacle standing over Jericho's body, screaming in victory.

Lightning cracked in the sky as the overcast skies thickened. The winds picked up and a storm erupted, more lightning cracking across Empyrean as if a fuse to the skies reached its end and a glorious explosion erupted in the heavens.

A few of the surviving Elites shot toward Pinnacle and smothered Jericho's body.

"We have to get him out of there!" Kira shouted.

"He's dead, Kira!" Kaden screamed back, the wind ripping at their words through the open window.

A lightning bolt cracked toward their shattered apartment, sending a flash against the wall of their building and igniting a fire the rain fought back against. The bolt sent both Kaden and Kira backwards.

As he flew backwards, he saw the brilliant bright light as it came down. It surrounded him and then snapped away, leaving his body in Empyrean unconscious, but his mind woke up in his old, familiar dream where he was running away from fire.

Once again, he chased after Kira, watching her run up over the horizon, and then Jericho stepped to Kaden. The heat felt like it was bubbling his skin as the flames licked his back, but he stood looking into Jericho's gray eyes.

"You're the fire," Jericho said, then he leaned back and the flame shot past Kaden and devoured Jericho. He felt the heat like it was a bottled-up fury finally unleashed, an explosion of torment. Soon, the fire dissipated, and ashes that were once Jericho floated in the wind.

The dream always ended with Kaden seeing the ashes float away, but this time, he stayed in the vision. The ashes danced in the air currents, rising up and spreading across the city and outward over the walls.

"You're the fire," he heard Jericho's voice say again, as if he were still right there beside him. "Now show the world what a righteous fire can do. Fight for those weaker, flip the tables of the wicked, and become a beacon of life to a world in need."

The vision of ashes floating away changed. Now Kaden was a young boy, back in the alley as the Elite's grip crushed his neck. He gasped for air. A figure appeared in a hood. The Elite threw down Kaden, but now Kaden's head didn't smash into the cobblestone. He went down gently and saw the Elite as it looked to the hooded figure.

Jericho stood, the wind whipping the ends of his jacket, and the Elite's hardened face – a face that shuddered at no man – was terrified.

Kaden saw the fear in its eyes before Jericho flicked his wrist and sent the creature soaring through the alley. He watched as Kira came out the creature's hand. They saw each other, in the bodies of children, but in her eyes, he knew that she was living out this vision just like he was.

With another flash of light, Kaden woke up. He looked at the purple couch that Kira prized, now broken in two as he lay in the middle. The blast sent him through the prized furniture.

Kira stood up. She had slid on the floor all the way to the kitchen, slamming against the wall.

"You saw it? They were scared of him?" Kaden said. "I never thought I'd see an Elite scared of anything."

"I did, but there was more. Where were you before the alley?" Kira asked.

"My dream, the wall of fire chasing me. You were there this time?" he asked.

"No. I was at the Lighthouse. He showed me what happened out there in the desert," she said, shaking her head as if not believing what she saw.

The floor of the ballroom that flew with them into their apartment was now burnt from the lightning bolt. A huge black scar covered it like a flaming sword from above cut into its surface.

They stood and the storm died down. They could see The Tower, full of cracks, now deserted where Pinnacle once stood, Jericho's body gone.

"What do we do now?" Kira said as she looked out of the open hole where a wall once held back the sky.

"He can't be gone," Kaden said. "He can't... He sacrificed himself for us, just like the dream. I brought the fire, through all these efforts of The Tower, but he took it. He took it all, for us, and... and now he's gone..."

They both stood in disbelief, looking out over the city and at the hole ripped through The Tower. The bodies of Agents and Elites dotted the streets below like frozen ants.

"Will you go back?" Kira finally asked.

"No," Kaden said, and he paused for a long moment, taking in a deep breath and releasing it. "The scales are off my eyes. My days as an Agent are over."

"We have the tunnels. Come hide with us," Kira said.

"They know about them. I saw a map before they took me. They know all of it."

"But we've moved positions, they couldn't have," Kira said.

"Where have you been going?" Kaden asked.

"Further down... Our space has been growing smaller and smaller, and we're further and further away, but they... They keep finding us," Kira said as a realization dawned on her. "They were forcing us back, herding us."

Kaden nodded solemnly.

"The Remnant will be wiped out, won't it? When they found me, there was nothing stopping them from annihilating everyone. Pinnacle wanted me first," she said.

Once again, silence filled the space in between the storm, then Kira turned to him. "Where will you run?"

"I'm not running anymore. The Remnant is on the run, but we'll find survivors. We'll regroup, then... We're bringing the fight to them."

"You're talking like someone in the Remnant," Kira said.

"If you'll have me, I'd be honored, and Kira, I'm sorry," he said, turning to look her in the eyes.

She saw his watering eyes, hers now welling up too.

"I'd like nothing else more," she said. She exhaled as if letting down a weight she'd been carrying for months. "But you have to fix my couch first. I love that couch."

Kaden smiled, looking down at the busted frame and ripped fabric. He nodded a few times, examining it. "You got yourself a deal."

Their apartment looked like a warzone. Broken glass, stucco, and concrete were scattered on the blackened marble floor that sat like an out of place, oversized throw rug near their window.

Seconds later, their door burst open. Elba and Enak flooded into the room. Elba's eyes wide.

"You good? Both of you?" Elba said. "It was you two floating through the air! I knew it."

"We are. Jericho saved us before, well, before..." Kira couldn't finish the sentence.

"I saw maps of the tunnels in The Tower," Kaden said. "We must be careful where you go. Any remaining Elites might come after–"

"Now you care, Agent?" Enak snapped bitterly, his eyes squinted sharply at Kaden.

"Hey!" Kira fired back.

"I'm sorry about joining that place. This world is a mess, and I thought... I'm just sorry, okay. And about your shoulder," he said, pointing to Enak's arm in a sling.

Enak looked at him, frustration hardened in his expression.

"You can see The Tower from here. You saw it. So, he really *is* dead?" Elba asked.

Kira and Kaden looked at each other, then to the ground. Elba soon did the same.

"If we count you two, there's twelve of us left," Elba said.

"We're not counting him," Enak interjected.

"Then why should we count you?" Elba turned, coming nose to nose with his brother. "Because if they really have maps of the tunnels, then I'm wondering where they got them. You were the only one drawing them out, so how'd they get in The Tower?"

"Guys, they have maps of everywhere. It doesn't mean–" Kaden tried to interject.

"I'm doing my best with what I have!" Enak snapped back, standing up straighter and confronting his brother.

"Seems like you're as much of a traitor as you accuse him," Elba said, and Kaden could see Enak's fist tightening.

Both brothers flexed their posture, their nostrils flaring.

"And you're *both* welcome here," Elba said, and his brother stepped back like he'd been punched in the nose, surprised at Elba's welcoming in the midst of his accusation.

"There's twelve left," Kira said, and the group diverted their attention from the standoff.

"Only twelve," Elba confirmed. Their heads bowed at the thought.

"Let 'em have the maps," Kaden said.

"What?" Kira mouthed.

"These demons have been ruining our lives. They're used to attacking, but not defending. We can strike," Kaden said.

The group looked at him, bewildered.

"There's a power in us all. Jericho didn't die in vain; he did it to show us what we have. If you'll stand with me, we're going to bring a righteous fire on that tower."

"And what will we do once inside?" Kira asked.

"We're going to get him. We're going to bring his body out."

"His body?" Elba asked.

"Jericho, Pinnacle, they both have roots in medicine, they were partners. There's no telling what Pinnacle and those demons will do with Jericho's body. We're getting him out of there," Kaden said, a fiery determination igniting brighter as he spoke.

The group's confusion began to subside. They stood up straighter as Kaden spoke with conviction.

Kaden took off down the stairs, the trio following behind. He remembered chasing after Jericho in the deep stairwells that led to the Pastures, how no matter how fast he went or close he came, Jericho was always a step ahead, just out of reach.

A moment later, Kaden burst out onto the chaos of the streets. The horror of The Tower's collapse was more apparent up close. Dead Agents with lines of blood trickling from their bodies dotted the cracked cobblestone alleys. Some squirmed in pain, crying out for help, with broken legs and other devastating injuries. Black clumps, like that of fallen boulders, were scattered in and around black robes. The pieces of the dead Elites pulsed, like a fading heartbeat coming from the matte-colored rock.

The four ran forward but stopped as another piece of The Tower fell from hundreds of feet above. A fallen Agent, screaming in pain, was silenced as the car-sized boulder crushed his body.

"Keep your head up!" Kaden cried out as he began running again.

They slowly approached the outer edge of The Tower, Kaden knowing he must find Jericho. Kaden hated him for all the pain and death in the world, but he also felt a calling from the man, as if he had reached out into Kaden's dreams of the past, the past where he was Darren, and planted a warm sense of belonging into Kaden's heart. Jericho saved him and Kira, facing Pinnacle and giving himself up in their place. Kaden had to reach his body, had to tell the world of the sacrifice that Kaden didn't deserve.

As they came closer, treading through the falling rocks and scattered bodies, a group came out of The Tower. Jace, Ryon, Aria, and Vala stood at the entrance. Kaden's heart leapt as he saw the familiar faces of his cohort, but as they took a defensive stance, hands hovering over their Spark Clubs, his heart sank.

"We need to get his body out," Kaden called out. But his former comrades only stood in silence, their faces steeled.

"You don't understand," Kaden pleaded. "Pinnacle is controlling all of Empyrean. He'll use Jericho to enhance his own powers. He'll strengthen the Elites!"

"Sounds like a good thing to me," Ryon replied.

"Only a traitor would speak against Pinnacle," Vala said.

"No," Kaden said, shaking his head. "We're a team. We almost died together."

"Because of the resistance trying to kill us!" Ryon snapped back, his eyes going to Kira, Elba, and Enak.

"You have to understand what it's like going against The Tower," Kaden said.

Both parties remained silent.

"Jace? Aria?" Kaden turned to them. Their faces flashed a sympathetic look, but their bodies didn't waver as they stood in opposition.

"It's four on four; we can get past them," Enak said.

"Try it," Vala said, pulling out her Spark Club and letting the crackle of electricity snap through the air.

Pieces of rubble continued to fall all around them as four on each side faced off.

"This is bad," Kira whispered.

"But we must. The Tower cannot oppress us any longer!" Elba shouted.

The rest of the Agents pulled out their Spark Clubs, tilting the odds massively in their favor.

"You don't want to do this," Kaden said.

"No, *you* don't want to do this," Ryon said, shifting his position to step in front of Kaden. "You're mine."

"They're ours," a voice called out from The Tower.

Beth-ell and her two Elites walked out of The Tower, standing with the four Agents.

"Four on four, eh?" Kira said.

"You shall not get in the way of the greater good," Beth-ell called out. Her two Elites now flanking her. The Agents and Elites stood in a triangle-like formation, the four Agents from Kaden's cohort in the first row of four, Beth-ell's two Elites behind them, and then Beth-ell the tip and last line of defense.

"Kaden, this is for another day," Kira said as she assessed the situation.

"No!" Enak screamed. "It ends today!" He shot forward in rage, scooping a jagged rock from the ground and darting at Vala. She cocked back her Spark Club, ready to unload on the charging Enak.

He threw the jagged rock like a pitcher unleashing a fast ball directly at the batter. Vala pivoted her club but couldn't react in time as the stone shot at her head.

But to her surprise, it stopped inches from her face.

Her face clenched, but then her eyes opened to see the rock floating in midair before her. Behind her, the Elite held up his hands, one holding the rock and the other stopping Enak. He stood midstride, both feet off the ground and anger across his face as his muscles twitched.

"You shall not get in the way of the greater good," Beth-ell called out once again.

The four Agents' confidence soared as Kaden and the others stepped back.

Beth-ell took a deep breath and looked across the four in opposition.

"You can end this. When you die, go end this before it begins," she said, looking directly at Kaden.

"Wha..." Kaden mouthed in disbelief.

"Remove them." Beth-ell sent a commanding order and her Elites flickered both wrists. As if a light switch turned them off, all four Agents, Ryon, Vala, Jace, and Aria, fell to the ground unconscious.

"End this before it begins. It is up to you now," Beth-ell said.

Kaden locked eyes with her and she reeled her hand back and then shot it forward. She moved as if she were an Elite controlling matter around her. As her hand shot forward, Enak, Elba, Kira, and then Kaden, all shot backwards in quick succession, their bodies falling on the hard, broken streets that were once pristine stonework. Beth-ell looked at her two Elites, the three in unspoken agreement, and then they went back into The Tower. Eight bodies lay spread on the battlefield behind them.

***

Darren jolted up from bed, his chest heaving and sweat pouring down his face.

"We're back," Kelly said.

He turned to see her. She took deep breaths just like him. They stared into each other's eyes, the dream of Empyrean rolling through his mind.

"She sent us back?" Kelly asked.

"She sent us back," Darren repeated as he thought.

A sound of footsteps grew louder from outside his bedroom door. The door flew open, Chris and Kirk crashing through, their faces covered in a bewildered expression.

"What was that?" Chris asked.

Darren looked at Kelly, and then back to the brothers.

"It was the future," he said. "And it's up to us to stop it."

End Book 1

***

ENJOY a special Pre-Release PREVIEW of Jericho Series Book 2 – Jericho's Heart.

***

Chapter 1

Jericho Book 2 Preview

"Tell me, Darren, what made you smile this week?" his mother asked as they rounded the corner of the supermarket aisle.

The five year old Darren hesitated, distracted by the colorful images and characters on the boxes all around him. The supermarket always seemed like such a joyful place to the young boy. There were boring aisles, of course, but the cereal and snack aisles were like a toy store. He couldn't wait to see all his favorites, smiling at him from the front cover.

"Answer your mother, boy," his father said sternly as he tapped the boy's shoulder. The nudge pulled Darren out of his imagination, where Cap'n Crunch sailed the seas, always with a full bowl of deliciousness and a jolly smile.

"What ma?" young Darren asked.

"What made you smile this week, sweetheart?" she asked.

"Oh," he said, then paused as he thought. "Lunch was great!" he finally erupted. "Matt had Oreos and he was eating ONLY the inside!"

"No way?" his mother said.

"He started stacking the cookie parts," he said, motioning with his hands as if he were building a tower. "But then Jimmy kept knocking the tower down!" he laughed as he spoke.

"Jimmy is sneaky, huh," she said.

"And then we'd all steal a piece before Matt could rebuild," the boy said in a whisper.

"Oh you're all being sneaky aren't you?" his mother said with a smile as she poked Darren's ribs, pulling out a giggle.

"Was Matt okay with all that?" she asked.

"Yeah, he doesn't like the cookie part," Darren said, an ear-to-ear grin covering his face.

"I always knew that kid was off," Darren's father said matter of factly.

"Oh, hush," his mother batted at the man's arms.

"Why does he get Oreos in his lunch if he doesn't like the cookie?" the father inquired.

"Because he LOVES the middle part!" Darren burst out.

"That's nice, sweetheart," his mother said.

"Sounds like a waste to me," his father muttered under his breath. An elbow shot out from the mother and the man winced as it caught his side.

"DunkAroos! Mom, can we, please, please?" Darren jumped forward and grabbed a box off the shelf.

"Speaking of waste," the father said.

The young boy heard and his body sunk over like a wilting flower.

"Always no," the boy whimpered as he put the box back on the shelf.

"Because it's garbage food," the father snapped.

The boy's mother stared daggers at him.

"Sweetheart, we're making No Bake Cookies. That's our treat this week," the boy's mother interjected with a sympathetic touch to the side of young Darren's head.

"More sug–" the father tried to say but she sent another elbow at him, this one more forceful instead of playful.

"I think we should grab some berries. Hun, can you go grab some? Whatever looks in season and only organic," she said, and Darren perked up a bit.

"You're making cookies but have to buy organic?" the father replied.

"Only organic, hun."

"No, the regular kind is fine," he protested.

"Would you spray weed killer on your salad before eating it?" she replied.

"I don't eat salad."

"Hun, organic only," she said, her expression inching closer and closer to more stern.

He took the hint and stepped back but couldn't stop the objection welling up inside of him.

"I pay for private school so he can learn to steal Oreos, his feelings get a boo-boo because he can't have garbage food, and now you want me to pay twice as much for the same fruit? I mean what are we doing here?" the father ranted. "Have you seen prices lately? My pay ain't keeping up with it!"

Darren's eyes went to the floor, avoiding his father's gaze as the man's stern look engulfed the boy like a spotlight in a dark room. Eventually, the look shifted to the boy's mother, who retorted with the raised eyebrows that only a disappointed wife can give to her husband. A thousand words, each sharper than daggers, impressed back on the man from her stare.

With an exhale of disgust, he slowly did an about face and then left the aisle, but Darren still eyed the floor.

"No DunkAroos, sweetheart," she said sympathetically. "But I'd love your help making the No Bakes later?"

"Okay," Darren said, his face rising to uncover a frown.

"I'd consider a peanut butter version too. What do you think?" the mother asked.

"Yes!" The boy's face lit up.

They moved down the aisle and soon turned down the next. As they walked around a football and BBQ themed endcap, the mother caught a concerned expression on the boy.

"Darren, what's wrong?"

"School wasn't all good this week," he sheepishly admitted.

"Tell me more, sweetheart."

"Stephen..." he said softly as if speaking it would give the memory life.

"Recess again?" she asked.

The boy nodded.

"The teacher?"

"She loves him, and never believes us."

"I'm sorry to hear that, sweetheart. That must be tough."

Young Darren exhaled, looking up and down the otherwise aisle. "Yeah..." he agreed and his shoulders dropped and rose again, finally allowing himself to breathe.

"What do you think you should do about it?" she asked.

"Can you call the teacher?" he pleaded.

"I could, but help me learn more. What's an action you could take?"

"Punch him in the face," Darren said through gritted teeth.

"Ehhh..."

"But Mom, he hits us and makes fun of us, it's awful!"

"I'm sorry you have to deal with him, sweetheart. Sometimes difficult people and situations come into our life."

"Why would God allow people like Stephen?" he asked.

The mother pulled back in surprise.

"Sweetheart, remember God made him too. And it's hard to hear, but God loves even the bad guys. I'm betting Stephen is scared or anxious or something, and he doesn't know how to act properly. Whatever it is, God loves him too."

"Yeah..." the boy dismissed.

"I think ignoring him will help. It's not good to be around bad people."

"But he's in my class, and he finds me every time."

"I love you, sweetheart. That's hard. Let's think on this more and talk later, okay?" She touched the side of his head.

"Okay, Mom."

They walked another aisle and passed by other shoppers. One woman was trying her best to ignore her young toddler screaming for their sippy cup. The child's binky fell and bounced in front of Darren and his mother. He instinctively picked it up and held it out for the exhausted mother. Her dazed look took a second to recognize the favor but she snapped back from her sleep deprivation and thanked Darren.

"That was nice of you," Darren's mother said to him as they moved down the next aisle. She grabbed an item here and there, slowly filling their cart.

Once again she noticed the concerned look on her son's face.

"You still thinking on Stephen?" she asked.

"Kind of," he said.

She gave an understanding nod and then turned to check their shopping list.

"Mom?" he interjected her train of thought. "Stephen reminds me of Dad. Why are you nice and Dad is mean?"

Her hand shot up and covered her mouth.

"Sweetheart, your dad loves you," she said.

Darren looked down and kicked at the floor.

"Can I not be around him? You said not to be around mean people," he said.

"Why do you think he's mean?"

"He's always telling me what to do, and I never do it right so then he gets mad and tells me more things to do, that I can't do!"

"I don't agree with everything your father says and does, but remember he loves you."

"I don't see it," he said under his breath.

"Don't talk like that," she snapped, but caught herself and squatted to meet her son at his level. "He has his own way of showing it."

"Can you just tell him to not yell at me or spank me?"

Her eyes watered as she looked at her son.

"Darren," she gently touched his chin and pulled up his face to make eye contact. "Your father and I are different. I'm more sensitive than him, and at your age, it's easier for me to cuddle you like crazy." She broke a smile that infected the boy, but soon the sadness returned. "But your father goes out and works hard to provide for us. I'm sorry he's rough around the edges. We've been through a lot together, and before God gave us you, your father's rough edges got us through some VERY rough times."

"I found his pictures," the boy admitted.

Her eyes widened. "From the desert?"

"Why were there all those bodies? They were cut apart."

She hugged the boy. "Sweetheart, your dad was in war. It was called Desert Storm and there were very bad people that your dad and his friends were trying to protect others from."

"He killed all those people. He's going to hell,"

"Sweetheart, I want you to remember two things. First, that your father loves you, no matter what. I'll talk with him about his words and I'm sorry he can act mean. And second," she pulled back his face as the boy tried to look away. "If there are bad guys, and there are, then good guys must kill the bad guys, otherwise there aren't really any good guys."

Darren gulped as he looked into his mother's watery eyes. His father came around the corner, holding a stack of plastic containers. They were all organic berries.

Chapter 2

Jericho Book 2 Preview

The four stood in the living room of the apartment, the excitement and confusion of each waking from the life-like dream of Empyrean.

"She killed us," Kirk said.

"She killed our future selves," Chris added.

"That's not me, that's some Enak guy, who might I add is more angry day-to-day than I've ever been in my life. That's just not me," Kirk responded.

The brothers looked at each other, waves of confusion still flowing over them. Meanwhile, Darren finally let his eye catch Kelly's. She'd been watching him, sensing something the brothers didn't know.

"You've been back and forth before, haven't you?" Kelly asked as Darren met her eyes.

He nodded yes.

"What?" Chris exclaimed. "And you?" he looked at Kelly.

"No, well in a dream, but it's hard to explain. Not like this, not putting on the glasses and being there."

"Glasses?" Kirk shouted, then he darted into Darren's room, quickly finding and grabbing the glasses before Darren could stop him. "So we have nightmares but these things are your virtual reality?" he said.

"More than that," Darren exhaled. "Guys you know I went to an eye doctor recently, right? Well, he put the photo-play thing over my–

"It's a phoropter," Kelly interrupted.

"Yeah, that. Anyway, he put it on and boom, I was there. It was like I was that person, Kaden, but everytime I died there, I woke up here."

"And how'd you get back?" Chris asked.

"I'd check on Kelly, who was always still peaceful, and I'd put my glasses back on and boom, again, right back to being Kaden," Darren said.

Kirk held up the purple glasses toward Kelly with a questioning expression.

"Yup, but this is the first time I died, or well, Kira died," she said.

"Well, I don't love having nightmares of those charcoal demons and some Beth-whatever lady putting me down like a suffering animal. Screw that place," Kirk said, tossing the glasses on the table. Darren and Kelly lurched as if pieces of priceless art work were carelessly handled.

"What happens if you put back on the glasses?" Chris asked.

"I think we go back," Kelly said, watching Darren's face grow stern.

"No way!" Kirk shouted. "Hallucinations!" he cried as he grabbed the black-framed glasses and moved them toward his face.

"No!" Darren and Kelly shouted, but they were too late, Kirk already had them on. He stood frozen like a statue, his eyes bulging and staring at Darren.

"His body didn't go limp like yours did," Darren said, as he and Kelly slowly crept toward the statue-like Kirk.

"Guys... What's going on?" Chris asked.

"He might be back in Empy–"

"Gotcha!" Kirk jumped and threw out his hands like a magician showing off the grand reveal.

"Ugh," Darren exclaimed. "I forgot our glasses only worked on each of us."

"Yours didn't work on me," Kelly reiterated.

"So what if you each put yours back on?" Chris asked, nodding to his brother. Kirk reluctantly gave them each their pair.

Darren looked down at them, thoughts of the Elites and Beth-ell waiting for him. "You can end this," Beth-ell's words echoed in his mind. Why would she say that before killing him?

"Do you go back to when you died?" Kelly asked, pulling Darren from his thoughts.

"I... Well, not precisely. Remember when you dragged me from the Outer Ring back to our apartment?"

"I sure do, ya heavy bastard," Kirk blurted out before catching himself. "I mean, Enak does... Not me."

"We could wake up right in front of the Elites," Darren said.

Kelly shook her head, now she took a turn lost in thought.

"I don't like those things," Chris added.

"I think only Thornhill does," Darren remarked.

The group looked at him curiously.

"Who's Thornhill?" Kelly finally asked.

"Oh, he's Pinnacle," Darren said.

"Ummmm," Kelly said as the three looked at each other, then back at Darren.

"The most powerful and evil person, if he's even a person, in all of Empyrean is here too?" Chris asked.

Darren thought a moment, trying to come up with the right words and wishing he could share the visions Jericho shared with him. Eventually, his head bobbed as he spoke.

"He's a businessman, I met him at the eye doctor's. He was friends and partners with Dr. Abrams," Darren said.

"And who's Dr. Abrams? The same guy who put the photo-bomb on you and gave you these glasses?"

Darren and Kelly both shook their heads yes.

"I get the sense he's not just an eye doctor," Chris added.

"Nope, he's... He's Jericho," Darren said.

"Oh great, we have the worst dictator of all time award winner in Pinnacle and the man, the myth, the legend himself crossing worlds with us. This all sounds lovely. Just a couple of jolly businessmen running an eye care shop here in Georgia. Why not?" Kirk said.

"You know those dreams were weird, and both of us having it, and matching theirs? Just try to listen and learn–" Chris said, before Kirk snapped, cutting him off.

"No, you listen and learn. Those dreams were freakin' wack–a-doo, and those demon things, scary. Yeah, I'll admit it, they were freakin' scary. I was scared and I don't want to go back there. So throw the dang glasses out and give the eye doctor hut a 1-star review. Done with all this," Kirk ranted.

"I'm sorry, bro. Once you see, you can't unsee," Chris said.

"What does that mean? Of course you can 'unsee' anything. I saw grandpa getting off the toilet when we were kids, I had to unsee that," Kirk said.

"I don't think you can unsee that," Chris said.

"Oh, shut up, you didn't see it," Kirk fired back.

"Guys, GUYS!" Kelly screamed. "You two don't have glasses, and regardless of what you think," she eyed Kirk. "Regardless, we've all been to

Empyrean. In our dreams or through these glasses, we've been there. Now we decide if we go back," Kelly said.

The brothers remained quiet, looking back and forth between themselves and Kelly. She met their eyes and reassured them with a confident look, then she turned to Darren.

"Hun, you've been a bit too quiet. What's on your mind?" she asked.

He took in a deep breath, his eyes on the floor, then he raised his eyes to meet theirs as he let the breath out.

"She said 'You can end this,' before we died. 'You can end this. When you die, go end this before it begins.' Why would she say that?" Darren said.

"Beth-ell is Pinnacle's next in command," Kelly said.

"You sure you heard it right?" Chris asked.

Darren nodded.

"I heard it too," Kirk said.

"Jericho showed me things when I was there. He showed me the history between him and Thornhill. I think Beth-ell wants me to kill him," Darren said.

"Kill Jericho? That's nuts," Kelly said.

"Hey, that's a pretty brutal world. One man for many?" Kirk said.

"No, I mean kill Thornhill. I think Beth-ell wants to end it all before it begins," he said.

"You can't do that," Kirk said.

"What happened to 'one man for many?'" Chris asked.

"Why we killing anybody here?" Kirk said. "You want life in prison because you knocked an eye doctor? I'm sure the judge will understand that he was a really bad guy in this dream world," Kirk said.

"We can't just kill people," Kelly said, touching Darren's arm.

"I know, but, what if we could stop the whole thing?" Darren asked.

"What if it is inevitable?" Kelly asked back.

"What would Jericho do?" Chris said.

Darren shrugged. "I don't know. He's the only person more powerful than Pinnacle. I'd ask why we'd let all this happen in the first place. He could have stopped him but didn't."

"And didn't Pinnacle just rip his heart out? I'd say Jericho is a distant second to that guy in the power race," Kirk said.

"Look, I'm not saying I'm going to, I'm just saying..." Darren paused.

"What are you saying?" Kirk asked.

"I need time to sort this out. My head is spinning," Darren said, turning and walking back to his room. Kelly took a seat on the couch while Chris moved back to his room.

"Okay, that solves a lot," Kirk said, throwing his hands up and slamming them down against his jeans.

"Just chill, bro. Take a power nap," Chris hollered from his room.

Kirk mouthed a mocking response then went back to his room. He looked at his closet door, wanting to see if the object he woke up with was still there or if he was hallucinating like his dreams. Moving to the door, he slowly opened it. There on the top shelf, right where he hastily tossed it when he woke up and found it clutched in his hands, was the worn, black leather moleskine journal. He took it out and held it to his chest.

"Darren, you okay?" he heard Kelly call out. Kirk jumped and hid the journal back on the top shelf, now pushing it behind other items.

Meanwhile, Kelly walked into Darren's room and closed the door. She stood in front of the walk-in closet, rapping her knuckle on the door. "You okay, hun? Let's take a nap and talk more after some rest."

"I think I need some fresh air," Darren said from behind the closed door. Thinking he couldn't let her know his thoughts or next actions. It'd be by far better if she didn't know.

He took out the hand gun stored in the small gun safe in the back of his closet where a watch his grandfather gave him and the american flag his dad used to hang outside their house rested. Sliding the gun in the back of his belt, he opened the door and was met with Kelly's eyes. The auburn haze of her hair, perfect curves of her lips, and her hazel eyes urged him to stay. He longed to kiss her and lay down, getting much needed rest, but the cold of the gun's handle pressed against his lower back.

"Get some rest. I'll be back soon," he told her.

"I'll come with you. Want to walk around the lake?" she asked.

"No, I'll be bad company, let me just... go for a drive. I need to shake some cobwebs in the fresh air," he said.

"Okay, I'll wait in here..." she said reluctantly, feeling passed off.

He didn't kiss her good-bye as he left the room, determined to find and kill Dr. Thomas Thornhill.

THANK YOU!

I hope you enjoyed the preview.

- Find it at **https://store.jamesbonk.com/** and enjoy a 15% discount with the code BESTSELLER when you buy directly from the author.

- You can stay in touch by signing up for my newsletter and getting special offers:

https://hello.jamesbonk.com/signup/

The Author

James Bonk writes Christian Fiction to develop his own faith and to share with others. He lives in the North Georgia area with his wife, two daughters, and fluffy Chartreux cat, Porkchop. When he's not writing, he's usually swimming or building forts with his girls!

His Light of the Ark book was the #1 New Release in its category upon release, with multiple five star reviews from adults and young adults alike.

Besides writing, parenting, and being a husband, James Bonk is a supply chain leader and business intelligence professional. He has a BS in Mechanical Engineering, MS in Industrial Engineering, and an MBA. He previously held his Professional Engineering license in Industrial Engineering.

Find out more at and get access to all his books at:

https://store.jamesbonk.com/

You can also find James by searching James Bonk Author on your favorite platform or following the below links:

- Goodreads (https://www.goodreads.com/author/list/21997660.James_Bonk)

- Facebook (search *James Bonk Author*' or go here: https://www.facebook.com/people/James-Bonk-Author/100092204034685/)

- BookBub (https://www.bookbub.com/profile/james-bonk)

The Author - James Bonk